LETHAL RHYTHM

PETER KOWEY MD
with MARION L. FOX

Pavilion Press, Inc.

Philadelphia • New York •

Copyright ©2010 by Peter Kowey

Lethal Rhythm

by Peter Kowey MD

ISBN: .

Paperback	1-4145-0718-6
Hard Cover	1-4145-0719-4

This book is printed on acid-free paper. Designed for readability

Library of Congress

Cataloging-in-Publication Data

1.Fiction 2. Mystery

Pavilion Press, Inc. Philadelphia, PA www.pavilionpress.com

Dedication

This book is for our patients, who, by their courage
and fortitude, motivate their physicians to learn more
about the diseases that afflict them. It is also dedicated
to Herb Denenberg, the ultimate advocate, whose kind
encouragement and support made this book possible.

Acknowledgements

We would like to thank Jim Kaufmann, Bob Hall and Avery Rome for their critiques, Sandy Goroff, Samantha Carr, Elyn Neilson and Allison Guarino for their tireless support, and our families for their patience and encouragement.

Disclaimer

The characters in this book are fictional. Any resemblance they have to real people is coincidental or because the authors lacked imagination. The exceptions are Drs. Michel Mirowski and Morton Mower. We couldn't escape the temptation to tell part of their wonderful story. We apologize if that part of our story is not completely accurate.

LETHAL
RHYTHM

CHAPTER 1

Screaming sirens shattered the early morning stillness as an ambulance with flashing lights sped down the posh tree-lined streets of Philadelphia's Main Line. There was little other traffic. Still, the driver had to be careful to avoid the few intrepid joggers in the legendary neighborhoods that have always been home to a unique mixture of landed gentry and nouveau riche. If they lacked commonality, most Main Liners were wealthy and privileged. To prove it, each street boasted its share of meticulously maintained homes, with an obligatory Mercedes, Range Rover, or Lexus conspicuously parked in the circular driveway. To go with expensive houses and cars, Main Liners enjoyed famous country clubs, world-class schools and great restaurants. And of course, they expected superb medical care.

Jack Creager and Mark Abrams, the emergency medical technicians dispatched by the local ambulance company, were usually capable of handling almost any situation. But today, they were in a serious hurry and barely noticed the lush surroundings.

This call had put them on edge. A highly distressed sounding man had called 911 begging for help for his wife who had collapsed in their bedroom. He said she was totally unresponsive. Madge, the dispatcher who took the call, could not give them much more information. She said a radio was blaring in the background, and she had a hard time communicating with the panicked husband.

The drive from Gladwyne Memorial Hospital to the Villanova estate took less than five minutes. The team had been summoned to countless "cardiac arrests" in the past that ended up being mere fainting spells or slip-and-falls that required little more than first aid. But today, Jack had the "pedal to the metal" after Madge told them the victim's husband clearly stated that his wife had some kind of long-standing cardiac problem. Getting to the patient and quickly beginning resuscitation was of paramount importance. Without CPR, the patient was already in jeopardy of brain damage. It only takes three minutes of zero blood flow to damage brain tissue, and they knew well that brain cells don't regenerate. Jack and Mark had bad memories of otherwise healthy people who didn't make it, or even worse ended up as vegetables doomed to a nursing facility. The possibility of that kind of bad outcome was squarely on their minds as they turned onto the Main Line's most fashionable address, Rock Ridge Road.

They identified the house quickly but were flabbergasted to find the tall ornate iron gates closed at the end of the driveway. They radioed Madge immediately.

"You aren't going to believe this, but the damn gates are closed!" Jack screamed into the handset.

Madge replied calmly, "Stay cool. I'll call back and get them to open the gates."

After what seemed like an hour, but was probably less than a minute, the black-iron gates yawned noiselessly open. Jack nearly took them off their hinges as he sped up the driveway. Both men jumped out of the ambulance, yanked open the rear doors, and took out their resuscitation gear.

Blonde and fit, Jack was the much more athletic of the two, but Mark, a skinny Jewish kid, grabbed most of the gear and bolted to the house. To their added dismay, the front door was also locked. They repeatedly rang the bell until it was pulled opened. Across the threshold, they encountered a scene they would later describe as "pure mayhem." Hapless servants who didn't speak English were chasing a gaggle of small, sobbing children. The EMTs struggled to find out where the patient was while barking dogs made communication impossible. Finally, one of the maids frantically pointed to the graceful sweeping staircase. "Upstairs," she managed to say in broken English.

As they entered the master bedroom suite, a stocky man in his underwear was holding an infant, and standing over a beautiful lifeless young woman who was lying on the floor. Her eyes were half closed and her skin dark blue. The man had a look of terror on his face.

"Her name is Moira," he said. "You have to help her, please! I found her like this when I came out of the shower. I tried to wake her, but she wasn't moving or breathing."

Mark established that the victim had no pulse or spontaneous respiration and used a bag and mask to administer oxygen. While he took care of the airway, Jack immediately started chest compressions to provide circulation to vital organs. After compressing the bag several times, Mark opened the external cardioverter-defibrillator they brought. This device was capable of automatically diagnosing a malignant cardiac arrhythmia and then delivering a series of electrical discharges to "shock" the heart back into a normal rhythm. After he had placed adhesive leads on her chest to deliver the shocks, he told Jack to stop the chest compressions and stand back. Jack knew what could happen if either of them were in contact with the patient when a shock was delivered—and it wasn't pleasant.

The machine went through its algorithm announcing each of its steps in an inappropriately pleasant female voice. Once it recognized ventricular fibrillation, the lethal rhythm responsible for this cardiac arrest, the device's batteries charged its capacitors and the voice warned everyone to stand back. The machine then delivered a high-energy shock and the woman's body leapt off of the floor.

The first shock did not restore a normal rhythm, so the paramedics continued their resuscitation attempts. The machine had to recycle and shock the patient three more times before a normal rhythm appeared. Once they had evidence of success on the monitor's scope, the paramedics quickly confirmed that the woman had a pulse and was breathing on her own, indicating that blood flow and oxygenation to her vital organs had finally been restored.

Jack continued to monitor the patient and started an intravenous line to administer medications. Their immediate task was to get Moira quickly prepared for the brief ride to the hospital. In addition to continuing to operate the bag that helped her breathe, they also needed to gather information for the team who would be caring for her at the hospital.

By this time, the husband, who identified himself as Hugh, was sitting helplessly in an armchair next to the bed. He had finally pulled on a pair of pants. In a few minutes, he was surrounded by his three older children who had filtered quietly into the room just in time to observe the dramatic finale of their mother's resuscitation. Hugh appeared to be in shock and had to be prompted repeatedly to answer the simplest questions.

Jack and Mark asked the servants to take the children elsewhere while they continued their pointed interview. They hoped Hugh would snap to with fewer distractions, and didn't want the kids to witness their comatose mother in this very sad state.

Mark began, "Sir, I need your full name."

"Hugh Hamlin."

"Mr. Hamlin, I need to know if Moira has been sick lately."

"No!" Hugh answered emphatically. "She has always been very healthy. Her allergies have been acting up lately but it is that time of year, and the antihistamine she took seemed to be helping. Otherwise she was fine."

"Mr. Hamlin, can you tell me what happened this morning?"

"Nothing unusual. I always get up early with the baby. I brought him into our bed for Moira to breastfeed, and she was lying peacefully with Nathan when I went to take a shower. While I was in there, Meghan, our six-year-old, yelled into the bathroom that something was wrong with Mommy. She said Mommy was acting funny. I ran into the bedroom. Moira must have lowered herself and the baby to the floor and then passed out. I couldn't wake her up and so I immediately called for help."

"Did you call 911?"

"No. The first person I called was Jim Flanagan, my neighbor next door. There was no answer. Then I remembered that Jim and his wife were away on vacation so I called 911."

"Why did you call your neighbor first?'

"He is a cardiac surgeon and I know that he keeps resuscitation equipment in his car. I thought it would be quicker to get him to come over."

"Mr. Hamlin, the dispatcher was concerned because she heard loud music in the background when she spoke with you. What was that about?"

"I guess that the clock radio alarm went off. I thought that I had turned it off when I got up but I must have forgotten."

"Mr. Hamlin, you told the dispatcher that your wife had a cardiac problem. Is that why you thought you needed resuscitation equipment from next door?"

"Yes, that is exactly why. My wife has been diagnosed to have the long QT syndrome. Dr. Philip Sarkis at GMH made the diagnosis and has been caring for Moira ever since."

Mark had heard of the long QT syndrome but had never seen a case himself. He knew that it could cause cardiac arrest, and that the team at the hospital was going to need some very detailed information about this patient's history.

"What was Dr. Sarkis doing about the problem?"

"Just keeping an eye on it—he said that she didn't need any treatment."

Jack was surprised. He had attended a lecture that Dr. Sarkis had given at the hospital. He knew that the condition was potentially fatal and that affected people needed aggressive diagnosis and management. They sometimes took medications but often needed pacemakers and defibrillators. He thought that just about everybody with the syndrome got some sort of maintenance treatment. Mark also remembered that certain medicines can further prolong the QT interval and are contraindicated in the syndrome because they can actually cause a lethal arrhythmia in susceptible patients.

Mark asked, "Was your wife on any other medications?"

Hugh was emphatic. "The only medication she took was an antihistamine, and Dr. Sarkis assured Moira and me that there was no problem with taking that drug. He also told us that Moira could still breastfeed Nathan since the drug doesn't get into breast milk."

Mark was reassured by the fact that Philip Sarkis was the physician on the case. He was a specialist and would certainly have known what treatment was best for her. His immediate concern was what to do for Moira in the next few minutes. Since his knowledge of her condition was limited, he was afraid that Jack and he were way in over their heads. It was time to call the physician in the ER to see if there was anything more they needed to do before the transfer.

Just as Mark started dialing, Moira's heart went out of rhythm again. The two medics looked on helplessly as the cardiac monitor started to alarm. Moira had two, then three, then multiple extra beats that were clearly coming from the ventricular or lower heart chamber. Her heart gradually then inevitably degenerated into the same chaotic rhythm. Since the external defibrillator was still attached, it again did its job and shocked Moira's heart to a normal rhythm, but the ventricular tachycardia came back very quickly. Mark, now in obvious panic mode, made the call to the doctor supervisor to find out what measures to take.

He was relieved when he was put through to Adam Wilkie, a rotund ER veteran who had treated just about every conceivable emergent problem including a host of potential cardiac disasters. In fact, Adam had a particular interest in cardiac arrhythmias. His Dad had one and so he read about them avidly and frequently conferred about the issue with his father's doctor, who coincidentally happened to be Philip Sarkis. When Mark carefully recounted the situation and told him the patient had the long QT syndrome, Adam wasted no time.

"Send me a strip right away and give her an amp of magnesium."

It took Mark a few seconds to transmit the EKG recording of the arrhythmia. But when Adam saw the strip, he yelled into the phone.

"Get her in here pronto! She is having torsade de pointes and you guys aren't going to get this thing squelched on your own. Give her at least two more ampules of magnesium sulfate while you travel and hurry the hell up!"

Mark had heard Dr. Sarkis lecture about torsade de pointes. He recalled that it was a particularly nasty form of lower chamber arrhythmia that patients with the long QT syndrome sometimes manifested. He also remembered that Dr. Sarkis had warned it was lethal unless treated promptly and that magnesium was the first thing to reach for. Mark prepared and injected the magnesium just as the ECD recycled and gave Moira yet another shock that worked transiently.

When Moira's rapid heartbeats recurred, Jack started CPR while Mark brought in the stretcher. Both of them were visibly rattled. None of their prior experience had prepared them for such a complicated and persistent situation. Most of the time, arrhythmias calmed down on their own. This one was a nightmare.

It took Mark a few seconds to lock the stretcher into position.

He could see that his always unflappable partner was beginning to unravel. Sweat was beading on his forehead and his compressions weren't as rhythmic as they had been at the start. Mark knew they were running out of time.

They loaded Moira onto the stretcher and began to move her out of the house. Hugh, the kids and servants were so distraught that the EMTs almost had to fight their way out the front door. Jack got into the driver's seat, and Mark took over chest compressions while maintaining communication with Adam on his headset. Adam instructed Mark to continue medications.

"Mark, this woman is sick as hell. I don't know if it will help but why don't you also go ahead and try some lidocaine. Give her a 100 milligram bolus and we will start an infusion as soon as you get in here."

Mark's well-honed skills kicked in as he continued to resuscitate and monitor Moira's condition while administering intravenous meds. He was the cerebral guy on the team, but the stubborn arrhythmia was beginning to rattle him too. Fortunately, the ride was short, and the last shock seemed to be holding, at least for now.

In the meantime, Adam decided to call Philip Sarkis, to let him know what was going on but more importantly to see if he could meet them at the ER. Adam knew he was facing a serious problem and needed all the help he could get.

The ride took less than four minutes and Moira's rhythm remained stable until the ambulance pulled up to the door. Then the tachycardia recurred with a vengeance, now looking even more disorganized and rapid. The ER staff was waiting for them in the driveway and took over the resuscitation as Jack and Mark maneuvered the stretcher into the cardiac room. Then, instead of getting out of there, they both decided to stick around to see how this one turned out.

The mobile crew had established a good stable IV line so Adam quickly inserted a tube in Moira's windpipe so that oxygen could be delivered efficiently. He knew it was critical to get her heart back into normal rhythm and to keep it there to normalize the amount of blood going to her brain.

Moira had been down for quite a long time before effective CPR had started. Adam and his ER crew realized that Moira's neurologic status was likely going to be the most important factor in determining her survival. Whatever they could do now to improve blood flow to the brain was critical. Adam began barking orders as nurses and technicians scurried about.

However, it didn't take long for Adam to experience the same frustration that Jack and Mark had felt earlier. When shocked into normal rhythm, Moira's heart would remain stable for a few minutes and then the arrhythmia would recur. "This is what they call 'electrical storm' boys and girls and you are seeing it in all of its glory!" Adam announced to the team. "I just hope the cavalry gets here soon."

He was referring to Philip Sarkis who luckily was already up, showered, coffeed, dressed, and heading out the door when the phone rang. He snatched it up quickly, hoping to silence it before it awakened his family. Although he routinely left before they were up, Philip had not always been an early riser. He remembered his surgical rotations when he was a medical student and how much he hated leaving for the hospital in the cold and dark of pre-dawn mornings. But over the years, he had come to cherish the quiet of the early part of the day, when he was able to think and write creatively before the crush of his usual schedule.

An urgent phone consultation from the ER was not unusual but what surprised him was that the patient was Moira Hamlin. She had been doing so well. He hadn't considered her case to be particularly dangerous and she was not at high risk for a cardiac arrest. When he heard the gravity in Adam's voice, he dropped the phone and shot out the door.

As he sped to the hospital, he tried to review the details of Moira's case from memory. His recollection was that she had a mild form of the long QT syndrome and that she had been resistant to the idea of being treated with anything, even a benign drug like a beta-blocker. Although Moira was a low risk patient, Philip had been an arrhythmologist long enough to know that anything could happen to patients like her. But the overwhelming probability in this case was that Moira should not have had a major cardiac arrhythmia, let alone a storm of ventricular tachycardia.

He sprinted into the ER and was directed by the desk crew to room three, where cardiac emergencies were usually handled. It was outfitted with an impressive array of state-of-the-art equipment that the hospital, at Philip's urging, had purchased. He had always felt it was important that GMH have the best tools if it wanted to have the reputation as the "go-to center" for cardiology problems. It had taken some teeth-pulling to get the hospital drones to ante up for the physical plant and equipment, but blessedly it was there.

All eyes turned to Philip when he entered the room. While he was anything but physically imposing, Philip really looked like a doctor. Slightly built, with thick, curly salt and pepper hair and a well-trimmed mustache, he projected the persona of someone born with a stethoscope around his neck.

At once, Philip could see why Adam was losing his grip. Moira's heart had just gone out of rhythm for the eleventh time. As she got CPR, the staff prepared to shock her yet again. Adam's face was so wet with perspiration that his glasses kept slipping down his nose

"Philip, I haven't been able to come up with a way to keep her heart from going back into VT!" he shouted to Sarkis who amazingly appeared as cool and collected as he might have been on routine hospital rounds.

"How is she doing otherwise? How are her blood gases?" Philip inquired. He needed to know if Moira was getting enough oxygen into her system and if the prolonged cardiac arrest was having a detrimental effect on other body organs.

"Well, she was down at least five to seven minutes before our crew got to her and the husband didn't know how to do CPR, so I have to assume that her brain and kidneys took some kind of hit. We don't have all of her labs back yet so I can't tell how badly her other organs might have been damaged. Right now, her gases are good."

"Did anybody do anything to resuscitate her on site?"

"No. The husband called his neighbor first, a doc of some kind or other, but he was away and the 911 call came in later. The dispatcher couldn't hear the husband—loud music in the bedroom for some stupid reason. Then the crew had trouble getting to her but Jack and Mark did an outstanding job once they found her. Her oxygen level was good when she hit here except that her carbon dioxide levels were a little on the low side." Philip understood that ambulance crews tended to overdo it in emergencies,

19

and in their exuberance might give patients too many breaths, and that can cause some low carbon dioxide levels. Normally, that was not a big deal, and it was certainly not contributing to the problem here.

"So she has been storming ever since?"

Mark Abrams was standing by and cut into the conversation. "No, she was quiet for the first ten minutes or so at the house while we got the history from the husband and then the shit hit the fan. She was shocked about six times in the ambulance and about 10 or 11 times total."

Adam chimed in. "She holds for a few minutes and then off she goes again. We managed to get a 12-lead cardiogram in between the events when her heart was stable. You might want to take a look."

Philip followed Adam to the counter and looked at all the recordings of Moira's heart rhythms that had been accumulated since her ER arrival. They were impressive to say the least. She had somehow developed massive QT prolongation that was directly causing her heart to go out of rhythm repetitively. The major questions were why, and how to stop it.

"What are her electrolyte levels?" Philip asked. He needed to know if there were any obvious causes for the very long QT interval.

"The electrolytes were a bit wacko. Her potassium was low and we are giving her a bunch IV now. The magnesium was low normal too—which is really screwy since she got enough magnesium in the field, and on her way in, to turn her into a magnet."

"And the drug screens?"

"We haven't sent the drug screen yet," Adam continued. "The lab's not fully functioning this early in the morning—surprise, surprise. There is no history of drug ingestion. The husband said her only medication is an antihistamine that she hits pretty hard this time of year. But apparently you said it wasn't a problem for her to take."

Philip remembered the conversation in which Moira requested help with her allergies. Philip prescribed Appel because it had proven to be safe in patients with Moira's condition, never having been reported to cause this complication even after a few million patient-years of use.

20

"Is she bradycardic?" Slow heart rhythms tended to make problems like this one worse.

"Just a little—her spontaneous rate is in the 50's. I put the Zoll on her and pumped that up to 80 just to be on the safe side. But she has blasted into the arrhythmia even with a faster baseline heart rate."

The "Zoll" was an external pacemaker developed in the 1950s that delivered electrical pulses on the chest wall to stimulate the heart to beat. The device worked but it caused such severe pain that after a few minutes, patients who were awake begged to have it removed. The subsequent development of pacemakers that were implanted under the skin and connected directly to the inside of the heart made the external pacemaker obsolete for long-term use, and the Zoll eventually fell out of favor for about 25 years. Then a clever physician in training at Harvard came up with the idea to use the device for emergency pacing. Now, every ER and ICU had the device for short-term rate support in unconscious patients who can't feel the pain.

As Philip left the cardiac room to clear his head, he ticked off the options. Conventional dugs were not an option with her QT interval already prolonged. After a few moments, he made a tough decision and hurried back into room three.

"Hold the fort, Adam. I need to go get some stuff. I'll be right back."

Philip knew all too well that "electrical storm" carried a terrible prognosis: only about 10% of patients who developed incessant arrhythmias survived. They either died of the arrhythmia or worse, died of the complications caused by extended periods of low blood pressure after the arrhythmia was under control. If Moira had any chance of surviving, he would have to use extraordinary methods to bring her rhythm under control.

In this instance, he felt compelled to try a radical new drug that Gladwyne Memorial's research review committee considered experimental. Philip knew that the data supporting its safety and efficacy was preliminary, but he had used it before for similar problems and it had worked. His experimental lab had proven it corrected the underlying electrical disturbance, so there was a good rationale for trying it. Under ordinary circumstances, he would need consent from the patient to use the new drug, but since

Moira was unconscious, this was impossible. He would therefore have to get consent from Moira's husband. This type of consent by proxy was generally frowned upon by review boards but acceptable in extreme circumstances.

He dashed to his lab, picked up the drug, then headed to the clinical arrhythmia laboratory for a piece of equipment. He raced back to the ER pushing the equipment cart in front of him, and then rushed into the waiting area to look for Hugh Hamlin.

Hugh had arrived shortly after the ambulance. When he reported to the ER desk, the receptionist asked him to wait in the family lounge area. "Just make sure they know that I'm out here!" he barked at her. The seasoned receptionist was accustomed to rude behavior from stressed families and she didn't respond.

Hugh paced in the waiting room. He wasn't used to being kept waiting, so he was in a rage by the time that he was joined by Moira's former college roommate, Bonnie Romano. Hugh had called her from his cell phone as he was driving to the hospital to let her know what had happened. Shortly after she arrived, Philip hurried into the consultation area. Hugh introduced Bonnie as a trusted friend who was there to support him, and said he wanted her to listen in. Philip couldn't help but notice her sensuous blonde looks, and wondered how she fit into this picture. He didn't have time to ruminate.

"Hugh, Moira is very sick. We are having a tough time keeping her heart rhythm stable with the medications and devices we have in the ER. You know that my lab does a lot of research in this field. This is why Moira came to me in the first place. But I need your permission to use a new drug to see if I can reverse the arrhythmia. Moira's problem involves the way her heart reactivates itself, and that is reflected on the cardiogram as a long QT interval. The reason for the long QT interval is that that the channels in the cardiac cell membranes that let potassium ions through don't work the way they should. Everything else is OK, but right now the potassium channel defect is the big issue.

"The drug I want to give her is called Naladil. The Japanese use it for other cardiac conditions including coronary artery disease but in the course of developing it, the scientists discovered that it opens potassium channels. It could help Moira's electrical system by restoring normal potassium flow. The company that produces the drug in Japan asked me to use it on a research protocol. As a result, I have tested it in my basic laboratory but we have only used it in three or four other patients, and none of them had a rhythm as bad as Moira's. It worked great for all of them but I can't promise anything. I also brought a new defibrillator from the arrhythmia laboratory. Once I administer the medication, I want to deliver a more powerful shock to get Moira's heart back into sync. I am hoping these things will turn the tide."

Hugh looked confused, and seemed to be having a hard time assimilating all the information. "I am not going to kid you or paint a rosy picture," Sarkis continued. "This drug has about a 50-50 chance of working and about a 10% chance of making the arrhythmia worse. I don't think there is much of a choice here, but you need to know everything before you sign the consent form."

Hugh turned to Bonnie. "You are so much more knowledgeable about these things. What should I do?"

She shrugged and pushed a large swath of dramatically highlighted hair off her shoulder. "Hugh, I'm not sure this drug is such a hot idea. Who knows if it will work, and as Dr. Sarkis said, it might make things worse."

Hugh turned pleadingly to Philip. "Can't I even have a few minutes to think about this?"

"Hugh, we don't have time for that. Every second we spend reduces the chances for Moira."

"But, damn it, I need time. Let me talk to Bonnie alone."

Philip didn't hide his frustration. "Look, while you two are talking, I'm going to go back in there to see where we are. I'll be right back." As he left the room, he watched Bonnie's arm tighten around Hugh, whispering something while he sobbed into a handkerchief. Philip wasn't optimistic about Hugh being able to make a rational decision. Getting "informed consent" under these circumstances seemed stupid to Philip.

Back in the ER, Philip gave the experimental drug kit to a nurse with instructions on how to mix it. He reasoned if Hugh ever got around to giving permission for the new drug, he would at least be ready. While that was being done, he wheeled his cart into the room and hooked up the new defibrillator. This machine was unique because it shocked the heart using a very different kind of pulse waveform. Philip had had enormous success with it in his laboratory and had tried to get the hospital to replace all the defibrillators in the hospital with this new biphasic waveform device, but it was expensive and not surprisingly, he hit the customary financial snag. Although Philip couldn't imagine what could be more important, he was powerless to do anything more than complain at every purchasing meeting. This did not endear him to the hospital administrators who didn't particularly like him and secretly thought he was just another pig-headed physician who wanted a new toy.

First of all, Philip didn't look like he belonged at a Main Line Hospital. His dark complexion and Middle Eastern features made him an anomaly among the Dr. Welby types at GMH. Even worse, he had a reputation of being overbearing and dismissive. But the administrators knew it would be hard to replace him with anybody as talented or successful in bringing in so much business. In the end, the hospital compromised and agreed to phase in some additional equipment, but the ER had not gotten its amazing new defibrillator yet.

Philip knew there was little time to spare. Adam and his staff were tiring, and Moira's metabolic situation was worsening by the minute. The staff in the ER watched in silence as he made preparations. Philip tried shocking Moira's heart with the more powerful defibrillator but got the same results. Her heart would stabilize for a few seconds and then go right back into the same ugly rhythm.

The clock above the door ticked loudly, reminding Philip that time was now the enemy. He looked at Moira's ashen face and made a decision that would haunt him for the rest of his life. He turned to the young ER nurse next to him, and quietly told her to administer the bolus of Naladil. Accustomed to taking orders, the nurse did not question Philip and started the two-minute infusion. Philip then asked everybody to move back from the table, placed the paddles on Moira's chest with firm pressure, and pushed the buttons to activate the device one more time. This time, the high-energy shock had a dramatic result. Moira's body flew up at least six inches off the table as the staff ran forward to keep her from falling to the floor. As soon as the amplifiers on the telemetry screen recovered, it was obvious that not only had sinus rhythm been restored, but the dramatically prolonged QT interval was now normal. Most importantly, Moira had regained her blood pressure.

For the next several minutes, the ER staff watched the monitor screen. The room was silent save for the beeping of Moira's steady pulse. After about five minutes, the tension eased as it became obvious that Moira's heart was finally electrically stable. Slowly, the business of post-resuscitation care continued. The extra staff whispered to each other as they filtered out of the room. Philip gave management orders for Moira's medications and ventilator care, then made a beeline to the waiting room to deliver the good news to Hugh.

In the waiting room, Hugh practically assaulted Philip. "Where the hell have you been? You said you were coming right back. How is Moira?"

At that moment, Philip made another tough decision and did not tell Hugh that he had injected the experimental drug. Without Hugh's consent, he had violated a fundamental principle of ethical medical research. He rationalized that he did want to upset Hugh, and after all, the drug had worked. It had a good effect on Moira's heart, and the crisis was over. Philip figured that he would have to do some creative paperwork and then hope that no one discovered what he had done.

"I am happy to report that we had a good result. Moira's rhythm finally stabilized and we were able to get her QT interval back to something like normal. We are going to move her up to the ICU soon and try to figure out what happened to her."

Hugh blurted, "Nothing happened! She did this on her own."

Bonnie vaulted out of her seat and put her arm around Hugh. "Dr. Sarkis knows that, Hugh. He is just trying to be helpful."

Her soothing voice quieted him. "I know, I know. It is just that people ask me the question and I don't have an answer."

Philip also tried to reassure him. "That's OK, Hugh. That's why I'm here. I am just glad things are better, but we are by no means out of the woods yet. We will have to wait to see how much organ damage was created by that period of cardiac standstill."

"We understand, Dr. Sarkis" Bonnie said. "And we want to thank you for all you've done."

While Philip appreciated Hugh's emotional state, he was grateful for Bonnie's support. However, he didn't understand how and why Bonnie Romano suddenly became the family's spokesperson. Something didn't feel right about the whole situation, but Philip couldn't put his finger on it. The waiting room scene would be temporarily forgotten, but remembered vividly by all three.

CHAPTER 2

After she was stabilized in the ER, Moira was placed on a ventilator and admitted to the intensive care unit on Dr. Sarkis' private service where he would assume responsibility for her care with the assistance of non-cardiac specialists. Once she was "tucked in" by the nurses, an internal medicine resident, intern, and one of his cardiology fellows recorded Moira's history and did a thorough physical examination. These doctors were in various stages of their training, and were assigned to the unit to help with Moira's management.

Lab testing indicated that Moira had suffered relatively little damage to major organs except for her brain. Her drug screen, as expected, yielded the antihistamine that Philip had prescribed. Curiously, she also had small amounts of a diuretic, or water pill, in her system. Philip had not prescribed that and he wondered if Moira had taken it on her own, or if it was just a contaminant in the drug assay. Importantly, there was no level of any drug that could have caused the QT interval to prolong. Her heart function, assessed by ultrasound, had recovered from the insult.

Philip was relieved that Moira's heart had not been damaged permanently by low blood pressure or by the multiple shocks that she had received. Her kidneys had been sluggish immediately after the arrest, but normalized quickly as did her liver function. Philip asked the pulmonary specialists to help with management of Moira's ventilator. They reported that her lung function was adequate although the part of the central nervous system responsible for driving respiration was not working.

By far, her brain loomed as the major concern. It had been deprived of oxygen for so long that it was showing almost no spontaneous function. Everyone including the nurses recognized this right away, and Philip asked Steve Goldstein, a staff neurologist, to evaluate her.

Philip respected Steve. He was no charmer and had little bedside manner, but he was a straight shooter who always delivered an honest—sometimes a brutally honest—opinion. Steve liked to wear a short white coat and a bowtie, and always carried his little black bag filled with his examination tools, like a country doctor. His gee-whiz persona caused him to be mistaken for a new medical student on more than one occasion.

Steve did his usual detailed neurological assessment that included a functional measurement of Moira's central nervous system. He ordered an EEG or brain wave test immediately to determine if her brain was able to generate any electrical activity.

After interpreting the results, he delivered his report directly to Philip by phone. "She suffered severe higher and lower brain damage from that long period of poor blood flow when she first collapsed and during the ensuing repeated arrhythmias. Her pupils react abnormally to light, and she has no spontaneous respirations, which means that her brain stem is shot. The first EEG showed little organized electrical activity so I'm not sure how much higher function is going to come back."

Steven admitted that it was too early to throw in the towel, but he also advised Philip that it would be good idea to "hang crepe" with the family, medical jargon for preparing the family for the worst. Simply put, Moira was probably never going to recover brain function."

"So what do you suggest I do at this point?" Philip asked.

"Well, that article in the New England Journal makes me think that hypothermia is definitely the way to go. Keeping her chilled should maximize the chances of brain recovery."

The idea to use total body cooling was a logical one and many people believed it could work. The concern had been that there might be some damage to other organs that could offset the benefits of cooling. In fact, GMH had been one of the enrolling sites for research studies to determine the relative benefits and risks of total body cooling in severe brain injuries. According to the study, there was little down side to chilling Moira's body to about 95 degrees for 24 to 36 hours using a cooling blanket and delivering ice internally through a stomach tube. The recent journal article reported a highly significant improvement in neurological recovery, as long as patients were closely monitored. After writing his consultation note, Steven called Philip again to apprise him of his findings.

"I put a fairly long note in the chart and went over all of it with the house staff and nurses. I also spoke with her husband to prepare him. He got really pissed off when I told him about the body cooling and said he didn't understand why everybody wanted to use his wife as a guinea pig. I had no idea what he was talking about, but I told him that her treatment was mainstream and appropriate. He is impossible to deal with. All he kept asking was when we would know if the brain damage was permanent. He wasn't happy when I told him that we wanted to give this protocol at least three or four days."

Philip tried to give Hugh the benefit of the doubt. "Yeah, he is acting strange, but I guess he has a right to be a little crazy right now. In a matter of minutes this morning, his life was turned upside down."

"I guess so," said Steven, "but I just got the feeling he wants to get this whole thing over with and that he isn't holding out any hope at all. That struck me as weird. And that bleached blonde who was with him kept butting in. She said she had a medical background, but I couldn't figure out what it was. Then she told me she works for a drug company."

A light went on in Philip's brain. "That's right; I thought she looked familiar. I must have met her at some drug company gig, but I couldn't remember where. She is a close friend of Moira's — went to school with her, I think. She tried to help in the ER too."

"Anyhow, the guy is strange, Philip. But he knows the story now. He is well prepared for the worst, and I am out of here. I'll stop by tomorrow and keep tabs on Moira for you. We will have to repeat her EEG in 48 hours or so to see if anything is stirring. Right now, the lights are off and no one is home."

Philip thanked Steve and hung up, but his comments about Hugh stuck in Philip's mind. Steve certainly wasn't the first person to offer this kind of assessment of Hamlin. He was identified as the youngest son of a man who started an extremely successful food processing company. As such, his plump visage was regularly featured in the society pages of the Main Line Times. That didn't mean he was respected. In fact, the "in crowd" knew his he really couldn't make it on his own.

Hugh had attended the best private schools, but despite his father's hefty donations, had failed to get into Harvard or Yale where his two older brothers matriculated. Hugh ended up at Penn State instead, a "second-rate state college" according to his father. Whenever Gene Hamlin was asked about Hugh's major, he quickly replied, "skirt chasing."

After a lackluster four years that were remarkable only for proving the resiliency of his liver, Hugh declared he was ready to join the family business. Gene Hamlin was less than thrilled. With a good deal of arm twisting, he put that off for a couple of years by getting Hugh into the MBA program at St. Joseph's University in the Philadelphia suburbs. It was a decent school, "but no Harvard," his father would say. But a business degree was a must if Hugh was going to be taken seriously.

After he graduated, Hugh was given an office, secretary, car, cell phone, and almost nothing to do. True to form, Hugh readily accepted his position in the family company since it would give him lots of time to play golf and generally fool around.

Moira Hamlin's background couldn't have been more different. The O'Sheas were solidly middle-class, rooted in Springfield, a blue-collar neighborhood in the southwestern suburbs. Appearing like a well-scrubbed Irish kid from that part of town, Moira's light brown hair framed a pale complexion and sparkling blue eyes. "Oh sure darlin'," her grandmother used to say, "you've got the map of Ireland on yer face."

But five kids are a lot of mouths to feed, and Moira's parents struggled to scrape together the pittance needed to send them all to the neighborhood Catholic schools. Both of her parents worked, her father Tom as a security guard at a local shopping center, and Mary, her mother, at a cash register in the cafeteria at the Franklin Mint.

Like most of the families on her block, free time meant pitching in to make ends meet. Her brothers delivered papers and did odd jobs. Moira scrubbed the floors and ironed everybody's school uniforms. Her grandmother cooked and they all cleaned up. Family dinners were followed by homework around the grey Formica kitchen table. When the chores were done in the summertime and during school vacations, Moira headed to the library where she read voraciously and learned about exciting worlds far away from her drab life in Springfield.

During school terms, Moira enjoyed sports and practiced hard to excel. In fact, her excellent academics and tennis skills were good enough to get her into Penn with a generous financial aid package. To save money, she lived at home and worked as a waitress and bartender at a campus hangout to cover commuting expenses. Even so, there was little money left over. Although she longed to be part of the chic sorority crowd, she always felt as if she were watching a foreign film she would never quite understand.

It hit home one evening when she was waitressing at Smokey Joe's, a local campus hangout. A bevy of expensively dressed girls in cashmere sweaters, suede pants, and high-heeled boots piled into a booth, followed by an equally attractive group of boys. One of the young men motioned for her to get them menus. As she approached the table, he said, "We need to order. A few of us have to get to a squash match. Oh, by the way, that's a game not a vegetable."

The insult and the resultant giggling found their mark, and she was grateful for the dark shadows and low lights that concealed her burning cheeks and brimming eyes. Someday, she vowed, she would get even. Moira knew a good education would be the ticket out of her parents' shabby three-bedroom lifestyle. So she plowed on and worked hard, and even dared to daydream.

After graduation, she decided on business school. The Wharton School acceptance was alluring but instead she settled on St. Joe's because they offered a full scholarship. That decision would ultimately change her life.

Hugh was immediately attracted to Moira's natural good looks and almost innocent persona. In turn, Moira was intrigued by his smooth come-on, his obviously expensive clothes, and his red Porsche convertible. "Oh Holy Mother of Jesus," her brother Don exclaimed when she described her new boyfriend. "Does he know where ya come from, Moira? Did you tell him about us?" The truth was she didn't, and because she was concerned, she was evasive when he inquired about her family.

One late spring day, about two months after their first date, Hugh said he had to detour home before dinner to pick up a tuxedo for a stag party at his club. When he turned onto the wide leafy road, then punched in the code at a gate guarded by two enormous stone lions, Moira thought they were at a club or a hotel. When Charlie, the groundskeeper, took his car, and Conchita, the parlor maid, greeted them at the door, she felt faint. How could she ever take him home?

Moira was shy, and Hugh's courtship overwhelmed her. When he boldly announced that he was going to marry her after a couple of dates, Moira was amused, flattered and intrigued. Secretly, she couldn't decide if it was Hugh or his status that really attracted her. The gifts were clearly overwhelming. The pale mauve cashmere sweater that appeared on the car seat after their third date somehow made up for the unforgettable insult at Smokey Joe's.

Moira thought Hugh was good-looking, in a beefy kind of way, and she tried hard to ignore his faults. That Moira was a fitness fanatic and in great physical condition and Hugh a couch potato didn't bother her. Eventually she learned that Hugh's father not only had a luxury box for all major sports events, but also owned a piece of the Eagles, Philadelphia's professional football franchise. Hugh had been the envy of his schoolmates since he knew many of the players personally and had their autographed photos in his bookbag.

Moira loved dancing and enjoyed tennis, hiking and almost any vigorous outdoor activity. Hugh loved golf, but his lack of skill and overall laziness meant he often lost large wagers and was considered an "easy mark."

If Moira and Hugh struggled to find commonality, they curiously found mutual satisfaction in a place Moira never would have imagined, Atlantic City. Hugh's parents had recently purchased a condominium at one of the new casinos, and Hugh asked Moira to accompany him there one weekend. Moira's initial reaction was negative but Hugh convinced her to give it a try. "I'll get tickets for one of the shows and we'll have a great dinner. You won't have to go to the casinos if you don't want to."

Reluctantly, Moira agreed and the adventure turned out to be a huge success. Hugh spent the entire day gambling in the casinos. Moira jogged on the beach and got her first-ever massage at the hotel's luxurious spa. She was glowing when they met for dinner and later sat stage-side for a Four Seasons revival. Hugh had even arranged for her to meet Frankie Valli, the lead singer, after the arranged for her to meet Frankie Valli, the lead singer, after the show. The sojourn set a comfortable pattern for their future relationship: days apart and evenings together.

Moira was anxious to have Hugh meet her family. When she asked him one evening what he thought the best venue might be, he said, "I have a great idea. Let's take them to an Eagles game. The first pre-season night game is next weekend. We'll do a casual dinner in South Philly and go to the stadium."

The plan worked. The dinner at Dante and Luigi's was initially strained, but when Moira's father got to meet the Eagles coaches and players and sit in a luxury box, he was as excited as a little kid. In fact, both Tom and Mary O'Shea were so impressed by the lavish night out, they quickly minimized Hugh's Jewish background. As Hugh turned on the charm, Moira's parents melted.

In contrast, the senior Hamlins were not so easily won over. They admired Moira's energy and intelligence, but the religious issue concerned them. Many of their friends reported that when their children married "goyim" there were inevitable problems when grandchildren came along.

Gradually, Moira managed to convince herself that she was in love with Hugh, and not his money. When he popped the question during a romantic candlelit dinner at an elegant restaurant, she blushingly accepted the four-carat yellow diamond.

The dazzling wedding occurred soon after Moira and Hugh graduated from business school. The reception at the Hamlin club was obviously more than Moira's parents could afford, so the Hamlins covered it. Afterward, the couple headed to New Zealand and Australia for a month-long honeymoon. Their marriage was off to an auspicious start.

Upon their return, Hugh and Moira moved into a new house, not far from his parents' estate. Moira accepted a job in the county tax office, and Hugh continued collecting a salary for showing up at the plant, and working on his golf handicap. It wasn't long before Moira was pregnant. Although she intended to take a short leave, she couldn't bear to be separated from her infant son, and with Hugh's blessing did not return to work. She sensed, however, that her decision diminished his underlying respect for her and that he consciously "dumbed down" their conversations to subjects that he really didn't care much about.

Day-to-day life was supported by a bevy of servants who took care of everything. Moira drove a black Range Rover with a blue ing with designer clothes, including cashmere sweaters of almost every color.

Another boy and girl arrived in rapid succession. The couple proved to be a formidable parenting team. Their children were well adjusted, successful in school and sports, and the pride of their grandparents with whom they spent a lot of time. Moira was out every day playing bridge or tennis, and working on her favorite charity events. Choosing a place to "do lunch" became her constant obsession, and a couple of glasses of wine, she rea soned, never hurt. She stopped exercising as often and didn't loose all the weight she had put on with her latest pregnancy. But Hugh wasn't paying much attention, and therefore neither was she.

Eventually, Moira's menstrual periods became erratic, and her birth control methods grew lax. At the age of 39, she was shocked to learn that she was pregnant with their fourth child, especially since sex with Hugh at that point was rare. The real surprise was Hugh's wildly negative reaction to the news. He accused her of intentionally becoming pregnant to keep him engaged in their marriage. It was a conclusion that Moira found ridiculous, because she openly preferred his absence.

Knowing that pregnancy at her age could be problematic, Moira consulted Natalie Gerson, GMH's bespectacled and dowdy head of Ob-Gyn, who took over her case from her regular obstetrician. Natalie was a renowned physician who specialized in caring for older women or those who had pre-existing medical problems. Initially, Moira's case appeared routine to Natalie, and she cheerfully took on this high-profile new patient.

But within a month of her first visit, Moira began to experience cardiac problems. She told Dr. Gerson that when she was in bed at night, she often had heart palpitations. "It feels like somebody is beating a drum in my chest and then suddenly decides to skip a beat or two. The pattern repeats itself for minutes to hours at a time," she explained.

Natalie asked Moira, "Have you had any other symptoms like blackouts, dizzy spells, chest pain maybe?"

"I have had a little lightheadedness sometimes, but only when I overexert."

Natalie knew that abnormal and forceful heart rhythms were very common during pregnancy. Moira was healthy and had no family history of cardiac problems. She was taking no medications except for pre-natal vitamins. So in the absence of more severe symptoms, Natalie initially decided to hold off on a cardiac evaluation. She preferred not to send patients to consultants unless absolutely necessary.

However, when Moira continued to complain of severe palpitations, Natalie caved in and called Philip Sarkis. Although not the most engaging person in the world, he was extremely competent. Like Adam Wilkie, she had sent a parent to Philip for some atrial or upper chamber arrhythmias. Natalie was pleased with Philip's conservative approach to her mother's problem.

When he answered the phone, she said "Philip, I would really appreciate it if you could see Moira Hamlin soon. She is 39-year-old pregnant woman and is having some kind of arrhythmia. It is making her crazy."

"That name sounds familiar. Have I seen her before?"

"No, you probably recognize her name from the society pages. Her husband's family is very prominent, and extremely philanthropic, so she is out and about at functions all the time."

"Great, a society maven. Can't wait to serve."

Natalie, who was also a dyed-in-the-wool Main Line socialite, decided not to react to Philip's comment. "OK, I'll have her call your office and set up an appointment and we'll send over the few records we have."

When he met Moira, Philip was pleasantly surprised. He had assumed that she was going to be just another society twit with an attitude. Instead, she was attractive, bright and had a sense of humor that put Philip at ease. He sat quietly and listened to her story, interrupting only a few times for clarification. He asked about any family history of rhythm or heart problems, and was interested to hear that there were none. When he inquired about other illnesses, he wasn't surprised to learn that Moira had a minor eating disorder in college. "I just didn't want to be fat so I starved myself most of the time and made myself throw up. Then I got tired of the way it made me feel so I stopped."

Aside from that, Moira had no other problems and took no medicines. "I took an antihistamine for seasonal allergies before my pregnancy but stopped it when I got pregnant." After a brief physical examination, Philip explained that Moira was clearly having some kind of cardiac rhythm issue.

"This kind of thing is common during pregnancy and it is rarely a cause for concern, Moira," he said in an even, non-threatening tone. "It is likely that the palpitations represent single premature beats coming from the bottom chamber of your heart called the ventricle. The 'skips' occur because the heart has to reset itself after the premature beat and so there is a brief pause. In most cases, treatment is not necessary, and it usually resolves following delivery."

To prove that the extra beats were benign, Philip suggested that Moira have a few tests, such as routine bloodwork and an EKG. Then he accompanied her out of the office and introduced her to his secretary.

Rhonda Simons had been with Philip for over 15 years. In fact, they had practically "grown up" together. When Philip had just completed his training and was the new guy at GMH, he was assigned the least experienced secretary in the department. Rhonda was a 19-year-old African American with a ghetto accent, fresh out of school. The prevailing theory among the office staff was that Rhonda wasn't too bright and was an affirmative action hire who wouldn't last too long in the job. Philip already had a reputation for being difficult so no one gave Rhonda much of a chance.

To everyone's surprise, Rhonda and Philip hit it off. In fact, for many years she was the only person who could tease him, and get away with it. A jewel with a photographic memory, superb typing skills, and a great work ethic, she admired Philip for his intelligence and his fairness, and managed to ignore his more than occasional gruffness.

Soon after she was hired, on a hot summer day, Philip invited Rhonda her husband and kids to his house for a swim and barbecue. This was a noteworthy event because Philip rarely entertained. That afternoon, he watched with amusement as his neighbors stared in horror as the group of attractive young African Americans sauntered up the driveway. After all, entertaining black people was not the Main Line way.

At work, Rhonda fit perfectly into Philip's office. She dressed conservatively, enjoyed meeting patients, and bantered easily with other physicians. Rhonda frequently chatted amicably with chiefs of other departments until Philip got on the line. Everybody loved Rhonda.

Rhonda made arrangements for Moira's tests and follow-up appointment. Moira later told her mother, "Dr. Sarkis wasn't exactly Mr. Personality, but he knew what he was talking about. And his secretary Rhonda was terrific."

Moira was so comfortable with the outcome of her visit that, after the tests, she slipped back into her routine and put the problem out of her mind for the few days it took to obtain the results. Hugh didn't take much interest in what was occurring. In fact, the only reason he even knew Moira had seen a cardiologist was because he too had palpitations but was afraid to have them checked.

When Moira returned to see Philip, she knew immediately from the look on his face and the tone of his voice that the news was not going to be good. She tried to remain calm, but could feel tension welling up in her chest. Philip pulled up a stool and sat next to her at the end of the examination table.

"Most of your tests were fine, Moira. In fact, your blood work checked out, with the exception of the potassium and magnesium levels, which were both a little low. Is your diet normal now or are you still having eating problems?"

Moira was defensive. "No! Sometimes I junk out, but I think I do pretty well with my diet over-all."

"Well, I don't have any other way to explain the low values right now— my nurse practitioner will give you some information about what foods you need to eat to supplement your mineral levels. The real issue, though, was your EKG. I found that your QT interval was prolonged."

"What does that mean?" Moira asked trying to keep the mounting panic out of her voice.

"It means that there is a problem with the way your heart activates and reactivates electrically."

Philip went on to give Moira a mini-lecture about cardiac electrophysiology. It was hard for her to understand the complicated terms, but she fought to pay attention and managed to retain most of what Philip told her. For his part, Philip wasn't the best at simplifying things, and often became impatient with slow learners. "I do my best—I can't help it if people can't keep up with me," he would often say in self-defense.

"The heart is an electrical pump, and the 'electricity' is generated by the movement of ions across the heart's cellular membranes," he said. "Once the heart activates and contracts, it needs to reset so that it can fill up with blood and activate again. Sodium ions move into the cell to activate it, and potassium ions move out of the cell to reset it. For reasons that are not clear to us, some people are born with an abnormality of potassium channels so heart cells can't reset, as they should. We can detect the problem by measuring an interval on the EKG we call the QT interval."

"So mine is long. Is that what makes the heart go out of rhythm?"

"Because some cells reset more slowly than others, this could create short circuiting in the heart, and that is what can lead to the development of a severe cardiac rhythm problem. The QT prolongation is a marker for an electrical condition you may have been born with. The truth is, I really can't be sure, based on what we have so far, if what I am seeing on the EKG is the cause of the palpitations you are having. I tend to doubt that, but I will need to order some more tests. If you do have the long QT syndrome, without severe symptoms or a family history of sudden unexplained death, the most we would have to do is treat you with drugs to prevent severe heart rhythm abnormalities from developing."

"I don't like taking drugs," Moira protested, "especially while I'm pregnant."

"Let's not get too carried away with ourselves. I am not sure this is actually the diagnosis. If you do have it, you can choose how you want to treat it, and if you wish, you can take your chances without any treatment. At this point I don't know what your real risk of a severe rhythm problem might be. We need more data."

Although Philip was fairly sure that Moira did have the long QT syndrome, he figured that he would need incontrovertible evidence that she did have the problem before she would agree to be treated. Besides, the tests would help him figure out how much treatment might be needed. There was a clearly recognized association between the extent of QT prolongation and the risk of sudden death. A monitor would allow Philip to quantify the risk. Then if Moira resisted treatment, he would know how much pressure to exert to convince her to do something. From the look on her face, Moira was going into panic mode so for the time being, Philip decided on a more direct approach.

"Let's do this," he said as kindly as he could. "We'll get some more tests. The studies I have in mind are fairly simple, but they will help us understand things better."

"OK, but can we get them done as soon as possible? This whole thing is starting to scare me."

"I am sure that Rhonda will be able to schedule them for you in our lab within the week. In the meantime, I want you to carry a heart monitor for 24 hours. This will allow me to see what happens to your QT interval as your heart rate varies throughout the day. You should also have a treadmill stress test to see if you have any arrhythmias when your heart is under stress. While you are at the lab, they will also do an echocardiogram, which is an ultrasound of your heart, just to make sure that there isn't anything wrong with the valves or other heart structures. None of these tests carry much risk and they will give us a lot of valuable information."

"All right, that sounds OK. When will we know the results?" Moira asked nervously.

Philip tried not to show his annoyance with a question he had heard a thousand times. He told Moira it would take at least a week to get the tests done and properly analyzed. But realizing her fragile state, he knew that emotional support was as critical as the evaluations themselves. For that reason he suggested that Hugh accompany Moira to the follow-up visit.

Tears welled up in Moira's eyes. "I asked him to come with me today, but he told me that coming to your office would just make him too anxious and upset. So I told him to forget it."

Not supporting your wife during a difficult evaluation seemed inconceiable to Philip. But this, and Hugh's subsequent bizarre behavior after Moira's cardiac arrest, convinced Philip that Hugh was not the kind of person he would ever want to get to know over a few beers. Unfortunately for Philip, he would get to know more about Hugh Hamlin than he could ever imagine.

CHAPTER 3

Philip didn't tell Moira about every nuance of her diagnosis because he didn't want to alarm her. He also hated it when doctors unloaded information on patients in an effort to make a "full disclosure." He had seen hundreds of patients who had been devastated by the "honest opinions" of doctors. Young physicians, who don't have a clue about the consequences, carelessly throw about terms such as "massive heart attack" and "severe heart failure." Patients need to have information filtered, and it is the skillful doctor who, without deliberate deceit, allows the patient to benefit from a therapeutic path. In Moira's case, Philip kept a lot of scary information to himself.

Philip had spent most of his research years trying to understand disorders that affect the heart's ability to re-excite itself electrically. He also had experience with applying basic research information in the clinic. This was an unusual skill. Not many physicians can take a clear understanding of basic science directly to the bedside. There was a lot he could have told Moira about the consequences of the diagnosis, but he knew it was always better to deliver bad news in small doses. For example, Philip knew that if he told Moira that her condition was hereditary, she would begin worrying about her children. Sure, they would eventually need to be tested, but he didn't want to bring that up now.

Besides, medical knowledge evolves quickly. Initially thought by scientists to be relatively simple, re-excitation of the heart is a complicated, genetically determined process. Just a few years before, a group of creative Italian investigators had published cases of sudden infant death syndrome that might have been caused by Moira's abnormality.

Although Philip considered himself an expert in the field, he leaned heavily on a team of foreign scientists to do much of the heavy lifting. They were bright men and women who never balked when he took the credit for their work. He almost never went to the lab himself and like other major "domos" relied on his team to generate data and add his name to the published papers.

As a group, the laboratory staff had a wonderful work ethic and labored efficiently on highly sophisticated projects. What took other labs weeks and months to investigate was carried off in a matter of days, and always with exquisitely analyzed data. As a result, Philip rarely had to critique their work. Grants and papers were almost always accepted without revision.

For example, Philip's laboratory explored the important question of what factors trigger a malignant arrhythmia in a susceptible individual. Since Moira had been born with a long QT interval, what were the chances that at some point her heart could suddenly go out of rhythm? What might cause that to happen? And if she had inherited the disease, why hadn't either of her parents had a similar problem? It was well known that abnormalities of electrolytes like low levels of potassium and magnesium were important predisposing factors, but they were rarely the entire explanation.

Philip's lab had also determined that some drugs—a long and growing list—further impeded the movement of potassium ions, exacerbating the congenital abnormality. Alarmingly, primary care doctors who were unaware of their patients' vulnerability prescribed many of these drugs for non-cardiac indications.

The list of agents included several antibiotics, antihistamines, and sedatives, some which were available over the counter. Philip's lab and others established that these drugs caused the deaths of many otherwise healthy people. Because of this, in an unprecedented decision, the Food and Drug Administration began to insist that any new drug approved in the United States must be analyzed for its effect on cardiac repolarization, placing this problem at the forefront of drug safety considerations.

At the clinical level, Philip had been working on ways to use the EKG to predict the risk of rhythm disturbances in patients with the long QT syndrome. He and a group of others had determined that abnormalities of the waveforms on the EKG could be a good indicator of how much risk there was for sudden death. Moira's EKG was particularly interesting in this regard. Her QT was only modestly long, but her T wave had a fairly large notch. From that tracing Philip suspected that Moira was at particular risk of having a severe cardiac arrhythmia if she took one of the drugs that were harmful, especially if her potassium or magnesium concentrations happened to be low at the same time. Philip knew that for Moira, strict avoidance of culprit drugs was a must.

Moira's situation made Philip uneasy for another reason: if something bad happened to a young patient like Moira, there was a good chance he would be sued. Bad outcomes prompt lawsuits all the time, especially since there are plenty of "experts" who, if paid enough, are willing to blame a doctor for just about anything.

Nowhere was that possibility greater than in Philadelphia, where there were more malpractice attorneys per square mile than anywhere else in the world. Philip knew all too well that a malpractice lawsuit was a nightmare that demands an inordinate amount of time and energy to defend. Worse, false accusations of incompetence leave deep psychological scars, severely damage good reputations, and skew patient management.

This situation was particularly egregious on the Main Line where the well-heeled clientele expect flawless medical care, and simply do not tolerate untoward outcomes. When something bad happens to an otherwise healthy individual, the first assumption is always that the doctor must have made an error. Malpractice attorneys, some of whom even retain billboard space to propagate their skewed views of medicine, dutifully plant that seed of doubt. Not surprisingly, Philip and his colleagues practiced CYA (cover your ass) medicine. This practice spurs high costs because doctors order more tests than they need so they could say they left no stone unturned. Errors of commission are easier to explain than errors of omission.

At the end of the day, Philip worried that he was overdoing Moira's testing and decided to run her case past one of the partners in his group. As a whole, Philip enjoyed collegial "curbside consults." He put Moira's chart under his arm and strolled into Milan Kuco's cluttered office.

Philip had recruited this junior colleague from his own training program. He respected Milan not only for his technical skill, but also for his sound judgment. Milan was a large, handsome, Eastern European man who had overcome personal tragedy in his native Yugoslavia before immigrating to the United States. He had worked his way up the Harvard training system before Philip asked him to run GMH's invasive laboratories. Not the most organized person, Milan was full of energy and loved to see as many patients and do as many procedures as he could cram into his busy schedule.

Milan's black eyes focused intensely on Philip. "I don't think you have any choice, Philip," he finally answered. "You have to get some more tests. But I think she should be at low risk of dying suddenly. She doesn't have a family history. She is 39 and has had no events in her life."

This was exactly the pragmatic answer he expected from Milan. "Yeah, but I don't like the look of her T wave. The big question is whether or not I have to treat her with anything or just follow her along."

Milan was quick to answer. "With her profile, I would just follow her along. As long as she stays off of the wrong drugs and keeps her electrolytes in line, she should be OK, no?"

"Well, we'll see what her test results look like and what she wants to do. She is pregnant, so she may want to avoid drug therapy until she delivers."

"Yeah, let it ride on the tests you ordered and see what her preference is, but I definitely wouldn't insist on treatment if I were you."

When Philip finally assembled all the test results, they looked very much as he had expected. Moira had a structurally normal heart, there was no evidence of coronary artery or valve disease, and her cardiac pumping function was normal. The stress test had been fine over-all, but the EKG and her 24-hour monitor provided indisputable evidence that she indeed had the long QT syndrome.

Philip brought all the data with him when he met with Moira and Hugh in his office a week later. Moira was again perched on the examination table while Hugh sat across from her on a roller stool. She had written out a long list of questions, which Philip answered patiently.

"Why did she have it?" She had been born with the genetic defect. "Why had it not been diagnosed before?" It was unlikely that Moira had had an EKG before (she couldn't remember having one). Even so, the abnormality was subtle and could have been missed by someone with less expertise. "What about the children?" They needed to be screened with EKGs, as did all of Moira's first-degree relatives. "Were there any other tests needed?" No, this was the diagnosis and nothing else would refine it further.

And then came the big question, which Moira asked in a tremulous voice. "What are we going to do about this?"

Philip did not hesitate. "Moira, you are not at high risk of dying suddenly based on what we know about you and your family history. You are nearly 40 years old and never had a problem. That is all to the good. With your profile, the most we would recommend is a drug to try to keep the heart electrically stable. The best prophylactic therapy for patients with your risk profile is a beta-blocker."

Philip went on to explain what beta-blockers are and how they reduce the chance of a severe arrhythmia by suppressing adrenalin's effect on the heart. High adrenalin, caused by things like fright, provokes arrhythmias in persons with the long QT syndrome. Philip thought that beta-blocker therapy for Moira was reasonable but he hastened to add that, like everything in medicine, there was a down side.

He explained, "Beta-blockers have side effects like fatigue and listlessness. In addition, beta-blockers in pregnancy can slow labor down and babies of mothers who have taken beta-blockers tend to be smaller and weigh less."

"Well, if I can't take them with absolute safety in pregnancy, is there anything else for me?" asked Moira.

"We sometimes recommend implantable shocking devices. But the patient really has to be at high risk because of a family history or because of extreme symptoms like blackouts. That's not your story."

Hugh jumped in emphatically at this point. "I agree with Moira. I don't want her taking drugs while she is pregnant."

Philip was a little surprised at the outburst, but noted that Moira was nodding her head in agreement

"Moira, I can understand your decision. But you must know that there is a small chance you could have an arrhythmia and pass out or die suddenly. It is very important that we keep a close watch on your electrolyte values, to keep your potassium and magnesium levels as normal as possible, and that you avoid drugs that could further prolong your QT interval. Water pills are particularly problematic. They leach potassium and magnesium out of the system when they remove fluid. And any kind of diet pill is bad because it has an adrenalin-like effect on the heart that could get you into trouble."

When Hugh asked what other drugs were prohibited, Philip reached into his lab coat and gave Moira a list of drugs likely to prolong the QT interval. Hugh asked for a copy. "I would like to keep one in my files." He folded the bright pink paper and tucked it into his jacket pocket.

Philip suggested that Moira see him every few weeks during her pregnancy and call him if her palpitations worsened. She agreed and even managed a nervous smile. However, Hugh barely said goodbye as he brushed past Philip and left the examination room.

Afterward, Philip sat at his desk and dictated a detailed letter to Natalie Gerson in which he explained that treatment had been offered and rejected by the Hamlins but that he would provide careful follow-up for the remainder of Moira's pregnancy.

As happened so frequently, Moira's symptoms improved significantly after the office conference. Philip knew that reassurance itself tended to improve things by making some patients less obsessed about their condition. During the following weeks, she had a few light episodes and called Philip's office to speak with his nurse practitioner. Her subsequent visits were brief and to the point. Philip was in and out quickly and didn't have much to offer.

Moira didn't know what to make of Philip Sarkis. She didn't like his gruffness but she did respect his expertise and resolved to put up with his abrupt personality as long as her pregnancy went well. When she asked Hugh what he thought of Dr. Sarkis, he merely grunted and said that the guy was a full of himself but he really wasn't surprised because that was the way most doctors acted.

As Moira's due date approached, Gerson decided to induce her when Dr. Sarkis was available in case there was a rhythm problem. Philip agreed and visited her as labor progressed. Drugs that Philip had approved were infused to stimulate labor and things went as smoothly as they had during Moira's previous deliveries when she hadn't been on a cardiac monitor.

On this day, though, the room was filled with sophisticated monitoring and resuscitation equipment as well as an additional cadre of expert staff. Throughout her labor, Moira asked the nurses, "Am I going to live through this?" In fact she did just fine and delivered a healthy boy they named Nathan.

Moira made a speedy recovery, and within a few weeks was back in Philip's office for a regular appointment. Philip and Moira had the same conversation as when she was pregnant, except this time she also asked about the effect of beta-blockers on little Nathan. Moira was breastfeeding and was concerned because she knew that most beta-blockers were secreted in breast milk and could slow Nathan's heart and drop his blood pressure. Therefore, she decided not to take them. In addition, she had read on the Internet that beta-blockers often caused people to gain weight, a side effect Philip acknowledged. Moira was fanatical about her weight, and was now on a mission to lose all of her "baby fat" and get back into her clothes. After adding up all of these issues, Moira felt that her decision not to take a beta-blocker was correct. She was self confident and adamant.

"No way Doc. Hugh and I talked this over and I prefer to take my chances, which you have told me are pretty good as long as I stay away from bad drugs and keep my diet on an even keel."

"It's your call, Moira. I can understand your decision, and we'll go with it if you wish." Nevertheless, once again Philip was careful to document their conversation in her chart, specifically that Moira had refused treatment The fact that she was not at high risk eliminated discussion about the implantation of a defibrillator.

"So what did your little bird decide after all?" Milan Kuco called out to Philip as he passed his open office door after Moira's visit.

"She wants to go bare," Philip replied.

"Is she going to be on any medications at all?"

"A vitamin and an antihistamine."

The antihistamine piqued Milan's interest. "Something safe, I hope."

"Damn right," said Philip. "The only drug I would dream of

giving her would be Appel."

Milan and Philip both knew about the complicated clinical trials in which Appel had been proven safe in patients with the long QT syndrome. This had been an important development since the precusor of Appel, a drug called Delcane, had been withdrawn from the market when several people who were taking the allergy drug suddenly died.

"So, it looks like this will work out OK, after all," Milan observed.

"God, I hope so," answered Philip. "I feel like I've put a ton of time into this damn case."

Milan nodded in agreement. "Yes, you are being very careful with this one, my friend, and I can understand why. She is a pretty high-profile patient. Even so, you can never be too careful."

Neither Milan nor Philip could have imagined how true those words actually were.

CHAPTER 4

After her cardiac arrest, Moira's early hospital course went according to plan. Following 24 hours of cooling, she was rewarmed to a normal temperature. During the process, she was carefully observed for complications of hypothermia such as liver shutdown and muscle damage. Her electrolyte levels were finally placed in normal range after large doses of magnesium and potassium. The amount needed to replenish those minerals had been far more than Philip would have predicted. Furthermore, he still didn't have a good explanation for the low electrolyte values the emergency room had obtained. After her pregnancy Moira had assured him that her diet was normal and she denied taking water pills. He came up with dozens of possible explanations for what had happened, but few made sense. The toughest question was why her cardiac arrest had occurred after so many years of stability.

Philip supervised Moira's case like a mother hen. He met with the staff in the nursing station at least twice a day to review her status. Her vital organ function, including her kidneys and liver, had returned to normal. Philip spent hours at her bedside, conferring with the residents, nursing staff, and therapists who had a hand in Moira's care. He also made a point of checking in each day with all the consultants on the case, in particular the neurologist Steve Goldstein.

Philip had learned from years of experience that it only took one slip-up to lose a patient as sick as this. He knew if Moira didn't make it, he could be blamed for her death. There were countless people at the hospital, who made a career out of cataloguing and reporting medical mishaps. Philip resented these "Monday morning quarterbacks." Anyone who cared for sick patients on a regular basis would know how brittle ill patients can be. Heart rhythm problems were the perfect milieu for a bad result. Cardiac arrest that occurs out of the hospital has a high mortality, with fewer than 20% of patients surviving with all of their faculties intact. The number fell into single digits in cases like Moira's, in which resuscitation was not begun promptly.

But Philip was determined to give Moira a chance to beat the odds by scrupulously attending to every detail of her care. He also took pains to inform Hugh and her parents regularly about her situation.

Hugh spent little time at the hospital, and didn't return Philip's phone calls. When Philip finally saw Hugh at the hospital, he asked if her diet had changed recently.

"I don't even pretend to know what you are talking about," Hugh answered. "Why do doctors always want to blame patients and their families when something like this happens? Moira had an excellent diet. In fact, sometimes I think she went overboard on the healthy stuff."

Each time Philip tried to discuss Moira's condition, Hugh was gruff and even referred to Moira in the past tense once or twice. Had Hugh already written Moira off?

Philip managed to track Hugh down early one evening to go over the drug question again, but he got yet another nasty response.

"I already told you what she took," Hugh barked in response. Philip swallowed his anger and chalked up Hugh's attitude to stress. He persevered because he needed the information. "Hugh, you have to know how important it is to get this thing right. The single most likely reason for Moira's problem would have been a drug that caused the QT interval to go way out on her. I am just trying to figure out if that is what happened and if so why."

When Moira was admitted to the ICU, Philip had insisted that another blood and urine specimen be sent to the laboratory, and specified that he wanted the most sensitive and comprehensive drug assay available. He knew that a QT prolonging drug, even when present in very small concentrations, could cause a disastrous arrhythmia. A relatively innocent drug, like an antibiotic, could produce a lethal arrhythmia. When the results came back a few days later, the only "hit" had been Appel, Moira's antihistamine. What had been surprising was the uncommonly high concentration of the drug in Moira's system.

Although he knew that his question would set Hugh off again, he had to ask why she had taken so much Appel.

"How the hell should I know? I didn't give her the damn drug! She took it whenever her allergies were bad, and they are pretty vicious this time of year. She was probably popping them fairly regularly. And why the hell are you asking me that anyway? You're the one who told her she could take the stuff. Or did you screw that up?"

In his early years, Philip was known to have a short temper and rarely took guff from anybody. His college roommates had nicknamed him "mad-dog," which stuck with him through medical school. He was known to go after people who were rude or who didn't do what he perceived to be the right thing. The nickname had been coined after he famously retrieved a piece of litter thrown out of a car window, chased down the driver, and delivered the refuse through the driver's window along with a lecture about not polluting the environment.

However age and experience had mellowed Philip and caused him to handle people more gently. He had learned to do otherwise was self-defeating in the medical profession. So with the assurance of his cutting-edge knowledge, Philip withstood Hugh's verbal diatribe. "No, Hugh," he said with deliberate calm. "There was no screw-up. Appel is safe for patients with Moira's problem at any dose. But the blood levels were at least 5 to 10 times higher than they should have been, even if we assume that she took the drug just before she passed out. That would mean she was taking a whole lot more of the drug than I recommended. And if she was not being compliant in that sense, it makes me wonder if she was making a habit of taking other drugs that weren't good for her."

"Look, I can't help you," Hugh snarled. "You guys are going to have to figure this one out for a change because Moira can't tell you what happened and neither can I."

This was the biggest problem: Moira simply wasn't waking up. Despite the hypothermia, ventilator management, and terrific nursing care, Moira's brain was not showing any signs of improving. Steve Goldstein, the neurology consultant, examined her daily. He was not optimistic.

"I haven't seen improvement in any parameter," Steve in-

formed Philip in a hallway conversation five days after admission.
"What do you suggest that we do at this point?"

"As that famous Vanguard guy Jack Bogle liked to say, 'Stay the course.' It is still too early to throw in the towel. What other metaphors would you like from me?"

Sometimes a little humor helped, but Philip couldn't loosen up. He knew that another family consultation was necessary, but he didn't have the stomach to lock horns with Hugh again.

"Steve, I have a favor to ask. Could you present all of this to her husband and see what he wants to do?"

"You mean take this to Mr. Congeniality? Sure, can't think of a more pleasant way to start my evening. You are going to owe me big time, and I think that a good stiff drink would be the most appropriate payoff."

Steve went to the family waiting room and caught Hugh just as he was arriving. Steve delivered the news succinctly and as honestly as he could. Hugh's reaction was hostile but not unexpected.

"So you guys want to give up on her? What's the matter, need the bed for somebody else you screwed up?" Steve had a higher threshold for abuse than Philip.

"Look Mr. Hamlin, we are doing absolutely everything we can to help your wife. It is an unfortunate situation. The ambulance guys told us that there was a long delay in getting your wife's resuscitation started and that is what caused so much damage to her brain."

"I told those people that I did everything I could," Hugh shot back. "I don't know how to do CPR and neither did anyone else in the damn house. If my neighbor had been home, maybe it would have been a different story."

"I understand, Mr. Hamlin. And there is still a small chance that Moira will recover at least some neurological function. I just have no way of knowing when and how much. We simply have to wait and see."

"Look, Moira has a living will and I am the trustee. Her wishes were clear. Under no circumstances did she want to be kept alive on a machine indefinitely. So at some point, we will have to decide if and when to remove her from life support."

Bonnie, who as usual was standing by, interjected. "In the

50

meantime, Doctor Goldstein, the family wants you to do everything you can to make her well."

"Sure, we certainly don't want to take her off of the ventilator prematurely. We need to do a brain wave test—an EEG—to see if brain activity is absent."

"OK, that would be very helpful. When do you plan to do that?" Bonnie asked.

"I can arrange for one to be done tomorrow morning."

"Fine, do it and then call me with the results," instructed Hugh.

Steve was relieved to return to the ICU, where he wrote an order for the EEG. While he entered a note in Moira's chart, he put in a call to Philip who was home with his family for the first evening in a week. Goldstein's call interrupted dinner, but Philip decided to take it. He was anxious to hear what had happened with Hugh Hamlin.

"How did it go?" Philip asked.

"Brutal. Philip, this guy is really pissed off. We're doing an EEG tomorrow and he wants us to call him with the results. That blonde woman keeps instructing everybody to keep trying, but he made it clear that Moira said she never wanted to be kept alive indefinitely on machines."

Philip could foresee trouble. Discontinuing life support was always a hot button in patient management, evoking strong, visceral reactions. Usually, however, the family would insist on going slowly to give their loved one every chance to recover. "I can see his point. But it has only been four days so there is still a chance she could wake up or at least get some function back."

"I guess so, but her brain was essentially fried and the chances of her getting significantly better are ultra-slim. Unless the EEG is definitively flat, we can keep going but only for a short while longer."

Philip agreed. "OK. Let's see what the test shows and we'll go from there."

"Philip, be careful with this guy. He is really angry, and I think he is the kind of person who could come after you when this is all over."

"You mean a lawsuit?" Philip had been thinking the same thing but felt obliged to deny the possibility with Steve. "I've gone out of my way to document everything in this case. There's no way."

"Come on, Philip, who are you kidding? Do you really think that there is any correlation between getting sued and good or bad

51

practice? Remember, anybody can sue a doctor for anything."

Philip knew that Steve was right. A large part of the malpractice mess was that any unprincipled attorney, supported by an opinion from one greedy doctor, could sue. There was no way to screen out frivolous cases. Pennsylvania had enacted changes in the law that required an expert to certify that malpractice had occurred before a case could be placed in suit, but there seemed to be no luck of unprincipled physicians who would sign any affidavit for the right price.

Philip, however, continued to protest. "Look, I've known these people for a while. It'll be OK. Anyway, we will handle this life support issue carefully and do the right thing."

To perform an EEG, the patient's hair must be shaved so that electrodes on the scalp can record electrical activity directly from the brain. It used to be a common test, but new imaging techniques like CAT scans and MRIs made it mostly obsolete. Only a few clinical situations called for an EEG. When there was a suggestion of a seizure disorder, an EEG was used to look for hyperactive electrical signals from the damaged area of the brain. It was also a good way to diagnose brain death so that life support could be discontinued, and that is how it was being used in Moira's case.

Moira's first EEG, carried out on her second hospital day, had shown very little activity from the brain's cortex, indicating that she had suffered severe damage. But it had been too early to declare brain death. The second EEG indicated that the brain's activity had declined even further. It was now clear that the brain damage was irreversible. Steve delivered the news to Philip as soon as he read the test. Philip was resigned. "Well, I guess it's my turn to get yelled at. I will tell Hugh the bad news and see what he wants us to do. I think we know the answer."

Philip called Hugh and asked him to meet him at the ICU visiting room. Hugh didn't ask for the results of the EEG on the phone, but said he would come to the hospital immediately. When Philip entered the consultation room, he and Bonnie were sitting together on the sofa holding hands and talking softly to each other. Bonnie had tears in her eyes and was obviously trying to console a distraught Hugh.

Philip sat across from them and began by relating the results of the EEG. In essence he told them there was little hope. "I know this must be shocking news, and you probably need time to weigh all of the consequences and decide what to do."

"I don't want my wife to die," answered Hugh slowly. "But if she is, it is going to be with dignity. So I will agree to taking her off the machines as long as you can assure me that there is no way she could recover."

Philip assured Hugh that the EEG was as definitive as it could be. "I suggest you talk to the rest of your family before giving us the final word."

At that, Hugh's temper flared. "Look, I don't need anybody else to help me. I have to make this decision, and as far as I am concerned, it is made."

Philip pushed on. "Have you spoken with Moira's parents? It would be a good idea to make sure that they agree with your decision." Philip's comments were especially germane given recently highly publicized cases in which family members disagreed with each other about continuation of life support.

"I did talk to them, and they told me to do what I thought is the best thing for Moira—and this is the best thing in my mind."

Philip continued. "I have one more question that I am obligated to ask. Moira indicated on her driver's license that she would like to be an organ donor if the opportunity presented itself. Well, this is the opportunity. In many ways, Moira is a perfect candidate. All her organs work great and they would help a lot of people who are on waiting lists for kidneys, livers, corneas, lungs. We couldn't use her heart for transplantation but we would like to take it for experimentation. It would help us enormously to understand what actually happened to her."

Hugh's previous temper tantrums were mere cloudbursts compared to the tornado that blew through the room at this suggestion. Though Bonnie tried to restrain him, Hugh rose and stood menacingly over Philip.

"You fucking doctors just never stop, do you? First you are so busy padding your wallet and making yourself famous that you let my wife have a cardiac arrest. Then when she is brain dead in the hospital because of your negligence, you have the nerve to ask us if you can keep experimenting on her. Well, the answer is no! You can't do an autopsy, and you can't hack up her body and take out all of her organs. I don't give a shit who needs them or what you think you will learn. Does that answer your fucking question?"

Philip was thunderstruck. Families had turned him down for autopsies and organ donation many times, but never so vehemently. He was particularly taken aback by Hugh's complete disregard for Moira's wishes. He also did not fail to take note of Hugh's terminology. Lawyers use the word "negligence" to describe care by a physician that is below the recognized standard, and thus indicative of malpractice. Maybe Steve Goldstein had been right and Hugh was already considering legal action. Had Hugh been talking to somebody about a medical malpractice case? Philip tried to process all of this very quickly and decided to move to the next topic.

Philip rose to face Hugh and spoke as calmly as he could. "In that case, I suggest that you get your family in here this afternoon. Everyone can say goodbye and then I'll take Moira off of the ventilator. If she doesn't breathe on her own, the end will come quickly."

Hugh stalked out of the consultation room without another word. Bonnie sheepishly apologized and followed him. Philip was relieved that their latest confrontation was over but the day's grief was only beginning.

The scene in the ICU later that afternoon was emotional and poignant for everybody. One by one, Moira's family, in-laws, and children spent a few minutes at her bedside, alternating between tearfulness and outright hysteria. The drawn curtains did nothing to shield the staff from the sadness that permeated the unit.

Hugh came in last and stood by the bed as Philip disconnected the ventilator. The nurse then turned off all the alarms and removed the tube from her airway. For several minutes, nothing happened. However, Philip could plainly see that Moira's breathing was shallow and inadequate. Slowly, her blood pressure and heart rate started to drop. Over several minutes, her heart rhythm slowed to a stop.

Philip could only shake his head and stand by the bedside with arms folded. Just before 6:00, he declared Moira Hamlin dead. Hugh said nothing. He waited a few minutes, expressionless, parted the curtains, and left the ICU. He told the charge nurse on the way out that the funeral director would be in touch to make arrangements for Moira's body to be taken from the hospital.

Philip thought about calling the coroner and appealing for an autopsy on the grounds that the cause of Moira's death was not clear, but he realized that such a maneuver would only anger Hugh further and set off legal wrangling that Moira would not have wanted. So he refrained; Moira's body was taken away that night.

Like many occasions during her married life, Moira's funeral was a notable Main Line event. In addition to fellow club members and families from the children's schools, many came from civic and social associations. Moira had been active in the local conservation society and public library, and had helped raise money to benefit parks and animal refuges. The high profile society funeral was an excellent excuse to see and to be seen.

The little Catholic church in Gladwyne was filled to overflowing. The viewing was held just two hours before the funeral mass, which then had to be delayed to give all of the visitors an opportunity to file by the casket. The sparkling clear day contrasted sharply with the sadness of the event.

Philip didn't go to many funerals. For one thing, he didn't have the time. Besides, doctors were taught to distance themselves emotionally from their patients. More importantly, these situations were inevitably awkward for the physicians and the grieving family. The question on everyone's mind was one that could never be answered: "Why didn't you do something that could have saved her?" This was especially true in a tragic circumstance such as this. Young people were just not supposed to die without cause.

In this case, Philip felt that he had to make an exception, and Natalie Gerson and he arrived together. He managed to convince himself that he wasn't going to the funeral because he had a guilty conscience, but because he had liked Moira. And so he endured the stares from the family when he entered the church with Natalie, and the fish-like handshakes and mumbled sentiments that Hugh and the family gave him in the receiving line.

The funeral mass was long and meaningless to Philip. He listened to the eulogies by Moira's relatives noting that Hugh was not among them. Each focused on the tragedy of losing such a young and talented mother.

Philip did not take communion. Though raised a Catholic, he felt estranged from organized religion and what he perceived to be its irrelevance and hypocrisy, so he rarely went to church with

Nancy and the children. It had been a source of sadness for him but something that he never took pains to resolve. Natalie and he endured more awkward moments as the mourners exited and watched the casket loaded for the trip to the gravesite. He saw the grieving children spirited away in a long black limousine.

The ceremony at the grave was brief. Moira's ornate casket was hoisted up on scaffolding suspended above the empty pit. As the priest prayed, several members of Moira's family cried uncontrollably.

As he left the graveyard, Philip saw Hugh talking to the caretaker. He overheard the caretaker tell his crew to hold off on the lowering of the casket into the ground until all the mourners had departed. Philip stopped briefly at the luncheon at the golf club, then hurried back to his office seeking the diversion that work would bring.

After Moira's death, Philip spent hours re-running the case in his mind, trying to understand what had happened to her. He kept going back to the drug screen and the assay results. There was something about the results that made him very uneasy, but he couldn't pinpoint it. He slept little and didn't return to a normal work schedule for days. Rhonda covered for him as best she could but the cardiac staff was anxious about his somber mood.

For his part, Philip's patterns changed. He slept later than usual and left work earlier than ever in his life. His time at home was less than idyllic. He spent little time with his family. Instead, he would routinely make a stiff drink and head out to the back terrace where he stared into space. Nancy pointed out that he was over-reacting to Moira's death. He was having way too many vodkas and "cocktail hour" was starting earlier each evening and extending later into the night. He had to admit that she was right. He didn't particularly like the way the alcohol made him feel, but it did numb the pain he was feeling over the bewildering death of that young woman.

After several weeks, Philip began to find an even keel at work and at home. Nancy was relieved to see him level off, and Rhonda and his staff breathed sighs of relief. Even so, Philip and his family knew that the Moira Hamlin case was going to haunt him for a long time.

CHAPTER 5

For the first few days after Moira's death, Philip thought a lot about Hugh Hamlin and remained uncomfortable with the way matters had ended. So many things were left unsaid, but to Philip's thinking, the most important outstanding issue was the future health of the Hamlin children. Since Moira had a genetic disease, it was important that they be tested to see if they also had the long QT syndrome. Philip needed to have a conversation with Hugh about that. Since he anticipated that Hugh wasn't going to be receptive to a random phone call, he needed to figure out the best place and time to seek him out.

Hugh and his family decided to sit Shiva for the week following Moira's death. This custom would give their Jewish friends and family an opportunity to visit, grieve, and celebrate the life of the departed according to their custom.

Philip saw the notice in the obituary pages and decided to attend with Nancy. He hoped to use this as an opportunity to have a short discussion with Hugh about the children's well-being.

As they cruised through the sylvan Main Line neighborhoods, Philip and Nancy took in one magnificent home after another. "I can't believe how much new construction there is in this area," Nancy observed.

"Land value around here is so high that they knock down modest houses built 40 or 50 years ago so they can build these palaces."

"I guess renovating is passé?"

"Why bother? These people can afford instant gratification, and there isn't much they like about some of the post-war houses. So they come down practically overnight."

When Philip and Nancy arrived at the Hamlin residence, they agreed it was a good example of the McMansions that were springing up on the Main Line — a massive, expensively decorated house filled with antique furniture, elaborate chandeliers, and thick oriental carpets. They handed over the car keys to a valet and followed other guests to the large living room, where they lingered on the periphery of the well-heeled crowd. Four bars had been set up, and waiters circulated with hot and cold hors d'oeuvres.

Philip observed Hugh for a while. He whispered to Nancy, "I want to pick the best time to speak with him so he listens for a change." From a distance, Hugh seemed sedate. He didn't look melancholy, but instead, almost lighthearted. Bonnie was a visible presence, acting as his hostess.

At the gathering, Philip and Nancy were shocked to hear that Moira's body had not been buried. Apparently, there had been an abrupt change of plans at the cemetery. Just before she would have been lowered into the ground, Hugh arranged for the body to be taken back to the funeral home to be cremated, claiming that had been her preference all along.

There was no explanation as to why Hugh had suddenly remembered this rather important request. Or was this an entirely new wrinkle? Philip thought Moira's Catholic family would surely object to cremation. Was the family's likely opposition the reason why Hugh had changed plans at the gravesite? In any case, the mourners had departed the graveyard thinking that Moira would be buried in the plot where the ceremony had taken place. But as it happened, Hugh had different plans for her. Philip wondered if there was a deeper, more sinister reason for the decision.

As they observed the crowd, Philip compared the Jewish gathering to the character of a very social Irish wake. Put off by the drinking, overeating, and general bantering, he whispered to Nancy that he wanted to leave as soon as he spoke with Hugh. At a seemingly opportune moment, Philip approached, but from the start, it was obvious he was wrong.

"Hugh, I just want you to know how terribly sorry we are about Moira's death. It was a tragedy. I know you are devastated and that it is difficult to focus right now. But I just need you to listen to me for a moment. There are some other things that need to be taken care of."

Philip was talking fast, not giving Hugh a chance to interrupt him. "I am convinced that Moira had a mild case of the long QT syndrome, but the fact that she had a sudden death puts a totally different light on things. Your kids need to be evaluated by a pediatric cardiologist as soon as possible. I am going to give you a card that has contact information for the person I would recommend. Her name is Vicky Vermeil. She is the chief of cardiology at Children's Hospital and a good friend. She is an expert in the field and a sensitive person. I have already talked to her and she is expecting to hear from you. I would strongly suggest that you call her as soon as possible."

Either Hugh was not paying attention or he was infuriated at this intrusion. He didn't take the card from Philip and didn't look him in the eye. "I am taking care of that problem myself."

"You mean that you are contacting somebody else, or you already contacted Vicky? There are a few other people in the area who are good, but some are not. You must get the right person. There is no room for error here, Hugh."

Hugh looked at Philip and spoke between clenched teeth, "I told you, I am taking care of it."

"Hugh, because Moira had the long QT syndrome, one or more of your children could be affected as well. You aren't thinking about letting this go, are you?"

Hugh snapped, "Look who's telling me what I should do? I know how to take care of my family. I would appreciate it if you would just get off my case so I can attend to the people I want to talk to. By the way, if you didn't guess by now, you are not one of them!"

Philip wasn't finished, and decided to endure one more insult. "And I am telling you that you can't drop the ball on this. Just make sure that Vicky, or anybody else you see, sends me a copy of their findings so I can keep track of this."

"Don't worry. You'll be hearing a lot more about this case, I promise."

Philip ignored the remark. He had to get his point across and he wasn't going to let Hugh derail him. "Look Hugh, there are many very good reasons why I am being so persistent about this. For one thing, I saved some serum from Moira and froze it away. When Vicky does genetic testing on your kids, knowing Moira's genotype will be critically important to interpreting the results."

Philip knew there were only about seven recognized patterns

of inheritance of the long QT syndrome, and each one had a different profile with unique treatments. To know which disease was in Moira's family was vitally important to the effective treatment of Moira's children who might have the genetic defect. It was also important to know the type of inheritance pattern. "Dominant" traits could be passed on if only one parent had a defective gene whereas "recessive" traits generally became manifest only if both parents had a defective gene, a much less likely occurrence.

Philip suspected from what he knew about Moira's presentation and her EKG pattern that she had a genetic type that was dominant rather than recessive. That meant the children could have it and in turn pass it on to their children if they lived long enough to have offspring. But to know for sure, the kids' test results had to be compared with Moira's.

"I don't remember giving permission for you to draw and freeze blood," Hugh stated in his most belligerent tone. "Is this an example of experimenting without permission?"

Philip was amazed at Hugh's objection and wondered where it came from. "We usually don't ask permission to have blood drawn. I came here tonight to give you some important information, and what I am telling you should be a help to you and your family."

Hugh was desultory as he backed away. "Oh yeah, a real big help. You've been real helpful all along, right to the end. I have to go now."

Stung, but not defeated, Philip turned to find Nancy. The interchange reinforced the nagging feeling that there was something very wrong about what had happened to Moira. But he was having a difficult time identifying what it was and if indeed it was real. Having learned through his training and practice to trust his instincts, Philip couldn't put this feeling aside. It was what good doctors did.

Philip had vivid memories of his mentors going to the bedside of new patients with a large entourage of residents and students. After a brief interview and examination they would walk out of room and make a diagnosis that no one else had even contemplated and some might have even thought absurd.

The first time it happened, Philip like other neophytes had doubted the accuracy of a senior doctor's assessment. But after they had been proven right on multiple occasions, Philip began to understand that experienced physicians were using the instincts they had honed by years of clinical practice and research experience.

Now as a senior doctor himself, Philip was able to intuit things that his junior associates could never know. And his instincts were telling him that there was much more to the story of Moira's life and tragic death than was obvious. Although he wanted to satisfy his curiosity about the case, one of Philip's cardinal concerns was the future of the Hamlin children if Moira's case remained an enigma. They could be susceptible to sudden death in the same awful way.

In the ensuing weeks, Philip heard nothing from Hugh. Rhonda called Hugh's home and office but he never was in, and the calls were not returned.

A few weeks later, he bumped into Vicky Vermeil at a meeting, and invited her for coffee to catch up on several mutual patients. Philip, who often made snap judgments about people, didn't know Vicky well but admired her ascent up the tough academic ladder. He had known many women who had lost their personality and femininity on that battleground, and wondered if Vicky was another example. Yet she was not only intelligent and successful, but also personable. Her southern drawl belied an energetic mind, and that laid-back, lady-like demeanor made her very popular.

They found a coffee shop in the hotel where the meeting was being held, and sat down at one of the window tables. After ordering a couple of frothy skim lattés, he asked, "Vicky, did you ever hear from Hugh Hamlin about getting his kids evaluated?"

Vicky nodded. "Oh yeah, we sure did. About a month after his wife died, his secretary called my office and demanded an appointment. He wanted all his kids screened for the long QT syndrome. And he made it clear that he didn't want us to request any of his wife's records. I managed to calm him down when we saw the kids in the clinic. Cute kids too. Two had abnormal EKGs with a long QT interval and so we started them on beta-blockers."

"I still wonder if beta-blockers would have helped their mother."

Vicky didn't know the whole story about Moira. She figured that Philip must have suggested therapy at some point. It wasn't going to help her evaluation of the Hamlin children and she didn't want to get into it with Philip who had never been overly cordial.

"Are the kids tolerating the beta-blockers so far?" Philip asked. Treating children with any drug can be difficult because of side effects. Beta-blockers were known to produce fatigue and nightmares.

"So far so good, but they haven't been back for a follow-up visit yet."

"Did the kids have genetic testing?"

"Yes, but it will be months until we get the results back."

Philip was painfully aware of the difficulties of getting genetic testing results in a timely fashion. Genetic science itself was very complex and only a few research laboratories had the capability of performing the testing procedures. Since the tests could not be done commercially, one simply had to get in line and wait for research labs to get around to it, and this could take months to years. Nevertheless, knowing the genetic pattern was critical in the prevention of a lethal arrhythmia.

"Well, at least you have Moira's serum sample so you can index the kids' results to her genetic profile."

Vicky looked surprised. "I thought you knew. Mr. Hamlin told us that he wouldn't give his permission to use her blood specimen either."

Philip was incredulous. "Why the hell did he do that? He must realize how important it is for the genetics lab to know Moira's genotype!"

"Philip, I don't know if he knows or even cares. He is a weird guy and I really don't like dealing with him. The woman who comes along with him seems like a good resource. She tries to keep him in check, but he goes off anyway. I punted the Hamlin family case to Joe Richardson, one of my junior guys. Now that the kids are being treated, there isn't a whole lot for me to do and Joe is very competent. He also doesn't take a lot of guff from parents so he should be able to handle Hamlin pretty well."

Hugh's behavior sounded familiar to Philip. Was there another agenda for this unreasonableness?

As time went by, Philip realized that his ruminations were getting him nowhere, and so he gradually re-immersed himself in his work. The Hamlin episode started to fade from Philip's thoughts. A request for Moira's medical records came across his desk months after she died. Even though it came from a lawyer's office, he paid little attention. Agents of deceased patients' families made such requests frequently for insurance purposes or to settle estates, so he suspected nothing sinister. When he saw Hugh and Bonnie at local school functions, they sometimes nodded woodenly in his direction. Their kids didn't hang out together, so there was little reason to connect.

Several months after her death, Philip saw Moira's mother in his office for an unrelated problem. Philip noted that her electrocardiogram gave no indication of the long QT syndrome. During his treatment of Moira, Philip had offered to screen other people in Moira's family. His offer hadn't been taken up so he had no idea who had the trait and how it had been passed on. That day, Moira's mother expressed gratitude for all he had done for her daughter, but she seemed like a minor, bewildered player in her child's life.

During that conversation, he also learned that Hugh and Bonnie had married about six months after Moira died. It was a small ceremony and Moira's family had not been invited. She told Philip that she rarely saw her grandchildren and had to make a fuss to get Hugh to allow visits. All in all, she and her husband were not happy with Hugh's behavior since the funeral. Moira's death had saddened and puzzled them, and depleted their emotions. They tried to pacify Hugh just so they could see the children.

Eventually, Moira's case became a distasteful but distant memory. That is until one afternoon, several months later, when Rhonda entered his office with a shocked expression, holding a thick envelope. Hugh Hamlin was suing him for malpractice. Philip sat at his desk for the next hour, transfixed, feeling like someone had kicked him in the stomach. He read the complaint over and over again, while patients stacked up in his waiting room and Rhonda held call after call.

Since the object of a malpractice suit is to win a monetary award, and since the amount of money is tied to the level of negligence, the complaint always makes the doctor seem like he or she is either a moron or the devil incarnate and frequently both.

The complaint alleged that Philip had "delivered substandard care to Moira" in several different ways. He had "not fully apprised Moira of her risk of sudden death and had not treated her with a drug or a device proven to prevent sudden death in patients with the long QT syndrome." He "should have prescribed potassium and magnesium supplements to Moira and his failure to do so was the reason that those mineral levels were low, contributing to the chances that Moira's heart would go out of rhythm."

Furthermore, Philip had "purposefully and negligently withheld therapy while not apprising Mrs. Hamlin and her husband of her risk of a lethal arrhythmia." Philip had "employed experimental therapy at the time of Moira's ER presentation without getting consent from Hugh," and "this recklessly negligent act added materially to the chances that Moira Hamlin would not survive to care for her children."

Another important part of the complaint was the allegation of economic hardships that the "wrongful death" had imposed on the family. Even though Hugh was fabulously wealthy, the complaint stated that Moira's children would be without their mother's upbringing and that resources would have to be found to pay for their childcare in addition to compensating them for the pain and suffering caused by their mother's death "in front of their eyes in their own home."

Included as defendants in the lawsuit were Natalie Gerson, Adam Wilkie, and of course the hospital itself for having an incompetent doctor such as Philip on its medical staff and for not policing his inappropriate behavior.

Philip was devastated. Throughout his career, he had practiced medicine with great intensity and never delivered sloppy care. Though not the most congenial person in the world, no one had ever accused him of being incompetent.

Beyond being deeply offended, Philip was furious that nearly everything alleged in the complaint was either wrong or incorrectly stated. He had spoken at length with Hugh and Moira about treatment options frequently, and at every turn had given them the opportunity to receive any or all of them. Moira's electrolyte values were fine when Philip evaluated them and so supplements were not only contraindicated, but might have been a hazard to Moira because high levels can be as dangerous as low ones. And clearly, Hugh was aware of what Philip had tried to do to resuscitate Moira in the emergency department, and had agreed with the treatment plan in Bonnie's presence. Moira's cardiac arrest was a tragedy, but it was unforeseen and not predictable.

Second-guessing has no place in medicine. Things can happen

without warning and without anyone's malfeasance. Philip was surprised that Hugh would turn on him, knowing how intense his efforts had been. It wasn't his fault that Moira had been left lying on her bedroom floor for so long without any help.

Philip had spent hours taking care of Moira after the cardiac arrest, and his family management had been exemplary. The one glaring glitch was the experimental drug administered in the emergency department without signed consent. Philip didn't know how Hugh's lawyers had found out about it, but he knew that he would have a hard time defending his therapeutic heroism, even though the drug had worked and Moira's rhythm had stabilized.

Philip visibly sagged as he was pulled into every doctor's nightmare. First he had to notify his malpractice carrier and then meet with a defense attorney. The insurance company assigned Daniel Edwards to his case. Dan called Rhonda to make an appointment to meet with Philip in his office and said he needed three hours. Philip seldom gave that much of his time to anyone, even for a fee, but he knew he had no choice. Planning his defense strategy was of paramount importance.

Dan was a few minutes tardy for his appointment but strode confidently into Philip's office and offered a firm handshake. He was clean-cut, well dressed, with slicked back, parted hair, like a 1920s movie idol. With his monogrammed cuffs and gold cufflinks, he looked like the GQ attorney he aspired to be. Philip thought he was horribly overdressed.

"Dr. Sarkis, I can assure you that you have little to worry about. I have reviewed the file and everything seems to be in order. It looks to me like you documented every event and that Moira Hamlin made some bad decisions about her own treatment."

Philip was not nearly as confident. "Maybe I am blocking out the facts that are too painful to remember accurately. I am going to have to pull the records myself and look them over carefully before I can make any sense of it."

Dan was only two years out of Yale Law School and had only a beginner's grasp of the legal issues. He had no medical background and no understanding of the complex case. One of the many unrecognized ramifications of large awards now commonly given to plaintiffs was that insurance companies no longer had the funds to employ top attorneys who had extensive malpractice case experience. Thus, Philip had been given a neophyte to work with, and it showed during this first interview. Dan was clearly in over his head medically and legally. But at the very least, Dan promised to represent Philip aggressively and was smart enough to say things to soothe his client, even if in reality he didn't believe them himself

Even Dan knew that this case could be a courtroom disaster. How would any jury react to the sudden and unexpected death of this attractive mother? Dan himself had a hard time understanding her diagnosis and the rationale for not treating her with medications, and he had completely missed the administration of the research drug without proper consent. But he was keen enough to be concerned about the venue.

"Dr. Sarkis, the suit has been filed in Philadelphia since the holding company for the hospital has its corporate headquarters in the city. Plaintiffs' attorneys always try to have their cases heard in a Philadelphia courtroom. The juries there are less sophisticated, less likely to grasp the medical subtleties, and more likely to be swayed by their sympathy for the 'victim.' In this case, the jury is going to have to understand the complexities of the diagnosis and the relative benefits and risks of the many medical management options. We are going to have to 'educate' them, which is going to be tough with a blue-collar jury. So I plan to petition for a change in venue to Montgomery County where the malpractice allegedly occurred. More often, Montgomery County juries are college educated and more sympathetic to physicians. This is a very important motion for us and will have to be crafted carefully."

Dan's second biggest concern was Philip himself. He'd have to endure a long legal process and like many good physicians faced with tough litigation, might want to take the easy way out and settle the case. Dan told Philip he wanted the process of discovery to proceed for a while so that the defense case could be properly assessed.

For his part, Philip recognized a new vulnerability. Aside from the horrifying facts of the case, he idly wondered if his fear of being sued would change the way he cared for patients. Philip could not have known that any differences in his approach to patient care would pale in comparison to the dramatic changes that the Moira Hamlin case would eventually cause in his life.

CHAPTER 6

Along the way, Dan would come to understand that Philip hated this lawsuit so much because he was a perfectionist who couldn't fathom that someone would accuse him of making an egregious and life-threatening mistake in the care of a patient. He had a high opinion of his skills and thought everyone else should too. Dan would also learn that Philip was not a stranger to adversity. In fact, Philip Sarkis had spent his life overcoming disadvantages.

He had been born to Lebanese immigrants in a poor area of South Philadelphia. Neither of his parents had more than a rudimentary education. Both came to America, driven from the poverty and turmoil of the Middle East, to join relatives and establish a new life in the land of opportunity. When Philip asked his parents why they left Lebanon, he always got a perfunctory answer. It was as if their memory of their homeland made them so sad they chose simply not to remember anything about it.

Philip's mother and father had emigrated separately and met in a tomato field in New Jersey where they toiled as migrant workers. Mutual friends had arranged the meeting and after a short courtship, they married and moved to Philadelphia.

Philip's father dreamed of advancing from picking the produce to retailing it. He was sure that the wives of blue-collar workers in the Philadelphia suburbs who did not have cars or supermarkets would appreciate the local delivery of fresh fruits and vegetables to their neighborhoods. Scraping together enough money to buy himself an old truck and garage, he launched the Sarkis Fruit Company. Eventually, through hard work and perseverance, his business instincts were proven correct.

Butrus Sarkis was a wiry man with boundless energy. He would awake in the very early morning and drive his dilapidated truck to the docks and the markets in South Philadelphia to select and load the best fresh produce. Then, he would head to the suburbs to "huckster" the fruit and vegetables for reasonable prices that provided him with a fair profit. Butrus and Catherine Sarkis had two boys, Philip and his brother, Brian, who was four years younger. Eventually, they moved their young family to Bridgeport, a small working-class town west of Philadelphia, where they sold their fresh goods. Eventually, Catherine learned to keep the books and manage the money, and she developed into a ferocious businesswoman.

Philip and Brian were expected to help with the family business almost from the time they could walk. As youngsters, they would organize the produce in the trucks and stack empty crates in the garage. When they begged for time off to play with friends, their requests were usually answered by silence and a scornful look from their mother that quickly caused them to stop asking.

As the boys matured, they joined their father and Uncle Norman on the truck, helping to load in the morning and unload at night. Weekends and summers were spent working and when they were in college, they drove the trucks themselves. Along with their cousins, they took more responsibility for the business and provided vacation relief for a few full-time employees. The work was hard but it became second nature for Philip. He developed a keen sense of quality; he could choose the best of what was to be had in produce, like a seasoned maestro. He also liked his father's workers and he learned lessons from them that would serve him well when he would later deal with similar folk as patients.

But as far as his parents were concerned, working in the family business was no excuse for skipping homework or not excelling at school. While his cousins seemed satisfied to join the family business, Philip's parents wanted better for their boys, so good grades were considered essential, and bad grades or mediocre ones were met with fire and brimstone laced with Lebanese epithets that Philip understood all too well.

As a result, the two bright boys did well at the local Catholic school. Because they didn't have time to have play dates or to join extracurricular activities, other students considered them "nerdy."

As a result, they turned inward, preferring to play at home with each other or their cousins, rather than explore a world full of strangers.

As Philip began his senior year, the only school that offered him a scholarship was LaSalle, a small college in Philadelphia. When his father heard that the school would help with tuition, he told Philip that there was no question about it—LaSalle was his next step. Not surprisingly, Philip complied, commuting and living at home to save money, and continued his role in the business.

In the end, LaSalle turned out to be an excellent choice. Philip enjoyed the simplicity of a small campus, and the school had an excellent biology department. He had a natural aptitude for science and aspired to be a doctor. His father considered medicine the most prestigious profession of all, and the thought that his son might achieve such an esteemed career brought tears to his eyes.

Philip performed well at LaSalle and his advisors encouraged him to apply to medical school. Once again, he elected to stay at home and commute to Hahnemann Medical School, a 20-mile jaunt each way. He found that he enjoyed cardiology for its integration of anatomy, physiology and bedside skills. Philip also liked to work with his hands, and the procedures that were part of cardiology allowed him to use his manual dexterity to its maximum potential.

After much soul-searching, Philip decided to begin his postgraduate training abroad. He was offered a slot at the Radcliffe Infirmary in England. This meant leaving his parents and brother for the first time in his life, and divorcing himself from the produce business. But Philip and his parents agreed that he had to seize this wonderful educational opportunity.

In the UK, Philip worked hard. The clinical training schedule was tough enough, but he also began to do clinical research, which he would continue throughout his career. His fellow registrars (as British residents were called) respected him but couldn't understand why Philip chose to spend so much time working and so little time enjoying himself. This, however, was his nature, and would be Philip's pattern throughout his training and career.

Philip's work ethic and clinical success attracted the attention of the venerable cardiology chief, Peter Blye, with whom he eventually published two important papers. Blye asked Philip one day, "What aspect of cardiology do you find most interesting?"

Philip replied without hesitation, "I really love cardiac arrhythmia. It intrigues me the most."

This new discipline within cardiology fascinated him and he eagerly expounded on the subject. "Patients with all forms of cardiac disease are susceptible to arrhythmia, some fast and some slow. I have read some early studies in which people are placing electrical catheters inside the heart to measure electrical activity to determine which patients might require drugs, surgery or specialized devices to prevent or terminate abnormal heart rhythms. It sounds extremely exciting to me, and I predict there will be much to learn on the subject."

Blye helped Philip find a training post in the States that would allow him to follow his dream. One of the few programs that offered specialized training was at Harvard and Blye's good friend, Dr. Bernard Lowenstein, directed it. When Lowenstein heard about Philip's interest, he agreed to take him on as a fellow the following year.

Philip's tenure in Boston was fulfilling. The contacts he made during those formative years were important to his future career, and would eventually help him launch many of his own research initiatives.

As Philip approached the end of his fellowship, he realized that he would have to make a difficult decision in selecting his first job. He received many attractive offers, including a flattering invitation to stay at Harvard, but his parents wanted Philip to return home. At the time, none of the Philadelphia hospitals had an arrhythmia program Philip could join. The idea of trying to launch a program in a relatively new discipline within cardiology, with little practical experience, was daunting. Philip accepted a position at Harvard, and thought after a few years, he might transition back to Philadelphia.

A few days after he agreed to the new job, Philip saw an ad for a position at Gladwyne Memorial Hospital, a good but relatively unknown private hospital in a Philadelphia suburb, not far from his parents. Almost as an afterthought, while home for a holiday visit, he met with some of the staff at GMH. During the meeting, he was impressed with the enthusiasm of the administration. They were absolutely committed to building a premier cardiology program and wanted Philip to join them. They were willing to commit resources and offered Philip an attractive package to come aboard.

Much to his family's delight and Harvard's consternation, he decided to accept the post after much soul searching. Philip joined GMH as the director of the coronary care unit or CCU, with the mandate to establish the hospital's first arrhythmia service.

His arrival was unheralded. In his quiet but logical way, Philip set about establishing a unit that would eventually become a preferred place to refer cardiac patients for complex rhythm problems. He didn't become pals with his fellow doctors, but his accomplishments spoke volumes. In a few short years, he became the head of the cardiology department.

Philip spent the next 20 years establishing his own reputation in arrhythmology. He wrote hundreds of papers and earned dozens of grants to study issues relating to sudden cardiac death and lethal cardiac arrhythmias. His personal success and aloofness made some consider him selfish or non-collegial. But Philip ignored the criticism and forged ahead.

Sometimes Philip thought of himself as a juggler at a circus. The juggler would start out with three or four balls that he could easily handle, then would exhort his assistant to add more and more balls that, to the delight of the crowd, he kept in the air with relative ease.

As a successful clinician, administrator, teacher, researcher, consultant, and mentor, he had no social life. In fact, to keep all of his "balls in the air" Philip needed extra work time. He sacrificed sleep, getting to work early in the morning and staying late into the night.

Philip's few friends were left over from school and training. Most new acquaintances were put off by his perceived abruptness and never went any further. Philip was well groomed, but was not handsome. In fact, his intensity and serious demeanor gave his dark hair and complexion a forbidding aspect.

Women in particular sensed that Philip didn't enjoy their company. He tended to treat them as inferiors, and would stop listening or visibly shut down when conversation turned to subjects that he found silly or uninteresting. He had dated a handful of women in college and medical school but had never had a serious relationship. Philip simply didn't understand how medical training and romance could mix. He was known to quip that doctors and not priests should remain celibate—a person's dedication to medicine made a good private life a tough proposition, so why even try?

When he met Nancy Whalen, there was no indication that his experience with her would be any different. He certainly noticed her good looks, but as usual, he didn't have time to admire her heavy mane of wavy blonde hair, nice figure, and bright green eyes before he got a big dose of her feisty personality.

Nancy was the head nurse of the coronary unit at GMH and by the time Philip had arrived to take his new job, she was weary of the quagmire of bureaucracy that was keeping the unit from getting what it needed. Nancy was exasperated with the directors who had preceded Philip. They had not done a very good job organizing medical care in the CCU. She complained bitterly about the administration's lack of responsiveness to her requests. She bemoaned the difficulty in reaching doctors in her unit to make routine management decisions.

In a torrid initial hour-long meeting, Nancy blistered Philip with the unit's problems, while he listened quietly and took notes. At the end, Philip agreed with most of her opinions and promised to try to solve the issues one at a time. It was a no brainer. If he was going to be successful at GMH, the unit had to run with the precision of a Swiss timepiece.

To Nancy's surprise, Philip delivered on his promises. He revamped the reporting structure in the unit and took personal responsibility for the day-to-day management of patients, so that the staff could always get questions answered. He also insisted that they function as a "unit" with nurses and doctors enfranchised as team partners rather than adhering to an outmoded pecking order. But Philip would be Philip and often intimidated the staff with his gruffness. However his aggressive, organized style enabled him to coerce the administration to build a new cardiac unit that he was invited to design with Nancy's help.

As Nancy observed Philip's performance, she couldn't help but be impressed with his patient interactions and teaching on the unit. She admired his breadth of knowledge in this new and exciting field. Patients with complex rhythm problems were now surviving and living full lives. The morale in the unit went from deplorable to excellent in a few short months.

Although Philip was attracted to Nancy, it took him over two months to summon up the courage to ask her out. She couldn't say that she liked Philip but she respected him. In truth, Nancy hated her job and had hoped to get involved with a successful doctor, so she accepted. "Nothing ventured, nothing gained," she said to the mirror as she slipped on a flattering sweater and zipped up form-fitting black leather pants.

Their first date was lunch at Valley Green, an 18th century inn in Fairmount Park that had been frequented by Washington and his generals during the Revolutionary War. In the room where they dined, it was said that Washington had mapped out many of his war strategies before the crackling hearth. The cozy setting was conducive to good conversation, and the comfort food delicious. Later as they tossed bread crumbs to the noisy geese that congregate on the picturesque Wissahickon Creek next to the restaurant, Philip found himself staring at Nancy's porcelain complexion and wishing he could touch it.

Nancy and Philip saw a lot of each other during that first winter. On their third date, she told him about her first marriage when she was in nursing school. Her husband was a fun-loving, solid guy who was a laborer for a construction company, but the couple grew apart as her education and aspirations changed.

Both of Nancy's parents were dead but she had siblings in the area. When she brought Philip to meet them, they were impressed with who he was, but surprised that Nancy was dating such an obviously humorless person.

Nancy's first visit with the Lebanese clan was an anxious moment for everybody. His parents had never met any woman whom Philip dated and they didn't know what to make of this Irish-Catholic person. But Nancy's charm managed to win them over in no time. Moreover, they were relieved that Philip finally had a relationship. They wanted him to marry an intelligent and attractive person so they could finally have grandchildren.

Nancy hated nursing from the minute she changed her first bedpan, but reasoned it was a way to make a living. She had been a Fine Arts major in college and enjoyed painting and sculpting. She even had a small studio in her apartment. With Philip, she re-discovered things that each liked to do but let lapse in favor of medicine. They went to movies, were frequent visitors to the Art Museum, and attended Philadelphia Orchestra concerts. They bowled and played tennis and grew to know each other's secrets. They tried to find ways to maximize their time together.

After dating for several months, they moved in together and began to plan their wedding. They decided on a simple and non-denominational affair at a local mansion on a crisp fall afternoon followed by a brief honeymoon in Hawaii. They bought a modest home and began a family. To the delight of Philip's parents, they had two girls who had Nancy's good looks and Philip's intelligence, but unfortunately, much of his personality too.

Their married years were ordinary. Philip's long hours at the hospital meant little time with his young family. Nancy happily abandoned her career to care for the children. At times she resented Philip's busy professional life and the limits it placed on their freedom. But she enjoyed pursuing her artistic interests and dove into school activities and local charities. Initially she was lonely when Philip traveled to glamorous medical meetings, but then she began to look forward to the times when he wasn't around.

Philip was a perfectionist, demanding that everything in the house be kept in order. The children begged for pets but Philip refused; he thought that it would make the house dirty and he didn't want the hassle. As he rose in stature, Nancy became jealous of his success, and felt he didn't appreciate what she did at home to support him.

The Sarkis marriage went from routine to less than idyllic. Philip and Nancy began to live in their separate worlds even though to others, their circumstances appeared enviable. Eventually, her concentration on the girls substituted for his affections. While Nancy's gaggle of friends and involvement in many volunteer activities satisfied her need for companionshi,. Philip's international jaunts and personal success fed his ego sufficiently.

It was into this rather superficial but serene existence that the Hamlin malpractice case exploded, affecting it in ways that neither Philip nor Nancy could ever have predicted.

CHAPTER 7

After the initial shock of the lawsuit, Philip continued his busy work schedule, in addition to the substantial amount of time to plan his defense with Dan. Although he had never been a defendant himself, he had reviewed a few malpractice cases for the defense in the past.

"The plaintiff's attorney is going to work this case to death," Philip asserted during one of his countless cafeteria lunches with Dan. "Their first step will be to assign an army of underlings to the case. They'll get some former nurses and medical personnel who work as junior associates and paralegals and charge them to scrutinize records for any evidence that I was involved in anything remotely questionable—ever. The more screw-ups they find, the easier to persuade a jury that I am incompetent. And believe me, the jump from stupid to negligent is not that big."

Over the years, Philip had several conversations about malpractice litigation with Scott Goldschmidt, the current chief of cardiothoracic surgery at GMH. A high-profile surgeon like Scott had learned to be sanguine and actually taught himself to view lawsuits as the price of doing business. "I've been involved in my share both as a defendant and as a witness," Scott boasted to Philip as they worked together in the OR implanting a device one afternoon. "Patients who have heart surgery, like this poor schmuck, are pretty sick to begin with, and people just don't realize that surgery is risky business."

Scott would frequently see patients rejected by other surgeons because they were too ill, but who had a chance to benefit from high-risk surgery. Scott was a superb surgeon who enjoyed taking on tough cases and beating the odds. Still, some of those patients who were hanging on thin threads simply didn't make it. Their deaths, inevitable or not, frequently precipitated lawsuits.

Scott tried to be reassuring. "Look, Philip, you are not alone. All of us have tried working to effect malpractice reform. Unless somebody in Harrisburg does something, it is going to be impossible to attract and keep good doctors in Pennsylvania."

"I know. But I just don't see how things can change. Plaintiffs' attorneys advertise on TV and billboards, for Christ's sake. And look how much money they contribute to the politicians who make the laws."

Scott nodded, as he sutured in a pacemaker lead. "The contingency thing has to go. The lawyers only get paid if the cases are successful, but they really need only one or two big wins and they're set for life. Without caps on awards for pain and suffering, there is no limit to what they can collect.

"And Philly has the highest premiums for malpractice insurance in the nation. Our neurosurgeons are paying over $200,000 per year for coverage. No wonder you can't find a neurosurgeon to see an emergency patient."

Though Scott was a veteran of malpractice wars, he retained a sense of humor about it. "Philip, their tactic is simple yet elegant. Just throw as much shit on the wall as you can and see how much of it sticks." While he set about fashioning a pocket for the implantable defibrillator that Philip was about to test, Scott went on to tell Philip about a case that illustrated what was wrong with the system.

"I once operated on a very sick 82-year-old man to repair a bad mitral valve. When the old guy died three days after the surgery, the family sued. They assumed that I had made a mistake. When the hospital chart was examined under the microscope, the plaintiff's attorney found out that the patient died immediately after receiving lidocaine to stop a post-op arrhythmia. In the complaint, they said that the lidocaine was given in the wrong dose and had caused the patient's heart to stop."

"Was the dose too high?"

"Yeah, but it wasn't enough to cause cardiac standstill. That happened because he was old and had a major operation. But the lawyers must have been relieved to find something, because the operation itself was fine. The other piece of good news for them was that they could access the hospital's malpractice policy as well as mine, and get to every other doctor who had seen the patient. The hospital of course has a much deeper pocket so this opened up all kinds of possibilities."

"So who won the case?"

"The plaintiff won, even though there was not a shred of evidence that the lidocaine caused his death. The fact that the standard of care hadn't been breached apparently meant little to the jury. They felt sorry for the old man's wife. I was of course included in the judgment because I was the 'captain of the ship' and thus responsible for everything that happened to the patient. It didn't really matter that I had been at home in bed and not on duty when the lidocaine was administered and that I didn't even order the drug myself."

Scott and Philip shook their heads. They both knew that experiences like that drove doctors to drink or to opt out of medicine entirely. Many ended up needing psychiatric counseling. For others, hobbies took the pressure off and restored some kind of normalcy. Scott's outlet was extreme skiing, which he pursued with a passion. People thought he had a death wish because he would fly down Vail's tree-lined black diamond trails at breakneck speed without a helmet. When asked why he was so reckless, Scott would merely shrug and bare his gapped-tooth smile and say, "It's my therapy."

Knowing what he did about legal tactics, Philip decided to do his own in-depth chart examination. He requested a copy of the records from the hospital and was frustrated when it took several days to get it. Why? When a hospital receives notification of a lawsuit, it sequesters the records to discourage document tampering. Although such cheating rarely occurs, such an accusation immediately casts the defendant physician as a fraud and turns the jury against him before the case starts. Quarantining the medical record precludes that kind of frivolous claim.

When he finally received the records, Philip pored over them, devoting evenings and early mornings to analyzing every single entry order, progress note, and lab test result from Moira's pregnancy and delivery to her final hospitalization. He took copious notes, but in the end couldn't identify anything substandard. Everything was appropriate. If anything, the consultation and nursing notes were unusually thorough, and Philip was impressed by the highly compassionate care Moira had received, especially at the end of her life. Administering Naladil was obviously the most damning thing, but he could find no entries in the chart about it. How had the plaintiff's attorneys found out?

Philip realized that his own review of the case was likely to be biased. After all, he was inclined to give himself and his colleagues the benefit of the doubt. He also knew that the case would have to be reviewed by experts who would then be asked to render a formal opinion and testify at trial if necessary. When Dan asked Philip who should review the case for their side, he chose Dr. Robert Myerstone, the head of cardiology at the University of Georgia. Bob was considered a world authority on the subject of sudden death and had a particular interest in the long QT syndrome. During Dan's subsequent call, Myerstone agreed without hesitation.

"Sure, I can take a look," he told Dan. "Philip is good. I would be surprised if he dropped the ball, but I will give you an impartial review."

"It is important that you not talk directly with Philip about the case," Dan warned. "A smart plaintiff's attorney will look for any evidence of bias or collusion and would exploit that if you have to take the stand."

"I understand and will be careful."

"And also remember that the plaintiff's lawyer will ask how much money you have been paid to appear in court."

"My fee is $500 per hour. It is what I can make in my office."

"I know that but it will seem like a fortune to the laborer or truck driver who is being paid $25 a day for jury duty."

Myerstone sighed. "Of course. But plaintiff's attorney will never divulge the terms of his contingency agreement and how much money he stands to gain from a successful verdict."

Dan was quick to agree. He suspected that Myerstone was savvy enough to handle cheap tricks. "Just be aware that they will ask about your fees, and above all answer honestly."

It didn't take long for Bob to review the case. His assessment: "Philip did a good job, and I don't think the lawsuit has much merit."

"Do you see any weaknesses in the defense case, Dr. Myerstone?"

"Well, giving a research drug without consent is going to be a sticky problem and could have ramifications for Philip beyond the malpractice case. The jury is going to have to be convinced that Moira was going to die without the research drug and that it was not a factor in her death."

"Is that something we can do?" Dan asked.

Bob was astute enough to know that the case was potential dynamite. "Maybe. But if not, and they start believing that the drug somehow contributed to Moira's death, this thing could simply blow up in your face. I have seen what happens when an unsophisticated jury is presented with the death of a young, attractive mother and when the medical facts of the case are highly complex, as they are here. This thing could go south real fast."

"So, what do you recommend we do?"

"I am sure that Philip didn't commit malpractice, and I will write a strong opinion letter. You have to be aware that the facts are so complicated there is a substantial risk that the jury could just go off."

When informed of Myerstone's opinion by Dan, Philip was mostly relieved. However, Dan took care not to alarm Philip with Myerstone's concerns. For his part, Philip was less than pleased with Dan's work on the case. He resented the younger man's inexperience and felt he wasn't proactive enough. Since Dan didn't know much about the topic, Philip thought he approached issues superficially. Philip wanted an attack dog at his side, a strong advocate with a better grasp of the science. He knew that an aggressive and knowledgeable attorney could easily turn a case around.

Philip recalled he had once worked with Joan Foster, a strong plaintiff's attorney who specialized in malpractice cases. Philip usually testified for the defense, but Joan had asked him to review a case for her. His initial inclination had been to say no, but when Joan described what had happened, Philip agreed to render an opinion.

Joan's client was a young man who had a procedure at a low volume, small, suburban hospital in Indiana, only 40 miles from a good metropolitan center. The healthy 45-year-old man experienced a few palpitations and made the mistake of telling his doctor about them. He was quickly referred to a local cardiologist who insisted the only way to sort things out was to do a heart catheterization. The doctor failed to point out that there were many other ways to treat the problem, including simple medications. He also neglected to say that it wasn't a life-threatening condition, or that the laboratory had performed only two such electrical procedures ever. The patient was frightened and agreed to the procedure without asking the right questions.

From the outset, it was clear that the staff was overwhelmed and the procedure took much longer than it should have. The doctor thought he had found an abnormal circuit, when in reality the wiring he traced in the heart was normal. By cauterizing normal rather than abnormal tissue, he caused the heart to go into standstill, and the patient ended up needing a permanent pacemaker. Even worse, the X-ray equipment was brand new and not properly calibrated. Consequently, the patient received about 10 times the necessary dose of radiation. This not only posed a cancer risk for the young man, he also suffered an incredibly painful radiation burn on his back that would take months to heal.

After Philip went through all the records, he was incredulous. He could not believe that any doctor would put a patient in such unnecessary jeopardy. Although he did not like to testify against other physicians, he agreed to write an opinion, which Joan said would result in a settlement. Philip was deposed, but the case never went to trial and the patient was given what Philip thought was a fair award.

Philip had watched Joan closely as she managed that case and was impressed with her polite firmness and quiet confidence. She was not exactly pretty, but was toned and dressed with flair. Most of all, she was a strong advocate, and her client was always her primary concern. Philip resolved that if he ever needed legal help, Joan would be his preferred counsel. So, as his confidence in Dan reached its lowest ebb, he telephoned her. After he described the situation, Joan got to the point.

"Well, the first thing you should do is petition your insurance company for a change of counsel."

"What are the chances they would do that?"

"Not great. They have already invested in Dan. If you were to get a new lawyer, that person would charge the insurance company for the time it would take to get up to speed. They certainly wouldn't want to appoint anybody more expensive than the person you have already. And it would be unlikely that they would let me do it by myself since I am mainly a plaintiff's attorney. I am clearly on the dark side as far as they are concerned."

"Joan, I am desperate. I need a good defense and I don't think that Dan can get the job done. Is there any way I could persuade you to help? How about if I just fire Dan and pay for my own defense? I would be willing to pay you your usual fees."

"Philip, that would get very expensive. How about if I do this for a reduced fee with the understanding that you will help me out sometime with the same consideration? We will call it partial payment in kind."

"That would be great. How do you want to handle it with Dan?"

"Let Dan be your first chair counsel on the case, and I will work in the background. I can help Dan apply pressure when it is needed and make contact with key people as the case progresses. If the case must go to trial, I will help him stay on course there as well. I know a lot of plaintiff attorneys and judges, and I should be able to leverage things without being out in front too much."

Joan was well connected. In addition to being a respected member of the Philadelphia bar and former officer of the Bar Association herself, Joan's father had been a federal judge. She had met many influential members of the legal community growing up. As a seasoned lawyer, she pretty much knew everybody. Her honest approach to complicated cases had gained her well-earned respect.

Joan wasted little time setting up a meeting with Dan over coffee in his firm's canteen. Joan had decided it would be better to have Dan on her side than to intimidate and upset him. She used a little diplomacy to help him understand why she had been called in to help.

"Dan, Philip asked me to help because he knows me well and we are good friends. I will channel all of my ideas through you and will not go around you on any issue. You will remain counsel of record but having said that, I do have some ideas that I think will help."

Realizing that Joan was on the case for the long haul, Dan was gracious. "Joan, I know your reputation and it won't be a problem. I am happy to have the benefit of your experience."

"Great. The first thing is the venue. Why is the case in Philadelphia court? This all happened in Montgomery County."

"I know. I had the same question myself. The holding company for the health system has their corporate offices in Philadelphia. So the plaintiff used this as an excuse to have the case heard there rather than in the suburbs."

Familiar with this tactic, Joan pressed on. "You know how important this is. The chances of winning a case like this in Philly are dismal. The jury simply won't grasp the nuances in such a complicated case."

"I agree. I think that they are much more likely to be persuaded by the emotional issues of a young mother's tragic death. The fact that Hugh is well off and could easily hire help won't be admissible. It will be easy for the jury to want to 'do the right thing' for the children, regardless of the merits of the case or the real economic issues."

"I know. It makes you wonder why Hugh Hamlin is suing Philip. He must be really pissed off or trying to prove some point. I doubt money is the issue."

Dan could only shake his head as he added cream and sugar to his cup. In his limited experience, money was the usual motivation. Hugh obviously had something else on his mind.

Joan asked, "So you filed for a venue change already?"

"I did but I have no idea of how the judge is likely to react."

"Who was the case assigned to?"

"Deidre Pleasance."

Joan's "ouch" response indicated her unhappiness with the answer. "Well, too bad it's someone so clueless. A janitor on the jury would be able to absorb more than she can."

As in many major cities, cases are assigned randomly by a supervisor judge who himself might be ignorant of the facts of each case. Assignment of trial judges is like a lottery in which you hope to draw somebody who is capable of learning something as the case progresses.

"I think we are likely to be stuck with her and with the Philly venue," Dan explained, "And I have been trying to do everything

I can to keep from pissing Pleasance off before we get out of the box." This was Dan's way of reminding Joan to tread lightly. Joan was experienced, but she did have a reputation for going off on judges once in a while, especially when she had to deal with one who was less than brilliant.

"I have known Deidre since law school," Joan offered as she sipped her brew. "She can be manipulated. We will work on that together as we get closer to the important motions or a trial. But I am actually more worried about the hospital. What is their take on the case?"

Joan knew that in malpractice cases, the attorneys for hospitals were generally reluctant to cooperate with doctors. In this instance, the hospital wasn't being accused of doing anything overtly wrong, but was being blamed for allowing "incompetent" doctors to practice negligently on its turf. To side with a plaintiff against the doctor minimized the hospital's liability, but this put the hospital and doctors directly at odds, creating the potential for ugly finger pointing. It also allowed the plaintiffs' attorneys to play one defendant against the other. This tactic could lead to a large plaintiff's verdict or contentious settlement with deeply wounded feelings after the case was over.

"So far, the hospital's attorneys have been cooperative," Dan told her. "I just don't know if they will stay that way. Philip is worried that the hospital is hanging him out to dry."

"Why does he think that?

"He is spooked because of the stuff in the complaint about his giving the research drug. Since that wasn't in the chart, he thinks the only way that the plaintiff could have gotten it is through the hospital."

"He might be right about that," Joan observed. "If the hospital sees any way of squeezing out of the case by putting Philip's head in the noose, don't think they won't try. They will certainly want him in the case as long as possible so that his policy can be used toward any settlement they try to pull off."

"Do you think Philip will want to settle?"

"He sure will be tempted when the case starts getting rough, but that has major repercussions for him professionally. We have to keep him in the game even if he gets cold feet. I really don't want his name in the data bank if we can help it."

The US Department of Health and Human Services had initiated a data bank listing all doctors who had verdicts against them in malpractice actions or who had put money up for settlement. It is accessible by the public and can be used by patients to help select a doctor, and by institutions during credentialing.

"I am going to advise him to fight this thing all of the way. He knows he didn't do anything wrong, and our expert agrees. I have been at this job for a long time, and I don't think he should have been sued in the first place. So my advice to Philip will be defend, defend, defend!"

As strongly as she believed in Philip's innocence, Joan knew they were going to have to use extreme care in case preparation and presentation. As they left the canteen and entered the elevator, Dan and Joan agreed that the case was rife with land mines. Joan knew the challenge was to pull the right strings at the right time, keeping the neophyte lead counsel in check, while helping Philip testify well and comport himself properly in the courtroom. No doubt about it, this was going to be a fierce battle—the kind that Joan, though she would never admit it, really loved to fight.

CHAPTER 8

Malpractice litigation is slow torture. First, with the courts jammed with cases, years can go by before the matter goes to trial. Although some states have mandated pre-trial screening, the plaintiff has a light burden before placing the case in suit. Furthermore, the panel's decision is non-binding, and a determined plaintiff can still take the case to court if they think it has "sex appeal."

Another sore point is the credibility of medical experts, those physicians and nurses who make themselves available to the legal community to review cases. Some like Myerstone are authentic leaders in their field. But others are either very young or very old, trying hard to supplement inadequate incomes. Most are not terribly successful in their own medical careers, and many don't even practice medicine.

In truth, though, experts wind up appealing to a group of totally naïve jurors. Some are good natural public speakers, others take acting courses to be more effective. Many professional societies have considered identifying physicians who abuse the system for personal gain, but sanctions are few.

Joan's favorite example of expert abuse was Dr. John Lee, an emergency room physician who testified in over 75 cases for and against physicians for seven law firms. The subject of the lawsuits ranged across almost all medical subspecialties, an amazing breadth of expertise for a 35-year-old. Lee was forced to reveal that he had only two years of residency training after osteopathy school, and that was at one of the worst hospitals in New Jersey.

Not surprisingly, he had never published or presented a paper at a medical meeting and had not achieved board certification in any specialty. His practice experience was in a "doc-in-a box" walk-in clinic two days a week. Joan told Philip that Lee worked on a sliding scale. "Not only does he get paid by the hour, but if his side wins the case, Dr. Lee expects a bonus."

Then there is the legal wrangling over every minute detail. The attorneys in Philip's case battled endlessly over the whereabouts and the interpretation of the EKGs obtained during Philip's original consultation. The tracings were not in Moira's office chart and no one was able to locate them. This led to plaintiff's accusations that someone had removed incriminating evidence. Philip told Dan and Joan, "There was nothing on those tracings that was different from what we saw in the hospital after the cardiac arrest, so why would I have ripped them out of the chart?" When Dan pointed this out to plaintiff's counsel, Len Barkley, at a pre-trial conference, his response was indignant.

"Our experts think that those tracings are important and we want to see them. If you can't produce them, we will simply have to assume that there was some tampering, and it will be our obligation to make sure that the jury knows that as well."

This incensed Dan, who was relatively new to the blustery tactics of plaintiff's counsel, and he immediately lost his cool. "That's bullshit and you know it."

"If you don't like our approach, take it to the judge."

Joan warned Philip to expect nasty confrontations with Barkley in the courtroom. Hugh had done his homework before he selected his legal representation. Len Barkley was widely known as one of the most aggressive personal injury guys in the country. His firm had handled some of the most highly publicized cases in the last 20 years, including representing disaster victims' families from the Las Vegas Casino fire and the World Trade Center attacks. Barkley had amassed a fortune that allowed him to buy almost anything his heart desired. In fact, he boasted about his collection of World War II airplanes, which he flew himself. A short, powerfully built man with coarse features, he was referred to as "Napolean" by his colleagues.

Barkley had no "partners" in the firm, only an army of associates. Though he was willing to take on any kind of personal injury work, he particularly savored medical malpractice cases. Many surmised he was wreaking vengeance on a medical profession that had refused him admission long ago. People said he liked to make doctors squirm even more than he enjoyed raking in the cash.

As soon as he met Hugh and heard Moira's story, Barkley knew he had landed a big one. It had many favorable ingredients including an inexperienced defense lawyer. Sure, Joan Foster was on the case, but she was a plaintiff's attorney at heart and could be neutralized if necessary. He put Hugh's case on the "A" list, which meant he would try it himself.

From his preferred list of experts, he selected someone he considered a star. J. Wilson Otley was a retired practitioner from the upper east side of Manhattan who had an adjunct professorship at Columbia Medical School maintained with two weeks of medical school student teaching a year, carried out cheerfully and punctually. A large annual donation to the medical school didn't hurt.

Bill, as he liked to be called, had married and invested well. He didn't need the money, but he testified in medical malpractice cases because he enjoyed having something exciting and challenging to do. His wife said it kept him from being under foot. He also relished having the opportunity to play the expert in front of a jury. Bill realized he was a small-timer in academic medicine. He hadn't published much, and most of his "work" had been "me too" research that hadn't moved the field of cardiology. But he knew juries were impressed with his Columbia appointment, his New York style, and his good looks.

Len Barkely told Bill that the six-foot, blue-eyed, silver-haired man looked like a "TV doctor" and why not? His perfectly groomed good looks were tweaked by twice-a-month visits to an expensive salon. His impeccably tailored suits were invariably complemented by bright silk bowties. Bill knew that his slick packaging never failed to influence female jurors.

And Bill certainly had a vivid sexual imagination, one that had almost gotten him thrown in jail. In his early years in practice, a female patient accused him of fondling her. With persuasion and money, he had been able to convince the woman, as well as her husband and the authorities, that it was just an unfortunate misunderstanding. Still, the rumors circulated and contributed greatly to the career inertia that kept Bill from achieving the academic heights he thought he deserved.

Knowing Bill's habits well, and that his review would be cursory, Barkley carefully distilled the Hamlin medical records and sent Bill the salient facts. When Barkely did call Otley to get his opinion, he listened to a disjointed redaction for a few minutes before interrupting with his usual solution. "Bill, it sounds like you have a great grasp of the case. It is exactly what my paralegals and I thought you would come up with. Look, I know you are really busy, so why don't I just have one of my people get down the first draft of an opinion. You can edit it as extensively as you like and send it back signed on your letterhead. Is that OK with you?"

Barkley knew that Bill would love the idea of having the paralegals do the heavy lifting. Meticulously reviewing a case and writing an intelligent iron-clad opinion was hard work he would just as soon pass on to someone else. Barkley also knew that Bill wouldn't change a thing in the document so whatever Barkley wanted in the opinion was sure to be left intact.

Barkley wasn't naïve about the importance of a sharply written expert report. Philip had done a good job of documenting in the chart all of the explanatory conversations that he had with Hugh and Moira. Barkley knew that he would have to stress the emotional issues of the case: a young dedicated mother, dead before her time; children left motherless for the rest of their lives; a stricken, hopelessly lost husband deprived of his true love. Philip would be cast as a scientist more interested in his professional advancement than his patient's welfare.

Barkley caught a break when the hospital attorney, Dylan somebody, let it slip that Moira Hamlin had an experimental procedure in the ER. Hugh was adamant that he had never signed a consent form and Barkley's staff couldn't find one in the chart. Barkley knew he could get the jury angry with Philip for using Moira as a "guinea pig." Furthermore, the cardiac arrest had occurred after Philip had "convinced" Moira that she didn't need to take medicine. That one would play well with the jurors too. Hopefully, they could be made to believe that Philip had been desperate to bail himself out after he found out about Moira's cardiac arrest, and ended up making one bad judgment after another, right to the bitter end.

Dan and Joan were surprised when, at a pre-trial meeting, Barkley announced he planned to amend the complaint to seek punitive damages against Philip. This meant that the plaintiff would attempt to prove that Philip hadn't simply been negligent, but that he had acted with a "willful disregard" for Moira's welfare by injecting a research drug into her system against her family's will.

"I also think that Sarkis tampered with the records and that's why we can't find all of the EKGs from Moira's office visits. That kind of behavior merits some extra punishment and punitives should take care of that."

Joan scoffed, "You don't have a prayer to get punitives here, Len."

"We'll see," Barkley replied confidently.

"I know what you're doing—you are trying to get Dr. Sarkis to settle the case before trial," Joan challenged. "I can tell you it won't work."

Joan wasn't so sure about that herself. Punitive damages frighten defendant doctors because malpractice insurance does not provide coverage and in the end, the doctor must pay it all. Doctors are averse to risk, especially if money is involved and having personal assets in jeopardy causes many to cave in. It was an old trick that Barkley didn't resort to often, but he knew with his wealth, Hugh would only respond favorably to a large settlement offer. Why not play the punitive card? He had nothing to lose.

"I am afraid that you are wrong about this one, Joan," Barkley said. "The jury will be very receptive to the idea that Dr. Sarkis acted in a reckless way. Giving an experimental drug without permission is going to be a big problem for him and for you. You will be getting an amended complaint soon. And by the way, we also plan to contact the federal authorities who were responsible for overseeing the research that Dr. Sarkis was conducting. I want them to know, if they don't already, that Dr. Sarkis didn't bother to get informed consent."

Philip unraveled when he got the news from Joan and Dan. "Everything I did was meant to save Moira's life, and now all her family and the legal system want to do is punish me." He was devastated.

Philip spent a large part of every day and night ruminating about the case, replaying each event like an old movie. He found himself staring blankly into space as black-and-white images of Moira in the examination room, in the ER, and in the ICU flickered across his memory. The shadow of the case cast itself across every aspect of his life and he couldn't escape its horrible impact.

A good doctor connects with patients with an upbeat mood and sense of humor, neither of which Philip had in abundance before this happened. Now he was surly with his staff, and viewed each new patient as a potential legal adversary. He couldn't reach out to anyone because he had so few relationships and because he was embarrassed by the case. On one occasion, he tried to open up to his brother Brian, but he couldn't grasp the issues or understand Philip's role in the case. After a couple of hours of explanation, Brian's attention wandered and Philip gave up.

Most of Philip's friends had similar malpractice concerns but when he sought commiseration, they didn't want to talk about it. "It is the price of doing business, old man," they'd say. He sensed that the pain of rehashing it all was too great for them too. He felt isolated and adrift.

But the major impact of the case hit home and Nancy in particular. Nearly every night, an angry Philip came home with some new piece of information that set him off. At first, Nancy soothed him with a vodka tonic to "take the edge off" but it gradually took more and more vodka to calm him, and after dinner, he would invariably fall into a stupor in front of the television set. Philip had no interest in sex and showed Nancy almost no affection. When she tried to discuss happier issues, Philip would launch into an angry tirade. He had almost no patience with the children. As painful as the trial would be, Nancy was anxious to get it behind them.

Despite all of this, Philip told Dan and Joan that he was not interested in settling. "I didn't do anything wrong," he insisted. "So if both of you agree, I will just have to put up with all of the bullshit."

The irony, not lost on Philip, Nancy and the attorneys, was that as Sarkis descended further into the depths of his despair, Hugh's situation was improving. After the funeral, he took time off to be with his family. His father was happy to oblige; Hugh was not important to the business the way his brothers were, and his absence was hardly noticed.

Bonnie's fortune likewise improved. Several years before, she had married John Romano, an Ob-Gyn doctor who was an heir to a South Philadelphia family fortune. Bonnie continued her business career as they planned to start a family. However, a strange set of circumstances changed everything. An otherwise healthy John Romano contracted a bad head cold. An antibiotic made him feel better until Bonnie found him dead in his recliner early one morning.

After John Romano's funeral, Bonnie rekindled her friendship with Moira Hamlin, her former college roommate who was now living a very glamorous life. Perhaps, Bonnie reasoned, Moira and Hugh would serve as stepping-stones to propel her out of South Philly into high society. Her plan worked and soon the trio was seen everywhere together, and eventually Bonnie bought a house close by on the Main Line.

After Moira died, Hugh and Bonnie spent even more time together. She enjoyed Hugh's children who by now called her "Aunt Bonnie." Eventually Hugh returned to work with renewed energy. His father, surprised by the change, entrusted him with new sales and marketing arrangements that he seemed to enjoy. After a few months of dating and being accepted as a couple, Hugh and Bonnie were quietly married in a small, civil ceremony, attended by family and close friends.

They decided that Bonnie's new home was a better place for the children, who still had nightmares and couldn't even pass the master bedroom without wailing. In one fell swoop, the entire household, including servants and pets, resettled without as much as a backward glance.

CHAPTER 9

After what seemed forever to Philip, the trial date arrived. When Judge Pleasance refused to allow a venue change, Joan spent several sessions preparing Philip for his stint in the Philadelphia courtroom. "You have to look serious and concerned, but not worried; confident but not cocky; sympathetic but not guilty. You should wear a dark suit and conservative tie. Get a haircut before trial day but no manicure. That would be overdoing it. A nice watch is a good idea but not too expensive and no other jewelry except a wedding ring. Patients expect their doctors to have money but not too much," she said.

"They want their doctor to drive a nice car like a Lexus — it means they are competent," Joan explained. But doctors should never be seen in a Bentley or Rolls Royce. That means that physicians are getting rich on the misery of their patients."

"Nancy wants to know if she should come to the trial."

"Nancy should attend court but not every day and not with the children," Joan replied. "Even Philly jurors are able to distinguish family support from blatant manipulation. But Philip, you have to be there every day no matter what, and you have to stay in the courtroom as long as the jury is present." Joan had seen juries turn on doctors who didn't take the trial seriously.

"You can try to work a little in the morning before you come to court but don't exhaust yourself." As Philip listened, he realized how dependent he was on Joan.

At the eleventh hour, the plaintiffs decided to let Moira's other doctors out of the case and concentrate on Philip and the hospital. At the settlement conference, it became obvious that the plaintiff's demands were larger than anything the insurance companies had to offer. The judge was not going to force any of the parties to settle so the matter would have to go to verdict. In addition, Joan and Dan were not successful in excluding any part of the plaintiff's case, including a video of Moira with her family that Barkley planned to use in his opening.

Dan and Joan were also not able to exclude the testimony of the plaintiff's experts. They had argued that Moira's disease was rare, and only experts in electrophysiology like Dr. Myerstone could understand its complexity. The judge ruled that the plaintiff's expert cardiologist was adequate to the task, and that it was up to the defense to cast doubt on his testimony. Joan didn't think bias to plantiff was unusual for Judge Pleasance, but it was going to make her work much more challenging.

The opening day was difficult for Philip. After a tough commute, he had to endure last-minute instructions from Joan and Dan about his behavior, as if he were a misbehaving child about to meet the headmaster. Then came the walk to the courthouse, between his two attorneys, like a convict being escorted to the gallows.

From the outside, Philadelphia's City Hall is an architectural delight, with high archways, dramatic statues, and ornate trim. Inside, it is a dreary dive with the smell of urine reeking from every destroyed phone booth. Rude security personnel rifle through bags and briefcases, while seedy criminals consult unsavory lawyers in the hallways and stairwells. For Philip, the bleak scene mirrored his mood.

Entering the courtroom, Philip bumped into Hugh Hamlin, and muttered a reflex "excuse me" before he realized who it was. As they moved in opposite directions, Philip noticed Hugh's hateful look. Try as he might, Philip could not empathize with Hugh. Earlier that morning, he had railed at Nancy, "This guy is crucifying me for no reason. He just doesn't understand what happened and I don't think he cares. His life is back together and he is taking mine apart. I hope I have the chance to make him pay for what he has done to us."

Jury selection became the immediate order of business. The initial panel was mostly African American and female. No one looked particularly happy to be there, and many were downright surly. Each juror had filled out a questionnaire that was distributed to the attorneys. Philip watched them pore over the sheets, conferring with colleagues, trying to discern which jury member might be sympathetic to their side. Philip doubted that any of them could follow the complicated medical issues in this case.

One attractive African American woman in the crowd looked familiar. When she said during voire dire that she had been a nurse in the CCU at GMH several years before, he remembered her as a skilled team member who left GMH for a position in industry. Nancy, the head nurse at the time, had attempted to talk her out of leaving and he learned later she was not happy in the corporate world. When the lawyers learned she knew Philip, she was disqualified.

Over half the panel had raised their hands when asked if being selected for the jury would represent a hardship with a myriad of reasons why they couldn't serve for two weeks. At two o'clock, the jury was impaneled. Judge Pleasance returned to the courtroom to deliver instructions, then adjourned for the day to get a "fresh start" in the morning. "I wonder if she wants to embark on that 'fresh start' from the first tee this afternoon," Philip whispered to Joan, who shot him a warning glare.

"Philip, I think you should go home and get some rest," Dan advised after the courtroom had emptied. It looks as if you haven't been sleeping much, and we don't want the jury to get the idea that you are overly worried."

"OK, but I have to stop at the hospital to do a little paperwork and check up on a few patients first. I know Nancy won't be disappointed. Having me moping around the house in mid-afternoon is not her idea of a good time."

Philip took a sleeping pill that night and managed a little rest, although Nancy told him at breakfast that he had fidgeted endlessly. He arrived in the courtroom prepared for opening statements, but found the attorneys loitering in the hallway. A male juror and a female alternate were AWOL and the trial couldn't start without them. The judge was preparing to issue a bench warrant when they wandered in two hours late, arm-in-arm, after a night of enjoying each other's company (courtesy of a bottle of Jim Beam). After a session in the judge's chambers, they were both dismissed. She was concerned that inappropriate fraternization would recur and threaten the integrity of the case. But that left 11 jurors and alternates. Given the unreliability of Philadelphia jurors, and the chance of a mistrial if more jurors were dismissed, the judge assembled another jury panel and identified two replacements. By then, day two of the trial was over.

Day three began with arguments of several pre-trial motions. Once again, nearly all of the decisions were in the plaintiff's favor, but Joan said that none of them really hurt the defense.

Len Barkley was then invited by the judge to deliver his opening. His forte was "speechifying" as Joan called it. He had been a theater major in college and enjoyed delivering an impassioned dissertation at the beginning of a case to put the jury in the right mood and solidly in his corner. Barkley stepped up to the jury box railing, surveyed the group with a paternal grin, and launched.

"Ladies and gentlemen of the jury, you will learn that Philip Sarkis is a cavalier, uncaring, highly ambitious doctor who recklessly deprived Moira Hamlin of therapy that would have prevented the disaster of her death. Then, he ruthlessly took advantage of his relationship with Hugh and Moira to do experiments that had no benefit for Moira and only increased her chances to die a horrible death. Because of his actions, sanctioned by his hospital, Moira Hamlin suffered terribly."

Philip listened trying not to make a face. Moira had been unconscious from the time of her cardiac arrest and aware of nothing. But Barkley was only warming up. "Philip Sarkis then deceived the family into believing that he had tried to help Moira, knowing all the while that what he had done was negligent. Imagine a doctor experimenting on one of your loved ones without permission." Barkley asked the jury, "How would that make you feel?

"Moira Hamlin was a wonderful, beautiful young woman. In addition to caring for her young children and husband, she was known in her community for selflessly giving her time and resources to those in need."

Barkley introduced Moira's parents and parents-in-law to the jury. "The Hamlin family grieving continues to this very day. Moira's loss was devastating to each and every one of them."

This concept was of paramount importance. Barkley knew that economic damages were going to be hard to prove. Moira did not support her family in any way and the Hamlins had a vast fortune. Caring for the Hamlin's children would be no problem. Thus, the jury had to be convinced that Moira's death had caused her family immense suffering for which they deserved compensation.

"We have to make that jury literally feel the pain of Moira's loss," he had lectured his staff before the trial. "Personalize it for them. Make them see Moira as a real person who could have been their spouse or sibling, and the best way to do that is to let them see Moira in action."

After Barkley's opening remarks, the lights went down and it was movie time. The professionally made tape began with still photos of Moira with her children, accompanied by sentimental Pachelbel music and narration by a commentator who sounded like God. Philip recognized the voice of John Fanfera, a popular TV news commentator. What some people wouldn't do for a buck, he thought. He leaned over and whispered to Joan, "Do you think that Hamlin advertisements on the TV station that Fanfera works for had anything to do with getting him to do this?"

There followed scenes of family celebrations with a heavy emphasis on birthdays and Christmas. Though the Hamlin family was Jewish, there was a notable absence of Jewish holiday coverage. Barkley knew that Jewish jurors were rare in Philadelphia so he wanted to play up the Christian holidays, which the Hamlins also celebrated. In all of these riveting scenes Moira was the central figure, smiling sweetly while she orchestrated things to the delight of everyone. Despite his cynicism, Philip had to admit that Moira was photogenic and epitomized the ideal young mother. But the knockout punch was the footage with her newborn, which reduced most of the jury as well as the gallery to tears. Even Philip found a lump in his throat as Fanfera, in a deep professional voice, identified the players and how each had shared Moira's life.

At the judge's instructions, the tape lasted less than five minutes and when the lights came on, everyone in the room was red eyed and sniffling.

Barkley finished his opening in a soft theatrical voice that intensified the jury's sympathetic mood. "Ladies and gentlemen, I will prove that by their negligent deeds, Philip Sarkis and GMH robbed Moira of a full and long family life. The facts are straightforward and will speak for themselves. Eminent experts will come forward to make certain you understand the medical facts so you can arrive at the only correct verdict."

Barkley told the jury he wanted their decision to be a dispassionate one. Philip and the defense knew that Barkley needed the jury to do just the opposite and make an irrational decision based on their sympathy. In Barkley's mind, Philip could not be perceived by the jury to be sympathetic in any way. The more he looked callous and uncaring, the more likely the jury would punish him with a large verdict. By the time Barkley was summarizing his opening, the jury was glaring at Philip. Barkley finished by entreating the jurors to "do the right thing and help Moira's family come to closure." Philip and his attorneys watched the jury nod in affirmation.

After Barkley's brilliant opening, it was Dan's turn. The young lawyer tried to capitalize on Barkley's speech by reminding the court that facts had to take precedence over an emotional response to Moira's untimely death. "Dr. Sarkis feels as bad as anyone about Moira's death," he explained. "But you have to remember that Dr. Sarkis delivered state-of-the-art care to Moira Hamlin. Furthermore, as you will hear, Dr. Sarkis regularly conferred with Moira and her husband about all aspects of her care including the things he did to try to save her life on the day she had her cardiac arrest. You will also learn that Dr. Sarkis documented all of his management decisions and the reasons he made them."

Philip listened intently, stealing furtive glances at the jury. Most were receptive although a few appeared bored and stared off into space. Dan plunged on. "We will be calling experts in cardiology or heart medicine who will testify that Dr. Sarkis did an admirable job and that Moira's death could not have been expected. By the time all the facts are presented, I am sure you will agree that Dr. Sarkis did not practice negligently, but in fact delivered excellent care to Moira in every respect."

Dan and Joan had decided in advance of Barkley's dramatic opening, to deliver an unemotional, simple message that was as plain as Dan's blue serge suit and light blue tie.

The hospital's attorney, however, came out swinging and it was clear from the outset that his style wasn't going to play well in front of this jury. Dylan McShane was a young, aggressive attorney who was eager to make his main point: Philip was to blame for what happened to Moira Hamlin. Philip's defense team knew that Dylan was not talented enough, nor was the hospital enlight-

97

ened enough, to argue the case on the issues of causation. They expected the simple argument that hospitals don't practice medicine.

McShane walked briskly over to the jury box. He was a big man who needed only a few strides to arrive in front of the wary jurors. He announced in a loud voice, "Our job is to provide an environment for our doctors to practice—we really can't control whether they deliver or don't deliver appropriate care at every moment."

Dan and Joan knew that if the jury was sympathetic to Moira's family, they wouldn't be in a mood to watch the defendants deflect blame. McShane may have sensed the same thing because he ended his opening comments fairly abruptly, almost in midthought, and promised the jury that it would hear more on these points later in the trial.

The next day, Len Barkley began his case, hammering away on the central theme of Philip's reckless disregard of his patient's welfare. He put Hugh on the stand first to create a firm foundation for his case.

Hugh did his job well, explaining how Moira had placed her trust in Philip and GMH. "I just couldn't understand why Dr. Sarkis picked the treatments he did," Hugh said, and added that he didn't remember any detailed conversations about therapeutic options. "As far as I could tell, Dr. Sarkis had pretty much told Moira what he wanted to do and then he just did it." Hugh said he remembered asking many questions that Philip merely brushed off and never answered. "I didn't know that Moira could have had an implantable defibrillator that might have saved her life because Dr. Sarkis never brought it up." He also said he couldn't understand why Moira had not been treated with beta-blockers if they might have prevented sudden death. "I really don't remember any conversations about using drugs or any other preventative treatment."

At the break, Philip told Dan and Joan that Hugh's testimony was inaccurate. "He almost never came to the office and when he did, he just sat there. It was Moira who refused the options I described. The guy is lying through his teeth."

Hugh's father, Eugene Hamlin, testified next. The old man's resemblance to his heavy jowled son was uncanny—just more wrinkled and gray. He walked slowly to the stand and eased himself into the chair, grimacing with back pain, but still smiling at the jury.

Gene's job was to point out what a wonderful daughter-in-law Moira was and how much she was missed. He described how he had met Moira, and how they had become like father and daughter. "Moira was the picture of health. She would have lived a long life if her QT problem had been treated correctly." This testimonial brought an immediate objection from Dan. Nevertheless, Gene played his part perfectly, quietly indignant that his daughter-in-law had received substandard care, and angry that she had died in such a horrible way. Then Barkley made sure that Gene pointed out the egregious effect the death had on his grandchildren. "They became withdrawn, like zombies sometimes. They walk around and don't speak or burst out crying for no apparent reason. It is awful to see how much they changed."

Dan and Joan had decided not to challenge these witnesses much. They were too sympathetic and attacking them would surely irk the jury. On cross-examination, Joan asked just a few questions to clarify things, but she didn't get too technical.

Dylan McShane, on the other hand, misread the situation again. He tried to get Eugene Hamlin to absolve the hospital of any wrongdoing, but Hamlin actually knew little about hospital policies. He made rambling statements about how doctors should be controlled by hospitals until the judge asked where all this was heading. When she snapped, "Gentlemen, we are simply not getting anywhere with this line of questioning," McShane abruptly concluded his examination and sat down.

Barkley had considered having Bonnie Romano corroborate Hugh's testimony about informed consent and the heroic treatments in the ER, but he decided to keep her out of the courtroom. He didn't want the defense to inform the jury about Hugh's remarriage. That tactic would have seriously weakened the "poor motherless children" argument. Instead, Barkley moved on to Bill Otley's testimony.

Otley would be the only expert witness because Barkley didn't want to confuse the jury with too much medical science. He just wanted someone who looked credible with proper credentials to tell the jury how negligent Philip had been. Dan and Joan knew that the jury might believe Otley, so their job was to challenge his qualifications.

Barkley started with the standard questions about Otley's education and training, his work experience and years in practice. In this phase of the trial, the judge permitted leading questions to speed the testimony.

"Dr. Otley, you have spent most of your career at Columbia Presbyterian Hospital in New York, is that correct?"

"Yes I have."

"And that hospital is considered one of the most prestigious in the United States, is it not?"

"Yes it is."

"And to this day, you see patients and teach students there, is that correct?"

Otley turned and gave the jury his most engaging smile. "Why, yes I do, and I enjoy that very much."

Barkley then introduced Otley's CV into evidence and asked Otley to describe his membership in professional organizations and committees. "Well, I am a fellow of the American College of Cardiology and the American Heart Association and have been for years." After a few more perfunctory questions, Barkley requested that Otley be qualifed as an expert and turned the witness over to Joan.

"Doctor, good morning. I just have a few questions. Could you do me a favor and go through your resume and point out any items relating to the long QT syndrome?"

The question didn't rattle Otley.

"You mean papers I have written on the subject?"

"Well, anything on the subject. Papers, lectures, special courses you have taken, anything. Let me give you the resumè so you can page through it and find what I am looking for. May I approach the witness, Your Honor?

"Certainly. Dr. Otley, do you understand the question?"

"I think so, Your Honor."

Bill Otley took the CV and started to page through it. He knew that there was nothing there to help him so he decided to wing it.

"Well, there are several lectures I have given on how to evaluate patients with cardiac disease that would have included information about the QT interval, I am sure."

"Perhaps Doctor," Joan said pleasantly. "But I am looking for some evidence that you know more about the QT interval than other cardiologists that makes you qualified to comment on Dr. Sarkis' actions in this case. Is there anything in your CV to prove that?"

Otley decided not to stretch things. "I don't think I can help you, counselor."

"Fine. Now Dr. Otley, you are not holding yourself out to be an expert in cardiac electrophysiology, are you?"

"If you mean am I board certified in that specialty, no, but I know a lot about cardiac arrhythmia and have taken care of patients with electrical disorders for years."

"You told us about membership in several professional organizations. Are you a member of the Heart Rhythm Society or any other society of doctors in the arrhythmia field?"

"Well, in my CV, you can see that I served on a panel on cardiac electrophysiology in 1987 and those proceedings were published in Circulation, the most prestigious cardiology journal there is."

"Really, Dr. Otley. Perhaps you can describe your contribution to the published paper. Did you actually do any of the writing?"

"No, I didn't do any of the writing myself." Philip had told Joan that Otley probably had been placed on that committee by a crony as a favor, not because Otley was expected to contribute.

And on it went, Joan trying to nail Otley down, and Otley trying to escape. But in the end, the judge qualified Otley. It was unclear whether the jury cared about his qualifications. Philip feared that Joan had angered them by holding up the proceedings and badgering this "mannered doctor."

The second part of Otley's testimony would deal with his opinion of Philip's medical treatment. Here, there was no equivocation on his part. When asked by Barkley if Philip's care had fallen below the accepted standard, Otley answered affirmatively. "Dr. Sarkis made many enormous mistakes in the care of Moira Hamlin. First of all, he should have treated her with beta-blockers, and later on in the case, he should have inserted an automatic implantable defibrillator. I could see no reason why beta-blockers were not prescribed; they are fairly innocuous and have been proven to reduce the incidence of sudden death in people with the long QT syndrome. I can understand why there may have been some hesitancy to use drugs or devices during Moira's pregnancy, but once she delivered there was no excuse for not recommending those treatments. Not to have done so constituted negligence and was clearly outside the standard of care."

Otley's criticism of Philip's interventions after Moira's cardiac arrest was even more strident. "There simply was no reason for Dr. Sarkis to administer an experimental drug to Moira Hamlin. He hadn't exhausted his options with approved drugs so I don't know why he insisted on trying something so unconventional. But what really stands out is that Dr. Sarkis did not obtain informed consent before administering a potentially dangerous drug. There is no way to know what damage that drug did to Moira Hamlin. That kind of behavior is simply reckless.

"Then to make matters even worse, the device that he used to shock Ms. Hamlin's heart was not properly inspected by the technical team at GMH. The inspection sticker on the device had expired, and Dr. Sarkis should have known that before he used it to deliver a bolt of electricity to Mrs. Hamlin's chest. Although it worked to get her heart back into a normal rhythm, it should never have been used and may have actually damaged her heart. The shocks may also have harmed Mrs. Hamlin's brain and may have contributed to the fact that she never recovered neurological function."

Joan knew that it was going to be tough for Philip to sit quietly and not react to this testimony. How had Otley found out about the device inspection issue? Like the experimental drug consent, this information was not contained in the medical record and would have had to come directly from hospital personnel.

Cross examination was going to be Joan's task. Philip had helped her understand the issues, and so she went on the attack fully armed. Her questions were rapid-fire, changing focus quickly to try to keep Otley off balance.

"Dr. Otley, just how effective are beta-blockers in preventing sudden death in patients with the long QT syndrome?"

"What are the side-effects of beta-blockers?"

"What are the complications of ICD implantation?"

"Were ICDs the standard of care for patients when Mrs. Hamlin had her problem, or is that a more recent development?"

Joan then asked how decisions about Moira's care were made.

"Dr. Otley, did you discover in your review of the records any evidence that the Hamlins were informed of their treatment options?"

"I do remember seeing that in Dr. Sarkis' office notes."

"And do you recall seeing that the Moira Hamlin had decided to go without beta-blockers or an ICD?"

"I do recall seeing that, but I didn't take it seriously. You see, it is important for doctors to guide their patient's treatment and to be directive if they think that there is a good reason to do one thing or another. In this case, Dr. Sarkis was not directive enough -- he should have insisted that Mrs. Hamlin have some kind of protection. If he had presented the facts clearly, I am sure she would have accepted his recommended treatment."

Try as she might, Joan was not able to shake Otley from his opinion: the therapy administered by Philip in the ER was experimental and never should have been given without Hugh's express permission. "There are guidelines from federal agencies on this topic, counselor. I would say that Dr. Sarkis' behavior was highly inappropriate. In fact, he failed to note what he did with the drug or the special shock device in the medical record and he didn't get proper consent. That not only constitutes negligence, but it is also a deliberate violation of the federal guidelines for the safe administration of experimental therapy. Dr. Sarkis has to be held accountable for that here and in other forums. It simply isn't the way it's supposed to be done."

At the conclusion of the redirect, Dan and Joan felt they had scored some points, but Joan was afraid that the jury wouldn't be able to understand what constituted good care in a dire situation. The jury would have to make a black-and-white decision about a complicated situation, and she feared all they would hear was that Philip had done something bad for which he had to be held accountable.

At the end of Otley's testimony, Barkley was almost ready to rest his case. Two more witnesses would describe the impact of Moira's death on the children. The first was Meghan Divan, a child psychologist from southern California who specialized in therapy for children who had witnessed a catastrophic loss of a parent or loved one. Divan, like many expert witnesses, tried to dress her part—charcoal mid-calf skirt, plaid blazer, white blouse and striped kerchief done up like a man's tie. Add mid-nose specs, and voila! Instant kid shrink.

"Ms. Divan," Barkley began, "could you please describe for the jury the psychological situation of each of the Hamlin children and the results of your interviews with them?"

"Their profiles are remarkably similar," said Divan. "All of them now have horrible nightmares that include the scene of the resuscitation. Any pleasant memories of their mother have been replaced by the grisly bedroom events. That is all that they can talk about."

"Is that unique for children who lose their mothers?"

"It is because they witnessed her death and attempted resuscitation. This shock can be described like a blowtorch wound on their little souls. It has become overwhelming for each of them. I suspect the trauma will linger for a long time, maybe forever."

On cross, Joan began by making sure that the jury understood how Meghan had found her way to a Philadelphia courtroom. "Ms. Divan, how did you come to Mr. Barkely's attention?"

"I really don't recall."

"Perhaps I can refresh your memory. Are you listed in any directories of expert witnesses for hire?"

Barkley immediately objected to the phrasing of the question as belligerent and the judge agreed.

"Let me rephrase," said Joan. "Are you listed in any directories of expert witnesses who might be available to review cases of child psychotrauma and testify at trial?"

"I am not sure. I may be."

"Allow me to show you a directory I found on the Internet that lists your name and contact information for the precise reasons I just described. Does this look familiar to you?"

"Yes, that is my information, but I don't know how it got there."

"Let's drill down further on this point, Ms. Divan. Did Mr. Barkley contact you about reviewing records in this case?"

"Yes he did."

"And did you ask him how he obtained your name?"

"I don't recall."

"Once again, your memory fails. Let me ask you if there was some other way that you know by which Mr. Barkley could have found you."

"Not that I know of."

"So would it be fair to assume that he got you off a list?"

Now Barkley objected that this question called for speculation on the part of the witness. The judge sustained the objection. Joan withdrew her question; her point had been made.

"Ms. Divan, how many times have you testified in cases such as this one?"

"I really couldn't say."

"You have no idea at all? Would it be greater than a hundred, greater than 500?"

"Probably in between those two numbers."

"So you have testified in hundreds of cases. Always for the plaintiff?"

"Yes, I think so."

"And in each and every one of these hundreds of cases, were you able to tell the jury that the children of a catastrophic event, such as occurred in this case, had been severely harmed psychologically?"

"To a variable extent, yes."

"And in any cases that you reviewed, were you able to arrive at the conclusion that the children in fact were OK and that they could go on successfully with their lives?"

"Yes, in some cases that I reviewed."

"Do you know what percentage?"

Divan was beginning to squirm. Her next reply, "No, I don't know" had a bite to it the jurors clearly noticed.

"OK, so you come in and render an opinion in a case such as this based on your training and experience. Do you have any way of validating that what you found is actually true?"

"I don't understand your question."

"You have been making these analyses for lawyers like Mr. Barkley for a long time, haven't you, Ms. Divan?"

"Yes, I have quite a bit of experience."

"Would you say for more than ten years?"

"At least that long, yes."

"So, have you ever gone back to find the children that you described as scarred, to see what happened to their lives?"

"No, it is not my place to do that."

"Weren't you curious?"

"Curiosity has nothing to do with my job — I am a scientist."

"So you are asking the jury to accept your non-validated opinions in this case? How are they supposed to decide if you know what you are doing?"

Barkley jumped out of his seat. "Your honor, this witness has been certified as an expert and Ms. Foster is badgering her."

"Objection sustained."

Once again, Joan had made her point. "I have nothing further Your Honor."

The last plaintiff's witness was a minor one on Barkley's list. The plaintiff would present the costs of caring for the motherless children. No reference to the plaintiff's net worth would be permitted. In effect, the jury would have to assume that there were economic damages to be assumed by the plaintiff unless they obtained a favorable verdict. The economic expert gave a short presentation. The amounts were fairly standard so Joan elected to forgo cross-examination. She didn't want to incur wrath from the judge, and the financial issues were not critical to the case. Len Barkley wanted a much bigger award than the economics would support. There was no point in nickel and diming the case.

CHAPTER 10

Barkley rested his case early on Friday afternoon, and the judge announced that the court would adjourn until Monday morning when the defense would begin its presentation. Philip had the weekend to replay it all, and to imagine the jury's reaction. Nancy had the weekend to listen to Philip's incessant ruminations so she suggested several diversions. None were acceptable to Philip, who retired to his den to watch sports while she cleaned out closets. Neither spoke more than a few words. Nancy would remember it as one of the worst weekends of their marriage.

Philip arrived at the courthouse on Monday looking wiped out and stressed. Despite this, Joan wanted the jury to hear Philip's account of the story as soon as possible. She had really wanted his testimony to begin before the weekend so that the jury could balance their thinking.

Nancy put Philip on the stand first thing and took him through his testimony exactly as they had rehearsed. He tried to be succinct and on point, and to keep his negative emotions in check.

Philip described his first encounters with Moira, explained the reasons for his recommendations, and tried to help the jury understand the nature and complexity of the problem he had been treating. He described how Moira had decided to forgo treatment, and ended with a detailed review of her final hospitalization and the measures he had taken to save her life. Then came the part they had rehearsed so carefully.

"Dr. Sarkis, as you sit here today, do you believe that the care you rendered to Moira Hamlin was negligent in any way?"

"No, the care I gave Moira Hamlin was at all times the best. I just wanted her to recover and lead a normal life."

"Is there anything you would do differently if the same case were presented to you again?"

"Not at all. I would approach things exactly the same way."

Next, Joan needed to convince the jury that Philip's recommendations had been acceptable to Moira and Hugh. "There were a number of difficult decisions that needed to be made in Moira Hamlin's case. Can you describe to the jury how they were finalized?"

"I saw Moira Hamlin many times. On each occasion, I presented treatment options to her. Since she was often alone, she would contact me after she had discussed the issues with her husband. Then Mrs. Hamlin would choose what she thought was best for her at the time, and we would go with it. The only exception was when she was unconscious in the hospital, and then I had only Mr. Hamlin to deal with. I used the same approach with him, and he seemed to understand that he was free to make whatever choice he thought was best for his wife. It is the way I have practiced medicine for my entire career, and it is the way patients of high intellect prefer to be treated."

"So you considered that the Hamlins were smart enough to make an informed decision based on what you told them."

"Yes, and I always documented the options I offered and choices made by the family or patient."

Joan walked to the witness box and paused dramatically. "Dr. Sarkis, why did you give Moira Hamlin an investigational antiarrhythmic drug without a signed informed consent?"

"That was a very difficult decision for me. Moira Hamlin was having repeated bouts of a life-threatening arrhythmia. Her heart was literally out of whack. I knew if I didn't get it stopped, she was going to die. I spoke with Mr. Hamlin about it but he couldn't make a decision. He was between a rock and a hard place. I intended to come back to him, but realized that if I did, it would be too late and she would die. So I gave it. I am sorry it happened that way, but I am not sorry I did it. It stopped her arrhythmias and stabilized her. She died despite the medicine, not because of it."

Joan nodded and handed over the witness to Barkley. "Dr. Sarkis, how much time do you devote to patient care as opposed to teaching, research and administration?"

"I put in about 30 hours a week on patient care in various venues, the office, hospital and in the laboratory."

"And how much time do you put into the other parts of your job, teaching, research, and so on?"

"About 60 hours per week," Philip answered.

"So it would be safe to say that patient care is not what you spend most of your time doing?"

Philip knew what Barkley was trying to do. "I do many different things, Mr. Barkley and I try to do them well."

Barkley quickly changed the subject. "Did you get Mr. Hamlin's permission before you treated Moira Hamlin with an experimental drug?"

"I tried to get a decision from Mr. Hamlin quickly since Moira couldn't sustain a normal heart rhythm. Because there was little time to lose, I tried to push him to make up his mind. In the end, he couldn't decide and I took a chance and gave the medicine. As a result, Mrs. Hamlin's dangerous arrhythmia was stabilized."

"But Doctor, Moira Hamlin died shortly thereafter. How do we know that your heroics did no harm?"

"I had no way of knowing at that time that her brain had been permanently damaged when she collapsed at home and had no blood flow to her brain. That is what caused her to die — not the drug I gave her to bring her heart rhythm back to normal."

Barkley shook his head solemnly and told the judge he was finished. During a brief recess, Philip gulped coffee, and Joan tried to calm his nerves. Then Dylan McShane took over the questioning. McShane, as he intimated in his opening, wanted the jury to understand that Philip had acted on his own. Consequently, most of his questions concerned the chain of command and authority in the hospital system and how Philip fit into it.

"Dr. Sarkis, when you cared for Moira Hamlin, did most of your contact occur in your office and outside the hospital?"

"I saw her in the hospital when she delivered her last baby, but most of our conversations occurred in my office."

"Was the hospital responsible for any of the decision making that went on in Moira Hamlin's case?"

"Not directly, but the same code of ethics and good practice were in effect no matter where I saw Ms. Hamlin. I have to conform to hospital medical rules just like everybody else. The hospital approved all research projects, including those I pursued in my office. I was also in compliance with hospital policies when I treated Moira Hamlin."

After several attempts to shake Philip's testimony, Dylan sat down.

The key witness for Philip's defense would be Bob Myerstone. Joan wanted to give Bob as much latitude as possible, but knew that the jury would be able to absorb only so much. It would be very important for Bob to hammer away at the key points so that the jury would remember what he said when they were deliberating. The verdict would likely come down to which expert the jury believed more.

Qualifying Bob was simple. His credentials were impeccable and he clearly knew more than almost anyone about the long QT syndrome. Barkley tried to cast doubt on his testimony by focusing on his compensation.

"Doctor, how much are you charging to be here today to testify on Dr. Sarkis' behalf?"

Joan objected to the line of questioning since it had nothing to do with Bob's credentials but the judge overruled the objection.

"I get paid $500 per hour for my testimony."

"And you also were paid to review the case, is that right? How much did you get for that?"

"It took me about eight hours so I was paid $4000."

Barkley pretended to have trouble with the mathematics. "So if my calculations are correct, and you will forgive me, Doctor, because math and science weren't my strengths in school, I figure that you must have been paid about $8,000 to $10,000 plus your expenses, is that about right?"

"Yes, about that amount."

"That is quite a chunk of money Doctor, maybe more than most of the jurors make in half a year, don't you think?"

Joan immediately objected and was sustained by the judge. Bob was qualified and his fact testimony began.

Joan took Bob through the case, as he understood it. She then came to the most important questions.

"Dr. Myerstone, were the treatment options Dr. Sarkis presented to Mrs. Hamlin reasonable?"

"Yes, the treatments that could have been used were beta-blockers or device therapy."

"Dr. Sarkis testified that he felt that defibrillator therapy was not required in Mrs. Hamlin's case because she had never had any blackout spells or severe ventricular arrhythmias. Do you agree with that?"

"I do. There are no data to support using an implantable device in patients with Mrs. Hamlin's clinical profile. It would have been acceptable to implant a device if Mrs. Hamlin had insisted, but there was no reason for Dr. Sarkis to push it."

Joan moved on to the more difficult question. "How about beta-blockers? Should Mrs. Hamlin have received one of those drugs?"

Bob turned to the jury and addressed the answer directly to them. "There is no easy answer to that question. There are data that beta-blockers provide some protection against sudden death in patients with the long QT syndrome. But the amount of benefit is not that large and beta-blockers have a lot of associated side effects, especially in active people. Mrs. Hamlin had never had any severe symptoms from the long QT syndrome, and she made it to her thirties without a problem so the odds that she would die suddenly were very low."

"Dr. Sarkis testified that Mrs. Hamlin declined to take beta-blockers. Was that a bad idea, and if so, what should Dr. Sarkis have done about that?"

"This kind of thing happens all of the time in clinical medicine. The doctor is expected to present the information about benefit and risk of an intervention to the patient, who has to make the ultimate choice. The doctor can only lean on a patient so much. It sounds to me that Dr. Sarkis did his job and presented the alternatives to Mrs. Hamlin and her family several times, and she flatout refused any medication. I don't think there was anything Dr. Sarkis could have done to change her mind. She was an intelligent person who knew what she was doing."

"Did Dr. Sarkis provide proper advice to Mrs. Hamlin in other respects?"

"Yes, he made sure that she knew to report any symptoms indicating she was having a serious arrhythmia, like severe palpitations or blackouts, and he told her to avoid medications that could exacerbate her condition. She knew about keeping her electrolytes monitored. He covered all of those bases well."

Joan segued into the second dangerous area of liability. "Dr.

Myerstone, questions were raised about the care Mrs. Hamlin received when she was in the emergency department. Can you tell the jury what happened at GMH and what Dr. Sarkis' role was in Mrs. Hamlin's treatment there?"

Bob recounted the events, being careful to emphasize the dangerous nature of Moira's problem and the high probability of a fatal outcome. "In my opinion, the chance that Mrs. Hamlin would have survived such an extreme arrhythmia was less than 10%. What Dr. Sarkis did was reasonable in light of that. He tried an investigational drug and then a special shock technique that did what they were supposed to do, which was to restore a normal rhythm."

"Did these interventions increase the chances that Moira would die?"

"Absolutely not! They significantly improved her chances for survival."

"Was Dr. Sarkis negligent in not obtaining consent to administer the experimental drug?"

"I don't think so. Although we would like to have informed consent from the patient or family, the patient's life always comes first. Dr. Sarkis acted quickly and saved Ms. Hamlin's life and so all other matters are irrelevant as far as I am concerned."

"So, Doctor, why did Moira Hamlin die?"

"She died because in the process of having so many episodes of arrhythmia at home, her brain was deprived of blood flow and it was damaged. In the end, she had suffered too much brain damage to make it through. It is the most common reason why people who have a cardiac arrest succumb."

Now the most important question: "Doctor, do you have an opinion, based on a reasonable degree of medical certainty, as to whether or not Dr. Sarkis rendered care that was below the accepted standard?"

"I do have an opinion. He did not. In fact, everything that Dr. Sarkis did was exemplary and reflective of excellent medical practice. Moira Hamlin died as a result of having an arrhythmia that Dr. Sarkis could never have anticipated or prevented."

"Thank you, Doctor. No further questions."

Len Barkley rose slowly from his seat, his half glasses on the edge of his nose as he carefully perused his notes.

"Tell me, Doctor, how do you know Dr. Sarkis?"

Joan objected. "That is irrelevant to Dr. Myerstone's testimony, Your Honor."

"Overruled. Doctor, please answer the question."

"I have known Dr. Sarkis for several years."

"In what capacity?"

"He and I have worked on some projects and I have been on some programs with him."

"Would you say that you are friends?"

"I think you could say that."

"Good friends?"

"Yes."

"So, when you were asked to look at this case, is it fair to say that you were anxious to vindicate Dr. Sarkis?"

"I looked at the case carefully and fairly. If I thought that Dr. Sarkis had not done his job properly, I would have declined to be here."

"Really, Doctor. So you don't think that you were biased at all during your initial and subsequent reviews of this case?"

"I don't think so. I think that the facts were straightforward and that I arrived at the only logical conclusion."

Len Barkley's body language and facial expressions informed the jury how skeptical he was about Bob's answers.

"Tell me, Doctor, have you ever been sued."

Joan objected. "Your Honor, what is the relevance of this question?"

Judge Pleasance wasted no time in her reply. "The jury is entitled to know Dr. Myerstone's background including malpractice history. Doctor, you may answer."

"If you practice medicine in the United States, you have a better than even chance of that happening, so yes, once."

"Can you tell us what that case was about?"

"I took care of a young man with heart failure and a severe arrhythmia who died while I was treating him."

"And did the case go to trial?"

"Yes, it did."

"And was there a verdict against you in that trial?"

"No there was not—the defense won."

"And did you have an expert witness testify on your behalf?"

"I did."

"That didn't happen to be Dr. Sarkis, did it?"

"It was."

Barkley let the obvious implications of the admission sink in.

"So, once again, Doctor, are you going to contend that you were not biased whatsoever in your review of the case, even though Dr. Sarkis came down to Georgia to rescue you?"

Joan turned to Dan. She had no idea about Philip's testimony on Myerstone's behalf, and judging from his expression, neither did Dan. Joan had to do something to protect Myerstone whose credibility was in jeopardy. "Your Honor, I object. Mr. Barkley is badgering the witness."

But judging from their expressions, the jury didn't think so and neither did Judge Pleasance. All she did was to ask Barkley to "tone it down" and then directed the witness to answer the question.

"Yes, I feel confident that my review was appropriate and impartial in all respects."

As Bob gave his final response, Barkley turned to face the jury and gave them a knowing smile. Of all of the evidence they would hear, this was the most understandable: helping a friend. Now they had an excuse not to pay attention to confusing and complicated medical testimony. Barkley could almost sense their relief. After a few points of clarification, Barkley dismissed the witness.

Dan and Joan had no other witnesses and rested their case. It was now up to the hospital to present its case. McShane called a witness who was an expert on hospital staff procedures.

Gary Crandle was a physician at a Philadelphia medical school, and he was known as a fiery hospital advocate who wasn't liked by physicians in the city. Philip, who had never met him, was aware of his reputation.

"Dr. Crandle, you are aware of the medical staff structure at GMH?" McShane asked.

"Yes, I have reviewed the bylaws in depth."

"When Dr. Sarkis administered care to Moira Hamlin in his office, was the hospital in any way responsible for his management decisions?"

"In no way whatsoever. Dr. Sarkis saw the patient in his private office and that interaction had nothing to do with the hospital."

"And when Dr. Sarkis elected to administer a potentially dangerous experimental drug to Moira Hamlin, did the hospital participate in that decision?"

"Of course not. The hospital has committees that are responsible for approving research protocols and this one was approved. However, the hospital has to trust the investigator to enroll appropriate patients and to make sure that the research is done properly."

"Now, Doctor, you are not here to comment on whether or not Moira Hamlin should have been enrolled in the experimental study in the ER, are you?"

"No. I don't have that expertise. I am just explaining that the hospital wasn't responsible for what Dr. Sarkis did or did not do in this regard."

"So when Dr. Sarkis gave an experimental drug to Moira Hamlin without permission, GMH was not responsible in any way for his actions."

Dan and Joan looked at each other. The witness was being led by the nose but they knew that their objection would be overruled. Better not to whine at this point. Barkley declined to ask any questions; the damage to Philip was obvious.

Joan's cross-examination was limited. She needed to make sure that the jury didn't think Philip had done anything wrong, but she didn't want to protest too much. In the end, she got Crandle to admit that the hospital had not brought any disciplinary action against Philip for his actions, at least not to date. "I suspect," said Crandle, "that they will wait to see how this trial ends before making any disciplinary decisions."

"But doesn't it seem odd that Mr. Barkley and Dr. Otley are claiming that Dr. Sarkis violated the standard of care, and yet no one called him on the carpet for what he did at GMH?"

"I wasn't there. If I had been, things would have been different, believe me."

"But you weren't there Doctor, were you, so you really have no way of knowing if the hospital considered Dr. Sarkis to have violated any research policies. In fact, you have to admit that there is not even one document that even remotely implies such misbehavior."

"That is correct."

After the hospital concluded its case, the judge made it clear to the lawyers that she was interested in getting the matter to the jury quickly. In her chambers, she strongly recommended that closings be kept short and to the point, and they were. No new information was forthcoming, and the lawyers, like the judge, could sense the jurors' impatience.

Joan's closing was brief and unemotional. "Philip Sarkis empathizes with Moira Hamlin's family, but just because there was a tragedy, that doesn't mean that somebody made a mistake. As Dr. Myerstone clearly stated, Dr. Sarkis did his job."

Barkley's closing was impassioned, reminding the jury of the terrible tragedy wrought on the Hamlin family by one man who had shown a fundamental disregard of Moira Hamlin's well-being. "This man first failed to treat Moira Hamlin with drugs that would protect her life, and then in an effort to save his own neck, gave the poor woman toxic mediations. And we all know what happened after that."

The judge's charge to the jury was textbook. They needed to decide first if there had been any malpractice. If there was, they would need to decide on the amount of the award, and they would have to apportion the responsibility among the defendants, in this case Philip and the hospital. She gave them the ground rules for deliberations and told them to begin immediately. They filed out as both sides tried to read their dispositions. Nobody in the courtroom thought they would deliberate very long.

Philip and Nancy had watched their share of legal dramas on television and in the movies where waiting for the verdict had been portrayed for all that it was worth. But they could never have imagined how stressful it was to be in the picture—in real life. The tension was palpable. Joan had told them that a short deliberation might indicate the jury had found for the defense. So when the call came on Joan's cell phone only six hours after the charge, Philip and Nancy re-entered the courtroom with some hope.

Everyone's eyes were on the jurors as they filed in. Some looked uncomfortable and others stared straight ahead. None of them looked at the plaintiffs or defendants. The judge had the defendants rise immediately, and then asked the jury, "Have you reached a verdict?"

The jury foreman, a matronly black woman wearing a hat with dark velvet flowers and strong perfume, responded that they had.

"What say you?"

"We find for the plaintiff, Your Honor."

Philip could feel his sensibility slipping away but he tried to stay focused since the next few sentences would change the course of his life and career.

"Have you arrived at an amount to be paid in damages?"

"We have, Your Honor. We find that the defendants should pay the sum of $5,000,000 to the plaintiff and an additional $2,000,000 in punitive damages for reckless negligence on their part."

"And how is that award to be apportioned between the defendants?"

"Your Honor, we believe that the full responsibility for payment should be borne by Dr. Philip Sarkis, with no penalty to Gladwyne Memorial Hospital."

Philip felt as though he had been struck in the stomach. He was having difficulty breathing and had to sit down. He could hear voices around him but nothing was making sense. Nancy had her arms around him and Joan was bending down to speak with him but the words were not penetrating. He barely registered Joan's request that the judge put the verdict aside, a request that was quickly denied. Then he heard Dan and Joan fuming about the injustice of it all and could hear Nancy softly crying. He processed little of the pandemonium in the courtroom as the Hamlin family cheered and congratulated each other.

His attorneys pulled Philip to his feet, and as he staggered into the hallway with Nancy, Joan, and Dan, a single thought reverberated in his mind: "I am ruined."

CHAPTER 11

The next year of Philip's life was a catastrophe. The carefully crafted facets of his once orderly existence unraveled precipitously after the verdict. It was clear to everyone who knew him that his decompensation was caused as much by his psychological reaction to the verdict as by its financial ramifications. Philip's large ego made it impossible to understand that he could be considered negligent, let alone responsible, for the death of a patient.

Although Joan and Dan had quickly filed motions to have the verdict set aside, these were rejected almost immediately. Philip was disheveled and exhausted when he arrived in Dan's office a few days later.

"Philip, I am willing to do everything we can to get the decision reversed but the chances are slim," Dan began. "And even if we do get a new trial, you would be responsible for the legal fees involved in the appeal, and they could be substantial. Appealing the verdict would also mean staying involved in the process and I know how much that has taken out of you. Your other option is to accept the verdict and get on with your life as best you can."

It took a long time for Philip to respond. "Fuck the appeals process then," he hissed finally. "I don't have the energy or the money anyhow. I just want to get my life back."

That wish would prove to be more difficult than his attorneys or Philip could have imagined. First, Philip found himself faced with enormous financial obligations that he could not possibly meet. His attorneys assured him that the property he held jointly with Nancy was not in jeopardy. However, Philip had never been careful with asset protection. It hadn't occurred to him that his malpractice insurance wouldn't suffice. His investment counselor had recommended placing all of his holdings in both names a long time ago but he hadn't done it and now disaster had struck.

While their primary residence was safe, Philip and Nancy's vacation home and a large part of their savings were seized to pay damages. In addition, the courts ruled that a significant portion of his salary would be garnished. What was left was clearly inadequate to maintain their Main Line lifestyle.

Divestment meant hard choices. Forgoing the country club membership was not a big deal; they didn't use it that much. But he had to tell his children that they could no longer afford private school.

"But Daddy, we don't want to leave our friends at school," Rachel pleaded as they sat on the sofa in the TV room. "I like my teachers. I don't want new ones."

"Your mother and I know what a disappointment this is to you," Philip gulped. "All we can ask is that you be patient and give your new school a chance. Lots of really nice kids go to public school. They have great activities and sports. Anyway, we really don't have a choice, Rachel. We just can't afford it."

"But why not Daddy? We used to have lots of money. I heard you tell Mommy that plenty of times."

"Daddy owes money to some people. So we will have less money to do what we used to do, and it is going to have to be that way at least for a little while."

Whenever he talked to Rachel and Jeremy from that point onward, money became the first topic of conversation, so Philip deliberately began to find ways to avoid his children.

The combination of financial woes and psychological upheaval also placed an enormous burden on Philip and Nancy's marriage. They spent most of their time together, at meals for example, in complete silence, a distinct relief from the bickering and sniping that went on whenever they did communicate.

Gradually, Philip lost interest in his family. He attended none of his children's school events, preferring to stay home and drink alone. He crept into bed long after Nancy was asleep and the subject of sex never came up at all. Some days he didn't even bother to shave. She finally confronted him one winter evening as he sat in his den watching a football game.

"Philip, I can't live like this any longer. You have become a person I don't know, let alone understand. I am not sure if you even love us any more. Something has to change and it has to happen soon."

Philip could not look at Nancy, but he did manage to answer rationally. In a soft voice he said, "Look Nancy, this is the most difficult thing that I have ever had to go through in my life. I know that I haven't been a good husband lately, but I am having a really tough time just coping day to day. Give me a break."

"Maybe you should see somebody. Maybe you need medication to get you through this." Philip had considered counseling but he had the same bias many of his colleagues had against psychiatry, feeling that it was a pseudoscience without much of chance of really helping people. Nancy's strong no nonsense message motivated him this time.

The next day, Philip called Chuck Wilson, a tennis partner, who specialized in treating depression on the Main Line. Chuck liked to tell Philip and others that he dealt a lot with "intrinsic personality disorders that were compounded by the pressures of modern life, especially in the electronic age." In reality, he was dealing with the issues of affluent clients who had no excuse for feeling blue, but had plenty of time to sulk.

Chuck was a good old boy from Mississippi who had moved to Philadelphia to get his Ph.D. at Penn, and liked it so much he stayed. Typically, Chuck wore jeans and crew-neck cashmere sweaters every day and was careful to leave enough clues around his office that he was a direct descendent of Johnny Reb. The audacious transplant maintained enough of his southern drawl to make him seductive to his female patients and a curiosity to their husbands. He was known in his neighborhood for "pig pickins" and flying the rebel flag over his front porch. In Dr. Wilson's case, "southern charm" was a good thing.

Chuck was happy to hear Philip's voice on the phone. He hadn't seen him in a long time. He had enjoyed watching Philip's transformation on the tennis court from an overly aggressive doctor to a kid having fun hitting the fuzzy yellow ball hard over the net. Chuck had heard that things weren't going well, and that the Sarkis family had to resign from the club, but he hadn't heard the details. He usually didn't want to hear about more grief than he was exposed to in his office every day, but he was genuinely concerned about Philip.

"What's up good buddy?" Chuck liked to believe that his drawl helped to relax his patients.

Philip was blunt. "Chuck, I am having serious problems and I need your help."

"Absolutely, come on over and we can hunker down over a beer or two and go over things."

"Chuck, I want you to handle me like any other patient. Will you see me at your office?"

"Why sure enough. Let's have you come over tomorrow at about five and we'll get the ball rolling."

Philip lasted about five sessions with Chuck. Since Philip's main problem was situational depression, Chuck was reluctant to recommend antidepressant drugs. When Philip insisted, Chuck relented but as he had anticipated, they had a marginal effect at best. On the other hand, the counseling sessions gave Philip a chance to ventilate. Chuck had a difficult time getting him to look inward to understand the reasons for his extreme reaction to the verdict and its consequences.

"What did the verdict actually mean to you Philip?" Chuck sprang the question during their fourth session.

With tears in his eyes, Philip finally answered, "It made me feel like a total fucking loser."

"Was there ever a time in your life when you felt that same way?"

"Yeah, I was a kid when it happened."

"What happened?" Chuck sensed a breakthrough.

"In seventh or eighth grade, I screwed up a math exam that was supposed to count for a large part of our final grade. I knew the stuff and I suspected that I just got the answers out of order or something like that. Anyhow, I totally fucked up the exam and got a D for the course. It was the only D I ever got in my life. My father went ballistic. He almost never raised his voice or used foul language in my presence but he really let me have it. Told me I was a loser and that he was disappointed in my work. That "D" word really hurt. I thought that I had lost his respect and I felt like crap. I felt exactly the same way after the verdict."

"Did you and your father ever talk about any of this later on?"

"Never, to the day he died. Too painful for me."

Despite medication and such momentary insights, Philip's mood and demeanor did not improve, and Nancy realized she had to take the children away. Explaining the situation to the kids was easier than either had anticipated. They told friends and relatives that they were just going to "get a little space" and that this was a temporary thing but they both knew that unless Philip had a dramatic turnaround, Nancy would not return. Her actual departure was as quiet as snow falling, cold and soundless but chilling for all them.

Philip drove Nancy and the children to her parents' home, said his goodbyes, and returned to a silent house, more depressed than ever. As he walked past the antique ice chest that served as a liquor cabinet, he opened it and took out a bottle of vodka. The vodka tonic, intended to take the edge off a bad afternoon, led to three more. He fell asleep on the sofa in front of a Saturday Night Live rerun. For the next several months, every day would end the same way.

Philip's medical career crumbled almost as quickly as his private life. He saw patients in his office and at the hospital, but was distracted and had difficulty focusing. He struggled with administrative responsibilities. Because he couldn't bear to talk to anybody from the hospital, his meetings were unnecessarily difficult and confrontational. There was no question that the hospital had leaked information about use of the research drug and device inspection to the plaintiff, and Philip was furious with everybody.

As a result, endless harangues with hospital administration prevented Philip from functioning effectively as the chief of the cardiology department. Jerry Santini, head of the Medicine Department and Philip's superior, finally requested his resignation.

"Philip, I really hate having to do this, but in the world we live, we have to play ball with the hospital and for some crazy reason, you are going out of your way to piss them off."

"You know what they did to me. How can I possibly be civil to those fuckers?"

"If you can't see your way to work with them, I am going to have to appoint somebody who can. They pay my salary—I have no choice."

"Do what you have to do. I really don't give a fuck anymore. This place has sucked me dry for long enough. I've sacrificed a lot to put this place on the map, and the thanks I got was getting screwed in the courtroom. They can go fuck themselves and the horse they rode in on."

Jerry liked Philip. They had worked well together and even played friendly golf matches once in a while. But Jerry was a realist. He was close to retirement age, and he had no desire to allow a major confrontation with the hospital to jeopardize his pension. If that meant Philip had to be sacrificed, so be it. Philip could be replaced, granted not by anyone as talented or energetic, but by somebody who could hold the fort while Jerry shopped around for a permanent successor. Somebody else who could bring as much money and prestige to the institution as Philip had. Making tough decisions was his job, and he had been doing it for a long time. Besides, Philip had always been high maintenance, so full of himself. Maybe he deserved to get axed. This was a chance to make Jerry's life a little easier and the idea didn't make him unhappy.

Then there was the matter of Philip's research violation. The research office at GMH had reported the incident to the federal agencies that were responsible for supervising funded clinical research projects. Because of highly publicized scandals that had occurred at several other prestigious centers around the country, their tolerance for research abuse, especially when evidence suggested a patient had died as a result, was low. Consequently, they elected to perform a full investigation of "the Sarkis matter."

For several weeks, representatives from the OHRP (Office of Human Research Protection), the arm of the NIH responsible for handling alleged breaches of this nature, were on site to conduct their investigation. This included hours of direct questioning of Philip and every person who had anything to do with the project.

Philip's interrogation took on the flavor of an inquisition. Ferguson Williams, the OHRP official, seemed to have already convinced himself that Philip was in the wrong, and he just needed data to confirm it. An athletic African American who had played college football, he arrived in spotless and standard government attire, blue blazer, gray slacks and striped tie, and conducted his interviews seated at the head of the table in Philip's cardiology conference room.

"How long did you spend with Mr. Hamlin when you talked to him about using the new drug in his wife's case?"

"I don't remember the exact amount of time. That was over three years ago."

"Was it five minutes, ten minutes, what?"

"Look, Mr. Williams, I don't recall. I was in a hurry because Moira was in the middle of a cardiac arrest. I tried to cover as much of the consent document as I could in the shortest amount of time. A life was at stake."

"Did you actually explain all of the risks involved?"

"I am sure I did—I always do. I know how important it is. For Christ's sake, I have been doing at for 20 years. Don't you think I would know what to do?"

"Dr. Sarkis, there have been serious allegations about your behavior, so I can't take anything for granted. Did you give Mr. Hamlin a chance to read the entire document?"

"I don't remember if he read every word. It was five pages of single-spaced text. It would have taken him a long time."

"So you really didn't make him read and sign it, did you? You just went ahead and gave the medicine without getting his permission."

"He read at least part of it, but no, he never signed it."

"Did you go back to him after you gave the drug to ask him to sign it after the fact?"

"No, I was busy trying to save his wife's life, and it slipped my mind."

And so it went. Accusation after accusation and with each one, the strong implication that Philip had played fast and loose with the ordinary procedures that were in place for human research. As they had in the courtroom, the GMH staff did everything it could to suggest that Philip had acted on his own. In fact, Philip had warned the research committee back when the study began, that obtaining informed consent would be difficult in such serious cases. Unfortunately for Philip, this warning was not reflected in the minutes of the research committee meeting and nobody from the hospital was about to tell Williams about it.

Following Williams' preliminary interviews, he went on to find several other irregularities in the research files. Most were typical minor transgressions like unsigned forms, or missing laboratory values.

In the end, the OHRP moved to censure Philip. In their official letter, the OHRP informed Philip that skipping informed consent was inappropriate and "egregious." They paid little or no attention to the fact that getting consent would have cost Moira her life at that point, or that informed consent had been obtained without a problem in the other patients, all of whom had done well with the treatment. The letter made it clear that Philip was not the only party at fault. The nurses and other investigators were criticized for sloppy paperwork. There were stern warnings to all parties that further violations would result in GMH losing its ability to conduct federally funded clinical research.

The FDA also took the matter under consideration and strongly considered disbarring Philip for his "reckless use of investigational drugs." Disbarment is an extreme action that effectively excludes the clinician-scientist from participating in any regulatory trials forever. Philip realized that he had to defend himself aggressively. He called Joan who agreed. "Philip, if you are disbarred, you won't be able to consult for any pharmaceutical company ever again. You have to fight this one."

Philip was asked to go to Washington to meet with Bobbi Woodstone, the deputy FDA commissioner in charge of compliance. The interview was strikingly similar to the confrontational meetings he had had with Ferguson Williams, and once again, Philip was not permitted to bring along an attorney.

"Dr. Sarkis, how do you explain all of these allegations against you with regard to how you conducted your research?"

"I did the best I could with a difficult situation. Moira Hamlin was going to die, so I had no choice but to give her the drug when I did."

"And that's the best you can do for an explanation?"

"I happen to think that it is the best explanation. Maybe if you and your drones down here took care of patients once in a while, you would understand what it feels like to see a young vibrant woman die with an arrhythmia."

"Do you think you are the only person in the world who takes care of sick patients? If this is your attitude, I am going to have to recommend severe disciplinary action. I find your behavior to be incredible. Your careless acts were bad enough but now you refuse to show any remorse whatsoever."

"Remorse. You want remorse? I spend every day feeling sorry for what happened to Moira Hamlin. If it ruined her family, it is ruining my life too. But the truth is that I would do exactly the same thing again, if I had the chance. There is no way I would ever just stand there and let a patient die to satisfy some dipshit regulation. So you can go figure out if that is remorse, Dr. Woodstone. I will leave it to you to decide."

Woodstone concluded the interview and in the end recommended disbarment for Philip. At the eleventh hour, the commissioner decided to stop short of inflicting the most severe penalty and opted instead for a five-year suspension. In reality, the suspension would have the same mortal effect on Philip's career. It would put him out of circulation as a pharmaceutical consultant or researcher for a long time. In the drug development business, it takes only a few months to lose touch, and Philip, who derived so much of his ego satisfaction to say nothing of his income, from his consultative work with drug companies had to deal with another major setback.

Reluctantly, but inevitably, Philip had to face the fact that he couldn't keep up his mortgage payments. With Nancy's assent, he put their house on the market and it sold fast. Then an auctioneer sold much of the furniture and other possessions. Philip stood miserably on the sidelines watching strangers bid on the things he and Nancy had so carefully accumulated over the years.

After realizing that the old train sets and toys would bring a good price, he even let the auctioneer sell some of his childhood treasures. The proceeds from the house and yard sales were protected from the lawsuit, and Philip gave most of the money to Nancy to buy a nice but modest home for the kids. That left him enough to rent a one-bedroom apartment in a borderline neighborhood and buy a beat-up Toyota to get around.

As his outside activities waned, he increasingly sought solace with his ever-faithful vodka bottle. Heavy drinking made it harder for him to wake up in the morning. Though he was no longer the head of the department, he was still seeing patients. But his increasingly sloppy demeanor did not go unnoticed. He was eventually called on the carpet again by Jerry Santini, who wanted to know if he could do anything to salvage his former star's floundering career.

"Philip, things are really slipping. I am getting complaints from all over the hospital about your behavior. The nurses and house staff feel you don't care anymore, and the patients and their families think you don't give a crap about them either. If you keep this up, you are going to get sued again, even if you don't do anything wrong."

"Yeah, whatever. I'll try to do better," was all that Philip could muster. Jerry could tell from the monotonic response that he really didn't mean what he said and was just trying to avoid the issue.

"No Philip, that won't cut it. You have given me that shit the last three times you were in here and it just isn't going to work this time. I want you to take a leave of absence. Give up your clinical responsibilities for a few months and see how you feel about things, and we can think about reinstating your clinical appointment."

"And what the hell am I supposed to do for all that time? I am damaged goods. I will have no way to generate any income. And even if I could find something menial to do, the plaintiffs get to garnish half of my earnings."

"I can't help it Philip. You are not doing anybody any good here, least of all yourself. Go play some golf or something and get yourself back on your feet and then we will talk again."

As he sat alone in his apartment that evening, Philip realized this was the end of the line at GMH and he suspected that it might be the end of his days as a physician. Under other circumstances, that would have been his major obsession. But as it had been ever since the trial, the only thing that he ruminated about now was Moira's death.

Try as he might, he just couldn't fathom why Moira had a cardiac arrest. He re-ran the case in his mind a million times, second-guessing every aspect of the care he had given her. He had a copy of the records on the coffee table of his apartment and he had read it so many times the pages were frayed and stained by the junk food he swallowed with his vodka.

Philip couldn't reconcile the facts of the case. Why had this healthy young woman who had gotten through multiple pregnancies and lots of other trauma, who was in magnificent physical condition, and who had no other reasons to have an electrically unstable heart—why did she suddenly have a major and lethal cardiac arrhythmia? Something that she did or didn't do had to have caused Moira's heart to go out of rhythm. But what?

Over the years, Philip had learned to trust his instincts. He believed that great clinicians, however knowledgeable, frequently make their best discoveries by using their gut. The truly great ones learned to trust their instincts even when facts pointed in a different direction.

He remembered one of his favorite Professor Lowenstein stories. One day, Professor Lowenstein went in with his entourage to see a middle-aged man who had suffered a cardiac arrest during an argument with his teenaged son. Fortunately, the man had been resuscitated and was being prepared to have a cardiac catheterization and possibly surgery to repair what was assumed to be blocked arteries. Philip and his fellow trainees had taken the case at face value: anger had triggered a high heart rate and blood pressure and his presumed coronary artery blockages had kept the heart from getting enough blood to keep up with the demand so a nasty heart attack had ensued.

Professor Lowenstein asked his residents and students to leave the room and then spent several minutes speaking with the patient alone. After that interview and a brief examination, he emerged from the room and announced that the cardiac catheterization scheduled for the afternoon would be negative and that the patient would not have significant coronary artery disease. Philip and his colleagues were incredulous. All the cardiogram recordings had pointed to ischemia or relative lack of blood flow to the heart as the mechanism for the event. How on earth could it be anything else?

When normal coronary arteries were discovered at the catheterization, as Lowenstein had predicted, Philip was stunned, and went to Lowenstein's office immediately. "Professor, how on earth did you figure that one out?"

"It wasn't that difficult Philip," Lowenstein answered, sitting back in his desk chair, hands behind his head. "The patient really never had any prior symptoms to suggest that he had coronary artery disease. I thought that the enormity of the issue that he was arguing about with his son could easily have thrown his heart into a major arrhythmia without invoking any actual compromise of blood flow to the heart. You don't know what they were arguing about, do you?"

"No, I never asked," Philip answered sheepishly.

"You didn't and no one else on the service did either. That was your mistake and the key to the case. The son barged into his parent's bedroom and found his father in bed with his next-door neighbor's wife. The father was mortified by the discovery and angry that he had been caught. The son then compounded the problem by telling his mother. Don't you think that was a major enough trauma to get his heart to go out of whack?"

"How did you suspect there was such an enormous set of issues here?"

"Instincts Philip, pure and simple. I suspected that he was holding back something that caused the cardiac arrest. You have to learn to trust your instincts in cases like this. It will never lead you down the wrong path."

The incident had taught Philip a valuable lesson. He tried to approach every case with an open mind, making no assumptions, and Moira's case was no exception. He felt sure there had to be factors involved that he just didn't know yet, but that if he kept at it, he would discover. Unfortunately, his one best source of information was Hugh Hamlin but he knew any dialogue with him was out of the question. Of all of the miseries in Philip's life at the moment, the most painful was not understanding why his patient Moira Hamlin had died.

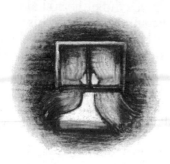

CHAPTER 12

With little money, and no one to hang out with, Philip had nothing to do. When his idle mind allowed disturbing thoughts like ending his life, he realized he had to get busy.

His first idea was reading. There was a pile of non-medical books on his end table. Or he could write up some completed research projects for publication.

Despite Philip's best intentions, his vodka habit got the better of him. He was dull in the evening and groggy every morning. After he did manage to rouse himself, he'd watch TV over multiple cups of coffee. Pretty soon, the daytime lineup of "soaps" sucked him in. He had to smile at the irony. He had pitied patients with little else to divert them other than daytime TV. Now, sapped of the energy to work or read, he kept a close watch on the latest romantic developments on Days of Our Lives.

He didn't venture out much. He tried to visit his kids, but they had new lives and frankly preferred their friends. He was embarrassed to bring them to his sloppy apartment, and he didn't have money for movies or other amusements. He had a hard time talking to them, and his moping scared them.

Philip's best diversion was Tavanos, an Italian bar/restaurant in blue-collar Norristown that he and Nancy had frequented when they were first married. It had good food and it was cheap. Best of all, there was a friendly bartender named Fred and a big screen TV that always played Philly sports events. Philip would have a plate of spaghetti and a draft beer while Fred did his witty color commentary. Philip was careful not to divulge his background, and no one asked or cared. He was just "Phil" who lived nearby, loyal fan of whatever Philly team was playing that night. It wasn't exactly "Cheers" but it gave Philip a new social life of sorts.

One night, after a particularly good plate of linguini, he felt a hand on his shoulder and turned to see Jim Flanagan standing next to him with a huge grin on his face. It took Philip a few seconds to focus in the dim light, and a few more to recognize the smiling Irishman and his wife Lisa. "Philip, how are you? I haven't seen you in years."

Philip thought Jim was going to blow his cover but fortunately the place was otherwise empty. The Phillies were playing on the west coast so the game wasn't on until later. Philip stood awkwardly and winced at Jim's strong handshake.

Jim Flanagan was a big man with a big life. The burly Irishman had grown up poor on the streets of Philadelphia, the son of immigrants who recognized the value of education for their six kids. They didn't have much money so Jim had gotten his college education and medical school training in the Navy where he also trained as a cardiac surgeon. When he left the military, he returned to Philadelphia and took a staff job at Temple University Hospital. His first wife was a pediatrician. Philip recalled the power couple had been featured on the cover of Philadelphia Magazine and often attended the city's most important social events.

In the late 1970s, GMH decided to challenge the large downtown academic medical centers and start its own cardiac surgery program. No one thought that a smaller suburban hospital could attract a good staff or patients, but GMH decided to recruit Jim Flanagan with a promise of a big salary and fabulous facilities. His reputation and good results proved to be the decisive factors, and the referrals flowed in.

Philip arrived shortly after that and together they developed a first-rate cardiology program. Soon their volumes and outcomes surpassed the traditional university programs. Jim was an aggressive character who jumped at any new opportunity, including the high-profile projects Philip brought to the table. It wasn't a big surprise that Jim started talking about their first big joint venture.

"Philip, just last week I was telling one of my golf partners the story about our first defibrillator implant. That was really something." If Jim was going to talk medicine, Philip had to get away from the bar. He managed to maneuver the Flanagans to a corner table so their conversation would be private. Jim asked, "What ever happened to that guy Mirowski? Is he still alive?"

"No, Jim, he died of a lymphoma a few years ago. I wrote a story about him for one of the cardiology journals. I will send it to you. You might enjoy reading about his career."

Philip had to agree that the story of the first defibrillator implant at GMH was fascinating and one that he had liked to tell himself. Philip had delivered a paper at a meeting in Miami Beach on a new method that he had developed in Professor Lowenstein's laboratory of shocking the heart out of ventricular fibrillation, the heart rhythm that was responsible for sudden cardiac death. When he finished, a shy little man in his sixties with horn-rimmed glasses approached him. He grabbed Philip's hand, shook it, and introduced himself in a heavy eastern European accent.

"Young man, my name is Michel Mirowski. I am the head of the Coronary Care Unit at Sinai Hospital in Baltimore. That was an excellent presentation and something I am very interested in. I wonder if you would be free to have lunch with my partner, Morty Mower and me. I have an idea that might interest you."

It turned out to be a lunch that Philip would never forget and it wasn't because of the food. In fact, once Mirowski and Mower started to explain what they were doing, he hardly touched his sandwich.

"Philip, I grew up in Eastern Europe, and had the misfortune of spending several months in a concentration camp, where I survived by my wits. After the war and medical training, one of my close friends from those horrible concentration camp days had a cardiac arrest at a cafe. I did what I could to resuscitate him but my friend died. I resolved then and there that I would dedicate the rest of my life to finding a way to keep this from happening to other people. I knew from the work of your mentor Dr. Lowenstein that an electrical shock applied to the chest through paddles can restore a normal rhythm. My idea was to invent a shock device small enough to be implanted in a person that would automatically sense when the heart goes out of rhythm and then deliver a shock internally to stop it."

"I have heard a little about this idea," Philip said. "But I have to admit that I really don't know much about it."

Mirowski nodded and continued on with his story. "I realized that my idea was going to take funding and other resources that I couldn't access in Europe so I began to search for a program in the United States that would be willing to help me. I found a small hospital in Baltimore where I started testing in various animal models. I had a lot of setbacks. Not only that, but when the scientific community finally learned what we were doing, they scoffed at our idea.

"I refused to give up and now we have a prototype that we think we can implant in people. We are looking for a few young investigators who may be willing to go out on a limb with us and implant our prototype in humans. Philip, after listening to your presentation at the meeting today, I am convinced you are the kind of person who could help with the project."

"Professor Mirowski, I am flattered by the invitation. You have to tell me what it is you want me to do before I can tell you if I can help."

"Fair enough, Philip. I want you to work with us to implant this new device. If you agree I will send you all the material we have gathered so far."

When he examined their early experimental results, it was clear to Philip that Mirowski had done his homework. He wanted Philip to implant one of the first devices at GMH. But since the implantation required opening the chest, Philip would need Jim Flanagan's help with the project. True to form, Flanagan nearly jumped out of his chair when Philip told him about it.

"Are you kidding me? This is a great idea and we have to pursue it. You have my total, unequivocal support. Just tell me what you want me to do."

Philip had to obtain permission from the GMH research review committee. The members agreed that the new concept had the potential for benefit but also for great harm. Eventually, they granted permission with the stipulations that patients selected for the implants had to exhaust all treatment avenues, and then be carefully informed of every potential risk, especially death on the operating table.

The next order of business was funding. Since this was "experimental treatment," insurance companies were not going to pay for the device. With Jim's help, Philip was able to obtain a small grant from a private foundation on the Main Line.

The first two implants in Baltimore and San Francisco went well. Michel told Philip and Jim that they could now select their first patient. Philip settled on a kind elderly woman who had severe heart disease and suffered through three cardiac arrests in ten years. Miraculously, she had been resuscitated from each and had not suffered any neurological impairment. On the day of the surgery, Philip handled the electronic equipment and coordinated the testing of the device.

Jim Flanagan arrived in the operating room glowing from the attention he was receiving from the hundred plus people who crammed the OR suite to watch. Jim did a standard mid-chest incision to expose the heart to allow the patch electrodes to be stitched to the surface of the heart. One by one, the components of the system were handed over to Jim while Philip directed where to place everything including the device generator. Through his equipment, Philip induced ventricular fibrillation and told Jim and his surgery team to stand back: the device should shock the heart in about ten seconds, the amount of time needed for the device to recognize the arrhythmia and charge its capacitors. Those ten seconds seemed like ten years to Philip and Jim but suddenly the patient's body jumped several inches in the air. The shock was followed by normal sinus rhythm greeted by a great cheer from the gallery. Flanagan looked over his mask at Philip, nodded his approval, and gave two thumbs up.

That had been the start of a productive relationship that ended with Flanagan's retirement in 1992 when Philip lost touch with him. Jim had remained active in his surgical societies while leading the good life on the Main Line. He divorced his first wife and married Lisa, one of his nurses. Lisa was about half the size of Jim and attractive in a flashy way. She spent much of her time trying to ingratiate herself with Main Line society where she really didn't belong. The couple liked to travel and dote on their grandchildren.

Though Philip liked Jim and was grateful for his early support, he was anxious about meeting under these circumstances. Jim had always regarded him as a top cardiologist and had continued to refer many patients to Philip even after retirement. Philip always went out of his way to see them promptly and to resolve their problems. Now all of that was gone and Jim and Lisa knew it. Besides, Jim was the perpetual "up" person and people with an upbeat attitude were hard for Philip to handle lately. They made him feel sad and lost. But he knew that Jim and Lisa wanted to chitchat and so he would have to go along for the ride, for a little while at least.

Jim didn't lose much time asking the obvious question, "What are you doing here, old buddy? I have never seen you in this place before."

Philip tried to deflect the question. "I was going to ask you the same thing. This joint doesn't seem like your kind of eatery."

"Well, we have been coming here for years now. Had our first date here, so it is just a little romantic kick. Besides the food is real good and the owner is a former patient. By the way, I heard about what happened to you, Philip. A rotten mess if there ever was one. I sometimes wonder what would have happened if we had been home the day that Moira Hamlin died."

"I don't understand. What difference would that have made? Do you know the Hamlins?"

"Man, didn't you know? We used to live right next door to them. Their kids were always running all over our property and breaking things, but the parents were nice enough in a haughty way and we managed to get along. We had them over a few times for cocktails and vice versa. Got to know them well enough to hear about Moira's long QT thing. I told them that I was happy that you were looking after her and I meant it. We used to kid around about my having to go over there to save her some time. That turned out to be a spooky premonition. I remember Hugh asking me, right before Moira had her problem, if I kept emergency equipment around the house. He was really surprised when I told him that I had an automatic external defibrillator in the trunk of my car specifically for emergencies. His eyes got real wide and he asked me if they really worked as well as the press said they did. I told him that they were a great potential help as long as the person using it was properly trained. That was why I didn't keep it out where any goof could get to it."

"So where were you when Moira had her arrest?"

"We were on a cruise in the Caribbean. We always tell our neighbors when we are going to be away so they keep an eye on the house."

"So Hugh knew that you were away when Moira had her arrest?"

135

"I thought so, but when we visited Moira in the hospital, Hugh said he had tried to call our house to get help. I told Lisa he really must have been in a panic mode."

"Why's that?" asked Philip.

"Well, when we get home from a trip, I always scroll through our caller ID list and his name wasn't on it. Maybe he called the wrong number. Since there was no message, it took us a couple of days to find out that Moira was in the hospital and in bad shape. By the time we got over there, she was just about gone."

Lisa chimed in, "When we actually saw Hugh at GMH, he looked terrible. His eyes were bloodshot like he hadn't slept in a while. He hardly spoke to us—just kept muttering about how his life was ruined. Boy did we feel guilty!"

"Yeah," Jim interjected. "I was surprised. He took it real hard."

"Oh. What do you mean?" Philip couldn't disguise his curiosity.

"Well, let's just say that Hugh and Moira were no Ozzie and Harriet."

"You mean arguing?"

It was Lisa's turn. "Oh yeah. More than once we heard them screaming at each other in the driveway. Once she chased him out of the house with a big silver hair brush, and then threw it at him. Another time he yelled at her and used some really foul language. We had the grandkids staying with us. They were playing out in the yard and I was worried they'd hear the ruckus. My daughter would be furious if they brought words like that home."

"Hugh would make a point of screeching his tires as his Porsche barreled out of the driveway. Then he'd pull back in the next morning."

"Did Moira ever talk about it?"

"Never," Lisa answered quickly. "I tried to give her an opening once but she never said a word."

Philip was amused by their tag team delivery, then realized they might have told this story a few times before.

"So what do you think was going on?"

Lisa tilted her head down and peeked out over the top of her glasses. "I think he liked to hit her."

"Lisa," Jim protested, "you don't know that. I hate it when you say that."

"Jim, I know what I saw—bruises under her makeup, those long sleeves in summer."

"Circumstantial evidence," Jim countered.

"I can tell when a woman has been battered."

"Lisa is just feeling guilty," Jim explained to Philip. "We both do. We wish we could have helped somehow."

The conversation moved on to small talk about kids, vacations, and sports. Philip did the best he could to dodge the big issues, like his separation and trial. As they got ready to leave, they made polite promises to get together again. Philip appreciated their kindness. He realized how much he missed old friends.

Over a couple more cold ones, Philip watched the Phillies game - - they blew a sizable lead in the late innings. As the unhappy patrons hurled their usual insults, he thought about Moira Hamlin in a new light. There had been those X-ray reports of healed fractures. He'd just assumed they were athletic injuries, maybe while she was biking, skating, or skiing. Now he had to wonder if Moira was a battered wife. Was their close marriage really a ruse? And were the video and family testimony at the trial merely a sham?

Clearly Moira had not been injured at the time of her death. According to the autopsy, the only fresh trauma had been from the resuscitation efforts. If Hugh had beaten Moira, he must have stopped so that the wounds had healed. Extreme stress could provoke heart rhythm abnormalities in patients like Moira, but she hadn't died in the midst of a slugfest. That she hadn't had arrhythmias while arguing with her husband was further evidence that her condition was relatively benign.

Once again, Philip's instincts told him to keep an open mind, and not jump to conclusions just because he hated Hugh. It was true that Hugh had spent a good deal of time trying to convince the world that he loved his wife. Philip and his attorneys rightly assumed that was to milk sympathy and a big award from the jury.

The whole thing just didn't hold together. Philip kept coming back to one of his favorite Mark Twain quotes, "Truth is stranger than fiction, but it is because fiction is obliged to stick to possibilities; truth isn't." Which of these was the story of Moira and Hugh Hamlin?

CHAPTER 13

Philip's financial crunch kept getting worse. Nancy had no intention of going back to work, and she hinted at legal action if he didn't keep her and the children comfortable. Their joint accounts would soon be depleted, and he wasn't able to see patients or to do any consulting work. He called several of his friends in the industry for whom he had reviewed protocols, organized data, and attended regulatory meetings to help get their drugs approved.

They owed Philip big time. Getting drugs approved is basically a high-risk game for pharmaceutical companies. The Food and Drug Administration demands the best data to put drugs on the market, in particular excellent proof of safety. Regulators routinely comb through primary source documents looking for inconsistencies or any sign of trouble. When a drug approved by the agency is later discovered to cause harm, the media's feeding frenzy inevitably brings the matter to the attention of legislators. Congressmen sniff out scapegoats and lay blame at the feet of the FDA administrator who gave final drug approval. After that, the drug company can look forward to a flurry of product liability lawsuits that could cost billions.

To protect middle-level FDA beaureaucrats and the drug companies themselves from heavy public and legislative pressure, the FDA and other regulatory bodies regularly solicit opinions from experts in the medical field. Philip had been an FDA advisory committee member for many years, and consequently knew a lot about drug development and approval. The agency scientists respected him because he gave honest opinions that were usually on point. With his help, a number of new cardiovascular drugs had been approved and marketed appropriately.

When Philip's FDA term expired, pharmaceutical companies started using him as a consultant. Philip helped them when he thought their products were worthwhile, and he never charged an exorbitant amount for his services. So it was not unrealistic for him to call in some chits now. But because the agency had censured him, they could never represent to the agency that his opinions had any weight, and he could not attend meetings on their behalf. And none of the people he called came forward to help him.

"Philip, you are asking me to put my freaking job in jeopardy." Gil Roberts whined when Philip got him on the phone. Gil had been one of Philip's good friends who had used his services on many occasions. Together, they had taken a new intravenous drug to the FDA that suppressed serious heart rhythms in patients who had a heart attack or open-heart surgery.

The drug had a number of serious side effects, but Philip and Gil argued that careful labeling would allow doctors to use the drug for patients who were in danger of dying. They had prevailed and it became the most commonly used drug for its indication in the world, arguably responsible for saving thousands of lives. This and other projects made it hard for Gil to level with Philip.

"I really hate telling you this but you are damaged goods right now, Philip."

"How about if I look at stuff for you and tell you what I think, and you can just tell your superiors that you thought of it. Hell, I don't care. I just need some income right now, Gil."

"It won't work Philip. The company is all over every consultant's contract. The Feds are accusing drug companies of bribing doctors and one way is by paying a physician for work that he hasn't actually done. Anyway, there is no way for me to sneak it through like I could in the old days. The company wants full disclosure to the regulators whenever we use any consultant, and they would go bonkers if they knew that we were using you and not telling them about it. If things loosen up here, believe me I will be the first one to call you."

Philip got several responses just like Gil's from his friends in the drug industry, so he finally had to conclude that mainstream consulting work was out of the question. So were lecture gigs. In his heyday, Philip turned down more lectures than he accepted. Now, he would take anything, but everybody was running for cover. Without being on the cutting edge of research, Philip didn't have much to lecture about and universities shunned him too. Nobody wanted the negative publicity of having befriended a defrocked physician. But Philip was desperate and had one more card to play.

Years ago, Philip had contracted out to read electrocardiograms for a company doing an early phase clinical trial in normal volunteers. The work was menial, and didn't pay much. It entailed reading EKG tracings for hours and entering data into a database, while being available if one of the subjects in the trial had a medical emergency. The EKGs were almost always normal, and real emergencies were rare. But since the studies were carried out by a contract research organization and not a pharmaceutical firm, Philip was technically eligible to do it. Most of the CROs paid in cash. There would be no paper trail so the income was tax-free and couldn't be garnished. The critical question was whether he could find something close by, and fast.

Philip called around and discovered to his delight that Kathy O'Hara was running a research company in North Philadelphia. That was good news. Kathy was the first person Philip had hired when he arrived at GMH. She had grown up in a family of eight kids in the northeast section of Philadelphia. All had gone to college, and Kathy earned a masters degree in laboratory science. When she applied for a job at GMH, she was fresh out of grad school.

Philip liked her immediately and hired her as a technician in his new basic lab. Competent and intelligent, Kathy was good looking in an Irish way, with freckles, corkscrew curly red hair, green eyes, and a bright smile. She was a quick learn and Philip rewarded her with responsibility and co-authorship on important papers.

Kathy was thrilled with her work. After a few years in the basic lab, Kathy requested a transfer to clinical research. She had excellent people skills and yearned for more human contact. Philip reluctantly agreed.

As expected, Kathy attracted the attention of drug company research personnel. It didn't hurt that Kathy was attractive and personable. It wasn't long before Kathy informed Philip that she had an offer from a drug firm.

"Well, I can't say I'm surprised, Kath," Philip admitted. "The drug company people hold all the cards these days. I'm sure they offered you a better salary and stock options."

When she thanked him and said it wasn't an easy decision, he countered.

"I appreciate that Kath, but it really isn't a difficult decision, what with the money and perks. I could spend the next half hour pointing out the potential downside of an industry job as opposed to working in academia. You won't have the same autonomy you enjoyed with me. It will be much more lock step, and you will be at the bottom of the pecking order for a while. Plus all of that travel—Charles will have to cover your daughter."

"I know, Philip. I had long conversations with Charles, and he seems to be OK with it. It is something that I really want to do and he understands."

"Well, I am not going to make us both uncomfortable with some crappy counteroffer. I know I can't change your mind, so I can only wish you the best."

Kathy lasted about eight months in her new job. Constantly butting heads with the drones who ran things made her miserable, but she never called Philip. She was sure that he would give her job back, but she wanted to stay in industry for a while longer and hoped to find a more appropriate environment. She eventually took a job as a project manager with an independent research company.

Kathy was a success there. She had the research skills for the job, and a mastery of detail, which is an important part of clinical trials. She also related well to the subjects who came back regularly to participate in the research. Her company operated in North Philadelphia for good reasons.

Phase one experiments are usually carried out in normal volunteers who are young and healthy. The goal is to understand a potential new drug's side effects, and to try to figure out the dose likely to be tolerated when it is given to patients with the target disease. Male and female volunteers are confined and monitored carefully for days or weeks. The usual participants are unemployed and unattached. The depressed areas of North Philadelphia was a fertile field, where making money for lying still, getting a drug, and having blood drawn is preferable to unemployment.

Almost all of the subjects used by Kathy's CRO were African Americans. Enrollment had to be handled carefully to avoid the appearance of impropriety. It would be easy to be accused of taking advantage of the poor, subjecting them to harmful experiments without proper consent.

Having grown up in a relatively poor neighborhood herself, Kathy was sensitive to these problems. She handled the ethics, the subjects themselves, and her workers so well that soon she was invited to run operations at the company. She had been in her position for nearly five years and understood the need to have excellent physician assistance. When Philip called to ask for work, Kathy agreed to have lunch to talk it over.

"So what took you so long to call?" said Kathy as they were seated at Jules, a cheesesteak place within walking distance of Kathy's office. Cheesesteaks are not just food in Philly, they are part of the culture. Many important business meetings, including presidential and papal visits, incorporate a cheesesteak event in place of a fancy meal. In Philip's case, it was about all he could afford.

"I heard about the garbage you had to put up with so I figured that you might need help with a job," Kathy offered.

Philip was grateful that Kathy didn't make him ask. "I can't say that I love the idea but I do thank you."

"And I am your last resort?" Kathy teased.

"No, I just love to sit in a dank office and count squiggles on a piece of paper all day waiting to prescribe an aspirin for a headache. It is why I spent all of those years in training."

"Well, I think we can be creative in getting some money to you. I suspect that cash would be preferred at this point?"

"Kath, you have no idea." Philip allowed himself a little candor. "It has been a real nightmare."

Kathy was sympathetic. "I can't say I'm surprised. This is really a rotten time to be a doctor. I know several who have gotten clobbered. I thought your case would be different. It's not like the husband was naïve to the medical issues."

"What do you mean? Hugh was pretty dense when I talked to him about medical issues. I thought that was one of the reasons he got so angry with me."

"Right, but I thought that Bonnie Romano would have provided some perspective on the thing. She was there, wasn't she?" Kathy asked.

"How'd you know that?"

"Bonnie's company uses my firm for phase 1 work, so I hear things."

"Well, in fact, she was in the ER and translated what I said to Hugh. I thought she understood and was trying to be helpful."

"Maybe Hugh fucked the common sense out of her."

Philip almost fell off of his chair. What happened to that good Catholic girl who rarely resorted to foul language? If that knocked his socks off, he was really taken aback by the suggestion that Hugh and Bonnie had been romantically involved when Moira was alive.

"You mean he was screwing Bonnie before Moira died?"

"Yes, you could call it that."

"I thought that Bonnie was Moira's friend."

"That is the most twisted part. Bonnie and Moira were close since they were kids. After Bonnie's first husband died, the three of them hung out regularly."

"So you think one thing led to another?"

"That's apparently what happened." Kathy focused intently on the straw in her iced tea. She appeared uncomfortable with the way the conversation was going.

"Kathy, how did you find this out? I never heard about an affair."

"As I said, we do a lot of business with Bonnie. Her secretary, Ros Wickman, used to work for my boss. Anyhow, Ros and I get together for drinks now and then. One night, she mentioned something about Bonnie and when I asked, she gave me all the detail about Bonnie's affair with Hugh. Poor Moira at home with the kids and Hugh bored with his job. It was the perfect set-up for adultery. After she'd gone on and on about all that dirty laundry, she caught herself short and asked me not to say anything. Bonnie wouldn't be happy to be portrayed as a home wrecker."

"So Bonnie was in the picture at the hospital not because of

Moira but because she and Hugh were having an affair? I sensed something was going on but couldn't figure it out. Are you sure about this?"

"Yeah," Kathy said, as she wiped ketchup from her chin. "Ros said it had been going on for quite some time. Ros thought that maybe Bonnie liked the danger of getting caught. One time she had trouble retrieving some panties she'd left in Hugh's car. She joked that she should have sent Ros to get them for her. She appeared to enjoy dropping hints about the affair with Ros. She trusted Ros wouldn't tell, and she didn't until she had a few glasses of wine with yours truly."

Kathy could see Philip becoming more distressed as she related her story. "Maybe I shouldn't have told you this?"

Philip shook her off. "No, that's OK, but obviously I am more than a little surprised. Who else have you told about this?"

"Just Charles. Most of the time, he falls asleep during our pillow talk. Stuff like this gets me excited and him drowsy."

"Did Ros say if Moira ever found out about the affair?"

"Apparently they went a little too far once. Moira came back early from a tennis lesson after turning her ankle and found them together. She went absolutely bonkers. After that, Hugh spent far less time at home, and Ros said that Bonnie was snapping at everybody at work. She overheard her screaming at Hugh on the phone several times. It seems Bonnie assumed Hugh and Moira were going to split up and was getting tired of waiting for that to happen."

"Moira finally cooperated by dying."

"Ros says it was hard to tell how Bonnie felt about that. She was out of work for a few days. When she came back, she didn't say much about it."

Philip just kept shaking his head. "Bonnie must have known that my care was reasonable."

Kathy shrugged. "I can't tell you what they were thinking. She is a control freak but who knows what her motivation was."

As they finished their "everything on it" cheesesteaks, Philip had a hard time concentrating, but thought it best to shift the conversation to business, research projects, and where he might be useful. Could he start next week, she asked. "Kathy, I'm sure I can clear my schedule for you." They laughed. Philip reached for

Kathy's hand. "Thanks, Kathy. I mean it more than you will ever know."

"Look, you got me started. I owe you my career. And now you will be a big help to me. Besides, it will be fun to work together again, like the old days." She couldn't resist one last tease, "Only now, I get to call the shots."

As he drove home, Philip had a chance to piece together what he had learned. Later, the burning questions rolled around in his brain as he lay sleepless that night and many nights after. What did Bonnie's relationship with Hugh have to do with the lawsuit against him? If Moira had discovered their affair that would explain the fights the Flanagans had described. If Hugh had battered Moira, why did he stop? Could the destination for the screeching tire exits have been Bonnie's place? And was Hugh's infidelity the reason for the driveway battles?

No matter what, Bonnie now had to be considered a pivotal figure in the Hamlin drama. Could Hugh and Bonnie have conspired in Moira's death? On one hand, Hugh and Bonnie had profited from her demise, but an unfaithful husband was not necessarily a murderer. Philip's racing thoughts were making his head spin. He vowed not to leap to conclusions. It was vital that he remain as objective as possible.

But try as he might, Philip's obsession with the possibility that Moira was murdered grew exponentially. What should he do and where should he start? Based on his medical training, his first reflex was to seek consultation with an expert, and he knew just the person who might be able to help him with this particular diagnostic dilemma.

CHAPTER 14

Philip never missed an opportunity to take on a new project, especially if money was involved. Now he was forced to take on projects of little value simply for the cash. Maybe it was his father's influence. His dad had loved making money; working two or three jobs didn't faze him. Now the son wondered if his father's motivation might have been more greed than selflessness.

Though Philip's work wasn't as physical as his father's, it required as much of his time and energy. On one hand, traveling to deliver lectures or attending meetings was more glamorous than servicing trucks, or selling fruit and vegetables. On the other, it meant missing many school and social events.

A good way to generate income was to review legal cases. Soon after he arrived at GMH, he was summoned to the office of Don Master, Jerry Santini's predecessor as Chairman of Medicine. Don was the long-time head of the department, an infectious disease expert, who had been instrumental in Philip's recruitment. Don wore the same grey slacks and white shirt combo with nondescript ties everyday, because he claimed, like Einstein, that he didn't want to spend any time thinking about his wardrobe. He had coke-bottle glasses, greasy, thinning hair, and a perpetual frown that kept people at a distance.

Don was also brilliant with a near photographic memory and knew the field of infectious diseases like few in his specialty. He started his illustrious career at Columbia and came to GMH to build the Medicine department.

Despite many academic duties, Don had a high-profile consultative practice, seeing patients from around the world with the most perplexing infectious diseases. He traveled internationally, authored textbooks and hundreds of medical articles, and did it all with great intensity. He recruited promising doctors like Philip, and gave the young Turks an opportunity to excel. So what if he took credit for their accomplishments? Don was selfish but had a knack for getting what he needed out of his "boys."

As a potential expert witness, Don reviewed dozens of malpractice cases every year. He was just as inclined to go after a physician, even a person he knew, as he was to defend one. Ruthless about everything, he broached no exceptions to his first rule of legal medicine: "If you screwed up, you deserve to get it up the ass."

Don's second rule, "I don't get involved in crappy cases" meant he rejected more cases than he accepted, and he made sure everybody knew it. "One thing that really pisses me off is some asshole lawyer trying to cram a case down my throat. I'll be fucked before I'll take a weak case." His secretary once said, "Nobody can tell somebody off like Don. I betcha he would ream out the Chief Justice of the Supreme Court if he got worked up enough."

Don charged huge fees, but lawyers who retained him didn't mind paying because good experts were worth their weight in gold. When Don saw a good case that was not within his expertise, he passed it on to a young colleague, and this was the reason for calling Philip.

Terrified that he he'd done something wrong, Philip was relieved that Don had a bone for him, a cardiology case that he wanted Philip to review and render an opinion.

"Dr. Master, this is something new for me. I really don't know what to do."

Don was his characteristically nurturing self. "Don't be a fucking wimp. Are you interested in doing it or not?"

"Sure, but can you just give me a little guidance?"

"All you have to do is go through the records, form an opinion about whether the doctor was negligent in the case, and call the lawyer."

Though it sounded pretty simple, Philip would find out that it wasn't that way at all. Legal medicine is a complicated discipline.

Don didn't tell him about the legal sharks who derive almost as much pleasure from making an expert look stupid on the stand as they do from suing doctors in the first place.

It took many years, but Philip established himself as a good defense expert witness, learning how to talk to the jury in a way they understood. He showed sympathy to the common men and women who sat in the jury box. It was a mortal sin to talk over their heads. He used props and visual aids and terms like "plumbing" and "electricity" to describe the complex workings of the heart pump and conduction system.

In a highly technical and complicated cases, Philip knew juries weigh personality and ethical behavior to guide their verdicts. Philip had seen that in spades at the Hamlin trial. The jury didn't believe Bob Myerstone because Philip helped him in a case of his own, not because the medical facts made a case against Philip.

Despite his talent for the task, Philip rejected the idea of working for plaintiff attorneys after a pointed conversation with his father. "I don't like the idea of you standing up in court and saying bad things about other doctors. As far as I am concerned, all doctors are heroes, trying to help other people. There's an old Lebanese expression that says 'you don't shit where you eat.' It will definitely come back to haunt you."

His father had been right. Doctors respected Philip for coming to their aid, and he alienated no one except the plaintiff bar. Like Don, he took only the best cases, those he felt passionate about. But Don never told him how to handle a bruising cross-examination. The only way to learn how to perform on the stand was doing it badly and paying the price.

Once he became familiar with opposing tactics, Philip was smart enough to counter, delighting in confrontations so he could pull the pants off the plaintiff's attorneys in front of the jury. One of his favorites was when they tried to paint Philip as an ivory tower academic.

"So tell me Doctor, do you actually take care of patients or do you have residents or students do that for you?"

"We have residents and students who work with us and they do have a major impact on how much time I have to spend in the clinic."

The plaintiff's attorneys would start to drool at the prospect of making it look like Philip didn't take care of patients himself. How could some professor know what a real doctor was supposed to do in the trenches? "Is that right, doctor? So you actually don't spend a whole lot of time with patients, do you?"

"No, I meant that because of the residents and interns who are constantly underfoot, I actually spend more time in the clinic, not less. Not only do I have to see all the patients, but I also have to answer a whole bunch of student questions. But I do it because our patients get better care by having the trainees around."

Sparring with attorneys had to be handled carefully so that the jury wouldn't think he was flip, but it served a purpose. Plaintiff's attorneys knew the danger of confronting a savvy physician in front of a jury and were inclined to settle a case before trial rather than take such a risk.

Over the years, Philip had come to respect attorneys on both sides of the fence. One of his favorites was Joan who had worked so hard in his own case. A few others stood out as particularly talented, not only in the courtroom, but in pre-trial preparation. Their research was meticulous, probing every aspect of the plaintiffs' case to leverage a settlement or to obtain a favorable verdict. Philip had never paid much attention to these tactics that seemed irrelevant to mainstream theories or issues of negligence. He was amused by the idea that invading someone's privacy was important to the outcome of a case of alleged physician negligence, never imagining he would need access to that same skill set.

But he began to think that peeking into Hugh Hamlin's private life might unravel the mystery that was plaguing him. There was considerable risk. But Hugh wasn't too smart. If Bonnie caught on they might press criminal charges, but Philip didn't have a whole lot to lose.

He considered the short list of people who might help him, someone circumspect and affordable. The name that kept coming to mind was Dorothy Deaver, but he was afraid that he was picking her for the wrong reasons. Dorothy was one of the most interesting women he had ever met. She practiced malpractice defense and toiled tirelessly for her clients, usually doctors who had been sued without evidence of negligence. She had a sparkling personality that she revealed in the courtroom. Jurors sat up in their chairs when they saw her bright smile.

Philip first met Dorothy when he was an expert witness in one of her cases. She had set up an appointment to discuss trial strategy and his testimony. When she walked into the room, Philip was so overwhelmed he had a hard time getting out a hello. During their hour-long meeting, he found it hard to concentrate.

When Dorothy suggested they meet for breakfast the day Philip was to testify, he readily agreed. He found himself carefully picking his clothes. When Philip learned Dorothy was neither married nor attached, she became his obsession.

At their meetings, Dorothy impressed Philip with how much she knew about the case and each of the principals. A man who had a heart rhythm abnormality called atrial fibrillation had suffered a stroke. The plaintiff alleged that the doctor should have prescribed a blood thinner. The patient and his wife stated that the doctor had told them it was too risky to use blood thinners in his case. The doctor countered that the patient had refused to take the drug, but his records were sloppy, failing to document his recommendations. Since the doctor had never written a prescription for the drug, the case was not going to be easy.

Dorothy had engaged Philip to verify that a blood thinner was necessary, and to give an opinion about the doctor's care. Philip thought that the doctor had been clear in his instructions and that the blood thinner was important to prevent a stroke. The plaintiffs had found a practitioner to argue that the doctor had not done his job, so it came down to whom the jury would believe.

As usual, Dorothy had gone one step further. She contacted several people who knew the plaintiff and his wife. Most refused to talk to her, but she finally found a disgruntled former caregiver who had overheard the husband tell his wife he wasn't going to take the blood thinner. "I don't care what that quack says. I don't want to bleed to death so that's that."

Dorothy also discovered that the patient had allowed his disability policy to lapse. She suspected he was counting on a positive verdict to compensate for the loss of an insurance payout. Although this hearsay information was inadmissible, Dorothy's skillful detective work made the case stronger.

After a ten-day ordeal, the verdict had gone in the doctor's favor. Dorothy called Philip to tell him the good news and to invite him to a celebratory dinner at Le Bec Fin, the finest restaurant in Philadelphia. Dinner at Le Bec was special. The master chef, Georges Perrier, was an international celebrity, and the cuisine and venue magnificent. To accept, Philip had to cancel meetings and tell his family that he would be home late. He worked at his desk until about 8:00, then headed downtown.

Philip expected to see the entire legal team, but a ravishing Dorothy was alone. "I decided to buy myself a little black dress for the occasion. What do you think?" Philip gaped at the whole picture—terrific figure, upswept chestnut hair accentuating high cheekbones and deep set, almost cerulean blue eyes. Philip was blown away.

They ordered cocktails. Sipping a vodka martini, Philip fantasized an angel on his right shoulder and a devil on his left, each whispering in his ear. Fortunately, he knew he would have time to figure things out; dinner at Le Bec typically lasts hours.

Dorothy was relaxed, and as they worked their way through appetizers, she told her story. "I really can't say that I pulled myself up by the bootstraps. Actually I grew up wanting for nothing. My father is a private investigator. He started the most famous detective firm in the city, debunking frivolous personal injury claims. One of his favorite subjects is injury on public transportation. If a bus happens to be involved in an accident, dozens of riders file whiplash injury claims to cash in on the situation."

Philip listened, chin propped on his hand, to the smooth, almost musical tone of Dorothy's voice.

"When I was in school and worked in his office, he taught me how to gather information about plaintiffs in the most discreet ways. Sometimes, he simply staked out the person for a few days. In more complicated cases, he would step it up with computer hacking, planting bugs, wire tapping, and a bunch of other sleezy tactics.

"He wanted me to take over the business, but I liked the legal end more than the life of a gumshoe, and so I decided to go to law school. I eventually joined a personal injury firm doing defense work and found out that I was pretty good at it. But the stuff I learned in my father's business was a big help, as you saw in this case."

After the sommelier brought out their wine selection, Dorothy told Philip about the case that had established her reputation. "I was asked to defend a company in a product liability lawsuit, something I had never done before. The case was a good example of how individuals abuse the system."

Dorothy leaned closer. "A healthy 24-year-old office clerk named Roy Boyd was plugging in a coffee machine at his job when he received a shock through the wall outlet. His hand and arm were sore, but he seemed to be all right and was returning to work when the office manager stopped him. She told him that since the incident had occurred on the job, he probably ought to have it checked out. She sent him to the neighborhood walk-in clinic where a nurse practitioner examined him.

"The nurse told him he was fine and that a 110-volt shock was unlikely to cause a real problem. Roy went back to work and seemed to have no physical limitations but continued to complain about vague pain in his chest and arms. He mentioned this to his family who were appropriately concerned and encouraged him to have a further evaluation. His mother was particularly worried and said something like, 'You never know how much damage electricity can do. Just remember, if you hurt yourself at work, they will have to make it up to you.'"

"I think I know what's coming," Philip interjected.

"You aren't going to believe it. Over the next three months, Roy began to tell his family about other symptoms, including shortness of breath climbing stairs. He was overweight and a heavy smoker, but he had never had ill health before.

"Roy went to the doctor and had some tests. The doctor told him that he had a reduction in cardiac function and referred him to a cardiologist who carried out a catheterization. Roy was diagnosed to have a mild enlargement of his heart, what do you call that, dilated cardiomyopathy, and the pumping function wasn't quite as good as it should have been. Anyhow, the obvious question was why? He and his family were told that in most cases, no reason could be found, that any one of a number of things could have damaged his heart, the most likely being a viral infection."

Dorothy wove her way through the story as the delicate coq au vin was delivered to the table. Philip was so fascinated with Dorothy and her story that he hardly noticed what he was putting in his mouth. "As the weeks went by, Roy continued to complain of not being able to exercise even though his doctors couldn't find anything else wrong with him. They all told him that his mild re-duction in cardiac function shouldn't cause exercise intolerance. He finally quit his job so he could figure things out."

"I am sure that it became a full-time occupation."

"It did. He took his records everywhere, including a personal injury attorney. He wanted to know if his job caused the problem and if he could be eligible for disability. The attorney had a staff of smart former nurses. One of them noted the electrical outlet in-cident and pointed it out to her boss. He called a doctor he liked to use for such consultations, one Giuseppe DiPietro."

"Skip, the Italian Stallion? I know that guy. What a sleeze!"

"You can say bad things about him, but the Italian population of Philadelphia thinks the guy sits at the right hand of God. And have you noticed that despite a fine education, he still sounds like one of the vendors at the Italian market. Skip knows how to talk the talk in South Philly. When he was asked to take a look at the case, he said. 'Sure counselor, I would be DE-lighted to take a look at it for yuz.'"

"That is quite an accent—you have spent some time wid doz guys."

"You betcha. Anyhow, Skip came back with the correct answer, as far as the plaintiff's attorneys were concerned. Electrical shocks could damage the heart. He said it was highly probable that Roy's heart problem had been caused by electricity entering the heart and damaging it, and he was willing to say so in court for the cor-rect fee.

"The lawyer filed suit against the employer and the manufac-turer of the coffee maker. My firm was asked to defend the com-pany that made the product. I called a physician friend of mine for an informal consultation, and he had a hard time answering because he was laughing so hard. 'Sure, you can damage the heart with electricity but not like that. You need to get thousands of volts to cause that kind of injury and it's called electrocution. A cardiomyopathy, even a mild one, from a wall outlet is total crap.'"

"Your guy was absolutely right—Skip was lying," Philip agreed.

"Well, I figured this could end up being one expert against an-other, and I knew DPietro's reputation for persuasiveness, so I decided to learn what I could about Roy. I checked several databanks and tried some soft surveillance myself. I figured I might save a little money for the firm. Maybe I watched too many Humphrey Bogart movies, but I imagined myself in a murder drama, desperately trying to prove the innocence or guilt of my client."

Philip interrupted, "Yeah, when I testify, I fantasize that I'm a knight in shining armor."

"Surveillance is not romantic. It involves interminable waiting for something to happen. I wanted to see what Roy did with his time. I had my trusty video camera with me just in case. The first two days, Roy was the couch potato that I expected him to be—didn't leave his place.

"On the third day, he walked out of his apartment building in sweats and sneakers and I finally saw him in person. Chunky guy who looked a little like Fat Albert from the Bill Cosby cartoon. Pudgy with fat cheeks and a rather large caboose.

"I let him get a sufficient head start on foot and then swung past him and around the corner in my car so that he wouldn't know he was being followed. He made a turn at the first street past his apartment and headed toward the neighborhood playground. By the time I spotted him, he had his sweatshirt off and was shooting hoops. Things still looked pretty innocent. I mean Roy wasn't moving much.

"On my next circuit, old Roy boy was in a hot pick-up game, running the court and circling into the lane for a sweeping hook shot. I switched on my trusty video camera. The camera was equipped with a clock that I calibrated by filming the PECO building in the background with that neon sign giving the date and time. I sat there and for the next 45 minutes taped Roy Boyd in a game worthy of ESPN."

Dorothy looked triumphant, and Philip's heart melted. "Wow! That must have blown the socks off the plaintiff's attorney."

"Yeah, he knew his case was cooked as soon as he saw the first few minutes of the tape. I told him that Roy Boyd could begin to look for a new job, and my client could scratch the case from their product liability log."

They spent the next hour finishing dinner and enjoying a luscious crème beûlée, talking about their lives and their careers. Philip took care to steer clear of his family, not wanting to ruin the mood. It was almost midnight before dinner was over. Philip and Dorothy strolled toward her Center City apartment. Later, Philip blamed Jim Beam for what happened when they reached the curb outside of her building.

"Dorothy, you are an unbelievable woman." She looked at him expectantly. "Incredibly bright..." He fumbled for words to convey what he was feeling. "Beautiful and talented and..." Suddenly, Philip pulled Dorothy close. They kissed long and yearningly. Without another word, they walked arm in arm into Dorothy's building and took the elevator up to her apartment and into her bedroom.

In the early morning, Philip awakened, dressed and left the apartment while Dorothy slept. He didn't see Dorothy again. Her secretary called his office a few times asking him to review cases, but he politely declined, deciding not to put temptation in his path again. He never told Nancy, and she never found out.

Now the situation was different. Nancy was gone, but he was still uneasy. He was thinking about calling this woman who had totally bewitched him. Was he calling her for assistance with a case that had ruined him, or to rekindle a relationship?

He thought about it for a few days and in the end decided he needed Dorothy's expertise. He would just keep the personal stuff out of it. What was so hard about that?

When Dorothy answered the phone, she sounded business-like. She listened patiently as he told his dismal story. He admitted that he had little more than circumstantial evidence that Hugh had committed any foul play. He didn't have a lot of money, so he would have to pay her in installments. When he finished, Dorothy responded in a soft and level voice.

"Philip, you know I respect you and that I care for you. But you need to know that you broke my heart. You were a happily married man, and I had no business tempting you like that. Your reaction in retrospect was completely understandable, so I really did it to myself. I also understand why you declined to take on any other cases for me for such a long time. Well now I am over all of that, and I don't want to open any old wounds, yours or mine."

Philip braced himself for the turndown, but Dorothy surprised him again.

"If we are going to do this, it will be only business, right?"

"Dorothy, I wouldn't have it any other way. Truth is, my personal life is already in the toilet and I don't need to make it worse. I want to find out about Hugh Hamlin and any leftover personal feelings can't jeopardize my chances of finding the truth. I am completely with you on this."

But even as he formed the words, Philip wasn't so sure if he was telling the truth or saying what he thought Dorothy wanted to hear. And he couldn't suspect that Dorothy didn't know either.

CHAPTER 15

Dorothy began by making some inquiries of several of Hugh's neighbors and acquaintances. She decided to take the "media" approach. When her father, Dick, first taught her how to do this kind of work, she was skeptical that anyone would open up to a stranger, even with authentic-appearing reporter credentials.

"You'll be amazed how much people will tell you," Dick Deaver had said. "You just have to get them at the right time and ask the right questions. It won't hurt that you are attractive and have a friendly smile. Just smile and engage them, and they will tell you more than they mean to or that you ever thought they would."

How right her father had been. A few people slammed doors in her face, but most were polite and many offered her a beverage and a seat. It was important to keep the interview as open-ended as possible, and Dorothy had to suppress her impulse to force the point. When she let the conversation meander, it was amazing how much juicy information inevitably came out. Talking to a reporter impressed people. It made them feel important.

Dorothy would tell the targets she was doing a story for Philadelphia Magazine on Hugh's family's amazing business success. Making the fake credentials was easy since nobody really knew what a magazine reporter's identification was supposed to look like. Dorothy also told people that their comments would be off the record, unless of course they wanted to be quoted. This made "confidential information" fair game.

Dorothy had followed a Hamlin maid into Gladwyne one morning, and saw her go into the dry cleaners. The clerk in the Gladwyne dry cleaning shop turned out to be a perfect target. She was an energetic lady, too bright for her job, who loved to observe her customers. Gladys Hutchinson had grown up tough in South Philly and still lived in the house in which she had been raised. Her husband left when she was only 30 years old and for the next 20 years she raised her three young children by herself, taking on three jobs including part-time at the Gladwyne cleaners. Gladys knew all of her clientele by name, who the tippers were, and how to give them good service. Big tips were what made the job worthwhile and justified the long bus ride from South Philly to the posh suburbs.

"Gladys, my name is Dorothy Frame, and I am doing a story about Hugh Hamlin for the Philadelphia Magazine." Dorothy flashed her fake ID, and Gladys didn't even glance at it. It also didn't occur to her to ask if Hamlin had approved the story.

"Mr. Hamlin is one of Philly's success stories," Dorothy continued, "and the issue will be on the top businesspeople in the city. I'm interviewing vendors who provided services for him and his family over the years. I want to hear the good and the bad. The Hamlins told me that they use your shop. Have you gotten to know them?"

"Oh, yeah! Everybody who lives in Gladwyne uses this place. I don't see Mr. Hamlin or his second wife very often, but I used to see his first wife a lot. She came in all the time and we would talk. She was real nice."

"Yes, I heard she died a few years ago. That must have been quite a shock?"

"It was a real tragedy. Mrs. Hamlin was always nice to me and asked me about my kids. She wasn't a real big tipper, but she never missed giving me a little something. You could tell that she wasn't used to having the big money. She paid attention to how much things cost. There are people who have accounts here, and I swear we could charge five dollars a shirt and they wouldn't care, as long as the starch was right. That wasn't her though—she kept track of all of it."

"Did she ever talk about her family?"

"Yeah, she had a Laura and so do I — mine is a lot older than hers — but we would trade a few stories about our Lauras. It was fun. You could tell that she really loved them kids."

"What about her husband? Did she ever say anything about Mr. Hamlin?"

Gladys got a funny look on her face. "She talked a lot about him when they first got married, and they even came in together a few times. They seemed real happy back then. But as time went by she almost never brought him up. I would ask about him, you know, if he liked the way the shirts were done and all that, but she would change the subject. At first I figured they weren't as tight as they were when they first got married, but that is no big surprise. Hell, I don't know too many married people who keep it up very long anyhow. But I guess there was more to it than that."

That comment got Dorothy's attention. "Yeah, marriage can be real complicated sometimes," she said trying to sound noncommittal.

"You can say that again. Before he ran out on me, my old man used to be real mean, even hit me a few times, so I could sympathize with Mrs. Hamlin."

"So it was pretty rough for her?" Dorothy tried to keep the excitement out of her voice.

"I guess you can say that. I saw a few bruises here and there, but maybe Mrs. Hamlin just hurt herself for all I knew. I really didn't give it much thought until Mr. Hamlin himself came in here in a huff one afternoon. I didn't recognize him right off and I know all of the customers. He started yelling about how his shirts had been delivered in boxes instead of on hangers like he wanted them. I tried to calm him down, and I went to the back to check to see what the order had looked like. I was so flustered that I had a hard time finding it. He just paced back and forth, fuming away. Man, I just couldn't understand what the big deal was but I saw the state he was in. I finally found the slip and, thank the Lord, it showed that Mrs. Hamlin had asked for boxes, just like we had done. I showed the slip to him and then he really went nuts, using foul language, called her a fat bitch, excuse the language."

"Who was a fat bitch?"

"His wife! I remember that really well because she was such a scrawny little thing. I was amazed that he would call her that, especially in front of me."

159

"Yeah, pretty amazing."

With a sudden start, Gladys realized who she was talking to. "I shouldn't be telling you this stuff. Is this going to be in the article? Are you going to quote me?"

"No, not to worry. This is all deep background. I just wanted to get a feeling for what the family was like and how they related to Hugh Hamlin. This helps me a lot."

"Well, I really didn't know them that well so I am not sure how they usually behaved. You shouldn't only use my word, you know?"

Gladys, however, had given Dorothy a glimpse of Hugh at an unprotected moment, and it made her believe that what the Flanagans had told Philip was accurate. She talked to a few other merchants in Gladwyne, but Gladys' information was the best. Dorothy didn't want to get too many people talking to each other about her research. Word might get back to Hugh.

Dorothy had heard there was a fast turnover among the Hamlin unskilled servants. Next, she called the agency that supplied most of the servants who worked on the Main Line and said she worked for Hugh Hamlin. When they confirmed Hamlin as a client, Dorothy told them that Mr. Hamlin was having an IRS audit. She needed a list of the servants who had worked in his home for the last five years. The agency immediately faxed the information.

Dorothy was able to identify the maids from the time before Moira died, and picked out those who worked for the Hamlins for six months or less. These would be the least loyal to the family. Dorothy discreetly called these women, again using the magazine story for cover, assuring them that she was only interested in background information. Three out of the four, with heavy Spanish accents, quickly hung up. Only one, a Portuguese maid named Isabelle Calvez, stayed on the phone. Dorothy proposed that she visit Isabelle for a brief interview.

"Well, I don't have too much time, but today is my day off if you want to come over now."

Dorothy quickly agreed, canceling her appointments for the afternoon. She drove to Isabelle's West Philadelphia address. The neighborhood was depressing, but Isabelle's little row home was a pleasant surprise. The outside was freshly painted white with neat bright red trim work on the windows and doors and the wood porch had been recently refurbished. Inside, the house was neat and clean, with mismatched furniture covered in plastic slipcovers. Isabelle didn't ask to see Dorothy's credentials but welcomed her into her house with a shy smile and an offer of coffee, which Dorothy accepted.

They sat in the living room sipping from their unmatched mugs, Dorothy careful not to drip coffee onto the highly waxed end table. They started with a little small talk. Dorothy learned that Isabelle was an only child whose mother had died when she was quite a young child. Isabelle and her father then immigrated to the US to join his extended family in Philadelphia. They were poor, but with odd jobs, her father had managed to scratch out a living.

Isabelle had performed fairly well in school, but as soon as she was old enough, she quit to work for the agency that supplied housekeepers to the Main Line. That was how she found her way to the Hamlins.

Dorothy gently directed the conversation.

"How long did you work for the Hamlins?"

"I was there for six months before Mr. Hamlin told me he didn't want me there anymore."

"Why? What happened?"

"I thought I was doing good. I really liked Mrs. Hamlin. Me and her talked every morning when I served her breakfast. I think that made Mr. Hamlin mad because he would always interrupt and change the subject. I thought he was rude."

"Did you get into a scrape with him?"

"No, but like my Dad told me, it isn't too hard to know what I am thinking; my eyes give me away. I think he knew that I didn't like him too much. So he ended up firing me without a real good reason."

This was a bonanza for Dorothy. Fired employees talk freely. Some information would be biased, but Dorothy found Isabelle credible because she corroborated Dorothy's other sources. Best of all, it sounded as if she had spent some quality time with Moira who may have been looking for someone with whom she could commiserate.

Isabelle continued, "He yelled at her a lot in front of the staff. He called her fat and disgusting. He went out of his way to tell her that she was a pig when she usually only had a few bites of anything. She was so scrawny."

Gladys had used the same word to describe Moira. "So he focused on her weight?"

"Yeah, he really beat up on her about that. He would order all kinds of diet magazines and would make her read them all the time. He would tell her that the food she ordered on line from the grocery store was fattening and that she didn't know nothin' about nutrition. Like he told her one time that grapefruit juice was good for losing weight, so why didn't she order it and stuff like that. It was really nasty how he talked about her body and being fat all the time. I think it really made her feel bad."

"Did she ever give it back to him?"

"It was amazing how much she put up with. He was a lot fatter than her and didn't do nothing to keep his own self in shape. In fact, I think he was the pig. She should have walked out on him, not the other way around."

"Did he walk out on her?"

"Yeah, he would get into his car and just take off without telling nobody where he was goin'"

"Do you know where he went?"

"Like I thought he was out cheating on her—but not everybody agreed."

"You mean other people knew about all of this?"

"Oh sure!" Isabelle had been right—her face did give away her feelings. Now she was amazed that Dorothy knew so few obvious things. "Everybody in the house knew that they were having problems. We just disagreed on whether he was messing around. I was pretty sure he was."

"How did you know that?"

"Just the look on his face when he came home the next morning. I also did the laundry. I could smell the perfume on his clothes."

"Did you ever confront Mr. Hamlin with any of this?" Dorothy knew that she was really pushing the edge—after all, what did all of this have to do with a magazine article about Hugh Hamlin the businessman? But Isabelle seemed to be enjoying the chance to unload her hostility. Dorothy was hoping she'd keep going.

"Are you crazy? He had a bad temper and I was scared of him.

No way I was going to pull his chain. I just didn't like the way he pushed her around."

"Did he ever hit Moira?"

"I never seen him hit her, but they fought a lot and I could hear them screaming pretty good. She sometimes had bruises here and there, and she didn't fall down or nothing. So I wouldn't be surprised if he was knocking her around a little."

"How did you get fired?"

"Mr. Hamlin came home early one night, and I was in the kitchen with Mrs. Hamlin. She was crying, saying that Mr. Hamlin didn't find her, you know, pretty or attractive because she was so fat. I said she wasn't fat at all and that I couldn't figure out where he got that stuff. Then he walked into the kitchen, and they really got into a big fight, screaming at each other like crazy.

"He called me into his study right after that and told me to get my stuff together and get out of the house, that I wasn't welcome there anymore. I tried to apologize — I didn't want the black mark on my record at the agency — but he said that he was tired of my interfering and that was the end of it. He was real red in the face so I knew that I was wasting my breath, and I just left."

"Do you still work for that agency?"

"Yeah. They were pretty mad about it at first, but then they said that they knew the Hamlins were a tough family to work for. I heard later that there were other girls who were let go for different reasons, so they just moved me to another position. Now I'm working for a real nice family in Chestnut Hill."

"Isabelle, did you know that Mrs. Hamlin died shortly after you left that job?"

"No! That's terrible! Nobody ever told me that. Oh, those kids. They really loved their Mom. What happened?"

"She had something like a heart attack and died at her house. Mr. Hamlin recently remarried."

"Was it that lady from the drug company?"

"You mean Bonnie Romano?"

"Yeah, she was always hanging out at the house and hanging all over Mr. Hamlin too. I figured she would get him if Mrs. Hamlin was out of the picture."

"Do you think she was the other woman he went to see when he left the house?"

Isabelle lowered her eyes,. She was clearly uncomfortable with the question.

"I don't know, but her perfume was pretty close to the laundry smell."

Dorothy backed off and asked a few questions about Hugh's business, not because she really cared, but she wanted the magazine excuse to seem credible. As she prepared to leave, Dorothy thanked Isabelle, reassured her that the information would be kept confidential. Isabelle's expression made it clear she knew that the magazine story was a ruse but she didn't mind.

"I am really sorry about Mrs. Hamlin dying. She was a sweet lady. But her husband wasn't very nice at all. You have to wonder if people like that ever get what's coming to them. Maybe they do sometimes."

Isabelle's interview helped to establish that the atmosphere in the Hamlin household had been an unhappy one. More importantly, Dorothy now knew that Bonnie Romano had been in the picture before Moira's death. It was now time to learn more about this intriguing woman and her relationship with the Hamlins.

Some of what Dorothy needed to know was common knowledge in the drug industry and would require little digging. She decided to call Al Kenworthy, a junior associate in her father's firm, to see if he could spend a few hours getting the skinny on Bonnie.

Al was a nerd, complete with crew cut, horn-rimmed glasses, and penny loafers, who also happened to be infatuated with Dorothy. He had asked her out a few times, but she had gently turned him down. She knew that he would do anything to spend time with her. The price of admission was going to be a background check, to which Al quickly agreed. He believed that when Dorothy called, you just did what she asked.

It took Al only a day to finish the task. Dorothy told him to meet her at Le Café on the Ben Franklin Parkway. The weather on that spring day was good enough to sit at a small sidewalk table. The lunch crowd made a good diversion. Dorothy was dressed casually in a skirt and sweater, while Al had on a sport coat and tie that he wore to impress the boss's daughter.

"Gee, Dorothy, it was really nice of you to call. I haven't had a chance to see much of you lately. How are things with you? Are you seeing anybody?"

Dorothy who had braced herself for Al's inquisition, calmly replied, "Well, no, I'm not, but work has been so very busy lately. I thought we should get together some time, and then this Bonnie Romano thing came up. I figured that we could kill two birds with one stone, if you know what I mean."

Dorothy didn't think that anyone could be naïve enough to fall for that line, but Al seemed fine with it. "You know that I am always ready to help you out. In fact, most of the information on Bonnie is public information. I went a little further for you, as you'll see."

"Well, why don't we get that stuff out of the way first, and then we can catch up on other things when we get our food."

"That sounds perfect, Dorothy." Al took out his notes and spread them out on the table. "OK, here goes. Bonnie graduated from college with a biology degree, and then she applied to medical school and for some reason didn't get in. She studied pharmacology but never finished her doctorate before she applied for a position with a drug company. Miracle hired her in an entry-level sales position."

"And that's the company she still works for, right?"

"Yes. But it wasn't a happy start. Being a drug sales representative is tough work, and Bonnie apparently hated it, all that kowtowing to docs to change their prescribing habits. But Bonnie was a shark. She was aggressive and worked like crazy. In addition, she learned how to manipulate male physicians, showing a little leg, and being suggestive in the cafeteria as she told them about the latest me-too antibiotic. She figured that was a small price to pay to get some doctors to use a new product."

"Does she have something against doctors?"

"Yes, and some think it's because she didn't make the team herself. She doesn't think they keep up with the literature, so they are easy marks for the first hard sell, even if there's little advantage to the expensive new drugs she was selling."

Dorothy listened to Al attentively, keeping good eye contact. Al struggled to maintain his concentration.

"It turns out that 'selling while seducing' got to be Bonnie's motto." Al was pleased that Dorothy chuckled at the remark. "However she did it, Bonnie rose quickly in the ranks to district and then regional manager and eventually landed a vice-president

Peter Kowey

position in charge of late clinical development of all new drug products."

"Sounds like a big deal for someone so young."

"It was. Any new pharmaceutical product had to pass through her office before going in for regulatory filing. She made a bunch of good decisions and became the highest-ranking VP in the company, reporting only to Jean-Claude Rømier, the company's president. Jean-Claude prefers the social scene and hobnobbing with politicos, so he left the heavy lifting to Bonnie. And Bonnie filled the bill as the beautiful, powerful woman that they love to put on the cover of business magazines as a paragon of feminine achievement. One of the rags called her 'a role model for a new generation of American businesswomen,' if you can believe that."

As their food was served, Al reviewed some details about Bonnie's current position that were less important, and then started to talk about himself. "I think that I am really starting to get a handle on this job. I can see starting an agency of my own some day."

Al went on trying to impress Dorothy with his accomplishments in the firm. This was the hard part of the lunch. Dorothy's father had already told her that Al was a good worker but "not the sharpest tool in the shed." Dorothy spent the last half hour of their lunch date itemizing the reasons why she couldn't have dinner with Al any time before the end of the decade.

Dorothy insisted on paying the tab, and they finally went their separate ways. The information Al had given her was useful but Dorothy needed something deeper. Philip had worked as a consultant for Miracle, so she conferred with him. Philip went back through his files to look for someone at the company he knew well enough to provide "insider" information. After making a few phone calls, he settled on Neil Eiserman. He called Dorothy at her office with his recommendation.

"Yeah, I think that Neil is ideal. He was a doc on staff years ago at GMH. Then, out of frustration with the medical medical profession, he decided to go to work in the pharmaceutical industry. A lot of people do that when the pressures of practice wear them down. They want a simpler life without the endless nights being on call for emergencies, and without the constant threat of malpractice litigation, even though the starting salaries aren't as good."

166

"I can see why someone in a pressurized practice might try to escape."

"Me too, but what most of them discover is that the drug industry is not that different from practicing medicine and sometimes the pressure is even more intense. They don't realize that they have to conform to production schedules and bring cash-producing drugs to market in a timely way. Since big pharma is multinational, they have to travel a ton and they end up taking even more time away from their families."

"It must be a rude awakening."

"You bet. Many of them move from company to company in search of the perfect work environment. That is what happened to Neil. He spent five years at Miracle in Bonnie's department before taking another job in New York at a smaller firm. I consulted on a few projects for Neil when he was at Miracle and at his new shop in New York. There was a rumor going around that Neil had left Miracle after a big public argument with Bonnie. Maybe his hard feelings will loosen his tongue a bit."

"He sounds perfect. Why don't you contact him to see if he would meet?

Philip agreed. "OK, he should be willing to do it for me."

When Philip reached him, Neil sounded happy to hear from his old friend.

"I kept meaning to call you, Philip, but I just didn't know what to say. What you're going through must be terrible."

Philip's voice was barely audible. "Neil, you have no idea."

"Yeah, we all heard about the malpractice case and the FDA thing. We really miss having you available. How are you holding up?"

"Well, there's a small chance that I can get myself off the hook. I can't go into details, but Moira Hamlin's case may have been a lot more complicated than you can imagine. I have a private investigator attorney, Dorothy Deaver, working with me. She needs information about Bonnie Romano. She married Moira's husband and she was real tight with the family just before Moira died. Would you be willing to have lunch with Dorothy? She is a very nice person. Of course anything you tell her will be strictly confidential."

"I don't know, Philip. Bonnie's very powerful, and the drug

167

Peter Kowey

industry is incestuous. If she ever found out, she would definitely find a way to screw me over. She already hates my guts."

"Neil, I wouldn't ask if I weren't, well, really desperate."

There was a pause as Neil considered his answer. Philip pushed harder. "Neil, I bailed you out a few times, so I'm just asking you to return the favor."

Neil had to admit that Philip was right. On a few occasions, Neil had research results that were difficult to decipher, and Philip had been able to help him prepare the results so that Neil could present them to Miracle management and then to the FDA, for the drug's eventual approval.

"OK, but you have to promise me that I'll be anonymous," he said slowly. "I don't want to meet anywhere near home. Have your PI come up to New York so that there's no chance of bumping into anybody from Miracle."

"No problem. Just tell me where and when, and Dorothy will meet you."

Neil picked a small Japanese restaurant on 45th Street near 6th Avenue. The entrance was easy to miss, a walk-down with a tiny sign. The main dining room was roomy and simply decorated. This was not a tourist trap—more a place frequented by locals who appreciated good Japanese food.

Neil asked Dorothy to meet him there at 11 o'clock on a weekday morning when he knew the place would be empty. He was pleasantly surprised to see such an attractive woman, while Dorothy was amused that Neil looked the academic part. He had the traditional tweed jacket, corduroy pants, button-down blue shirt, and striped military tie that preserved his link to the scientific community. No executive uniform for him. He ordered tea and an assortment of sushi to get them started, and got to the point fairly quickly.

"So what do you want to know about Bonnie Romano?"

Dorothy could sense that Neil wanted to direct the interview, so she elected not to take any notes or to use a tape recorder. She wanted him to feel at ease. She would make some notes later on her train ride back to Philly.

"Well, we already know about her public persona. What we want is any information you have about her private life."

"I really can't tell you a whole lot. Bonnie and I weren't ex-

168

actly bosom buddies. I wasn't in her department so I didn't work with her directly. Ros Wickman was Bonnie's private secretary and a gossip. The story of Bonnie's first marriage got a lot of play in the office."

"I haven't heard much about her first husband."

"I think that she met John Romano when he was a resident at GMH. Philip probably doesn't remember him—he only spent a year there, and then transferred out of the program and finished down at Pennsylvania Hospital in obstetrics. He was pretty good-looking, and his family was loaded. They dated while he finished his training and Bonnie was just a new drug rep."

"I heard she was quite the tart."

"Maybe, but Bonnie apparently really went after John big time. In fact, that was what got him bounced out of GMH. A cleaning woman found the two of them going at it in the on-call room one night, when he was supposed to be taking care of a sick patient in the unit. They warned him, but it just kept going on in closets, empty patient rooms, wherever. Bonnie either really loved the guy or was after his money or both."

"Did Bonnie get into trouble over this?"

"No, somehow she covered it over. Don't ask me how. Anyway, they got married just as he started in practice. The wedding was postponed twice because of haggling over the pre-nups. Ros found out that John, on the advice of his family, had held firm and insisted that in the event of a divorce, Bonnie would only get a million bucks, and would not be entitled to any of his property or other assets. Bonnie was really pissed off about that, but Johnnie's father and uncle were good businessmen and wouldn't let him compromise. There were rumors that they had organized crime connections, but that may have just been gossip."

"Did they have a happy marriage?"

"That depends on who you ask. Bonnie made it look that way. Whenever they were together, she was all smiles, hanging on to him and being affectionate. Ros overheard lots of arguments, mostly about money and Bonnie's wild spending habits. She apparently is not shy about living the high life, and John didn't like it at all. He cut off some of her credit cards, and that really got her going."

"They were only married a short time, right?"

"Yeah, a little over a year, and then he died suddenly. A real shocker."

"Did he have any health problems?"

"Just a few allergies according to Bonnie, but they were controlled with antihistamines. After he died, we heard that he had a couple of female cousins who had died at a young age several years before. One of them had been found at the bottom of a pool. But his father and brothers were fine and didn't have any heart problems."

"How did he die?"

"He apparently came down with a heavy head cold and started coughing. Bonnie told Ros that it had organized into pneumonia and got some antibiotic and decongestant samples to take home to him. He stayed out of work for a couple of days but told his office the day before he died that he was feeling better and that he would be back to work the next day. That night he stayed up to watch Letterman, and Bonnie went to bed. She found him the next morning dead in his chair."

"Did the autopsy show anything?"

"He had clean coronaries and nothing was wrong with his heart or brain. They didn't find any illegal drugs or other substances, just a little alcohol and the antihistamines and antibiotics he was taking."

"What was Bonnie's reaction?"

"How would you react if you just inherited several million dollars and a couple of mansions from a man you were fighting with all of the time? She put up a good appearance, crying at the funeral. I went to the graveside service to show my respect for Bonnie. John's family just kept shooting daggers at her the whole time.

"What was their beef?"

"Since the pre-nup hadn't put any restrictions on what Bonnie would get if John died while they were still married, they couldn't help thinking that Bonnie had something to do with his death. But there was no evidence of foul play or infidelity. I know that the family made some "inquiries", but little came of it. After John's funeral, they had nothing to do with her. There were no grandchildren, so they were just as happy to pretend that she was dead, too. They were really pissed that she got John's share of the family fortune."

"Did Bonnie take a leave of absence from work?"

"For a week or two, and then she came back in a pretty good mood, considering. She didn't waste any time getting rid of John's stuff at their house in Bryn Mawr and at the beach house in Cape May. She had both places redone within a few months. That was when she began to spend a lot more time with the Hamlins. Moira and Bonnie went way back, and I heard the three of them apparently got along real well."

"Anything else you can tell me about Bonnie?"

"No. I haven't seen much of her since I left Miracle. Ros quit a few years ago so I don't have a good information source anymore. I know that Bonnie is a regular on the Main Line social scene. I still live in Narberth, so I see her mug in the Main Line Times all the time. She and her new husband support lots of charitable organizations, but they always have shit-eating grins on their faces, like they have it all over everybody else. In a way, I guess they do. Maybe I'm just jealous."

Neil and Dorothy finished their lunch and were out on 45th Street just as a blast of arctic air made its way into Manhattan. Deciding to forego the 15-block walk to Penn Station to get her train back to Philly, Dorothy hailed a cab. Neil turned in the other direction to walk back to his office.

As they parted, Neil requested Dorothy's personal assurance one more time that nothing he had said would be made public. Dorothy said his information would be highly confidential. Neil had one last thought.

"You know, I could never convince myself that Bonnie was a straight shooter. She always seemed to come at things with an angle that favored her own interests. But she was very clever and played things well. She had a way of manipulating situations and people like chess pieces, and I never saw anybody catch her at her game. I wonder sometimes if anybody ever will."

As she bumped along the crowded streets of Manhattan her taxi, gazing out the window at the brave pedestrians, Dorothy wondered exactly the same thing.

CHAPTER 16

Dorothy spent the next few days synthesizing information. Maybe Hugh had been up to something before Moira's death, but she was a long way from understanding the full story or proving foul play. She called Philip and proposed that they meet for lunch so he could help her with some medical questions. He eagerly agreed and proposed that they meet at Jake's. He was anxious for an update, and a lunch date with an attractive woman was not an ordinary event.

Jake's was one of several excellent restaurants in Manayunk, a rediscovered part of Philadelphia and a good example of successful urban renewal. It had been an industrial community by the river, and an eyesore in the first half of the century. New enterprises including a number of furniture and home remodeling warehouses began cropping up there in the 1970s, and as shoppers entered the area, so did new eateries. The solid brick row homes on the hills leading up from the river were renovated inside and out, and sold to baby boomers who wanted to be close to the next new hot scene.

Manayunk was a Philadelphia success story. As the site of the premier American bicycle race every summer, bikers from around the world challenged the steep hills of the tiny community for a rich purse. For that weekend, Manayunk was the center of the sports world. As he drove from his apartment, Philip imagined that if such a tattered place could make a comeback, maybe a down-and-out doc could do the same.

Philip arrived at the restaurant first and sat at the bar. Typical of spring in Philadelphia, the weather was blustery, and he was chilled after his long walk from the parking lot. He ordered a coffee and nursed it for a few minutes until, through the storefront glass, he saw Dorothy walking across Main Street. He could feel his pulse quicken. Dorothy had a confidence about herself that he found attractive. When she arrived at the bar, they were whisked to a table in a rear corner of the restaurant, where they could have a quiet conversation.

The waitress asked for drink orders, and Philip asked for an iced tea. Dorothy was pleased that he was making good on his promise to abstain from alcohol. He was also beginning to get back to his regular exercise program and was looking better overall.

"You clean up well, Philip," she observed. Philip nearly blushed. Conservative dress meant wearing a tie, so he had difficulty trying to figure out how to dress casually. Dorothy ordered green tea and quickly got down to business.

"We have been lucky so far. A few people were forthcoming, so I got more information than I expected. They corroborated the Flanagan and O'Hara stories pretty well. I think that we can be sure that Hugh and Moira were not getting along well at all before Moira died, and I think that we can conclude Hugh was fooling around."

"With Bonnie?"

"A good bet. One of their maids, Isabelle, was fairly sure that Bonnie's perfume was on Hugh's clothing when he returned from his nights out. Bonnie was in the picture back then and was playing along as one of the Three Musketeers. I think that Moira bought that routine, at least for a while. I am not positive that Moira knew early on that Bonnie was the other woman, but she would have had to be thick as a board not to have known that Hugh was fooling around."

"If that's true, Hugh and Bonnie had the oldest motive known to man to get rid of Moira. But how can we can tie either of them to her death?"

"Don't know yet. Can you explain a little more about Moira's heart condition?"

"It really was simple. Moira was born with an abnormality in her electrical system. The heart activates electrically by the flow of sodium ions into the cardiac cell and then recovers its ability to excite again when potassium ions flow out of the heart. Moira didn't have proper function of her potassium channels, which meant that her cells were not all ready to get re-energized. So when the next impulse arrived, all the cells were sent into chaos, generating a serious rhythm disturbance in the lower heart chambers. In essence, the pump stopped working, and that is a 'cardiac arrest.'"

"Is this a common problem?"

"It depends on whether you are talking about the full-blown problem that kids die with spontaneously, or a milder case like Moira's that is rarely lethal. The first kind is rare, although it might be one of the causes of crib death. The kind of QT problem that Moira had is a lot more common and probably represents a mild version of the same disease that kills young people."

"How do you know it was milder?"

"It all boils down to the QT interval on the EKG. Full-blown cases have a very long QT interval, which means that the potassium channels are really out of whack, and mild cases have a slight prolongation, which is what Moira had."

Philip had to work hard to explain things to lay people. Dorothy suspected that Hugh's assertion that Philip didn't explain issues clearly might be accurate. Dorothy had more questions.

"If people are born with this problem, how is it they can get to be teenagers or adults before the heart arrhythmia develops?"

"We were studying that in my lab. We think that as the heart matures and gets bigger, something happens to the potassium channels that makes the heart go out of rhythm. We just don't know what it is. Like I said, the rhythm may go haywire any time after birth. Some patients don't present with their first rhythm problem until their fifties or sixties."

"You thought Moira's chance of having a problem was low?"

"Her QT interval was only minimally prolonged, and she didn't have anybody else in her family who had died suddenly at a young age without an explanation. Sudden death in relatives would suggest a severe genetic abnormality."

"They criticized you for not ordering genetic testing. Why did you not do that?"

"Moira would have had genetic testing when her children were checked at Children's Hospital. I didn't do it because I knew that they were going to test all of the samples there. You can only interpret somebody's results if you know the family pattern. Besides, I can't think of how it would have influenced my treatment recommendations. It takes a long time to get results and in a lot of cases, they aren't definitive anyway."

"Do you know the genetic pattern in Moira's family?"

"As I suspected, a couple of the kids had a long QT, but the genetic testing did not yield a specific pattern. So she had something wrong with her potassium channels, but it probably was some kind of spontaneous mutation in her family, a piece of bad luck, since no other family members had the same mutation."

"OK, so here's Moira with this problem lying dormant. She comes to see you for palpitations that you thought were innocent. Your learned opinion, and that of your defense expert, is that she should have done fine. So can you think of some way that Hugh and Bonnie could have caused Moira's cardiac arrest or made it more likely to occur?"

"A number of things have been shown to screw up the heart rhythm in patients with this problem, like an adrenalin surge or drugs or electrolyte abnormalities. We've tried to figure out if that can apply to cases like Moira's where the QT interval is a little long but not too bad. We presume that those same factors would be likely to stimulate an arrhythmia in cases like hers, but no one has proven that conclusively. But experiments would be hard to carry out; who wants to be a human guinea pig and be exposed to the chance of dying suddenly for the sake of finding out if a drug can put your heart out of rhythm?"

"Your research board would have a field day with that consent form."

"So, we really don't have a firm idea why the heart becomes susceptible to going out of rhythm. In the end, it may have just been a piece of rotten luck."

The waitress came to the table to take their orders. "What can I get for you and your wife?"

Philip blushed, and Dorothy didn't rush to correct the mistake. They both ordered the specialty of the house, Cobb salads.

Dorothy waited until the waitress left. "Hugh was giving Moira a hard time about her weight and her diet. It kept coming up in the interviews."

Philip nodded. "Hugh knew Moira had an eating disorder, probably bulimia. She mentioned to me during her initial visit that she had a weight problem in college but that she had recovered."

"People I talked to said Hugh tormented her about her weight."

"Patients with eating disorders have a distorted body image and when anybody, especially a spouse, tells them they are fat, they can relapse into old eating patterns."

"I knew a lot of girls who had eating problems in college, but I thought people outgrow it."

"Sometimes people get better in their twenties and thirties, but they still have the body image problem. It isn't hard for them to fall back into the same old routine of binge and purge."

"So, do you think any of this weight thing could have killed her?" Dorothy asked.

"In extreme cases, like the liquid protein diet, people clearly had bad rhythms because of the metabolic problems the diets caused. But we don't have any indication that Moira was using any of that stuff. It would be a real stretch to conclude that her eating behavior caused her heart to go nuts. An electrolyte problem could have been a contributing factor, but not the root cause."

Dorothy couldn't help being a little disappointed. She had been hoping that the diet thing would unlock the case. "So it sounds like we have to keep digging?"

"I'm afraid so. If Hugh and Bonnie conspired to get rid of Moira, they did one hell of a job of hiding how they did it. Maybe Moira was frightened or angry when she keeled over at home? Hugh said that she was sitting quietly, breastfeeding the baby when she collapsed."

"Didn't you tell me something about loud music at the house that morning?"

"Yeah, the ambulance crew said that the radio was blaring during the 911 call. I don't know if the radio alarm went off or what. I did go back and double-check the blood work that was done when Moira came into the ER. We were so concerned that a drug had precipitated the arrest that we ran a comprehensive screen. The only thing we found was alfenodine, the antihistamine I prescribed for her."

"And that drug is safe in patients with the long QT?"

"You bet. After all that happened with earlier generation antihistamines like Delcane, the FDA was taking no chances. Every new drug, especially antihistamines and antibiotics that are used on a wide scale, has strict testing to prove that it won't prolong the QT interval before it can be put on the market. Alfenodine was whistle clean. There was nothing unusual in its safety evaluation."

"OK, we obviously have to work harder on the method," Dorothy concluded "The good news is that the motive side is building very nicely."

"What's the latest there?"

"Well, I was able to prevail on an old law school friend, Betsy Childress, who works in the firm that handles the Hamlin family affairs. I got her to take a look at Hugh and Moira's pre-nuptial agreement. Copying was out of the question—her firm now keeps track of document copying to prevent confidentiality problems. But she was able to give me a few interesting details. The agreement was just the opposite of John and Bonnie's. Remember that his family sat on him about giving her too much in the agreement in the event of a divorce? Well, in Moira and Hugh's case, he went overboard. Men do think with their members sometimes."

Philip laughed nervously, and Dorothy noticed his embarrassment. She wondered if he was thinking about their one-night stand. She plowed on. "In essence, Hugh agreed to surrender half of his estate to Moira should they divorce for any reason, and he also agreed that he would not contest her having custody of their children if she wanted to keep them."

"Holy mackerel," Philip exclaimed. "He really gave away the ranch, didn't he?"

"You can say that again. My friend said that there were disclaimers in the file by the attorney handling the agreement so there would be no question of whose idea it was to make the agreement so lopsided. If there were ever a divorce, he didn't want to get his ass sued for legal malpractice. The notes also indicated that Hugh's father went postal when he heard about the pre-nup and tried to get Hugh to change his mind. Hugh wouldn't hear of it."

"Amazing. When Hugh falls for a woman, he doesn't go halfway."

Dorothy nodded. "Happens to some women, too." She wondered if Philip recognized the irony of that statement.

"So that means if Moira had called it quits, even if she was screwing around or just got tired of Hugh, she would've walked away with millions, some nice digs, and the kids to boot?"

"Yep, that about sums it up," Dorothy agreed.

"A pretty powerful motive for offing her."

"I also asked my friend Betsy to do the usual life insurance search. Hugh did take out a fairly large policy on Moira's life, worth a couple of mil and purchased shortly after they were married. It would be hard to argue that he killed her for the policy since he was worth about ten times the payout even without Bonnie's money, but it was icing on the cake."

As their food was delivered, Philip thought of another question. "Speaking of Bonnie, how does she fit into the picture at this point?"

"There is the obvious motive of wanting Hugh all to herself, though God only knows why. But you know, her first husband's death bothers me. John was apparently a healthy person who went to sleep and didn't wake up. At some point, I am going to have to talk to his family. If there was foul play in Moira's death, no way was Hugh the mastermind. It had to be Bonnie who put it all together and talked Hugh into it. She has a shark-like personality, and of course the professional background."

"You mean the pharmaceutical business?"

"Yeah, it's hard for me to believe that she wouldn't have fallen back on her knowledge base to get what she wanted. So you, Philip, have a homework assignment."

"Yes?"

"Research everything you can about the drugs that Moira received before she died to see if there is anything you forgot or someone else prescribed. When I talk to John's family, I'll get a copy of his medical records to see how that fits into this."

"So as you said, we do have a lot more digging to do." Philip sounded resigned.

Dorothy nodded. "Yeah, we're just getting started. All we have so far is a manipulative bitch, a fat, stupid husband, a dead woman, and a dead man who, as far as the authorities are concerned, died of natural causes. Pretty pitiful for a murder case, wouldn't you say, Sherlock?"

Philip nodded. He understood Dorothy's point and his downhearted expression prompted a Dorothy pep talk

"Look, you hate Hugh Hamlin," Dorothy continued, "and I understand why. He sued you, you didn't deserve it, and it ruined your life. You're angry, and you want to get back at him. That's all understandable. But you can't drive a square peg into a round hole. You can't force a case of murder if it isn't there. You have to remain as objective as if you were doing a scientific experiment. You have to be dedicated to knowing the truth, not proving your pre-conceived notions. If you let yourself get biased, you'll fail. And not only will you fail, but you will place yourself, and me, in jeopardy of being attacked for making false accusations, and then Hugh and Bonnie will have an even larger victory. Do you understand that?"

"I guess I do."

"You'd better keep these things firmly in your mind, Philip. We can't let anybody into this except our sources, and even then we have to be sure that we give them no reason or opportunity to rat us out. You must talk to no one about this and only do those things I specifically tell you to do. I don't want you going off on your own and playing the sleuth."

Philip knew that Dorothy was right. He needed a stern lecture but at the same time was grateful for a positive spin.

"Look, the case is shaping up pretty well," Dorothy went on. Consider where we started. Just be patient, and it might fall into place. The key will be getting Hugh and Bonnie to spill the beans. How we do that I can't fathom at this point, but they're arrogant and confident that they got away with murder. It's that kind of attitude that brings people like them down in the end."

"OK, you're right," Philip admitted. "I'll start my homework project first thing tomorrow."

Philip's face brightened as he looked at his watch. "But it is already two o'clock, and I think that we've earned some R and R. What do you say we take a stroll down Main Street to the Cineplex, catch a movie, and then have supper at that new Chinese restaurant on Green Lane?"

Dorothy shook her head. "Philip, I thought that we had an understanding. Keep this professional with no personal stuff. I'm not going to let it happen to me again."

"You're right. I just wanted to do something fun with someone I like."

Dorothy hesitated, obviously weighing the risks of saying yes and getting caught up in another difficult romantic situation. "Well. I'll accept on three conditions."

"Name them."

"One, I get to pick the movie; two, no more talk about the case; and three, at the end of the evening, we go our separate ways."

"All are acceptable to the gentleman."

They left Jake's and took a leisurely walk down Main Street. The afternoon was cold, but an occasional softer breeze reminded them that spring was on its way. At first, Philip had a hard time keeping off the forbidden topic, but as the afternoon and evening went on, conversation flowed. They were surprised by the number of things they had in common, despite diverse backgrounds. Philip was clearly suffering from his estrangement from his wife and children, and Dorothy's quiet understanding was soothing.

"Are you visiting the kids?"

"Yeah, but I really can't bring them back to my rat hole of an apartment, and they get tired of being out all day. They also miss their usual playmates."

"Why don't you bring them to my place some time? I love kids, and it would be fun to have dinner and watch a movie or play video games with them."

Philip was pleasantly surprised by Dorothy's offer. He worried how his kids would react to another woman, but he was desperate for some quality time with them. "That would be super. I'll definitely take you up on it."

Dorothy settled on a mindless Adam Sandler comedy, and the film was a perfect escape. They shared popcorn and laughed for a couple hours before a Chinese dinner, for which Dorothy insisted on paying.

After supper, Philip walked Dorothy to her car. He was grateful that he wasn't taking her home. Separate cars made it easier to keep his promise about ending the evening. He didn't think that either of them was ready to be intimate, but there had been an obvious change in the way they related to each other that afternoon.

They spent some time saying good night and making plans for their next meeting to discuss the case. When he moved close to kiss her good night, she didn't balk or back away. The kiss was short but intense. Dorothy had a hard time croaking out "good night" as she opened her car door. Stunned and speechless, Philip remained planted in the street as she drove away into the misty evening. Yes, things were getting interesting indeed.

CHAPTER 17

Philip's library about the long QT syndrome was extensive, but he also had years of experience. As he sat at his dilapidated kitchen table with a pile of articles and Moira's hospital records, he went through them page by page, searching for anything that might explain her arrhythmia. Her potassium and magnesium levels had been very low in the ER. Now, it seemed likely that Moira's electrolyte abnormality had been self-imposed. If she had been using laxatives and purging after she ate, those numbers would have been low. A lack of minerals made cardiac membranes highly unstable.

He reasoned that if Hugh was goading Moira into an inappropriate diet, he had to be doing it with Bonnie's instruction, and knowledge that a low mineral level might be contributory, but would not jeopardize Moira's life.

That left the drug question. Bonnie's company, Miracle Pharmaceuticals, manufactured alfenodine, marketed under the trade name of Appel. It was a non-sedating, once-a-day antihistamine that had captured over half of the "runny nose" market with direct-to-consumer advertising. Patients asked for it by name, and since doctors viewed antihistamines as interchangeable, they were inclined not to argue. The marketing success of Appel was even more remarkable since its predecessor, Delcane, had been a disaster.

Seasonal allergies are a nuisance. People simply don't like the sneezy-coughing-watery eyes thing, so like many other companies, Miracle marketed a number of antihistamines in the 1960s and 1970s, including Delcane, a drug with a complicated regulatory history.

The head of the FDA section that reviewed Delcane was Red Lomansky. Everybody, even the FDA Commissioner, called him Red, and nobody remembered his real name. Red was a legend in regulatory medicine. He dressed sloppily, drove a beat-up car, smoked and drank heavily, and was brutally frank at every meeting, whether a CEO or a Senator was at the other end of the table. Everyone excused his eccentricity because he was a brilliant physician and scientist.

At a relatively young age, Red had been put in control of the drug review division and held that job for three decades. During his tenure, several new drugs with cardiac safety issues had been reviewed, including Delcane. Red had retired and was now in the consulting business. Maybe there was something relevant about Delcane that Red might be able to tell Philip. It was worth a phone call.

"Good to hear from you, Philip. I heard that you got nailed by the yo-yo's down here." Red lived in the D.C. area but made it a point never to visit the agency. "I have a lot of bad memories of the people in patient protection. They think everybody is the bad guy until proven otherwise."

"I know. I trust you are enjoying life after the FDA?"

"Yes and no. I miss the control, but I get paid a lot more for doing pretty much the same thing for the other side."

Red had been one of the most powerful people in American medicine, controlling the approval of hundreds of drugs, including almost anything that had the potential for cardiac side effects. Now he consulted for drug companies that were trying to get drugs approved.

"I am sure you don't miss the pressure."

"Actually, some of it was fun. In the old days when I first got to the agency, it was possible to get a drug approved even if there was a safety concern as long as the sponsoring company could prove the stuff worked. By the time I left, the whole picture had changed. Now companies have to prove that their drugs aren't going to hurt anybody, especially if they treat a life-threatening condition. It's pretty nuts."

"Well, that's sort of why I called you. I want to get your perspective on the cardiac safety of Delcane and what you guys found out about its tendency to cause rhythm problems."

"That was quite a story. Why do you want to know about Del-cane? It's ancient history."

Philip had to think of a plausible excuse on the spot. "I am writing a review article for the Annals of Internal Medicine about cardiac safety, and I have a section on antihistamines. Just wanted to make sure I had it right."

The answer seemed to satisfy Red. "I remember how badly Miracle wanted that stuff to go over-the-counter. They pushed like hell to get us to agree. That's when the shit hit the fan."

"But the drug had been approved for prescription use long before that, right?"

"Yeah, the market for antihistamines back then was good, but not terrific because the early antihistamines caused sedation. So, unless you were bothered by allergies or had a truly serious case, you put up with the symptoms. Drug companies knew if an antihistamine didn't cause sedation, it could make billions. It took their chemists years to come up with candidate compounds. Many never got out of the animal labs, and a few of them didn't work on people. Finally, Delcane made it through to late-stage development.

"I understand that Miracle got their drug approved initially based on some fairly flimsy efficacy data?"

"Yeah. Back then, all you had to show was that the drug dried out the nose and kept tissue counts down compared to a placebo, and that's pretty much what they did. Delcane sailed through its approval process without a problem.

"It was an immediate hit with doctors who were impressed with the company's propaganda about how sedation induced by conventional antihistamines caused automobile accidents and work-related injuries. Sounded like a bunch of bullshit to me."

"Why?"

"Because they didn't have any data to prove it, but still, they were allowed to claim it in their advertising. And even though Delcane cost more than older agents, like Benadryl, patients were willing to pay to get rid of their stuffy noses without feeling drugged. Sales went nuts, and the company raked it in. In its second year on the market, Delcane became a billion-dollar drug with expectations that it would hit five billion dollars in four years.

"So what happened?"

Peter Kowey

"I guess you can say it was greed. In the clinical trials, Delcane's adverse effects were rare and not serious. In fact, just as many placebo-treated patients had side effects. So the company applied to sell the drug 'over the counter' and without a prescription."

"And that is where they hit the wall?"

"When Miracle first came to the allergy division with the idea, the reaction was cautious but positive. But as part of due diligence, the division reviewed all the serious adverse effects reported to them by physicians and pharmacists or by the public since the drug was approved."

"I thought that the system for adverse effect reporting was not so good."

"Well, it actually is a pretty good way to track serious safety issues after FDA approval. Some problems are pretty rare and may only be detected after millions of patient exposures, compared to the few hundred patients studied in pre-marketing clinical trials."

"But most doctors don't bother to file reports when they observe bad outcomes with drugs."

"Right, and so the system underestimates the incidence of drug complications. In this case, it didn't matter. When the allergy guys pulled the reports on Delcane, they saw a number of deaths. In almost all cases, the victims had either overdosed on the drug or had been taking anti-fungal agents at the same time, mostly ketoconazole."

Philip knew about this drug interaction. "So they had to suspect that the drug's metabolism was being interefered with by ketoconazole."

"Yep, they reviewed the original pharmacology studies, and, sure enough, they found that Delcane was metabolized in the liver by an enzyme system that was inhibited by ketoconazole. So taking both drugs together could cause extreme concentrations of Delcane in the blood, just like in a suicide case. They worried that Delcane at high levels might be inducing cardiac rhythm abnormalities, especially since most of the deaths had been sudden."

"Suggesting that the heart had gone out of rhythm abruptly?"

"Right. The agency sent a letter to the company outlining their concerns. They wanted the company to come up with some answers before the OTC application could go further."

184

"What was Miracle's response?"

"Oh, they didn't take it too seriously. They thought that the FDA was just being alarmist, and that they would eventually be able to prove that the deaths were coincidental and not really caused by the drug. A pretty amazing attitude when you figure that they had billions of dollars at risk. They kicked it around internally and dragged their feet. They had some woman there, I forget her name, who was the director of the team at that time. She wasn't responsive at all—just really obnoxious."

"Was it Bonnie Romano, by any chance?"

"That sounds familiar. Anyhow, the allergy guys were fairly sure she told her staff to slow down the OTC application and to let things cool off. They probably figured that as time went by, things would straighten out and that the FDA would drop the whole thing. They might lose the OTC claim, but at least the prescription business would be spared."

"But it didn't work out that way, right?"

"No, it didn't. The whole thing might have gotten buried had it not been for Jason Wemblay."

Philip knew Jason Wemblay and had worked with him in the past. He was an MD/PhD at the University of Virginia who specialized in the cardiac electrical effects of drugs and frequently worked with the FDA. The Delcane project was right up his alley. Wemblay put together a series of cases that he gathered from his colleagues at other institutions and published the results in the New England Journal of Medicine, proving that Delcane, in high concentrations, prolonged the QT interval. He concluded that the deaths that had occurred in previously healthy people were caused by an associated lower chamber arrhythmia.

Red continued his recounting. "That article came out just as the agency was looking at the Delcane data, so it went off like a bomb. Because Delcane was Miracle's highest revenue drug, the whole company was on the ropes."

"Panic at big Pharma?"

"You could say that. They decided to bring in a panel of consultants to address the issues and to advise the company on what their best course of action might be. We eventually got a copy of the minutes of that meeting—I guess we were supposed to be impressed.

"At the meeting, they told the consultants what they knew

185

about Delcane's cardiac effects, which was pitifully little more than what the FDA and Wemblay had come up with. At the end, the majority opinion was that Delcane was responsible for a few deaths and that the likely mechanism was prolongation of the QT interval and resultant ventricular arrhythmia. The good news for the company was that all the experts believed that the drug itself was safe unless given in suicide doses or combined with a drug like ketoconazole that blocked its metabolism."

"So now it was time for damage control?"

"For sure. The first thing they did was try to keep the drug on the market. By this time, I was involved. I told them that they were going to get a black- box warning in the product labeling that would advise docs in pretty explicit language about the effects of too much drug. Everybody agreed with this plan, and a letter was wired to all doctors with the new information."

"I got that letter."

"Unfortunately, docs either don't read warning letters or forget what they said. In fact, we continued to monitor for adverse effects for the next several months, and the sudden death reports continued. We also pulled Medicare prescribing records and found out that the simultaneous use of Delcane and ketoconazole actually went up after the 'Dear Doctor' letters had gone out."

"What was the company's response?"

"Much different. They knew that they had a real product liability problem on their hands. It was becoming clear that Delcane's days were numbered. Even worse, their competitors were marketing the older antihistamines as a 'safe alternative' to Delcane."

"The company must have gone berserk!"

"Not really. I think they had anticipated the worst. Back when the safety reports started coming in, the leadership had called in the formulation chemists and told them to get busy looking at the chemical cousins of Delcane to find a safer alternative that still had non-sedating properties.

"The head of the formulation team had a brilliant but simple idea. If Delcane was changed in the liver to a similar compound, why not find out if it had the same antihistamine effect as the parent drug, Delcane, without cardiac toxicity? The principal liver product of Delcane was alfenodine. It had been formulated years before and patented along with Delcane. To the company's delight, alfenodine was just as potent as Delcane, but even in massive concentrations, it had no effect on the QT interval or any other cardiac parameter."

Philip listened intently. "The company jumped on that idea."

"They expedited the clinical trials of alfenodine, making sure to feature a very comprehensive cardiac safety package, so by the time Delcane was on its deathbed, they were ready to send the new drug application in.

"The allergy guys at the FDA already had egg on their faces from Delcane's approval, and they were anxious to get the whole thing behind them. They put the new drug through an expedited review, and despite intense scrutiny over those six months, alfenodine came up as clean as a whistle."

"I remember seeing a news conference that Miracle put on to announce the new drug's release and the withdrawal of Delcane."

"They made a big splash and made it look like public safety was their main concern in drug development. A load of crap, but it sold on CNN."

"Quite a story, Red. This will really help me with my paper."

"No problem. Most of this is on the public record, so I didn't give any confidential information away."

They said their goodbyes, promising to keep in touch. "I hope that we can work together again sometime, Philip."

"I hope so too, Red."

After he hung up, Philip sat deep in thought. Bonnie had obviously pulled off a real coup for her company. She had been able to announce that Delcane would be replaced on the doctors' shelves by the much safer drug Appel. She explained to the press that the new drug had been extensively tested and that it was "absolutely safe as well as terribly effective."

Appel went on to have an ultra clean record, with no cases of death, even with overdose. It had been a remarkable industry save and earned Bonnie the admiration of her company, as well as the respect of her competitors, not to mention a few more promotions.

Appel was the drug that Philip had prescribed for Moira. He had given it to dozens of patients with the long QT syndrome who also had bad allergies, and it had worked well every time. Although Philip measured the QT interval compulsively at every patient visit, he never saw a problem. He pulled all of Moira's EKGs. Her QT interval measurements on Appel in the office were not different from what they had been before she started taking it.

Philip sat for hours trying to understand how Moira had a drug-related cardiac arrest if she was only taking Appel. He reclined on his Salvation Army sofa, closed his eyes, and nodded off for a few seconds. Suddenly it came to him, almost like a bolt of lightning that jarred him awake.

He rolled the thought around in his mind for a few minutes, and then got out of bed and started scribbling notes, addressing every aspect of his new theory. At first it seemed almost ridiculous, but as he continued to ponder the idea he realized he wasn't going to be able to dismiss it.

Suddenly, he stopped writing and stared at the empty wall for a long time as he considered his idea and what it might take to verify it. He reached for the telephone. He needed to talk to Dorothy right away.

CHAPTER 18

Dorothy sat at her cluttered office desk and listened carefully to Philip on the phone. Though a little far-fetched, his idea could not be dismissed. He wanted to hack into the records of Gladwyne Pharmacy where Moira and Hugh had their prescriptions filled. "Jesus, Philip, that sounds radical. Don't you have that information in the charts?"

"All I have is information for the last two or three years of Moira's life. And I don't know what Moira was actually taking, just what I prescribed."

"What about other doctors' records? You have most of her hospital records from the lawsuit don't you?"

"I looked hard, believe me. I don't have the medication information from the doctors' offices. I guess they didn't copy everything or the lawyers didn't think it was relevant. Some doctors' offices don't keep good records. Notes are often handwritten and unreadable. I don't have the stuff that was locked down tight when the lawsuit was filed, and doctors don't keep the real old stuff. It's either archived somewhere or destroyed. Anyway, even if I had those records we'd have the same problem. The docs only know what they prescribe, not what the patients take."

"Philip, you are talking about a federal offense. Everybody is concerned with the confidentiality of medical information, even for dead people. Health care providers, including pharmacies, have put in extra security to protect patient data. I don't have the expertise to hack into those systems, and even if I did, I wouldn't do it. It's too risky."

"Look, I wouldn't be asking if it weren't critical. There's no other way."

"I understand the dilemma, but if they catch you, I would be disbarred and we could both be prosecuted. Given your recent track record, there would be no mercy."

During the ensuing silence, Dorothy sensed that Philip was going to proceed with or without her help.

"OK, let me think about this some more, and I'll bounce it off my dad. Why don't you come to my place this evening, say about eight o'clock? Bring a pizza, I'll get some beer, and we'll discuss it further."

Philip was pleased for several reasons.

After Dorothy hung up, she weighed the pros and cons. She needed advice, and she knew that her dad would put her on the right course.

Dick Deaver had enlisted in the Marines after high school and had served in Vietnam for a few months before getting shot in the leg in a firefight. After his return to the States and a medical discharge at 18, he got swept up in the anti-war movement. During an odyssey of protests around the country, he supported himself with insignificant odd jobs.

As much as he resented the government, he used the GI Bill to pay for college. When asked why he picked Temple University, he quipped that the ghetto surrounding the campus reminded him of the bombed-out villages of Viet Nam and that his Marine training came in handy with his commute.

Dick did well in college, even though he rarely studied. He was more interested in student government and being a gadfly. He scored high enough on the LSAT to get into Penn law school, but after a month he quit in disgust. His excuse was, "I can't work in a system that is more interested in preserving a stupid set of rules than protecting clients' rights."

He took a job in a sandwich joint in the Frankford section, making Philly-style hoagies. Lively debate with customers about national news was just about the only thing he liked about the job.

One afternoon he got into a heated conversation with one of the regulars who also happened to be a private detective. They argued about a rape case that had just been heard in Municipal Court. The case hinged on the admissibility of evidence obtained during a questionable search of the defendant's car. As usual, Dick had a strong opinion.

"The pigs had no right to open the trunk. I don't give a shit if the search came up with bloodstained clothing that the driver couldn't explain. The arrest, conviction, and the death sentence all came from an illegal search. That's wrong."

The private detective disagreed. "The court said that there was sufficient rationale to search the car because they thought the perpetrator had drugs. It didn't matter that they didn't find drugs; they found something more important — the victim's friggin' underwear. What the hell else do you need?"

The spirited argument went on for so long that the shop's owner told Dick he had enough of his loud mouth. "Just clear the hell out and don't come back."

The gumshoe felt responsible and waited for Dick outside. "Look man, I was just having some fun in there. I feel real bad about your getting fired."

Dick was dismissive. "That's OK; the job sucked anyway."

"Well, maybe I can make it up to you. There's a vacancy in my office. It ain't much, but I bet that it will pay more than you were making here and the hours are likely to be better."

"What's the gig?"

"Gofer. You know, get the mail, run messages, filing, stuff like that. Not hard, but you'll get to see how the business operates. Who knows, you might like it."

Dick took the job and proved to be a quick study. Within a couple of years, he was licensed, conducting his own cases, soliciting new business, and opening new offices in the suburbs. When the owner died a few years later, Dick bought out the widow. Now he made a really good living and thoroughly enjoyed his work. He frequently told people that dropping out of Penn saved his sanity.

While doing a background check on a doctor who allegedly examined sedated female patients using body parts other than his hands, Dick met the girl of his dreams. Janey was the doctor's receptionist and actually was the whistleblower.

Dick fell hard the moment he saw her. After a brief courtship and a small wedding, Janey got pregnant on their honeymoon. But their ecstasy was brief. Within months of Dorothy's birth, Janey started losing weight and was diagnosed with metastatic breast cancer.

Dick never recovered from Janey's ugly death, but dedicated his life to his little girl. The spitting image of her mother, Dorothy was the only person Dick allowed into his heart. The two had a tight relationship, and Dorothy even worked for him for a while after college. But she quickly became disillusioned with the work and ironically headed off to law school.

Dorothy and Dick met regularly for lunch in downtown Philadelphia. So when Dorothy called to suggest a lunch date for that afternoon, Dick was delighted.

"Let's meet at the Ritz Carlton, across from City Hall. I'm testifying in a crappy case, and could really use some time out with my little girl."

They met in the cavernous lobby. He walked briskly past the doorman, looking fit in a well-tailored pinstripe suit and bright orange silk tie. A bushy moustache matched his thick gray brown hair. He gave Dorothy a bear hug and peck and directed her toward the lobby restaurant.

Dorothy expected her Dad to tell her about his case. After beverage orders, Dick gave her his impression of the defendant. "The shithead was caught in the act and ought to take his medicine. It really pisses me off that he's pretending his partners are screwing him."

Dorothy knew her father had to get it out of his system. And his "colorful" language, which was always directed elsewhere, didn't faze her at all. "Dad, why don't you back up and tell me what this person was caught doing?"

"My firm was hired to conduct surveillance on the senior partner of an architectural firm. The other partners suspected he had been bleeding money out of the corporate accounts, and they wanted me to find out why he needed extra cash.

"Sure enough, my guys observed the mark making frequent midday visits to a condominium building in Rittenhouse Square, just down the street from our offices. Not exactly the low-rent district. Anyhow, our surveillance spotted him taking strolls in the square with a woman about half his age, and definitely not his wife. She had gams that ran up to her ears and major cleavage to match. It didn't take an Einstein to figure out what was going on.

"So I called this guy's partners and had a little show and tell with my digital prints. I also reviewed his 'creative financing.' The fling was pretty damn costly. They were pissed off, but didn't press criminal charges because they felt pity for the old fool. But they did bring a civil suit to recover the money he embezzled. And they wanted him out of the firm permanently."

"Sounds reasonable."

"You bet it does. But you know what the guy does? The schmuck puts up a fight! So your dear old dad is in court, on a very nice day I might add, as they are trying to figure out how much the moron is going to cough up."

"Yeah, that's frustrating but you aren't doing it for nothing."

"No, the idiot is going to end up paying my bill, too."

After her father settled down, Dorothy got to the point. "Dad, it's my turn. I need your advice about a case."

"Happy to help. Do I get paid for this or is it pro bono?" he teased.

Dorothy laughed. "No, Dad, I will be happy to retain you at your normal rate."

Then, Dorothy described Philip's situation in detail as they ate their salads. By the time the entrée arrived, Dick understood the issues.

"You can't help this guy, Dorothy. The new legislation about keeping medical records confidential is serious business. They put real teeth in the law. You could easily get disbarred, and maybe do some time, even if all you did was give this poor soul advice."

Dorothy lowered her eyes and nodded. It was what she expected to hear.

"But why do I think you are not giving me the whole deal here? What aren't you telling me?" Dick asked. When she couldn't hold his gaze, the light went on. "Aw shit, Dorothy, are you involved with this guy?"

Dorothy blushed.

Dick slammed his fist on the table. "Damn it, Dorothy, you should know better! He's your client, for Christ's sake. You lose your judgment, and you lose everything."

Whether she chose not to react, or was simply in a different place, Dorothy seemed to be focusing on a delicate white piece of Dover sole sprinkled with tiny bits of parsley. Dick grinned inwardly as he stared at the porcelain face that was the mirror image of her mother.

The poignant moment was fleeting, and when Dorothy spoke, her tone was a soft, almost reflective murmur.

"I can't explain it. He isn't particularly good looking, and when he was on top, he was clueless and self-centered. But he seems different now, sweeter and more caring. He needs to find out what happened to this patient before he can move on with his life, and I am his only hope. What am I supposed to do?"

Dick could sense her inner torture. Truth be told, he had a similar problem when he met Janey. "If you can't back away from the case, I guess I'm going to have to help."

"How?"

"There are some independent computer hackers we can access. Some of them are pretty greedy and will do crazy stuff. They all work under the table since most of what they do is illegal. You have to realize that almost anything they get for us isn't usable in court, but maybe it will help your boyfriend."

Dick scribbled a number on a notepad. "Have him call this cell number in Torresdale and tell them what he needs. Make it clear to him that if he is ever questioned about this, he found the name on a bathroom wall, right?"

"Absolutely."

"I will make sure that his contact expects the call. She is a good egg and hopefully won't let this get back to us. Just make sure that your buddy boy knows he is taking a huge risk and if he is caught, he has to go down solo. Can you trust him to do that?"

"I think so, Dad."

"Look, little girl, when the feds put on the squeeze, there are few real heroes. If this is a not a stand-up guy, we'll both be in hot water."

They finished lunch and said goodbye on Broad Street. Dorothy processed the conversation on her way back to the office. Her father had decided to help against his better judgment, and she could never let him regret it.

Philip splurged and picked up a fancy pie at Peace of Pizza for their meeting, then, on a whim, added a bright bouquet of flowers to the equation. Since their one-night stand years before, Dorothy had moved to Rosemont, a pleasant community in the heart of the Main Line. Her building was 1960s vintage, with small balconies, inner courtyards, and fireplaces.

The apartment was charmingly decorated with lots of dark wood and comfortable furniture. Philip arrived at the crack of eight, nervous as a tick but looking relaxed in sweater, jeans, and loafers, matching what Dorothy had chosen for the evening.

Dorothy was obviously surprised and pleased by the flowers. "Philip, you didn't need to do that."

"It's the least I could do. Your apartment looks great." He noticed that she'd lighted some expensive French scented candles.

"How about a cold beer?" she asked, as she hung up his coat.

"That would be perfect."

They sat on the sofa and before the crackling fire dove into the pizza. Between bites, each recapped the day. "I spent the morning reading EKGs at the Phase one unit and supervising a clinical trial. I have to tell you what happened. It'll crack you up."

Dorothy was only remotely interested but pleased that Philip was actually engaged in his work and feeling better about himself. A positive development.

"The study is evaluating a drug for erectile dysfunction. This trial is supposed to look at the cardiac effects of the drug because old guys with cardiac disease will take it and might get into trouble. The company had a few clues that the drug might affect the cardiac electrical system and cause arrhythmias. Judging from the EKGs at the center, the likelihood of a serious problem is probably remote. But in this study, the normal male volunteers are going to get big doses to exclude an effect on the heart by looking at their electrocardiograms and blood pressures. It is something that the FDA wants to know."

"Gee," said Dorothy, "isn't that dangerous?"

"It could be, but that is why the study is being carried out in a special unit with a lot of medical personnel around to watch the subjects."

"I bet they enjoy the attention."

"You can say that again. The drug is meant to arouse the subject to have an erection but only when stimulated sexually. The volunteers all signed consent forms that stated this clearly, so they knew what to expect."

Dorothy started chuckling, "I bet I know what you are going to tell me."

"Well, these guys decided that they had a duty to not only be guinea pigs for the cardiac stuff, but also to see if the drug worked. They had a field day with the nurses on the unit, chasing them around with their you-know-whats poking through their pajamas, asking to be evaluated to make sure that the drug was 'having its correct effect.'"

By now, Dorothy was laughing uncontrollably while Philip enjoyed playing the entertainer. "They were making a big joke out of the thing and really pissing off the staff. The idiots didn't remember the fact that half of them had gotten a placebo. Anyhow, it was hard to get the blood draws and the EKGs done with all the mayhem."

Pleased that Dorothy enjoyed the story, he went on, "But, I digress. How was your day?"

"Pardon the pun, but it was not nearly as 'stimulating,'" she shot back. "I had lunch with my father, then took a deposition in the medical malpractice case that I am defending. This one is really sad, Philip. A relatively young woman with chest pain went to an ER. She was only there for about 15 minutes before she had a cardiac arrest."

"Uh-oh!"

"They called a cardiologist to the ER in the middle of the code, and the poor guy did everything he could think of to help, but she didn't make it. So he got sued, and I'm defending him."

"Sounds disturbingly familiar," Philip observed.

"The plaintiff's attorney is a real horse's ass and brought in an all-purpose expert who started testifying to the standard of care of every doc in the case, including my guy. This jerk isn't even a cardiologist, so I had to say objection about a million times to make sure that it was on the record for the judge to look at later. Hopefully, I can get the expert disqualified.

"In the meantime, the deposition was supposed to take two hours and lasted four. The plaintiff's attorney kept having sidebars with his expert. The principal defense attorney who was taking the deposition had a sappy grin on his face because he knew his clock was running. I am telling you, Philip, the system is broken."

"Nothing definitive is going to happen as long as the trial lawyers contribute as much as they do to the legislators, who by the way are lawyers too."

"At some point, the public is going to have to rise up and scream bloody murder about not being able to get the care they need after all the docs leave."

Philip agreed and was warming to the conversation as he always did when this subject was discussed. "There are already doctor shortages. People up north can't find general practitioners or obstetricians, and around here you better not get a head injury on a weekend because a neurosurgeon is nowhere to be found."

"There is no question that the malpractice situation has driven doctors out of the state, and malpractice insurance premiums are off the wall."

"It was a real problem when I tried to recruit young docs at GMH. No matter how many incentives we provided, I was successful only when the candidate had some other reason, like family ties, to want to live in the Philadelphia area. Otherwise, they went where incomes are higher and threat of malpractice lower."

They took their plates into the small white kitchen and opened second beers before heading back to the living room sofa. Dorothy added a log to the fire and decided to broach the topic of the evening.

"Philip, I have given your idea a lot of thought and then reviewed it with my father. I know you need this information to prove your case. Are you certain you have really exhausted all other ways of getting it? What you're asking is dangerous."

At this, Philip was immediately agitated and his answer edgy. "Dorothy, I have racked my brain, but I just can't come up with anything else. I know it's a risk, but I can't live my life like this. My family is gone, I lost my job, and my reputation is shit. I have to prove that I am not responsible for Moira's death. That's all there is to it. My instincts tell me she didn't die naturally. I can't sit on the sidelines and let somebody get away with murder."

Dorothy wasn't surprised by Philip's emotional outburst. She desperately wanted to allay his anxiety but also wanted to be clear in her response. "All right, I understand, but I can't be involved. If you decide to go ahead, you are on your own."

Angry and powerless he blurted, "Well why don't you just tell me what I can do?"

"My father suggested that you use an anonymous computer hacker. Some of his clients have chosen that route in the past. Unfortunately, most of the hackers are scum and will flip over on you if they are caught. As you will see, they put you through some paces to contact them and then do everything they can to hide their identity so you can't finger them if you get caught.

"My father gave me a contact, but he doesn't know the person you would be working with. And if by some chance you are

197

caught, you didn't get any information from me or from my father. Engaging in this could result in more litigation and/or serious prison time. If they ever found out, the Hamlins would happily crucify you."

Philip appeared unfazed by her dire warnings. "Dorothy, I'm desperate. Like I said, my life is already ruined, so I don't have a lot to lose. If I go ahead, I promise to keep you and your father out of it."

Dorothy was relieved that Philip was calming down, but she needed to spell out what was expected of him. "Philip, you may meet my father someday, but it's very important that you not make contact with him now. The only thing that I'll give you is a cell phone number—after that you are on your own. Got it?"

"I understand, believe me."

"They are be expecting you to request pharmacy records. Don't get greedy. Ask only for the things that you absolutely need."

"OK. I just need to know the drugs, the doses, the dosing frequency and how often the prescription was re-filled." Philip paused. "Oh yeah, remember that you found out that the Hamlins used to order food on line? Do you think the hacker could also get me some information from the Gladwyne Supermarket?"

Dorothy laughed in surprise. "Why on earth do you need to know their grocery list?"

"I know it sounds funny, but I want to get more information about their breakfast juice selection."

"Fine, I'm sure your hacker can do that too. Nobody gives a rip about supermarket records."

"I don't think we should discuss the case any more tonight. I have a pretty good idea of what I have to do, and you don't need any more details about why."

"I agree."

Philip moved ever so gently closer to Dorothy. For the next few hours, they snuggled in front of the fireplace, listening to jazz, and talking about nothing in particular.

"I am about as relaxed as I have been in months," Philip admitted. "Sitting here with you and watching the fire kind of hypnotizes me."

"I am glad, Philip. Really, really glad."

His fingers seemed to remember the softness of her pale hair and as she drew to him, her lips welcomed him back.

CHAPTER 19

This is pretty bizarre, Philip reflected. He was about to participate in a flagrantly illegal act, enlisting a lowdown criminal to be his accomplice. Dorothy was right: he was taking an enormous risk. He would have a hard time explaining to any rational person, let alone somebody in law enforcement, exactly why he was doing this. All he had were strong suspicions. He had yet to uncover one piece of evidence to prove that Hugh and Bonnie had done anything other than have a fling, something that was so much a part of the Main Line scene. Philip himself had wandered off the straight and narrow with Dorothy, so why not Hugh? Just because he was playing around didn't make him a calculating killer who did in the mother of his children.

All these thoughts swirled through his mind as he dialed the cell phone number Dorothy had given him. Before Philip had a chance to utter anything more than his name, the person hung up. He put the phone down in astonishment. Then his phone rang and an elderly woman's voice said, "Destroy the number you were given. Never call it again. Go see the Liberty Bell at Independence Mall today at two o'clock." The line went dead.

Philip stared at the handset for a few minutes. His first reaction was to smirk at the cheesy melodrama. Then it dawned on him that he had just witnessed a standard criminal operating procedure. Somebody was taking extreme precaution not to have the call traced. He had stepped into the inner circle of a very dangerous game. If he answered the directive and went to the meeting, he knew he was in for good.

How ironic that his encounter would be on such hallowed ground in the city where the United States had been born, within shouting distance of the residences of patriots like Betsy Ross and Ben Franklin. Most Philadelphians, including Philip, visited the historical sites rarely. Since it was a favorite stop for school trips, his kids came more often, but Nancy and he only occasionally dragged visiting relatives here.

The attacks on New York and Washington on September 11, 2001 had a major impact on the landscape of Independence Mall. Security was turned up several notches so getting into the historical sites required a security check worthy of a Middle East airport. Philip often wondered if terrorists ever plotted to destroy a monument like Independence Hall. They didn't really have to; the mere possibility was enough to make access an inconvenient and unpleasant experience.

The Liberty Bell, which had been removed from the old Pennsylvania State House, now called Independence Hall, was now housed in a secure and attractive pavilion across the street. Each day, long lines of tourists, many from other countries, waited patiently to get a glimpse of the international symbol of freedom. But first, metal detectors and bag searches had to be endured. It was exhausting.

Ironically, the only truly malicious attack on the Liberty Bell predated 9/11. A lunatic had decided to go at the Bell with a hammer. He had done some fixable damage before several shocked and out-of-shape security guards wrestled him to the ground. He said he had only wanted to hear what the Bell sounded like, a curiosity that cost him his own freedom and kept his picture on the front page of the local paper for several days.

Philip parked his car a few blocks away, then walked to Sixth and Market to join the admission line. Since the Bell Pavilion closed at 3:30, the wait would be short. A young mother and her two small children were in front of him. They all spoke Spanish.

A few minutes later, a young, slight, Hispanic man dressed in jeans and turtleneck, stepped over the rope to join his family. He was carrying a couple of sodas and gave them to the kids. "Drink fast," he told them. "They don't let you bring food or drinks inside."

The man nodded at Philip, who was busily looking for his contact person. From the voice on the phone, he expected an old lady, but everyone in the line was young or male. The longer he waited, the more anxious he became. How would his contact know him? Distracted, Philip shuffled ahead in the line while the family's chatter got more animated. Soon they were ready to be ushered into the Bell viewing area. The father took the forbidden soda away from the older child, and the cup fell to the floor, splattering the bottom of Philip's trousers.

Luckily, Philip's khakis were only wet at the cuff, but the young father apologized profusely and gave him a wad of paper towels he was holding to dry them. Philip patted the cuffs and put the towels in his pocket. The family left, but Philip took his time, circling the Bell until it was time to close.

Philip walked slowly out of the exhibit and back to his car, expecting to be approached by every person he saw. Frustrated and angry, he was convinced he had been stood up. Reaching for his car keys, he found the wet paper towels and was looking for a trash can when he noticed a note written on red paper in between the towels. On the paper were big block letters: "FOURTH BENCH BEHIND INDEPENDENCE HALL."

Philip sighed audibly. He was impressed, and his heart raced in anticipation. He pocketed his keys and sprinted back to the park behind Independence Hall where there were lots of benches. They were used by the hordes of tourists who came here, and by the lunch crowd during the business week. Late on an off-season weekend afternoon such as this, the park's principal inhabitants were a few homeless people and scads of hungry pigeons.

The young father never looked up from his newspaper. Philip wondered if the woman and kids were his real family. He couldn't imagine putting kids in harm's way, but then again he wasn't an experienced criminal. Philip sat down next to the man.

"Take a section of the newspaper, hold it in front of your face, look, straight ahead, and pretend you are reading. You can call me José. Now tell me what you want."

Philip detected a hint of a Spanish accent, but the diction was precise.

"A woman named Moira Hamlin was a customer at the Gladwyne Pharmacy a few years ago. I need to know exactly what drugs she was taking. I need her complete pharmacy records for the last five years of her life."

"Do you have her social security number and birth date?"

Dorothy had warned Philip he would be asked for some personal information about Moira. She had told him to have them memorized. Philip gave him the required information. José didn't write it down.

"OK, as long as the records were computerized and they used a central server, we should be OK. Both are likely, but some of these small pharmacies can be pretty backward. A drug store in Gladwyne should have fancy electronics, don't you think?"

Philip heard the sarcasm in Jose's voice. "Anything else, Mr. Big?" Jose continued.

"While you're in the pharmacy records, can you also get a list of any other stuff that the Hamlins purchased? I am particularly interested in any dietary aides, protein supplements, stuff like that."

He caught the smirk on José's face out of the corner of his eye. "That stuff will come with the drug purchases if it was all one account. So, is that it?"

"Well, there is one more thing. I know the Hamlins ordered groceries from the Gladwyne Supermarket, and I am pretty sure they placed their orders online. I need to know what kind of juice the Hamlins ordered for the last two years."

José half turned to see if Philip was serious. Philip had been afraid that he would get this reaction. To a pro who was used to cracking into financial and corporate records, this request must have sounded ridiculous.

"I'm not kidding. I need to know if the Hamlins changed their juice purchase pattern—you know orange juice, grapefruit juice, that kind of thing."

José's demeanor took a severe turn south. Through clenched teeth, he snarled, "Man, I'm telling you, you better not be yanking my dick. This is no fuckin' game we're playing, you understand? What I am going to do for your white ass is il-fucking-legal, man. If I get caught, we both go to jail, so you better be straight with me now!"

Philip's newspaper inadvertently rustled as his hands began to tremble, but he steeled himself and tried to sound tougher than he felt.

"Look, I am aware of the risks. My neck is on the line, too. You are going to be well paid for the information, and it won't be hard to get. I am not fucking with you. This stuff is important, so I need to know if you are going to get it or not."

José adjusted his newspaper slowly and methodically. "All right motherfucker. Just get your ass down here to this same bench three days from now at exactly 7:30. Reach under to get the envelope stuck underneath. Come alone and make sure that nobody is around when you pull it out. Don't talk to anybody about this. If you do, you will be pulling shit out from under the bench. And if you fuck with me, even a little, there won't be any place for you to hide. Got it?"

"Got it."

"And let's not forget my fee. That will be two large, and it will be in cash and in small bills. You will take your stuff out of the envelope and then put the money in it and drop the envelope in the trash can sitting right next to the second bench over there."

"OK. Anything else?" Philip was already intimidated by this man who appeared ready to murder him at the drop of a hat.

"No, asswipe, just don't ...," Philip stared at José. "Don't," repeated José, "screw with me or I'll rip your head off and shit down your neck."

With that, José left. Philip sat in amazement. What had he gotten into? He put the newspaper down and walked away as nonchalantly as his wobbly knees would allow.

For the next three days, Philip fearfully anticipated his next visit to Independence Mall. Wouldn't using the same meeting point twice be dangerous? Dorothy reassured him that if José weren't savvy, he would be in jail. Besides José had been recruited by her father's contact person, so he had to be competent. Philip hoped that José meant that two "large" was $2,000 because that was about all he had saved up.

"Look, it's not like you're buying heroin," Dorothy pointed out to Philip when he called her. It's just papers that nobody else cares about." Despite having her own fears, Dorothy thought it best to reassure Philip. "Besides, that part of town is dead on a weeknight. Women, including me, are scared to death to walk around there after that rape last year—they never did catch the pervert. So the only people you might see are dog walkers or joggers, and they are usually in their own little worlds. You have a better chance of getting mugged than arrested. Just do what José told you, and everything will be fine."

Philip was not happy with the alternatives of rape and mugging, and his trip to the bank to get the cash only made him uneasier. The friendly assistant bank manager insisted on making small talk. He even asked Philip why he wanted the money in small bills. Philip had to make up an answer, but it worked to shut the guy up.

The evening of the pick-up was chilly. A persistent rain left puddles that glistened in the glare of the old city streetlights. A light fog imparted a dreamy unreality, and his brisk footsteps echoed eerily around the empty park.

He located the stuffed envelope under the bench, and was dying to examine the contents before making the money drop. But he knew that would be dangerous. Jose was undoubtedly hovering. He slipped the papers inside his coat and placed the cash in the envelope, furtively checking to see if anybody was watching. Then Philip stood up, walked to the trash container, and dropped the envelope inside.

As nonchalantly as possible, he walked away, trying to look casual, overcome with terror that someone was going to spring out of the darkness to attack, arrest, or kill him. He was tempted to bolt but resolutely slogged on, and slowly his senses began to return. His car appeared like a shrouded hulk in the fog and mist. Once inside, he breathed a sigh of relief. Though feverishly anxious to see what information he had paid for, he decided to open the envelope later, in a much safer place.

When he got home, he replaced his wet clothes with cozy sweats then laid out the data sheets on his makeshift kitchen table. First he examined the grocery store orders, amazed at how organized the records were. Far from his own haphazard grocery buying patterns, the Hamlin family had standing orders they rarely strayed from including everyone's favorite foods. Since Philip had requested information about juices, José had obligingly highlighted the beverage sections. Philip had a hard time reconciling that angry man with a computer wizard who had generated these data. Apparently, José was good at what he did.

It was easy to see that the Hamlins liked orange juice. They ordered it in quantity every week. But about six months before Moira died, a puzzling new weekly order for two gallons of grapefruit juice appeared. One person would have to be drink about a quart of grapefruit juice a day to consume it all.

Philip scanned the other orders and found nothing else notable. It was apparent that the Hamlins ordered large quantities of junk food straight out of the "Unhealthy American Diet Cookbook." Was the concern about her weight real, or was Hugh just trying to drive his wife crazy?

The pharmacy records were less voluminous, but they required more time to dissect. They were poorly organized, without summaries of drugs ordered over time. Philip managed to find the Hamlin deliveries and saw that Moira was a frequent purchaser of dietary aids, including many expensive but unproven homeopathic preparations.

As he scanned through two years of records, he discovered that Moira had purchased diet pills, even though Philip had clearly instructed her to stay clear of all over-the-counter drugs. Ephedra and other diet pills dull the appetite and increase metabolism, but also render the heart more electrically vulnerable, especially in patients like Moira. After Moira's death, Ephedra had been pulled from the market for precisely that reason. Moira wasn't stupid, so how to account for this reckless behavior?

The prescription drug records were exactly what Philip needed to see, but they didn't make sense. He pulled Moira's medical records and tried to synchronize drug purchases with her clinical course.

Moira had used Benadryl for many years until her allergies worsened. She then started to take Appel. She used it for several months until she got pregnant. Then her obstetrician likely had told her to stop all medications unless they were absolutely necessary.

Philip found his notes from her first visit after the delivery. She was bothered by allergies, and he hadn't seen a problem with restarting Appel. For two months, regular orders were placed and filled and then everything stopped. From that point until Moira died, the Gladwyne Pharmacy delivered no more Appel to the Hamlins.

Philip ticked off possible explanations. Had the family changed pharmacies? That was unlikely, since all the other orders were intact. Had Moira's allergies improved? Hardly. Every time he saw her she complained about her runny nose and watery eyes. Was she getting free samples from somebody? Although the affluent Main Liners didn't mind taking handouts, what doctor would hand over that many sample drugs to a single patient?

Yet, Moira had large concentrations of alfenodine in her blood when she hit the ER. She had to be getting Appel from somewhere. Was Bonnie the source? And if so, why was she giving out free drugs?

Philip sat immobile. His detective work had opened up as many questions as it had answered. He was going to have to dig even deeper, and his quest was going to place him at odds with some powerful and evil people.

CHAPTER 20

Philip realized he was going to need José's services again. When he told Dorothy the next evening at her apartment, she was obviously concerned. "You are really pushing your luck. You saw how nasty these people can be."

"The last thing in the world I want to do is to put either of us in harm's way, but I have no choice. I need you to make sure it is OK for me to contact José. I was told never to call that number again, and I don't want to piss them off."

"Philip, you haven't seen your kids in days, the only work you have is at the clinical testing site, and you are consumed about Hugh and Bonnie. I'm really worried about you. Are you sure you want to keep going after these people?"

Philip turned on the sofa to face Dorothy squarely. "If I tell you what I think Hugh and Bonnie did to kill Moira, will you stay on board and help me out?"

"I guess that would help."

For the next thirty minutes, Philip laid out his theory, reviewing what he suspected, and what he could prove. At the end, Dorothy's skepticism fell away, and she had to admit that Philip was on to something.

"You see, their plan was simple but brilliant. It lets nature take its course, and each of them has an alibi to boot."

"Whose idea was it?"

"Well, the plan needed Bonnie's knowledge and contacts. But there are still some holes to be filled. Jose can help with some.

We also need more details about John Romano's death."

Dorothy was intimidated by the idea of talking to the Romano family but she knew she was the person to take that one on.

"OK, here's the deal. I will talk to my father about José and visit the Romanos, although it's all against my better judgment. When the information draws a straight line to Bonnie and Hugh, we go straight to the authorities. If what we find out doesn't get us that far, you have to promise me that the witchhunt is over and you'll move on. Agreed?"

"You have a deal."

Dorothy was so certain of her father's negative reaction that she decided to send an email rather than make a phone call. Dorothy's message carefully omitted names. It would be unpleasantly ironic to get busted by somebody else's hacker at this point.

Dorothy could picture her father's reddened face as he typed out an expletive-filled answer. He would then soften the language before sending it off.

"Are you sure that he understands by going back to the same person he's multiplying the risk of getting caught? I'll only go ahead if he clearly realizes this."

Dorothy read the message and paused to consider the circumstances. Was her attraction to Philip corrupting her judgment? He'd promised this was the last shot before quitting his amateur sleuthing. "Go ahead," she typed, then paused before finally tapping the "send" key.

The next evening, Philip found an unmarked envelope in his mailbox, setting up his next meeting with José. This time it was the Italian Market in South Philadelphia, another busy meeting point, early on a Saturday morning.

Unlike Independence Hall, the Italian Market consistently draws more locals than tourists to its open-air storefronts. The original vendors had been Italian, but over time, new ethnic groups joined the lineup and now the market offered every kind of food imaginable. On weekends, the streets are closed to traffic as throngs of shoppers work their way from store to store, buying cheeses, lunchmeats, olives, coffees, and delectable confections.

It was in this neighborhood that Philip's father began his fruit business and where Philip had been brought as a child. He loved the sights, sounds, smells, and the noisy bartering that distinguishes regular shoppers from naïve tourists. In fact, Philip's father often bragged about how much he saved on every item he bought.

The note in his mailbox instructed Philip to purchase an apple at Mirabile's fruit market at Ninth and Christian. At 8 a.m., a short, smiling, elderly Italian woman shopkeeper with a wisp of a mustache handed him a rich red apple wrapped in tissue paper. Remembering his first encounter, he crumpled up the wrapper and put it into his pocket as he strolled away from her fruit and vegetable stand.

When he was far enough from the stand, he read the message on the back of the wrapper. Once again, it was printed in block capital letters. "Alley between 8th and 9th—now." Philip wasted no time heading in that direction while nervously checking over his shoulder. Suddenly, there was Jose, leaning against a garage door in the middle of the block, a cigarette hanging from his lips.

"So, white boy, you want some more?"

"Something like that." Philip answered quietly, determined not to let Jose provoke him. But this time he summoned up the courage to ask Jose a question.

"Is there some reason you seem so angry with me? I thought this was your, let's say, occupation?"

"That's none of your business. Let's just say that I don't like uppity white guys and leave it at that. Don't worry, my man, this little spic has the tools to get you what you want."

Obviously, getting personal with José was not a good idea, so Philip quickly returned to business.

"I need you to get some information from Miracle Pharmaceuticals about a drug called Delcane. It was taken off the market about four years ago because it caused heart problems. I need to know what the company did with the drug inventory and if there is any more of it around."

José stamped out his cigarette out and replaced it with a toothpick, which he slowly moved from corner to corner. If he didn't seem to be paying attention, his response indicated differently.

"Getting information from drug companies is hard, man. I manage to do it from time to time, but they are real protective about products that have been yanked. So this one is going to require a 50% surcharge. It will cost you three large."

Philip wasn't surprised; he was prepared to hock a few remaining pieces of jewelry.

"I also need you to look up one of their senior executives, Bonnie Romano, and find out what she had to do with Delcane."

"Bonnie Romano, huh? You got the hots for her? Don't matter, boss man. You need anything else?"

"No, that should do it."

OK, same procedure as last time, except we'll make the exchange at the Sixers-Celtics game on Tuesday night. Here's your ticket. Get there as soon as the doors open. There will be an envelope velcroed to the seat bottom. Pull off the envelope, take out your goodies, put my money in, and then stick the envelope back under the seat and get out. Sorry you won't be able to stay for the game. Should be a good one. You think I should put some money on the Sixers? Want to wager my fee double or nothing?"

Philip did his best to ignore José's taunts. When he was certain José didn't have any additional instructions or conditions, he turned back toward the market.

While Philip was in South Philadelphia with José, Dorothy was only a few blocks away. She had parked her car on Broad Street and was looking for the storefront that served as offices for John Romano's family. She had an appointment with John's father and uncle, a meeting that she was dreading.

As usual, Dorothy had done her homework. She had combed through decades old newspaper stories, and thick files she found in after-hours searches in her father's office. Included were dozens of interviews about assorted crimes investigated by his firm and the police. The file was rich with stories and opinions from people who knew or worked for the Romanos, and who were more than anything else desperate to remain anonymous.

The Romano family owned a successful chain of regional appliance stores. John's father, Giancarlo, emigrated from Sicily to join his brother Vincente in the 1940s. Their family played the ethnic loyalty card that caused just about every Italian family in Philly to buy their appliances from them.

Amazingly, their market dominance continued even as low-budget superstores came on the scene. The quality of the store magnetized three generations of Italian families to come back for more. Not surprisingly, local politicians considered the Romano empire an integral part of South Philly's complicated tapestry.

When he arrived in the United States, Giancarlo Romano had two priorities: to become a successful businessman, and to start a large family. Vincente, his senior by five years, was resigned to bachelorhood, but motivated to help his younger brother's search for an appropriate wife.

Giancarlo liked the idea of becoming an "American." But he understood that his core values were Sicilian. That meant finding a wife would proceed according to Italian tradition. Although he was not handsome, he had striking dark features and a dashing presence. Vincente was expected to arrange family-supervised "dates" with potential mates.

The women whom Giancarlo met during those arranged encounters had several things in common. They were all Sicilian and essentially uneducated. Subservient and respectful, all lived with their parents, helping to run households and raise younger siblings.

The first dates always occurred at the young woman's home and revolved around a Sunday midday feast. The women served, while the men smoked, sipped red wine and discussed the business of the day, religion, sports and politics. The elder women supervised and otherwise hovered to make sure everything was perfect.

After dessert, usually fresh, homemade cannoli, the men had cigars and espresso in the living room, and the potential suitor and young lady donned their coats for a stroll through Washington Park. They were permitted to walk by themselves to get to know each other, although for the sake of propriety, a few of the older women followed several yards behind. After this introduction, the young man's father or older brother would confer with the girl's father to determine if the relationship should be pursued.

Giancarlo was pleasantly surprised by the grace of the women he met. His preconceived idea had been that Italian-American women would somehow be less attractive and refined than the women back home. He was pleased to have been proven wrong. "Vincente," he exclaimed after one encounter, "these women are all beautiful! Every Sunday I meet one who is more lovely than the last."

"Yes, my brother, you seem to have a hard time finding one

you would like to pursue. The people we have visited like you too, but grow impatient."

"The truth is," he sighed, "they are all very nice, but none of them have taken my breath away."

"With God's permission, I hope that happens soon. I enjoy eating well, but a few more of those fabulous Sunday feasts, and I am going to have to buy some new suits."

The very next week, Giancarlo was indeed rendered breathless by a dazzling beauty named Adalina Sicaranza. She was the fourth child of Michael and Mildred Sicaranza, who had immigrated to the United States at the turn of the century as newlyweds and eventually established the first gelati store in South Philadelphia.

In the early 1900s, good ice cream was cherished. Michael started with a small window in the front of their South Philly row house. In short order he expanded to three stores and two horse-drawn carts. He was the forerunner of the "Good Humor Man," ringing a cowbell on the back of his cart to announce his arrival.

Mildred concentrated on their family. Within a span of fourteen years, she gave birth to eleven children, two of whom died in infancy. The remaining seven girls and two boys attended the parish school until they were old enough to help around the house or in the family business.

There was no doubt Adalina was the beauty of the family. Even though she wore dowdy clothes and no makeup, her thick raven-black hair resembled a silky mane, and high cheekbones defined her aristocratic good looks. When Adalina married, her father vowed, it would be to a man of his choosing.

Vincente knew Michael both as a loyal customer at the appliance store, and as a purveyor of fine gelati. When he asked Michael if he and his brother might call on Adalina. Michael felt proud that the owner of a successful business was interested in his daughter. The following Sunday after their initial introduction, Adalina and Giancarlo hit it off.

Their one-year courtship was followed by a grand wedding that launched a deeply happy marriage. They bought a modest but roomy row house in the heart of South Philadelphia, a block from the Romano appliance store.

Shortly after the wedding, Adalina developed a cough, accompanied by fevers, and night sweats. At first, they assumed she had a cold, but because her symptoms progressed, they visited their family doctor who ordered a chest X-ray. When the doctor confirmed she had tuberculosis and recommended six months in a sanitarium, the young couple was devastated.

The nearest facility was deep in the Pocono Mountains, three hours from Philadelphia. Instead of the few months of confinement they expected, Adalina ended up staying nearly two years. Giancarlo bought a used car and visited every weekend, sitting at her bedside, reading to her, and providing encouragement. At night, he slept in the car to save money.

Antibiotics that kill the tuberculosis bacteria had not been discovered yet, so care was supportive and usually ineffective. There were a few interventions, like collapsing and resting the infected lung, but these techniques were unproven and dangerous. When victims survived, they were left with damaged lungs and the possibility of disease in other organs that might not surface for years.

Both Giancarlo and Adalina worried about her ability to have children. The doctor admitted he didn't know if Adalina's reproductive organs were damaged. But that became a moot point since sexual relations were forbidden for at least a year.

When Adalina retuned home, hosts of well-wishers volunteered to help out. Her obvious weight loss prompted her family to ply her with plenty of macaroni and gravy. But Adalina sank into a horrible depression. No longer was she the bouncy person Giancarlo had adored. She withdrew and became a frightened little bird who was quick to tears.

For the next several years, Giancarlo and Adalina tried to have children. Doctors blamed her infertility on fallopian tube scarring from TB. Even the specialists had no solutions.

Their fertility became an obsession for everyone in the family. Countless novenas, votive candles to the Blessed Virgin Mary, and rosaries did no good

After much soul searching, the couple decided to adopt, and arranged a meeting with the one person who controlled the process, the parish priest. Father Piazza counseled the couple and sorted through the legal work. There was no "waiting list." The priest was the final arbiter and made all decisions.

After two years, the call came. A young immigrant Italian family had a house fire. The father had evacuated the children, but perished trying to rescue his wife. A boy of two and a girl of ten months had to be adopted together. Giancarlo and Adalina raced to the rectory to fetch the children before anyone changed their minds. They renamed the boy John, after his new father, and the little girl kept her original name, Maria.

John finished high school and stayed in Philadelphia for college. He was expected to enter the family appliance business, but he was attracted to medicine and decided to pursue obstetrics and gynecology. Ironically, he established a practice seeing women with fertility problems.

While John was a dedicated physician, he had a weakness for the ladies. He dated extensively and was one of the most eligible bachelors in the city. He had no plans to settle down until he met Bonnie Squardito.

Bonnie was a drug representative at Miracle Pharmaceuticals when John met her at a watering hole in Center City. She was a striking woman, with classic Italian features, bright eyes, and a good figure. But her utter self-confidence and quick wit are what got John's attention.

When he sat down next to her at the bar, she turned and said, "I hope you're not going to use some tired come-on line. I've heard them all and they all turn me off like a switch. If you want straight talk and want to know something about me, just ask."

John smiled and lowered his eyes while deciding if he should just move down the bar. He finally looked up and said, "OK, let's play 'This is Your Life.' Give me your life's history in a hundred words or less while I buy us both a drink."

Bonnie laughed. "OK sailor, here goes. I was born in West Philly and attended Catholic schools all the way to college at Villanova. I hated the mainstream courses so I decided to go to their nursing school. Don't ask me why, because I didn't really like taking care of patients, so I transferred into the biology program. Afterward, I went to work for a drug company in sales. I anticipate climbing the corporate ladder fairly quickly. I am obviously single, have no main squeeze, and really don't want one. But I like sex with the right person now and again, so this might be your lucky night. Your turn."

John was taken aback by her brashness, but was an even match for her clever bantering. He didn't get lucky that night, but she rewarded him with her phone number and a promise that she would go out with him on a real date if he chose an appropriate venue.

Their romance progressed quickly. Although they saw each other nearly every day Bonnie wasn't traveling, they rarely visited John's family. To his clan's dismay, after a few months of dating, they decided to live together and moved into John's stylish center city condominium. Within a year, Bonnie and John were married in a non-sectarian ceremony in South Philadelphia, with a grand reception at the Four Seasons.

After a honeymoon in Belize, it didn't take long for problems to surface. Bonnie was promoted to an "inside" job at Miracle, which entailed lots of overseas travel and long hours even when she wasn't on the road. John found himself spending a lot of time alone. He put up with it for a few months, then started visiting his old haunts.

That got Bonnie's attention, and when she accused him of "dipping his wick" in some familiar places, John didn't deny it but reminded her of her frequent absences. Soon, their late-night shouting matches became a scandal at the condo. On more than one occasion, police had to be summoned. When his family tried to intervene, they were told to mind their business.

Almost a year later, John Romano, the successful, young fertility specialist, died one night while sitting in his favorite chair. He had been battling a respiratory infection, watching late-night television. Bonnie found him in the morning. She called 911 and started resuscitation, but the ambulance team wasn't able to restart his heart. An autopsy showed nothing.

Armed with her research, Dorothy was ready for her coffee meeting with John's father and uncle. The Romano business headquarters was on the second floor of their largest appliance store, on Broad Street only a few blocks from their original site.

Giancarlo and Vincente had aged gracefully. Their thick black hair had turned gray but they both looked healthy and fit, still fully involved with the business. They politely asked Dorothy about her educational background and her law firm. They even discussed the nice spring weather and Philly sports teams before Giancarlo finally leaned forward, elbows on table.

"Ms. Deaver, forgive me for being forward, but Vincente and

I want to know why you need information about John."

"I am not at liberty to give you details. I have to respect the privacy of my client. I can tell you that Bonnie Romano may have had something to do with the death of a woman on the Main Line. The police are not investigating because they have no way of implicating her, but my client has reason to believe she was an accomplice. I am just trying to get some background, including her relationship with John."

"Ms. Deaver, we never really got to know Bonnie well. She worked long hours and traveled, so we didn't see her much. My daughter brings her family to see us every week, but John and Bonnie didn't come often."

Giancarlo's piercing gaze and the silence that followed made Dorothy understand how much the brothers resented Bonnie. She decided to move on to the point of her visit. "What can you tell me about John's death?

John's death came as a shock. He was healthy. He had nasty allergies as a youngster but never any heart problems, and he never used illegal drugs."

The papers said that the autopsy was inconclusive. Do you have a copy of the report?"

We can get you a copy, but I can tell you that it was as negative as it could be. The only thing they found was antihistamine and antibiotic in his bloodstream. There was nothing wrong with his heart or brain."

Dorothy's didn't hear the last sentence. The mention of the antihistamine had grabbed her attention.

"The police conducted an investigation?" she continued.

"Yes, if you want to call it that. We were very disappointed. Once they knew the autopsy results, they said there was no evidence of foul play, and they refused to investigate further. As far as they were concerned, John's heart stopped for no good reason."

"Have you seen or talked to Bonnie since John died?"

"No. The only time we heard from her was when the will was in probate. We have not heard from her again. It left everybody in the family with a bad feeling."

Vincente had been quiet, but he obviously had strong feelings about John. His eyes misted over when Giancarlo spoke about his nephew. He pointed a finger at Dorothy.

"Look, Ms. Deaver, in this part of the world, the police aren't really that important. When something like this happens, and somebody so dear dies without a reason, inquiries are made privately and discreetly. And they were made in this case. Anybody found responsible for what happened to John would receive appropriate treatment, if you know what I mean. But despite the best efforts of professional people, we found no evidence of wrongdoing. So, reluctantly, we let the matter rest."

Dorothy processed what she had just heard. Vincente indicated there had been a private investigation that had failed to implicate Bonnie. If Bonnie had known about the Romano family's "resources" and still murdered John, she was either raving mad or had the courage of a veteran assassin.

Vincente watched Dorothy's reaction and was pleased that she had gotten the message. He took in a deep breath and then continued.

"All right, Ms. Deaver, I think that we should put all of the cards on the table. After you called us to set up this appointment, we did a little checking of our own. We know who your client is and that Bonnie married Hugh Hamlin after the death of his wife Moira. It is only logical that you would want to know about John Romano."

Dorothy nodded. There was no point in denying the truth.

"You probably think that these two elderly men and their families have grieved for John and we have moved on. Maybe you are considerate and you don't want to open up old wounds. But let me be clear, Ms. Deaver. John Romano's death is not a closed issue. There is no statute of limitations on the way we feel. So we intend to help your investigation."

When Dorothy's color drained, Giancarlo moved his chair closer to hers and took her hand, which was slick with sweat. "Now, don't be upset, Ms. Deaver. We mean you no harm. We promise to stay in the background. All we ask is that you give us a call once in a while on a secure line and give us an update. And if the time ever comes when you solve the riddle of Moira's death, we would like to hear your conclusions. Is that fair?"

Dorothy was reeling as they handed her a phone number to use. Vincente had one last request. "I must remind you that everything we have said today must be kept in utter confidence. If word got out, there could be some unfortunate misunderstandings. Also, we must ask you to go into the ladies room with Gina, one of our clerks, to make sure that you are not wearing any recording devices. We regret this, but if we are going to work together," Vincente explained, "we have to be extra careful."

Giancarlo patted Dorothy's hand. "Many people would like to prove we are violent people. Can you believe that?" Both men chuckled almost on cue.

"Now, we will get you those autopsy and police reports. Please do not divulge where these documents came from. Shall we expect a call from you in about a week or so?"

Giancarlo sat back and smiled at Dorothy in a fatherly way. She nodded yet again, as Vincente showed her to Gina's office. After a polite and efficient search, she found herself back on Broad Street. She couldn't decide if she was elated with the information she had just received or petrified that she had wandered into the lion's den. Her mind raced much faster than her car as she drove back to her office. She couldn't wait to phone her father.

Dick Deaver listened to her story with his customary grunts. When she paused, he delivered his opinion. "Well, it appears that you have good news and that you have some bad news. The good news is that you may be on to something with this anithistamine thing, but you will need more information to say that for sure. Hopefully, Philip will be able to help you with that. The bad news is that you now have some potentially violent people who will want you to implicate Bonnie in John Romano's death."

"I know," Dorothy said.

"Make sure you keep Philip on a short leash. You are going to have to walk a very narrow line between fact finding and obeying the law. In fact, you might want to talk to some law enforcement folks soon. Do you have someone you can call? I know lots of people in Philly, but you need somebody in Montgomery County."

"Yeah, lots of people, but we have to come up with someone who will be discreet so we don't get into hot water with the Romano brothers. I'll talk to Philip about it."

"Keep me posted. I'm here to help you as best I can."

Like a good dad, Dick resisted the temptation to say, "I told you so." Instead, he decided to lighten the mood.

"Look on the bright side. You're drilling down into an interesting case, and meeting some really fascinating people."

CHAPTER 21

While Philip waited to pick up the newest information from Jose, he read EKG tracings for the research center and obsessed. The television was blaring, but his mind was racing. He was still furious with the hospital, and narcissistically allowed his anger to dominate his emotions. He recalled a number of run-ins with the board at GMH who basically hired accountants to run the place, who in turn underpaid the physicians who were responsible for patient care. Philip and many other doctors believed management had kept GMH from blossoming into a premier institution, and as a result, many doctors just gave up and either left the hospital or withdrew into their own practices. He fought hard to keep the doctors on board, pointing out that good patient care mandated that they stay engaged. But the majority ignored him. Now he understood why.

Philip watched the clock. He thought about Dorothy and her meeting with the Romanos. She had been an enormous help, but he wondered why she was willing to interrupt her practice and spend so much time on his case. Were they foolish to get romantically involved? Would she tire of helping him and eventually go back to her own life?

Desperate to hear the full Romano story, he thought of calling her. He worried about another exchange with José in a public place, and what the Miracle records might reveal. There was a lot riding on what they contained. Would he be able to figure them out?

Finally, it was time to leave for the Wachovia Center. He knew that he would be hitting horrible traffic enroute to the South Philadelphia Sports Complex, but it was crucial to be there when the doors opened. The city of Philadelphia had pumped over a billion dollars into three beautiful sports facilities that housed the Phillies, Eagles, Flyers, and Sixers. Philip remembered that Hugh Hamlin's family was part owner of the football team, and he mused about the perks of reserved parking and a luxury box. And if you don't like the person you're with, kill her, get a replacement, and ruin her doctor in the process.

He arrived just as the doors opened. To blend in, he went to a concession stand and bought a hot dog that was mostly bun, and a overly sweetened Coke that was mostly ice for seven dollars. The facility was almost empty. It wasn't like the old days when Philip had bugged his father to get him to the game two hours in advance to see his favorite players warm up. Now there was pitifully little to watch. The players walked around the court for a few minutes in their colorful warm-ups, stretched, pretended to practice foul shots, and rapped with their buds. Not much reason to come early.

Philip made his way to his assigned section, cup in hand, trying to look as casual as possible. A young girl in red satin hot pants showed him to his seat. She bent over at a provocative angle when she wiped the seat with a chamois cloth. Philip gave her a buck for her trouble and sat down.

His heart pounded as he nonchalantly leaned over and felt under the seat. A thick paper envelope rewarded his effort. Slowly, he eased it loose and inched it under the coat on his lap. Once the wad of papers was safely inside his jacket, he inserted the money, and resealed the package securely. He slapped it back under the seat.

He watched the listless shooting for a few more minutes, left the building and, looking neither right nor left, headed to his car. Jose was certainly watching.

He drove swiftly to Dorothy's office, and was grateful to find a parking space outside her building. She greeted him, smiling brightly, and chatted while opening the packages she had picked up at Latimer Deli, a Philly institution around the corner from the new Academy of the Performing Arts, where well-dressed people add bibs to their attire and proceed to slurp up juicy deli sandwiches before attending the orchestra.

Dorothy liked Latimer's take-out, and the reuben concoction topped her A list. However, no single human being could consume the mass of corned beef, cole slaw, and gooey dressing that oozed out of the freshly baked slices of rye bread. So they shared one with some extra slaw, pickles, and chips. Two icy beers were the perfect accompaniment.

After a breezy kiss, they dove into the food as Dorothy related her Romano story. Philip wasn't surprised about John Romano's autopsy, the antihistamine, or the antibiotic. Even the Romano's willingness to use violence didn't seem to faze him.

"I am not surprised they came clean with you. You have the potential to nail Bonnie for John's murder, and they want you to know what they can bring to the task. I think this will be OK as along as we keep them on our side."

Dorothy was amazed by Philip's detachment. "That's easy for you to say. You aren't the one who has to report in every week."

"Look, if we don't get enough to put Bonnie and Hugh away, the Romanos are no worse off than they are already, right? How can they hate you for that? We have to be very discreet. As long as they are in the background, we should be all right. And if it bothers you that much, give me their numbers and I will call them with news bulletins."

Dorothy wasn't happy but agreed. "I guess that makes sense. And yes, I wouldn't mind staying away from Dad and Uncle Vince. They scare me."

Philip wanted to move on. "The key to this case is probably in the papers I picked up at the stadium tonight. I need to go through them ASAP."

"OK. Let's finish eating, and I'll set you up in one of the back offices. I have a ton of work to catch up on myself."

Philip sat back. "Sounds like a deal. Pass the cole slaw, will you? And I wouldn't mind a few more chips."

As usual, Philip's appetite reflected his mood—when he was up, he was voracious. He scarfed down everything, including Dorothy's leftovers. After finishing their messy feast, and dusting off another beer, they adjourned to their respective offices. Dorothy tried to do some of her own work but couldn't help wondering what was in those papers.

She looked in on him a few times to find him poring over the documents. Why she was attracted to this man? Was it pity? He was not the best-looking guy in the world, and he certainly had his quirks. He had a gift for learning things quickly, and his ability to discern the kernel of truth was astounding. He wasn't a people person, yet he had dedicated his life to helping others. How devastating to be rejected so decisively when he'd worked so hard to do the right thing. No wonder he had sunk into depression. If they could prove their theory, Philip might be able to recover some of what he had lost. Dorothy wanted to be part of that redemption —if she could just keep from getting killed in the process.

She went back to her office, sat on the sofa, and opened a hefty brief. The next thing she knew, Philip was gently nudging her awake. He had a smile on his face. "You are so adorable when you are asleep. I love that mug of yours."

Dorothy sat up, rubbed her eyes, reached out for Philip, pulled him close, and kissed him tenderly. "Thanks for letting me sleep — guess I needed that. What time is it?"

"After midnight. José got us what we needed. Come on back and bring some tea. I'll fill you in."

Dorothy heated up some water in the microwave and brought the cups, tea bags, milk, sugar, and spoons on a tray into the back office. Philip was immersed in a stack of papers but looked up with a grin.

"Stop me if you have any questions. It is a little complicated. I have pieced it together from what I learned from Red and José, plus what I knew myself, so it might be a little disjointed.

"So, Delcane is on the market and is doing well. Miracle is piling up the dough. The drug made $3.5 billion in its third year on the prescription market. The company launches a series of direct-to-consumer TV commercials, particularly notable since they were one of the first companies to do that. The campaign was an enormous success.

"Everybody is talking about this new non-sedating antihistamine, and everybody wants it. They market it aggressively to the primary care docs whose patients hate to feel sleepy all the time. They spare no expense, setting up lavish dinner programs, and taking docs to posh resorts. Delcane pens appear in every doctor's office. It was an impressive marketing blitz."

"The drug companies weren't regulated as much back then, right?"

"They would never get away with that stuff now. Anyway,

there were no safety issues they knew about. In fact, there was very little difference between the drug and placebo in clinical research trials, so the docs felt secure in letting it rip. The company even gave them pre-printed prescription pads and lots of samples to make it extra easy."

"Did the company know the drug wasn't really all that safe?"

"Well, they knew as much about Delcane's safety as we knew about any drug back then. If you look at the data that supported the approval of 'tried-and-true antihistamines' you would be amazed at how little there was. In the Delcane clinical trials, about 4,000 patients received the drug, which is about ten times the number that was in older antihistamine trials. In retrospect, there were a few deaths in the trials and some of them were sudden and could have been due to an arrhythmia. Most of the folks who died had some kind of heart disease, so it was impossible to know if the drug caused it or not.

"But, in the great scheme of things, even 4,000 patients is a drop in the bucket. There was a one in 5,000 or 10,000 chance of dropping dead from an arrhythmia with a drug, in clinical trials that enrolled only 4,000 patients, you might not see it. About 15 times that number of patients received the drug within a month after the FDA approved it, and the number grew exponentially for the next three years. As many as 35 million people were probably exposed to the drug in the US and 100 million worldwide before it was pulled from the market."

"So how safe was Delcane when all those people were taking it?"

"It's hard to be precise. There's no organized system of surveillance for drug safety after market approval. The FDA has to depend on receiving spontaneous reports from docs and other health care professionals. There are no teeth in the program; it's all voluntary. The system doesn't work well. We figure that for every reported case, something like 99 are not."

"So why don't they fix it?"

"That would literally require an Act of Congress. The laws would have to make drug companies responsible for gathering post-marketing information on any drug with safety concerns, and that might mean just about all of them."

"But it's not impossible."

"Of course not. Cardiac safety is an important problem. Think about Vioxx. Here you had a drug that may have been causing strokes and heart attacks in thousands of people, but it wasn't until a large study was done for a completely different reason that they had enough data to pull it off the market. If we had some way of tracking those problems in a comprehensive registry, we would know a lot more about a drug's safety before it did so much damage. And maybe then we wouldn't have to deprive the public of drugs that can be used safely in most patients."

Dorothy watched Philip carefully as he related the story. He was clearly excited by his discovery. "So, what happened with Delcane?" she prompted.

"Well, the company just kept promoting the drug and raking in the cash. They even managed to tack on another billion or so by combining Delcane with a decongestant. In retrospect, the added adrenalin effect of the decongestant may have actually made the cardiac situation worse. But the company didn't know that and they weren't looking for problems."

"So, how did this juggernaut finally fall apart?"

"Well, Miracle got greedy. It wasn't good enough that they were making billions with a prescription drug. They figured that if the drug was safe, it could go OTC."

"You mean over-the-counter?"

"Yeah, and on the face of it, it didn't seem like a big deal. Lots of drugs have made the transition to OTC including antihistamines like Benadryl. The main concern is safety. Will anybody, God forbid, die from the drug? If the drug doesn't work so well, so what? The public is used to buying crap that doesn't work—look at how much money people spend on unproven homeopathic drugs. To maximize safety, the manufacturer will put the lowest doses of their products over the counter, since most of the toxicity for drugs occurs at higher doses."

"What did the FDA think about the OTC application?"

"Not much. Based on the safety officer's initial report, the allergy division started to process the application. But then a novice reviewer was told to check the spontaneous adverse event reports. These come to the agency when a doctor, nurse, or pharmacist—anybody really—thinks a case represents a problem with the drug. It was pro forma stuff except for the reviewer, a guy named Gan

Oh. He apparently didn't speak English very well, but he was pretty smart, and as tenacious as a pit bull.

"Dr. Oh found a few dozen cases of people who died suddenly on Delcane or Delcane-D with the decongestant. He brought this information to his supervisors. They blew him off at first, but his persistence paid off. at every allergy division meeting, he would bring his Delcane transparencies with him and show them to the crew, and each time he added a few more suspicious cases. The Director of the Allergy Division finally cried 'uncle.' They decided to get a consult from the cardiology division at FDA."

"You worked with most of those guys, didn't you?"

"Yes, Bob Fennister got the case for review. He is the assistant division director. Bob's a character, a Renaissance man. When he isn't working at the FDA, he camps in the wilderness, or does an iron man competition in Hawaii. He even writes poetry during boring meetings.

"Once Bob got the file, things started to happen. He was particularly concerned about the overdose cases. Those patients were on monitors and had some really ugly cardiac arrhythmias at the same time they had QT prolongation on their EKGs. He called a series of meetings with the company and demanded they go back to find out more about the death cases."

Dorothy was resting her head on her hands, trying to stay awake. Philip noticed a few suppressed yawns. "I know you're tired, but you need to hear the whole story."

"I'm OK. Keep going."

"Well, as more information came in, it became clear the drug was doing something bad. Bob and the FDA staff finally challenged Miracle to explain what was going on or to withdraw their application, which the company did. But by then, the damage had been done. About a year later, the drug was yanked from the market altogether.

"In the meantime, the company sent out warning letters to doctors, telling them to respond aggressively to symptoms like blackouts that could potentially indicate a nasty arrhythmia. Of course, the letters didn't work. Doctors just kept prescribing the drug, and people kept dying until the drug was finally pulled completely."

"What did you find out about Bonnie's involvement? Isn't that why you needed José the second time?"

"Yeah, that was the point, wasn't it? When I looked at the minutes of the meetings with the FDA, Bonnie's name was on the list, so she was there. She was a junior person when the problems were first recognized, but she handled herself so well she eventually took over the project. The Miracle brass recognized a disaster when they saw it, and Bonnie became the 'go-to' person for damage control. She did one hell of a job."

"When a drug like Delcane is withdrawn, the shit generally hits the fan, doesn't it?"

"The lawyers line up at the courthouse to file class action suits, not to mention claims brought by individuals. Look at what they did to fen-phen and Vioxx. Potential litigation would cost the company billions, but Bonnie managed the withdrawal of Delcane so well that lawsuits were kept to a minimum and the company lost comparatively little."

"Those cases can kill a drug company if they are not managed properly. Lots of people end up losing their jobs."

"For sure. Bonnie took the offensive, and it worked beautifully. The stockholders asked lots of questions about what Miracle employees and directors knew and whether or not they withheld information to protect the stock price. Bonnie took that problem on too. The best thing she did was to make sure investors stayed the course and didn't sell off. They all got their money back and a lot more."

"The stock rebounded quickly when Appel came out."

"It did, and Bonnie was on a roll. She made the most out of an adverse situation."

"If Bonnie was doing so well at Miracle, what was her motive for killing John? Why not just divorce him and move on?"

"A woman back then made a salary that was peanuts compared to the male brass. She stood to get a few million from John's estate. So she probably figured she could be successful and rich, too."

"OK, so she is the Miracle heroine. What does any of this have to do with proving that she helped murder Moira Hamlin and John Romano?"

"That's where it gets interesting. When a drug is pulled from the market, public advocacy groups push the company to keep making it for those poor souls who have serious diseases and can't be treated with anything else. Miracle had Appel nearly ready to go, and they knew that Appel had almost identical effects to Delcane. So anybody who took Delcane and had a good result with it could easily get switched over to Appel. But they decided to play the good guys and keep Delcane available at no charge for people who had severe allergies and for whom the drug worked well.

"It was a great public relations move that diffused a lot of the public's anger. I remember thinking that myself. Even groups like Public Citizen that were after Miracle had to admit that the company was doing the right thing. Bonnie took personal responsibility for the 'compassionate-use' program."

"Isn't that a little strange? She was pretty senior by that time. Why would she want to run that small program, especially if it was actually worthless?"

"Precisely the question I asked. It gave her immediate access to the drug. If she took a few samples to give to somebody in her family, for example, there would be absolutely no paper trail."

"So how much Delcane was given out?"

"Not much that I could see, but unlike everything else she ran, the records for that program were hideously poor. The disbursements looked random, and the accounting was crappy. Who knows how much of that was on purpose? All I can say is less than 5,000 doses of Delcane were dispensed until the program was closed about two years later."

"I bet that wasn't long after Moira died."

"You're right, about three months to be exact. Bonnie didn't really explain why they pulled the plug, and, unlike the decision to continue the compassionate use program, this move wasn't publicized. Nobody batted an eye. By that time, Appel had replaced Delcane anyway, so patients could get an effective drug no matter what."

"That helps explain how Moira got the drug. Where does John Romano fit into the Delcane story?"

"That took a lot more digging. It wasn't just a matter of his taking Delcane. The drug was available for general use back then, and the Romanos said his autopsy report clearly showed antihistamine in his bloodstream. I predict that when you get the actual copy of the report it will be Delcane's metabolite, which is alfenodine or Appel. And I also suspect you will find he had a

Peter Kowey

quinolone antibiotic in his system that slowed the liver conversion of Delcane to Appel."

"How do you know that?"

"I was about to give up and conclude that John's antihistamine use was just a coincidence and that we weren't going to be able to implicate Bonnie in his death. Then I found a little Delcane study that was carried out right around the time they began to suspect a problem with the drug. One of the company's bright young scientists proposed a study in which they would take a bunch of normal volunteers, give them Delcane in the highest recommended dose, and then measure the subjects' QT intervals to see what their responses were."

"How come we didn't know about this study before?"

"It was an internal study that was never published, but the FDA must have seen it at some point. They gave 60 mg of Delcane, the highest tablet size, to 30 men and women, and took EKGs every 15 minutes for six hours. Most of the data came from one of the centers like I work in now, but the company also enrolled a few patients in their own clinical trial unit downtown."

"What was Bonnie's role in the study?"

"She was the immediate supervisor, so all of the data went straight to her. As expected, the average increase in QT interval was pretty modest, less than ten milliseconds or so. Remember, they didn't know back then that inhibiting the drug's metabolism would push the QT way out. But they did discover something about the drug's effect that was very important. Of the 30 people in the study, 28 had modest QT prolongation, but two had whopping QT increases. Judging from their blood levels, because of their genetic makeup, they were probably poor metabolizers of Delcane."

"What does that mean?"

"These two would eventually convert the Delcane to Appel, but it would take them longer and the effects of Delcane would be bigger for the first hour or two after dosing Since there is no practical way to know who the poor metabolizers are ahead of time, the fear is that these people will have a lethal rhythm even at normal doses of Delcane, especially if they are taking another drug, like an antibiotic, that inhibits its metabolism."

"Did either of the two patients actually have an arrhythmia

228

during the trial?"

"No, the conditions weren't right and their levels probably weren't high enough."

"So what happened to the study report?"

"As far as I can tell, nothing happened. The company knew that they had a problem, and they were on track to yank the drug anyway as soon as Appel was ready."

"OK, so I'll repeat my question: What does this have to do with John Romano?"

"Well, one of the other subjects was a woman who never came back for any follow-up. She was studied at the outside trial site, and I don't have those records. The other was a guy who was studied at the downtown facility, so we have a little more information. He was recruited at the last minute because they were in a hurry to finish the study and they had some dropouts. All they needed was one more warm healthy body to take a few pills and to sit around and have EKGs and blood tests for a few hours. They finally collared somebody who was related to a Miracle employee. His initials were JSR, and his birth date was June 5, 1958."

Before he finished the sentence, Dorothy was hurrying to her office to check John Romano's demographic information.

CHAPTER 22

Philip and Dorothy stayed up late piecing the story together. Bonnie and Hugh had figured out a way to give Moira large doses of Delcane, to prolong her QT interval and send her heart out of rhythm. Bonnie knew from the normal volunteer study that Delcane in large doses would kill John, especially if it was given with an antibiotic that also prolonged the QT interval. And because Moira had a mild case of the long QT syndrome, Delcane would push her over the edge, too. Just to be on the safe side, Hugh continued to hound her about her weight so she would take over-the-counter pills that contained ephedrine, which would further irritate her heart. Extreme dieting would lower her potassium and magnesium levels and render her heart even more unstable.

Philip told Dorothy, "I distinctly remember the ambulance drivers telling me that their dispatcher had a hard time hearing Hugh on the 911 call because a radio was blaring in the background."

"What does that have to do with anything?"

"Patients with the long QT syndrome sometimes have arrhythmias when they are startled by a loud noise. Hugh made sure she got plenty of the drug and then turned up the volume on the clock radio."

"Right. When it went off, he was in the shower, and it jolted Moira awake."

"And presto, instant cardiac arrest. All he had to do was stand there and watch her die while he pretended to call his neighbor, whom he knew was away, then 911, figuring they would never get there in time to save her."

"But they did get there and restarted her heart."

"Bonnie must have told Hugh that if he just delayed a few minutes, Moira's brain would fry."

Dorothy asked the logical question. "So why didn't they pick up Delcane in the drug screen?"

"This was the most brilliant part of Bonnie's plan. Because Moira didn't die right away, Bonnie knew that her liver would convert Delcane to its metabolite. That happens to be Appel, the antihistamine we thought Moira was taking. By the time her blood was drawn in the ER, the only thing to detect was Appel. No surprise, except for how much."

"That also explains why the Gladwyne Pharmacy had no record of Moira getting an antihistamine all that time."

"Exactly. Bonnie had access to Delcane. Moira thought she was getting free Appel from Bonnie and couldn't have known the difference, especially if Bonnie packaged the Delcane to make it look like Appel."

"And the grapefruit juice?"

"Grapefruit juice blocks the metabolism of Delcane to Appel. Just another way to make sure that Moira had killer levels of Delcane in her system long enough to destabilize her heart rhythm. Hugh told Moira that grapefruit juice had fewer calories than other beverages and would help her lose weight if she drank a ton of it."

Dorothy shook her head. "Your case sounds logical, but the whole thing is built on circumstantial evidence, almost all of which you gathered illegally. This stuff would never hold up to legal scrutiny. There isn't a shred of physical evidence. Moira's body was cremated, and the 'murder weapon' doesn't exist."

"I know. Bonnie covered their tracks well."

Dorothy put her head in her hands. "I don't know where we should go from here."

"Would it do any good to get another opinion? That's what I did when I was practicing medicine and hit a snag."

Dorothy thought for a moment. "Maybe you can organize all of your findings in a brief, and we can show it to a few people with legal experience to see if they find it credible."

"That should be pretty easy."

"But remember how sensitive this material is. We have to carefully pick who sees it."

"Sure. I'll get it together and give it to you."

In a few days, Philip had assembled a seven-page brief that Dorothy agreed summarized the case well. Dorothy wanted to show it to her father first.

"Philip, I don't want you around. I think your presence might inhibit him, and I want his brutally honest opinion. He will be stopping by this evening, and he can read it then." Philip was clearly disappointed that he was being left out but didn't press the issue.

When Dorothy's father arrived, he flopped down on the sofa in her office. "Man, am I tired. Had a surveillance today, and the mark wore me out."

"Dad, do me a favor. Read this brief and tell me what you think."

"Sure, honeybunch. Anything for you, especially if you throw a beer into the deal."

After he finished reading, Dick Deaver looked up over his half glasses. "That's quite a story. Basically, you're using rumor, hearsay, and illegally obtained information to accuse two prominent people of conspiring to kill the mother of small children by using her own disease against her. And you have no hard evidence, is that correct?"

Dorothy nodded.

"Dorothy, these aren't career criminals here. I bet they never even received a speeding ticket. You're just going to look damn foolish unless you have an airtight case against them. If you go after them and you're wrong, they'll sue you and likely clean your clock in court. Philip doesn't have a lot to lose now, but you certainly do, especially if they get wind of the computer hacking."

"So, what do you propose? Philip won't drop this thing."

"I am not an expert with this stuff, but you'll either have to find physical evidence, or they must confess."

"Everything happened so long ago," Dorothy explained. "The people we interviewed never saw Hugh abuse Moira. They say he treated her like crap and was probably having an affair, but that's still a long way from proving he had anything to do with her death. Her disease regularly kills people on its own."

"And remember that Philip wouldn't have a lot of credibility. He has an axe to grind, and any prosecutor with a brain will toss the case."

Dorothy believed in Philip, but even she had to wonder how much Philip exaggerated the facts to make Hugh and Bonnie look like the criminals he believed them to be. "What do you think about our theory of John Romano's death?"

"Intriguing. What happened in John's clinical study suggests that Bonnie had a good way to kill him. But the autopsy didn't yield anything."

"Bonnie is a smart gal."

"It's a good thing, because if the Romano brothers can link her to their bambino's death, they'll arrange a nice long dive for her into the Delaware with a bullet in her head and concrete boots on her feet."

"So, do you have any suggestions about what to do next?"

"First of all, you can't get involved."

"I realize that, Dad, but I already am. Philip is friends with an assistant DA in Montgomery County. Do you think it makes sense to talk to her?"

"I guess so. Just tell him to be extra careful. You don't want the Romanos to accuse you of betraying their confidence."

"This would be handled discreetly, but I think the Romanos expect me to use their information to move ahead. I did tell Philip to keep the Romano information out of the final draft of the brief. The Hamlin case has to stand on its own."

But the next day at Dorothy's office, Philip disagreed vehemently. He wanted to include everything to make the brief as compelling as possible. The issue sparked a short but intense argument.

"Look, Philip, if you put that stuff into the brief and it gets back to the Romanos, there will be hell to pay. Why risk that now?"

"But don't you think that knowing that Bonnie killed John Romano would make the authorities take the Hamlin case more seriously?"

"Maybe. Why don't you just tell the DA without writing it down?"

After arguing about it a little longer, Philip agreed to do as Dorothy suggested. He didn't want to put her in harm's way. Besides, the person he was going to consult was a good friend, and he knew she could keep a confidence.

Judy Thomas was an assistant District Attorney and Philip's former neighbor. Judy's kids went to the same school, and their families became friends. Philip and Judy discovered they both had Lebanese ancestors, and shared many childhood memories. Judy was close to her family and was helpful to her aging parents. Judy was a sixties throwback, preferring frumpy long wollen skirts and heavy sweaters in earthern tones to dark lawyerly business suits with white frilly shirts. She had a friendly face and a sweet smile that she tried to suppress at work, but rarely succeeded.

After law school at Penn and clerking for two years for a federal judge, she took a job in the Philadelphia District Attorney's office. But after two years, she decided there were too many scummy criminals in the grossly overloaded system and she resigned.

She and her husband, David, moved to Montgomery County, where she accepted a job as an assistant DA. In this more orderly environment, she quickly became one of the "go to" people for murder cases in the county. This got her a good deal of media attention, and Philip liked to tease her about getting her autograph.

David was a hard-driving businessman who worked for a New York brokerage firm. He smoked, seldom exercised, ate poorly, and had a spare tire around his waist. He played doubles tennis on the weekends, and invariably finished off those afternoons with a plate of wings and a few cold ones with his tennis partners. Though every male member of David's father's family had heart disease, David quipped, "I must have gotten my mother's genes or else I would have a stronger serve."

Late one Saturday afternoon, David was splitting firewood in the backyard. A cigarette was hanging out of his mouth as he used the maul and sledge. Their kids had left for a sleepover, and he and Judy were looking forward to an evening alone. David wanted a fire to set the mood. Flitting about the kitchen, Judy watched him stop and rest a few times.

When David brought the logs in, he told Judy his chest had

been aching when he was chopping, but that it eased up when he rested.

"Should we go to the emergency room?" Judy asked.

"I'm not used to swinging that damn axe, and I think I just pulled a muscle. Christ, I've been waiting for alone time longer than I can remember. We are not spending it in the friggin' ER."

So instead, they opened a bottle of merlot and enjoyed a delicious meal. After dinner, David started a fire in their bedroom fireplace and switched on some music. They were just beginning to make love when David moaned, clutched his chest, broke into a sweat, and lost consciousness. Judy scrambled to the phone, called 911 and then Philip.

Philip and Nancy were watching an old Mel Brooks movie with the kids. Philip had dozed off, but the ringing jarred him awake. He saw it was Judy on the caller ID screen. Good thing, because Judy could barely get the words out of her mouth.

"Philip, come quick. It's David. I think he is having a heart attack."

"On my way," Philip said, and ran out the back door.

The quickest way to the Thomas house was over the fence. Somehow, he managed to avoid tripping over dog and kid toys or slamming into the swing set in the darkness. He took the fence like a champion hurdler and was in the Thomas kitchen before Judy had been able to button her robe. "Hurry Philip, follow me."

Judy led Philip to their bedroom where David was lying on the floor, naked and blue. Philip immediately cleared his airway and began chest compressions and mouth-to-mouth resuscitation until the ambulance crew arrived a few minutes later. The paramedics gave David an electrical shock that restored a normal heart rhythm. But the ensuing EKG showed a large amount of damage to the heart muscle.

"It looks like a coronary blockage caused his heart to go out of rhythm," Philip observed. "We have to get the vessel opened quickly before the muscle is permanently damaged."

Nancy arrived and embraced Judy as David slowly recovered consciousness. Philip hopped into the ambulance and called ahead to the catheterization team at GMH, led by Sean Marshall one of Philip's staff cardiologists who specialized in procedures to open blocked arteries.

"I want to have everyone there and ready to go when we arrive," he told Sean.

Philip supervised David's transfer to the cath lab where Sean and the team were setting up. The nurses moved David to the catheterization table and began to prep the groin area while Sean explained what was happening to Judy who had arrived with Nancy. Within five minutes, Sean and the cardiac fellow had inserted a needle into the femoral artery, and had threaded a guide wire up the aorta.

Philip stood in the control room just outside the lab and watched. "I think that you should go to the left coronary first," Philip suggested. "The EKG at the house looked like the damage was on the left side."

Sean positioned the catheter perfectly in the left coronary artery, where they were able to visualize a tight blockage. He opened the artery and placed an expandable metal device called a stent to ensure that the vessel would stay open. The procedure was finished within 75 minutes of the time David had collapsed. By the time he was sent to the observation unit, David was cracking jokes with the nurses. Judy alternated between laughing and crying hysterically.

David made an excellent recovery and was home in a few days. As Philip's patient, he heeded suggestions about diet, exercise and smoking. Like so many others, David's potentially catastrophic fright was necessary to get his attention. Judy thanked Philip dozens of times and told him she would return the favor some day.

So, when Philip called Judy to ask for a meeting, she readily agreed. Judy had been crushed when Nancy and he had split up. Even though Nancy lived in a house in the same neighborhood and the kids played together, it wasn't the same, not to mention that her husband had lost his cardiologist.

Judy had no idea why Philip wanted to meet with her. He had merely said he needed help with a legal matter. They agreed on lunch at the Mediterranean Delight, a small eatery three blocks from the county courthouse. The family-run restaurant wasn't much to look at, but the service was fast, the food was homemade, and it came in big portions. Philip arrived first and ordered a selection of his favorite starters. When Judy arrived, they ordered a couple of iced teas, and decided on baked kibi as the main course with baklava for dessert.

"So what have you been up to, Philip?" Judy asked while they munched. "David and I miss seeing you across the back fence."

"I am living in an apartment and doing what I can to make a little money. Mostly, I have been trying to find out what really happened to Moira Hamlin. Judy, I have a strong suspicion that her husband and his mistress conspired to murder her."

Judy stopped chewing and stared at Philip. Had her friend lost his mind? She answered slowly. "Philip, that sounds pretty far-fetched. I can't believe that Hugh would do something like that. It looked to everybody around here like he loved Moira."

"It was the world's oldest motive—Hugh had an affair with Bonnie Romano who is now his wife, and I think that the two of them engineered the murder."

Judy had never met Bonnie Romano, but she had certainly heard of her. After all, Bonnie had been featured in the newspapers and magazines as a shining example of what women can accomplish. Judy just couldn't understand how Philip had arrived at this bewildering conclusion, let alone why he took her to lunch to tell her about it.

"Are you all right, Philip? You've been through a lot."

"I'm fine, and this is not a delusion. It would take a long time to explain everything to you. I've written down most of what I know, and I'll give you a copy of the brief. I'm sure you realize how important it is to keep anything I share with you confidential."

"You know you can trust me, Philip."

"OK, fair enough. But in addition to what is in the brief, I need you to know that Bonnie Romano probably murdered her first husband a few years ago in a similar way. I can't tell you too much more about that case. But believe me, my suspicions about Bonnie Romano are well founded."

Judy had heard about the John Romano case when she worked in the Philadelphia DA office. She knew there had been a lot of angst in South Philly's Italian community. The detectives had worked the case hard, and had come to the strongly supported conclusion that John's death was from natural causes.

"Is somebody helping you with this investigation?"

"Dorothy Deaver. Know her?"

"I've heard of her and her father. She's a good lawyer, and her father runs a reputable private investigation firm. Do you have any hard evidence in either of these cases?"

"Not really. We have interviewed some people and pieced things together pretty well. The circumstantial case is strong, but much of our evidence came from what you might call unconventional sources."

"You obtained the evidence illegally?"

He nodded. "But the information wasn't hard to access, and no one knows we have it."

"Well, I really don't want to know more about that. As an officer of the court, if I learned about illegal activity, I would have to turn you in."

Judy was concerned to see Philip agitated, much different from the calm and confident physician she had talked to across the back fence. "Philip, what do you want from me?"

"Your opinion about what to do next. What else do we need to nail Hugh Hamlin and Bonnie Romano for Moira's murder? What kind of information will withstand legal scrutiny? I don't want to get myself or anybody else in trouble, but I can't stand the thought that they might get away with this. It's not right, and I won't let it happen."

Judy had a worried look on her face. Philip's intensity was disturbing.

"Look, Philip, maybe I can help, but we have to set ground rules. I'll review your brief and, if appropriate, I'll help you bring your case to the correct people. I owe my husband's life to you, but we have to play this one exactly by the book."

"I understand completely. Can I call you tomorrow?"

"Sure, but not at the office. Call me at home tomorrow evening. In the meantime, please don't talk to anyone else, and please, no more 'fact-finding' until I have a chance to go over all of this. I need to see if there is anything that can justify an indictment, short of a confession."

Philip and Judy finished lunch and said their goodbyes. Judy watched Philip leave the restaurant. She realized that just as Philip had saved her husband's life, he was asking her to do the same for him.

As he drove back to his apartment, and all the next day, Philip's mind whirred. Judy had mentioned a confession. Was there some way to get Hugh and Bonnie to confess and how could that be done legally? A wiretap or illegal listening device would be out of the question, inadmissible in court, and possibly dangerous to Dorothy and him. There had to be a way.

Dorothy met Philip at her office the following evening for the call to Judy and used her speakerphone. Judy had reviewed the brief and could find little usable in court. "There just isn't enough here. You're going to need a confession of guilt by Hugh and Bonnie or your case is cooked."

Philip was sitting across the desk from Dorothy with his feet up on an ottoman, looking surprisingly relaxed. He didn't look like a person who was scrambling to answer a difficult question, but more like somebody who already had the solution. He spoke in a disturbingly quiet voice.

"I spent most of the day trying to figure this out. Judy, as I understand it, a wiretap or bug are out because they are secret and invade privacy. But what if the recording device belonged to the Hamlins or was in their possession voluntarily, and what if they were informed ahead of time and in writing that the device could record what they said? Would that change things?"

Judy was intrigued. "You can't invade their person or their property. They would have to accept the device, be aware that it was activated, and then talk into it. How in the world would you get them to do that?"

Dorothy looked at Philip. He wore a big smile. "Judy, would it be possible for you to run this by a few of the people in your office or maybe one of the common pleas judges? Ask them to assume that the perpetrators took possession of a device that they knew could record their conversation. And then ask them to assume that while the device was activated, the targets actually spilled the beans voluntarily, without any coercion whatsoever. Would their 'confession' under those circumstances be admissible in a court of law?"

Judy thought for a moment. "I will run this one by Judge Silverburg, our resident legal scholar, but there isn't a whole lot of case law. I can't see why their statements would be inadmissible if they were not coerced or deceived."

"That's all I can ask, Judy. Thanks for your help."

After he hung up, Philip was grinning, but Dorothy was scowling. "Do you have any idea what the hell you are talking about? I really don't think it's a good idea to waste Judy's time, let alone Judge Silverburg's."

As the words came out of her mouth, Dorothy thought she had hurt Philip's feelings. But his shit-eating grin had not faded one bit.

"So you think my idea is ridiculous? Well, first of all, you probably don't know that Judge Silverburg came to see me a long time ago with a heart problem that I solved for him PDQ. So I figure that if he knows I am the requesting party, he will at least hear Judy out."

"Yeah, but no matter how much he likes you, he's still going to say that information obtained illegally is flat out worthless."

"Well, if we need a legal admission of guilt, I guess I am just going to have to pull another rabbit out of my hat, won't I?"

"Philip, are you going to come clean and tell me what you are thinking, or are you just going to torture me?"

"Tell you what. I have to talk to some people about this tomorrow. If you have dinner with me tomorrow evening, I'll fill you in. What do you say?"

"OK Philip, if you are well behaved, clean, and shaven, I will go out with you. But please, don't get into trouble."

"Trouble my dear? Trouble is my middle name."

At least he was right about that.

CHAPTER 23

Philip was now convinced that nobody in law enforcement would agree to question Hugh and Bonnie based on what he had obtained so far. Judy had been clear about the illegality of eavesdropping. So what was left? It would be necessary to get Hugh and Bonnie to admit to the crime, ideally at the same time to eliminate the possibility that one of them could roll over on the other.

Philip tossed and turned the night after seeing Judy, trying to come up with a way to solve the problem. He wanted to have some ideas before his next phone call with Judy and Dorothy the next morning. As he sat at his kitchen table in a semi-stuporous state, sipping coffee, he flicked through a pile of medical journals. He always enjoyed the advertisements and was amazed at how much drug companies were willing to pay for dramatic print advertising that most docs ignored. He had to admit that they were well done, always featuring healthy-looking people who were clearly benefiting from whatever therapy was being sold. If only his own patients looked that good.

As he paged through some of the glitz in the American Journal of Cardiology, he came across an advertisement for MCM, a company that Philip knew well. He had vivid memories of how he had first learned about MCM.

A few years before, Philip had been supervising his kids going door-to-door in the neighborhood on Halloween night. It was damp and dark, but the adults in his group seemed to be the only ones who were cold; the kids were racing around seeing how much candy they could collect. He was holding a bag of loot when his cell phone rang. He answered by reflex, then immediately regretted it.

On the other end was a cardiologist from Indiana who rarely called him at work, let alone in the evening. Eric Purcell had worked with Philip on several academic projects. If Eric was calling off hours, it could be important, but Philip didn't want to be distracted from his children. He didn't get a chance to do this very often.

"Eric, I'm with my kids, and they're trick-or-treating. Can I call you about this in the morning?"

"I know this is a bad time. My kids are all grown up, but I remember how important Halloween was. What I need to know is if you can be in Washington tomorrow afternoon."

"I have a full day of patients in the office tomorrow. What's so important?"

"Here's the deal. I have been consulting for a new company called MCM—Mobile Cardiac Monitoring. They are based in California, and they have this terrific new technology that allows patients to have their heart rhythm monitored continuously out of the hospital or wherever they go. They do it online with technicians who watch the heart rhythm from a central facility and can respond immediately to an emergency. Pretty cool, don't you think?"

"Swell, Eric. But what does that have to do with my being in DC tomorrow?"

"They're going to present their data to an FDA advisory committee tomorrow for approval, and they need a doc to go with them. I was supposed to do it, but Gloria is in the ER with a bad urinary tract infection. They need somebody with regulatory experience who can hold their hand and help to answer questions, and I thought of you. You know the guys down at the FDA better than anybody, and you know how they think. I told them you are their man."

"Eric, I don't know anything about the company or their product."

"Already thought of that, my friend. MCM will arrange to have one of their executives pick you up at your office at the hospital at nine o'clock. He will brief you on their system and data on your way to DC. You should get there in plenty of time for your after-

242

noon meeting, and they'll drive you back afterward."

Philip started to give in. "How much information is involved?"

"It really isn't that complicated. The system is pretty self-explanatory, and the data are straightforward. The device does what it is supposed to do, so they are not really expecting much of a fight at the FDA."

"Eric, you are a good friend so I will say yes, but this is going to create scheduling problems for my office."

"Philip, I know how big a pain in the ass this is, but I have invested a lot of my time, and I'd like to see them succeed. I am sure that the company will pay your usual rate."

Rhonda managed to clear his calendar, and he was at the main entrance of the hospital in time to meet the stretch limousine that pulled up to the door. As he stepped into the back seat, a distinguished, nattily dressed, middle-aged man greeted him with a cup of coffee, warm pastry, and a briefing book.

"Philip, I am so glad to meet you. I am Perry McSwaine, the CEO of MCM, and I have heard a lot about you. I really appreciate your help with this meeting. Take a few minutes to look over this material while you have your coffee, and then I'll answer your questions."

Perry pulled out a USA Today and paged through it, glancing up from time to time as Philip studied the document.

As he would soon learn, Perry was a high-energy person. When he was just eight years old, he organized a lawn mowing service in his neighborhood. Since he was too young to mow the lawns himself, he enlisted some older kids, scheduled the clients, and collected an agency fee.

At just about every phase of his life, Perry had come up with a new way to make money. He had been successful with small projects and moved on to bigger things after high school. His parents insisted on college, but he quickly tired of wasting time acquiring information he would never need. He was a born innovator, and traditional education wasn't for him.

Perry eventually concentrated his skills on health care. He had correctly surmised that health care was going to be big business with the maturation of the baby boomers and their increased interest in healthy lifestyles. Over the next 25 years, he started seven health care companies, all of which had gone public and turned a profit within five years, and all were still in existence. His latest brainchild was MCM an idea that came to him in a hospital bed in his hometown of San Diego while he was recovering from a heart attack.

The attack had been a real shock to Perry who, at 55 had taken very good care of himself and thought himself "immune" to heart disease. He was standing on the first tee after hooking a drive into the woods. He felt terrible chest pain and slumped to the ground. Fortunately, there was an automatic defibrillator in the clubhouse, and the pro and staff members had been trained. They quickly came to Perry's rescue and began CPR. They placed the device on his chest and activated it, sending a high-energy shock through his thorax. The electrical charge activated all of the cells in his heart simultaneously, allowing the normal pacemaker cells to take control of the heart rhythm.

Perry awakened just as the ambulance crew arrived. Because of the quick response, he suffered no brain damage. He had a catheterization to fix his coronary arteries, after which his doctors told him that he would have to remain in the hospital a few extra days so they could monitor his heart rhythm. Perry had gone berserk over the prospect of being stuck in the hospital so somebody could watch his heartbeats.

He began to ask the nurses about telemetry monitoring, how it was done, and why it had to be carried out in patients like him. Why couldn't monitoring for low-risk patients be done outside the hospital? There would have to be some way to transmit the signal, so why not use cell phone technology? Perry started calling people he knew who had expertise in electronics, data processing, and cellular communication.

By the time he was discharged, Perry was well on his way to creating MCM. He called Eric Purcell, with whom he had worked on a previous start-up. Eric had good business sense, and was enthusiastic about the idea. Perry was right; many patients had to remain in the hospital just to stay on a cardiac monitor. Keeping track of a patient's rhythm on a continual basis out of the hospital would be valuable, especially to insurance companies.

"You'll have two major hurdles," Eric predicted. "The first will be convincing the insurance companies to pay for a new technology. The second will be getting doctors to change over from their old methods to try something new." The two obstacles were connected. "Until the docs know that they are going to be paid at a reasonable rate for this service, they won't order it."

Perry aggressively pursued his idea, even though his cardiologist and his family told him to take it easy. He thrived on work, and the new project ended up being a great way to rehab. Within six months, he had patented his idea, established a company, bought a building in downtown San Diego, and hired key personnel. By the end of the year, he had a prototype device to test. And now, 18 months after his heart attack, Perry was on his way to an FDA hearing to get market approval.

Philip closed the briefing document. "Quite an idea. I've seen a few prototype monitors, and their problem was that they didn't record clearly. How well does this one work?"

"We still have a few glitches, but almost all of the tracings are readable. I think that the real challenge is going to be hiring and training technicians who can watch the monitors and know what they're looking at."

"What's the patient reaction to it?"

"Patients love the idea that someone is watching them. They like to call it their guardian angel."

"I understand the monitoring part, but what happens if the technician sees something important?"

"We are working on several possibilities. First, the technician will call the patient and doctor. The device can work as a cell phone, so we can call the patient or they can call us. If the rhythm is really bad, the technician can also enlist emergency help. The device has a GPS guidance system, so the technician can give emergency help an approximate location."

"That will be important," Philip agreed.

"We're also working on a kind of walkie-talkie system. We hope to allow the patient and technician to talk to each other with an activation button or when the patient has a serious arrhythmia."

"Sounds like you have big plans."

"Yes, we just have to get the basic device FDA approved so we can start marketing it. And that's where you come in. We need you with us at the advisory committee."

The FDA regularly convenes advisory committee meetings in which they solicit opinions from experts about the approvability of drugs or devices. This takes pressure off the agency when difficult decisions have to be made. Having buy-in from thought leaders before approval helps to diffuse criticism from the public and Congress when products are pulled off the market.

"I don't think we'll have a problem today," Philip predicted. It looks to me like the system works. The big question is how quickly doctors will assimilate this new technology. Physicians tend to be slow to change, and they won't take a financial loss to switch over to a new idea."

"That's what Eric said. We understand that, and have some plans that I will share with you later about both issues."

Philip had been right about the meeting. The group assembled to review the MCM application consisted of renowned cardiologists, statisticians, and basic scientists. There was also a consumer-nominated representative to look out for the public's interests.

The committee was as critical as usual, but they were impressed with the work Perry and his company had put into the project. In the end, they were satisfied that patients could be monitored safely. When they asked Philip, as an expert familiar to most of the panel, for his thoughts, he gave a balanced opinion about the potential limitations of the system as well as its clinical value. After a full afternoon of deliberations, the committee recommended that the agency approve the device.

But physician acceptance was slow, and insurance company approvals didn't come immediately. Nevertheless, Perry was grateful and retained Philip as an advisor for MCM. Philip supervised a series of studies proving that the device shortened hospital stays without compromising patient safety.

The studies were the final piece of the puzzle for MCM. With approval for payment by insurance companies came physician buy-in. It was another success story for Perry McSwaine. This time, he decided not sell the company. He wanted to expand monitoring capabilities to other parameters like blood pressure and body fluid levels.

Philip learned a lot about business from Perry and his crew. He took special interest in training the monitor technicians to read the array of arrhythmias their patients generated. Many pleasant memories replayed in his mind as he read the ad in the journal, but he remembered what Perry had said about the device's ability to voice transmit. Was that a capability the device now had?

Philip called Perry in San Diego. Perry's secretary said Perry was out on the links. "But I can give you his cell phone number, Dr. Sarkis," she quickly added. "You can call him there."

Most golfers hate to get interrupted, but Perry never minded. Philip had played with him a few times, and was amazed at how Perry could put the phone down, hit a terrific shot, and resume an important conversation. When Philip reached him this time, Perry was standing on the tenth tee getting ready to play the back nine at Pelican Bay.

"So Philip, what's it like there weather-wise? It's 75 degrees here, sunny and beautiful, and I'm in the middle of shooting my best round of the year."

"Yeah, the weather is terrific here too—if you're a duck. I'm jealous."

Perry laughed. "I told you to take a job with us and move out here. So what can I do for you, Philip?"

"Perry, I just have a quick question. You told me a few years ago that MCM would eventually incorporate a walkie-talkie feature? What happened to that?"

"The device does have a cell phone built in now. It doesn't have the walkie-talkie feature yet. We are going to set it up so a severe arrhythmia opens the line and lets the patient and the monitoring center talk to each other. The software to do that is already in the device, and the engineers have given it a name—IVT for instant voice transmission. It's just a matter of putting another button on the box."

"Have you tested it?"

"Yes. It's actually child's play for engineers, but it just hasn't been a priority. I have been concerned about privacy issues. I don't think that patients would appreciate a technician recording some pillow talk or such. That part will have to be handled carefully."

"Could you produce some devices with IVT for a special project?"

"I guess so, but we'd have to be careful to explain the feature to the users since it has not passed the regulators yet. What do you have in mind?"

"Not sure. I just need to know if I can get my hands on a few of them."

"Philip, after what you did for us, there's no way I could turn you down. If it weren't for you, there might not be an MCM. My biggest disappointment is that you didn't get to share in our success."

"That was a shame but it wasn't your fault." Philip had lost his MCM stock in the malpractice verdict. Perry knew about Philip's case, but had been embarrassed to bring it up. "How soon could the modified devices be ready if I need a few?" Philip asked, ending the awkward silence.

"Just a few days. Whoever uses it must be fully aware that it's a prototype and has this capability. Things have been going well lately, and I don't want to screw it up with a legal problem."

"Gotcha. I promise that it will be done on the up-and-up. I have a few special cases, and the new feature would be perfect."

"If you want to pursue this, call Jamie Ascot. You remember her?"

"Sure. She was the general manager of the monitoring facility when I consulted."

"I put her in charge of all operations. She'll be able to authorize the prototype and get it for you."

Having Jamie Ascot as his contact was a break. She was competent, and Philip had worked well with her. She ran MCM's monitoring center with an iron hand. Jamie had been a nurse before going to industry, so she knew what patient care was all about.

After he rang off, Philip spent the next few hours sitting on his sofa, staring into space, and making notes on a legal pad as he prepared for his teleconference with Judy at Dorothy's office. The device modification would allow him to record a conversation between Hugh and Bonnie. But how would he get Hugh Hamlin to accept the MCM device? And how could he record something that would prove the couple's guilt? Philip was going to need some help if he was going to set an effective trap.

CHAPTER 24

Philip awoke the next morning, his mind instantly churning with ideas. He was reasonably sure that his appeal to each of his colleagues would succeed, but he needed all the details to be worked out.

Philip had learned additional things about Hugh Hamlin that might help in setting the trap. Henry Wong was Philip's internist and also saw Hugh as a patient. Henry liked to talk, and told Philip that Hugh was paranoid about getting heart disease. He was a hypochondriac who constantly reported every ache and pain to his doctors, begging assurance that he was healthy.

Henry Wong was a legend at GMH. He was the first child of Chinese immigrants, and had graduated at the top of his medical school class at Penn with an added doctorate in microbiology. He decided against a high-salary subspecialty, choosing to be an old-fashioned general internist. Within a year at GMH, he had one of the best internal medicine practices on the Main Line. When his photo appeared on the cover of the Main Line magazine as the area's top generalist, his office was overrun. Previously, the idea of an Asian garnering a top doctor award on the WASPish Main Line would have been laughable.

Henry accepted the accolades with customary humility. He continued to take a full hour to see a new patient and sat with established patients as long as they needed. This wasn't a way to get wealthy, but Henry had decided long ago that money was not his motivation for practicing medicine. He worked long hours, meticulously checking laboratory tests and talking to patients on the phone well into the evening. He loved his solo practice and refused to hire associates. He had a small staff, and his wife Sadie worked at the front desk greeting his patients like family members.

The problem was that an appointment to see Henry was harder to get than 50-yard-line tickets to the Superbowl. Henry gave priority to his GMH brethren, so Philip had been able to see him as a patient. Ironically, Philip had called Henry personally on Hugh's behalf. During one of Moira's visits, Hugh said he needed somebody good to help him with his medical problems. After Henry saw Hugh, Hamlin called the office almost every day with pesky questions.

Henry and Philip had shared the care of dozens of patients, and they discussed cases on a regular basis. Henry briefed Philip on Hugh's neuroses and pseudo-illnesses after Hugh's first few office visits. At that time, Philip was more focused on Moira's health, so he didn't make much of it. He listened to Henry's opinions of Hugh more out of courtesy than interest.

"I am telling you, Philip, the guy's some kind of a nut. He must call my office every day with a new ache or pain. I can't imagine what the guy would do if he actually had anything wrong with his heart."

"Well, is there anything wrong with him?" Philip had asked.

"The only thing has been a few ventricular premature beats now and again."

"Can he feel them? Does he have palpitations?"

"Actually, he can feel them, and they drive him crazy. I sent him over to see somebody in your group once. I think it was Milan. He had a stress test and an echocardiogram. They were normal, so Milan sent him back and said that nothing further needed to be done."

Philip wondered how much of Hugh Hamlin's paranoia had come from concerns about Moira's problems. He decided not to bring it up to Moira and that had been the end of it.

Then Hugh sued Philip. Henry called Philip several times to offer sympathy, but Philip never returned the phone calls. He was embarrassed by the entire affair. During his recuperation, Philip needed a check-up, and Henry was happy to see him. "I have to say I was ashamed to be Hugh's physician. I felt like a traitor,"

Henry observed.

"He isn't a sweet person," Philip had replied.

Henry described how he had been conflicted. "I really wanted to dump the son-of-a-bitch. But I have made it a policy not to fire patients unless they are just totally non-compliant or they choose to end the relationship. I don't see Hugh doing that, do you?"

"No. He needs someone with your patience. I respect your principles and your loyalty to your patients, Henry."

Philip now remembered that conversation, and knew he was going to have to depend on Henry's relationship with Hugh to hatch his plan.

Philip decided to stop by Henry's office at lunchtime. He knew that was when Henry did paperwork and his office staff would be in the cafeteria. Philip didn't want to scandalize Henry's nurses and secretaries. Besides, he had some tough things to ask Henry and he didn't want to be interrupted.

Philip found Henry on the phone with a nervous patient, reassuring her she didn't have cancer. He finally extricated himself and greeted Philip in his usual white starched shirt, regimental tie and sweater vest. With coke bottle lenses, he looked the part he played.

"You know, fear of disease is almost as bad as the disease itself," Henry observed. "Thank God I took all those psychiatry courses in medical school. I spend so much of my time reassuring healthy people. Now, to what do we owe the great privilege of your presence today, my dear Doctor Sarkis?"

They'd always spoken to each other with exaggerated civility. It reminded Philip of happier days.

"Funny you should ask, my dear Doctor Wong. I have come to ask you if you would deign to wreak revenge on one of your most paranoid patients. I am about to offer you an opportunity to let a prick live his worst nightmare."

"Hugh Hamlin, by any chance?"

"How perceptive of you, Doctor Wong. I came to ask if you would be willing to make our old buddy Hugh believe that you are finally worried about those damnable premature beats."

"And might I be able to learn what this is all about?"

"Certainly. Let's say that I have information that links Hugh Hamlin and his second wife to the death of Moira Hamlin."

Henry nearly jumped out of his chair. "His first wife? You mean he murdered Moira?"

Philip smiled. "I knew you would have that reaction. It makes for a pretty amazing story."

"That's an understatement. And he brought a lawsuit against you?"

"Yes, and ruined my life in the process."

Philip watched Henry doodle on a notepad with a lead pencil as he slowly composed himself. "Now, just suppose, for the sake of argument and my affection for you, my esteemed colleague, that I was willing to help. Exactly what course of action would this bring us to?"

"It is really very simple, Dr. Wong. All I ask is that you advise Mr. Hamlin that he needs to go back to see the good Dr. Milan Kuco for another evaluation."

"That's all I have to do?"

"Well, I'd like you to do it soon. Does the eminent Mr. Hamlin have an appointment coming up?"

"Soon, I think. I can have Sadie call him and say I need to see him next week."

"That would be delightful. You could do an EKG and 'see something' you don't like. That would be your excuse to have him see Milan."

"All right, Philip," said Henry thoughtfully. "I will do this for you. But is it possible to ask how you came to suspect Hugh of wrongdoing?"

"No—it's too complicated, and I don't want to put you in a bad position. Why don't we just say that Hugh Hamlin needs to pay for what he did."

"Well, retribution is one of my favorite themes. I will have to assume you have a good case?"

"Let us say that I have a lot of circumstantial evidence but I need to get him to hang himself. That's what this is all about. Henry," said Philip, breaking from their formal banter. "This is not revenge run amok."

"Look Philip, we'll probably violate every principle of medical ethics by doing what you suggest. I know what you have been through, and I feel terrible about it. But I am going to have a hard time taking advantage of one of my patients."

Henry's response didn't surprise Philip. But his next few words did.

"On the other hand, I trust you Philip. You are a good person, so if you suspect that Hugh hurt Moira, I have to believe it. I will help you as best I can."

"Henry, I owe you big. Just let me know when you send the referral, and I will make sure that Milan is ready for it. And when all of this is done, if there is any flak, I promise you I will take full responsibility. You will be able to say you simply made the referral and that you knew nothing more."

"Look, I don't want to get into trouble, but what happened to you sounds terrible, and if there is a payback possible, I understand why you would want to pursue it. I will take my chances."

Philip felt a lump in his throat. He resisted the impulse to give Henry a hug and instead lapsed back into their familiar banter. "Well, my dear Dr. Wong. This has been an extraordinarily valuable session, I must say. I will have to find a way to return your generosity."

Henry nodded. Philip left the office quickly. He needed to compose himself before moving on to the next person in his plan, his former partner, Milan Kuco.

Milan's story was another example of the American Dream. Born in Yugoslavia, Milan was educated there before the country was ripped apart by civil war. Following high school, Milan was drafted into the army and served in the infantry as a medic. When civil war broke out, he served in a field hospital. The carnage was terrible, and Milan was forced to care for hundreds of mutilated boys who mostly died after suffering horribly. It was during this service that Milan resolved to leave the country at his first opportunity.

After two years in the army, Milan was permitted to go abroad for college. He applied to colleges in Germany and France, was accepted into a program in Hamburg, and graduated with a medical degree in six years. He worked at several jobs to pay his tuition at the university. When he finished, he decided to study in the US. After hundreds of letters of application, he latched onto a third-rate residency in a small community hospital in Connecticut.

Once he saw what the American system had to offer, Milan wanted to stay in the States, but this was no mean task. Thousands of physicians emigrated from other countries with similar aspirations, and there were a limited number of positions. What distinguished Milan were his iron will and a clever attorney. It didn't hurt that Milan had published some important research on cardiac arrhythmias. After training at some of the country's best hospitals, Philip offered him a position at GMH.

Milan was a gentle giant, with a heavy Eastern European accent, a good sense of humor, and a positive attitude about nearly everything. His years of turmoil and adversity had left him grateful for every day.

Milan was also technically gifted, able to maneuver catheters to just the right place to cauterize the most resistant arrhythmias. Philip had groomed Milan to succeed him as chief, but Philip's professional demise had thrown the cardiology department into turmoil. Milan was neither a strong political in-fighter nor eager administrator. He finally lost out to a senior, though much less talented, member of the department. Milan accepted the decision gracefully.

Unlike Henry Wong, Milan did not spend long hours at the office. He usually went home as early as possible to his family and his dogs in New Jersey. For an uninterrupted conversation with Milan, Philip knew he'd have to go to Milan's home. When Philip called, Milan's wife, Christina, answered.

"Philip, how have you been? We have missed seeing you. It's been too long."

Philip didn't pay much attention to most faculty spouses, but he had taken an immediate liking to Christina. She had come from a moneyed family in Eastern Europe, was gracious, and doted on her family. She respected Philip and had been grateful for all he had done for Milan.

"Christina, it's good to hear your voice. I am getting back on my feet. How are you and the children?"

"Good. We had my family over for the holidays, and now we're back to our usual routine. The kids are involved in a million activities. You wouldn't believe how big they're getting. Are we going to see you?"

"As a matter of fact, I was going to ask if I could drop by this evening to talk to Milan."

"That should be fine. He's picking up Alex at tennis practice

254

now and should be home soon. Can you stay for dinner?"

"Christina, that's so nice of you. But I have to meet someone back in the city tonight, so I'll take a rain check. What time would be convenient?"

"Make it about seven. We'll see you then."

As Philip drove across the Ben Franklin Bridge to South Jersey, he started having second thoughts about his "brilliant plan." What if something went wrong? Although he would take full responsibility, he didn't know if he could keep Henry and Milan safe. And how fair was it to place them in a risky situation just because he couldn't think of any other way to nail Hugh and Bonnie?

The Kuco home was situated near the Pine Barrens, about 25 minutes from the bridge. Milan and Christina had bought land in a new development and designed a roomy, comfortable house to accommodate their children as well as Christina's large family who visited frequently. They had a spacious backyard and a tennis court, as well as plenty of open space for their three big labs. Alex, their only son, was a tennis phenom, ranked nationally as a junior player.

Milan was relaxing in the living room with a scotch and classical music. He gave Philip a bear hug. Christina swept in from the kitchen and also embraced Philip with tears in her eyes. Philip sat on the sofa with a glass of white burgundy and gave them a brief synopsis of his life since the verdict, then summarized what he was doing to prove his innocence. He had intended to exclude Christina from the conversation for her own sake, but he saw that Milan was not going to do anything without discussing it with her. She might as well hear it directly from Philip.

At the end of the tale, Milan shook his head. "So you think that this guy Hamlin schemed with Bonnie Romano to kill his wife and they laid the blame on you? That's unbelievable."

"Right. It's such a fantastic story that we're going to have a hard time proving it. All the circumstantial evidence points to them, but there is no body, no murder weapon, and no physical evidence. My only hope is to get them to confess."

Christina chimed in. "How?"

"Well, it will have to be 'extracted,' as they say, but I am struggling to do it legally so that their confessions won't be thrown out in court. I have an attorney assisting me, and her father is a private investigator. We have some help from an assistant DA in Montgomery County. They all think that planting a bug or tapping a phone line would be a bad idea. But we might be able to use MCM."

Milan had used the device to decide if, after a procedure, patient symptoms could be due to a recurrent rhythm problem. His curiosity was piqued. "I don't get it. How on earth will recording somebody's EKG prove they are guilty?"

Philip explained the walkie-talkie capability of the MCM device. "If we can place a device in his home when Hugh has an arrhythmia, the IVT feature will activate and tape his conversation with Bonnie."

"And you want me to get Hugh Hamlin to agree to use the device at home?"

"Yes. He will also be asked to sign an agreement with a clause about voice recording. I'm banking on his not reading it carefully."

"So, how will I see Hugh Hamlin to make this recommendation?"

"That's the easy part. Henry Wong has been noticing premature beats on his EKGs. He's going to tell him he needs to come back to see you, and the MCM device is what you will prescribe."

Christina was taken with the idea. "Philip, that's brilliant. It could work."

Philip was delighted to get some positive feedback, but Christina and Milan needed to understand the risks. "If something goes wrong with this, these people will come after us. I'll take full responsibility. You must deny that you knew anything about the special device. You merely did your job as a consultant."

Milan sat quietly in his easy chair. Finally, he put down his drink and leaned forward. "Look Philip. Until you have been shot at and nearly killed, it's easy to be frightened by people like this. I lived through terrible situations, so this is nothing to me. You're my friend and you are asking for my help. I will do this for you, and if something bad happens afterward, we'll simply have to deal with it. That should be the last time that we have to say this to each other."

Philip was touched. "Milan, I really appreciate this. I only hope that someday I can repay your kindness."

Christina rose and gave Philip another hug. Philip said his goodbyes and left with tears in his eyes. He called Dorothy from the car and asked her to meet him at the 16th Street Bar and Grill, a favorite of the late-dinner crowd. The bar was noisy and smoky, but Dorothy arrived first and found a table in the back, where the lights were low, and the music a bit softer. From Philip's jaunty walk, Dorothy could tell he had good news.

"Well, you look happy. You had success?"

"I did. My faith in human nature isn't totally restored, but it's been repaired."

Philip ordered a bottle of white wine, then told Dorothy about Henry and Milan. As Philip explained his plan, the concern on her face became more distinct. When he finished, she reached across the table and took his hands.

"Philip, I know how hard you have worked on this, but I am worried about its legality."

Philip snapped, "I don't understand what you're talking about. There's going to be a clear disclaimer. How could that possibly be illegal?"

"Don't get angry. It all has to do with deception, Philip. They will be able to argue they weren't aware of the invasion of their privacy."

"Well, I don't agree," he said vehemently. "If we put this plan into place as I described, and the technician at MCM records conversations when she legitimately thinks she must, it should be admissible."

Dorothy was getting tired of being the naysayer and thus the object of Philip's anger. She had looked forward to a romantic evening, and now Philip was on edge. "OK, let's drop this. We'll run it past Judy first thing tomorrow, and maybe she can see how Judge Silverburg would rule."

"Fair enough," Philip agreed. "We'll call Judy tomorrow morning, and I will lay it out for her as fairly as I can." His mood changed abruptly again, this time for the better. "How was your day otherwise?" Philip asked in a desultory way.

"It actually was good until right at the end. At five o'clock, Vincente Romano called me on my cell and wanted to know what was going on."

"What did you tell him?"

"What could I tell him? Nothing, of course. But he's on my back and insists that I update him in a few days. He said that his family just wants to make sure justice is done."

"That sounds reasonable."

Dorothy almost came out of her chair. "Reasonable! Have you gone totally nuts? These people play for real, Philip, and having them contact me regularly is weirding me out. I'm frightened, no matter whose side they say they are on. I didn't want to have anything to do with them, and now they are my new cell phone buddies."

Philip peered into his wine glass, avoiding eye contact. He was exasperated. Through clenched teeth he said, "Look, just tell them the truth. Give me Vincente's number, like I said before, and I'll call him every few days, and that way you won't have to worry about it any more."

"That would help. I mean it; these people scare me."

"I'll be careful. Now, let's take a look at the specials, have some dinner, and I'll get you home. You're getting wound up about all of this and need to relax."

"God, Philip, I don't know how much more of this I can stand."

"I know. Hopefully we'll get to the end of this ordeal soon," Philip said, patting Dorothy's hand, not sure if even he believed what he'd just said.

CHAPTER 25

Philip and Dorothy spent the night together but didn't get much sleep. Long ago, during their first encounter, each was plagued by guilt. Philip couldn't stop thinking about Nancy, and Dorothy, who never imagined herself a home wrecker, regretted seducing a married man. Their lovemaking had been marred by loads of emotional baggage.

This night was another story. Dorothy responded to Philip in ways she hadn't thought possible, and her pleasure further excited him. As she turned to watch the sunrise from her window, she wondered if Philip's aggressive approach to sex had anything to do with his hostility toward the people who had effectively ruined his life.

They were both exhausted but in good spirits when the alarm went off at 7:00. In the kitchen, Philip drank coffee at the counter in his boxers, watching Dorothy toast bagels. "That's the first all-nighter I've pulled in quite some time," he observed.

She smiled at him quizzically.

"You are the only woman I ever met who could keep me awake that long."

"It's too early for such a big lie."

"I assure you, lies are the purview of lawyers. We doctors are always sincere."

"That is not exactly my information, but we can argue about that later — another thing that lawyers do, by the way. Why don't we just call Judy soon so I can go make a living. I have a ton of work waiting for me."

Philip explained the "MCM plan" to Judy, and laid out the roles his friends would play. "It's going to be essential that Hugh believe there's a good reason to have the device in the first place. That's where Milan and Henry come in. Then Hugh will have to be frightened enough to blurt out what we want to hear."

To Dorothy's amazement, Judy was optimistic. "There is an element of deception, but that's not totally outside the scope of the law. For example, when federal agents conduct a sting operation, the targets are deceived, but as long as their privacy is not invaded, and they speak voluntarily, their admission of guilt is allowed as evidence."

Dorothy wasn't persuaded. "But isn't this like wire-tapping or planting a recording device in someone's home without their knowledge?"

"Yes and no. It is, because they might not realize all that you're recording. And it isn't, because Hugh Hamlin will sign an agreement letter that will clearly state, in bold and not fine print, that the technician may activate a voice channel if there's a need for communication. If he knows that, and if Hugh and Bonnie happen to have a recorded conversation that implicates them in a capital crime, I think the courts would rule favorably on having their 'confession' admitted as evidence."

Dorothy persisted. "But he's being duped by two doctors, and the MCM people will be alerted to activate the device pretty much on command. Doesn't that bother you?"

"Only to the extent that you are placing these helpers of yours in harm's way. Theoretically, they could be called to task for deliberately deceiving Hugh Hamlin in the guise of being his doctor or a service provider. As long as the two doctors can say, truthfully, that they were only doing their jobs and making appropriate decisions about medical care, they will be fine. I would never tell them to lie about the 'sting,' but if they deny knowing about it and there's no documentation that they did, it will be their word against anybody who wishes to challenge them."

Judy paused to see if Dorothy and Philip were absorbing her opinion. "The people at MCM are in a more tenuous situation. They're going to give Hugh a device that every other patient gets, but it's going to be modified to communicate in an immediate way should Hugh Hamlin have a problem. It is reasonable for those communications to be tape-recorded; ambulance and police dispatchers do that all the time, and those recordings have been used in criminal cases. So that part is OK. The question is why did Hugh Hamlin, of all people, get the new version of the device?"

Philip nodded. "Yes, I anticipated that question myself."

Judy smiled. "Well, if the company decided to do a little study and give such a device to, say, a couple dozen consecutive patients, and Hugh Hamlin happened to be one of them, it would be hard to blame anybody at MCM for entrapment. Mind you, I'm not advocating such a thing, I'm just telling you what the safe harbor might look like."

Philip liked the idea of other patients receiving the device. "That would also give the technicians some experience with the new gadget to make sure that they knew how to use it."

"When you say a study, you mean a feasibility test on a feature of the device that is already invented but not yet utilized, correct?" Dorothy asked.

"That's a good way of putting it," Judy replied. "If you think about it that way, it looks less like you're going after Hugh Hamlin."

Dorothy listened attentively as Judy laid out the legal issues. Maybe the plan could work after all. "So, Judy, where do we go from here?"

"I scheduled a meeting with Judge Silverburg this afternoon to run this past him. Philip, I think it would be best if I told the judge who's involved in the case, rather than presenting the case as a hypothetical. I will, of course, make sure he understands that anything I tell him will be in confidence and that he will have to recuse himself should the case ever come to court."

"Judge Silverburg seemed like a pretty nice person when I saw him in the office that one time. What do you think, Dorothy?"

"It doesn't thrill me. But the most important thing here is to get an accurate opinion from somebody with experience. Judge Silverburg should know what he's talking about. Judy, as long as you can guarantee confidentiality, I suppose you can go ahead."

"Absolutely. I will call you two when I am finished."

Judy Thomas had had few one-on-one meetings with Judge

Silverburg. It wasn't common for an assistant district attorney to conference with senior judges. So she was understandably anxious as she entered his chambers for her three o'clock appointment. The judge had shed his robe and was poring over documents in shirtsleeves behind his large antique desk. He was an imposing figure, a former athlete still in good condition. He looked up with a welcoming smile."

"Would you care for a beverage, Ms. Thomas?"

"No, thanks, Your Honor. I'm fine."

"You want to ask me about a hypothetical case and how it might be viewed legally?"

"Well, if it's acceptable to you, your Honor, I would like to present the case as it really is and identify the players. It might help you put it into a better perspective."

"I have no problem with that. You have my promise of confidentiality."

"Thank you, Your Honor. That helps. The person who came to me is Philip Sarkis. Perhaps you remember him?"

"The cardiologist at GMH?"

"Well, he was a cardiologist at GMH before he was sued in a nasty malpractice case and lost his livelihood."

"I remember. The wife of Hugh Hamlin died and the case was heard in Philadelphia, if I am not mistaken. It was an outrageous verdict with punitives?"

"Correct. Philip Sarkis lost the case, his savings, and his marriage, and has been pretty much run out of his profession."

"I saw him as his patient a long time ago. His demeanor was professional but slightly aloof. I was surprised to hear about what had happened."

"Well, Your Honor, according to information that Dr. Sarkis and his own attorney have been able to gather, Moira Hamlin did not die a natural death. He has good reason to believe that Hugh Hamlin actually killed his wife."

"What? You can't be serious! That's a prominent family. What possible reason could Mr. Hamlin have to do something like that?"

"The oldest reason known to man — Hugh Hamlin was having an affair. Philip Sarkis thinks that he killed his wife so he could marry his mistress."

"Why not just divorce her?"

"Good question. Hugh had signed an overly generous pre-nuptial agreement and stood to lose more than half of his wealth. Since he was involved in an affair, and Moira was the victim, there was a good chance he would have lost custody of the children as well. It looks like Hugh Hamlin conspired with his mistress to come up with a scheme they thought foolproof."

"Who was this mistress mastermind?"

"A woman named Bonnie Romano, Your Honor."

Judy went on to review the evidence. She was careful to exclude any mention of the Romano family and John's death, but otherwise tried to make Philip's case as strong as possible. The affair, she said, would be easy to prove.

As to method, Judy emphasized the importance of Bonnie's drug company connection and the unexpectedly high antihistamine blood levels Moira had when she presented with her cardiac arrest. She explained the complexity of Moira's medical problem carefully to Judge Silverburg, realizing that if he didn't understand the long QT syndrome, he wouldn't be able to grasp how she had been killed.

Judge Silverburg listened quietly, taking no notes and not interrupting. He raised his eyebrows and nodded now and again, but gave little indication of what he was thinking. When Judy finished, he came around from behind his desk and joined her in the second visitor chair. He leaned forward with elbows on knees.

"Judy, this is one of the most unbelievable stories I have ever heard. If it is true, a heinous crime has been committed. It would make me sick to think that these people not only got away with it, but also ruined a great doctor. But Judy, what you have so far isn't going to prove their guilt, not by a long shot. I know you realize this."

"We all do, Your Honor, which is why I am here today. Since much time has passed and Moira's body was cremated, finding physical evidence is unlikely. At this point, I don't think that the DA would authorize an arrest. We could issue a warrant, conduct a search, and question Hugh and Bonnie, but all that would accomplish is to put them on alert. The only way to bring these people to justice is to get them to confess. Dr. Sarkis has come up with an unconventional way of getting that done, and I can only describe the method as questionably legal. I am here to ask if evidence gathered in such a way would be admissible in court." Judy then explained the MCM technology and focused on the instant voice transmission feature Philip had such hopes for.

Judge Silverburg responded slowly and deliberately. "This technology is beyond anything the law has ever had to deal with. But let me make sure I understand; the fundamental question is whether or not a statement from Hugh and Bonnie about their roles in the death of Moira Hamlin gathered using the voice activation feature of the MCM recording device would be admissible in court and usable against them. Is that right?"

"Yes, Your Honor, understanding that Hugh Hamlin would have to agree to accept the device while knowing that the feature was available and could be used at the discretion of the monitoring staff at MCM."

"And you say that this feature is going to be implemented for other patients at MCM so Hugh Hamlin will not be a special case?"

"That's correct. And the feature will only be activated if the staff observes an arrhythmia and believes it is important to communicate with Mr. Hamlin."

"And Hugh Hamlin has a legitimate cardiac problem that will make this device necessary? And there are doctors who are going to provide the device to him for his benefit?"

"Correct. Mr. Hamlin has a rhythm problem for which he has seen a specialist in the past, and his internist is about to refer him back to that person for help once again."

Judge Silverburg sat back in his chair, absorbing what he had been told. Staring at the ceiling he said, "I don't want to know how you know that, and I don't want to know who those doctors are, but I will assume that they are not operating under any instructions from Philip Sarkis or anybody else?"

Judy avoided the question. "Dr. Sarkis did not breach patient confidentiality by getting medical information from those doctors. Hugh Hamlin solicited Dr. Sarkis' advice about his rhythm problem many times in the past. So the arrhythmia is not new information for Dr. Sarkis."

"What makes you think you will get a statement of guilt? Isn't that a little far-fetched?"

"Your Honor, that is an important question and one I posed myself. Dr. Sarkis believes that many cardiac arrhythmias are triggered by psychological stress. Dr. Sarkis believes that Hugh Hamlin may be having rhythm problems now because of guilt over the murder of his wife. If that's true, conversations with his accomplice about the matter might stimulate an arrhythmia and, if so, some information about what they did might be forthcoming at that exact time."

"It appears you have done your homework, Ms. Thomas."

Judy looked down at the floor and blushed. "Yes, Your Honor, I believe this is an important case. Nevertheless, it is a bit of a long shot."

Judge Silverburg smiled. "Yes, it is. Have you considered the consequences if you are wrong?"

"If it doesn't work, we are no worse off, and Hugh Hamlin's civil rights would not have been compromised. On the other hand, as you pointed out, if we don't do this, it is possible that Hugh and Bonnie will get away with murdering the innocent mother of small children."

Judge Silverburg stroked his chin while he looked out his window. After a minute of silence, he turned back to Judy.

"There is a lot to assimilate here. I need some time to think and to do a little legal research of my own. What is your time frame?"

"Hugh Hamlin is scheduled to be referred to a specialist after he sees his internist early next week. The device will be ready by then, so Dr. Sarkis would like to implement the plan within seven days."

"OK, it's Wednesday. I can get one of my clerks on this today, and I will have some time to read and reflect on the research tomorrow afternoon. How about if you come back on Friday, and I will give you an opinion then?"

"Your Honor, that would be fabulous. I couldn't ask for more."

The judge held Judy's gaze. "I want to help you, Judy, but this isn't going to be easy. We have to weigh the civil rights of the alleged suspects against the desire to solve a terrible crime and bring the perpetrators to justice. We have a new technology that is going to be used for several purposes, some of which are helpful to the recipient, and some of which invade his privacy. I will do what I can to search for a precedent, but I wouldn't hold my breath."

"I know, Your Honor, Dr. Sarkis has agreed to abide by your decision and will go forward only with your assent."

"That is fair, but it won't be my assent as much as my admitting I have no reason to say no. I suppose that if such a recording is obtained, you will go forward with an indictment?"

"Yes, Your Honor, I have already spoken to my superiors and they are comfortable with seeking an indictment for murder in the first degree for both Hugh and Bonnie, should we record an admission of guilt."

"Very well." The judge rose to signal the end of the meeting. He put a hand on Judy's shoulder to emphasize what he was about to say. "Judy, it should go without saying that everything we have discussed here must be kept in confidence. I know that you will share what we have discussed with Philip Sarkis and with his personal attorney, as you should, but that's as far as it can go. I will issue no court order in this matter authorizing the recording. So, we will agree that no one will ever know that I had any knowledge of this case whatsoever. Is that clear?"

"Yes, I understand."

Judy left the judge's chambers with an appointment to return at eleven o'clock on Friday morning. After she left the court building, she called Dorothy's office and set up a meeting with Philip and Dorothy for six that evening.

Philip and Dorothy were waiting anxiously when Judy arrived at the office. She threw her coat over a chair and immediately got to the point. "The judge was rather blown away by the whole thing. He knows the Hamlin family by reputation, but I didn't get the impression he has ever had any dealings with them. His initial reaction was exactly what we all predicted—disbelief. That's bad because it places a large burden on us to prove our case. On the other hand, he clearly understood the rationale for an aggressive approach to getting an admission of guilt."

Philip couldn't restrain himself. "So what did he say? Is the plan legal?"

"Well, he admitted there is little legal precedent, but he wants to do some research and think about it some more."

"Oh, great; more waiting."

Judy was soothing. "Easy does it, Philip. The judge understands that he needs to give us his opinion soon. He scheduled some time to talk to me again on Friday morning. I'm hoping we get a definitive answer then."

Philip was bouncing around the office. Everything Judy said made him feel fidgety and raw. Two years had elapsed since the lawsuit had been filed, but as far as he was concerned, it was an endless ordeal. Dorothy tried to stay calm. "So, Judy," she asked, "what do you predict he will come up with?"

"Well, he has three options. He could tell us to forget about the whole deal; he could tell us that we have a chance to survive a legal challenge; or he could issue a court order that would authorize our voice recording. The last one is out of the question. Our consultation with him will be kept strictly confidential, and he will deny hearing about any of this.

"I also don't think that he will advise against your plan. He doesn't want to see a criminal get away with murder, so he'll let you do the dirty work. Keeping things hush-hush is to his advantage. If the plan blows up somehow, he can say he had no knowledge. That's how I read it, anyhow."

Philip was distracted as he began to tick off all of the things they had to do in the next week to implement their plan. Dorothy wanted Philip to stay focused. "Philip, you have to be cool. You're the person who will make or break the plan, and you have to have your wits about you from now on. We're only going to get one shot at Hugh and Bonnie. If we don't get the recording we need, we will be finished, and they'll walk. Even worse, if they find out about any of this or if you make one mistep, they will come after us. The more jittery you are, the more likely you are to blow it. Do you understand?"

Philip plopped into a chair and nodded. The message had gotten through, and he realized that the success of the plan meant placing himself, and many people he cared about, in jeopardy. They had to hope that the weight of his responsibility, and stress of the case, would not interfere with his ability to function at the critical time because, against all odds, the moment of opportunity was finally upon them.

CHAPTER 26

Judy met with Judge Silverburg on Friday morning. As expected, he had not been able to discover a precedent. He told Judy he believed the taped conversation might be admissible.

"As you know, when there is little or no legal precedent, a lot depends on who hears the case. If it's someone who places a high value on civil liberty, the tape will be excluded. On the other hand, if the person wants to bring the alleged murderers to justice, he or she might let it in. Personally, I wouldn't exclude it, but that's not relevant since I won't be hearing the case."

It was the non-answer Judy expected but still she wanted to cover all the bases. "If the decision is so arbitrary, would an appeals court strike it down?"

"I have been wrestling with that question myself. Looking back over past cases in which taped conversations have been contended, appeals courts in this state have been more likely to sustain a judgment for the defendants. It is just another indication of how liberal the courts have become in dealing with felons. So even if the evidence is not excluded, the defendants would have a pretty good shot at getting the judgment overturned."

"Will that influence the decision of the lower court?"

"Of course. No judge wants to be overturned. But the judges here in Montgomery County are anti-crime and their constituents like it that way. So as a group, they would be sympathetic. I can't speak for all of the judges, however."

"I don't suppose that you would have any way of knowing who

might get this assignment."

"No, I couldn't tell you that. The cases pretty much go in rotation, although as President Judge I have some discretion. I can tell you right now that I will not interfere with the assignment of this case in any way, given that we have had these conversations."

"Thank you, Your Honor. I would expect that."

Judge Silverburg sensed Judy's anxiety. "I am truly sorry I can't be more definitive, Judy. I guess if I were in your shoes, I would go ahead with your plan, as long as the DA agrees. If you don't get anywhere, your client will have to accept the fact and move on. If you do get recorded evidence, and I think that is a long shot, I expect the DA will issue warrants. Then the courts will decide if the case goes to a jury."

Judy was relieved. "That's pretty much how I see it, Your Honor. Without a clear stop sign from you, I am pretty sure the plan will go forward. I want to thank you again for your help and time." When she naively uttered, "I will make sure you find out what happens," he countered, "I usually do, Judy."

As she left the courthouse, Judy knew it was up to Philip now, and she was fairly sure what he would decide.

In fact, Philip had already asked Perry McSwaine if he could meet with Jamie Ascot, the director of the monitoring center for MCM, to begin to map out their plans. Perry informed Jamie that Philip wanted to do a feasibility study of the IVT (instant voice transmission) feature of the MCM device. He told Jamie that Philip Sarkis was coming back on board as a consultant to help implement the study, format the system, and put the proper documents in place.

Jamie was surprised. "I heard that Philip had run into some legal problems and was barred from working with industry."

Perry reassured her. "This is going to be an off-the-record consultation and won't jeopardize the company or you, I promise. I just need Philip to come in for a few days to help out so we can get this off the ground quickly. Officially, we will be doing the project on our own and processing the results without his input. But I still want you to work with him. Let him be your primary contact for questions and the like."

Jamie was reluctant. She hadn't liked Philip when she worked with him in the past. Though he was clearly knowledgeable, she had found him to be cool and distant. When Perry told her Philip needed the work, Jamie agreed to cooperate. Perry did add one important disclaimer.

"It's important that we keep Philip's work quiet. The only person he will actually meet with is you, and if you are asked later about any of this, you won't recollect anything. I don't want to jeopardize the center by using a disbarred consultant. Is that OK with you?"

"Sure, Perry, that's really swell. You are asking me to work with some guy I don't like, to meet with him off site and off hours when the place is empty, and to pass along whatever hair-brained scheme he comes up to the appropriate operations people as if it were my own."

"Perfect," Perry said, ignoring her sarcasm. "And keep me posted."

Jamie and Philip decided to meet around the corner from the MCM facility in West Conshohocken. Philip had urged MCM to place their first monitoring facility in West Conshy, as the locals called it. They had wanted to launch their company in the middle of the East Coast, and metropolitan Philadelphia had the country's highest number of arrhythmia specialists, the largest users of the MCM device. West Conshohocken was an up-and-coming business hub of Philadelphia, a beehive of new office construction. Since real estate costs had not caught up with the rest of the area, MCM got a cheap lease on a large office building, which had been converted from a warehouse on the river next to the train station. The company had since expanded, but the West Conchohocken facility continued to be the center of their national operation. It was the place where new ideas were presented and fleshed out before global introduction —the logical place to test out the IVT system.

Jamie Ascot met Philip at Ted's sandwich shop on Elm Street. Although a little overweight, Jamie spent a lot of money on clothes designed to cover her flaws. At work, she functioned as one of the guys, but out of that setting she was a lady who clearly enjoyed a good time. She had been responsible for the development and refinement of the MCM device and was now in charge of the monitoring facilities. It had been her idea to incorporate the IVT feature, but she was anxious about this meeting given

Philip's status with regulatory agencies, not to mention the aloof attitude she poignantly remembered.

Jamie gave Philip a perfunctory handshake before they found their way to a booth. Although she flirted with ordering a meatball sandwich, both settled for Italian salads and Diet Cokes.

"Perry filled me in, Philip."

"Good," Philip said. "Then you realize I have to stay in the background?"

"I understand."

"Great, but I do have to tell you two important things. First, Milan Kuco is putting a patient named Hugh Hamlin on the system. He has to get one of the IVT devices. Second, your technicians must have a low threshold for activating the IVT feature and recording what is happening on the other end. We would prefer that they not transmit to the patient unless there is an urgent need to do so. So, for example, if the patient has a high heart rate, the technician should plan to listen and record without interrupting what the patient is doing, unless of course the patient decides to talk to the technician. Is that clear?"

Actually it sounded bizarre, but Jamie was a good soldier. "I think so. How will the patients be enrolled in the study?"

"You should plan to do about 30 consecutive patients from a few selected local practices in the next two weeks. How are the patients currently put on the service?"

"Like we always have. Once the doctor gives the order, one of our technicians goes out to the patients' homes, installs the system, and shows them how to use it. The patients sign an agreement and that's about it."

"OK, but we will have to add a clear statement in the agreement that the IVT is being tested and that a technician may elect to activate it when they see an important cardiac rhythm problem, just in case the patient needs to communicate any symptoms or needs help. Since this is not a research project in the classic sense, this new clause in the agreement letter should cover informed consent."

Jamie had several questions. Why did this guy Hamlin have to get the device, and how did Philip know he was about to be placed on the service? She knew better than to ask, and then there was more.

"Jamie, there is another twist to this. When Hugh Hamlin gets his device, he won't need to be told about the IVT feature. Milan will take care of that in the office, and he shouldn't be reminded about it. He is very skittish, and I don't want him to be spooked. In fact, to make sure that Hamlin's installation is handled properly, could you do it yourself?"

Jamie was now certain there was more to the Hamlin situation than she was being told but Perry had requested her cooperation. "I haven't done many installations myself lately, but I don't see why I couldn't do this one. I take it that you want me to show him how to use the device, get the agreement signed, and get out of Dodge?"

"That would be great. Obviously, we want all voice transmissions to be tape— recorded so we can correlate them with the patients' rhythm abnormalities."

"I don't see any problem with that. We record all conversations with patients anyway, so I will just make sure the technicians know about the need for hard copy."

As Jamie and Philip finished lunch, she asked Philip if he wanted to stop by the monitoring center some evening to see their new facilities.

"No, I am not supposed to be doing anything on the record. This project is kind of a special favor from Perry, and I don't want to get any of you in hot water. Anyway, we have everything covered. I will call you next week to see if you need any help."

"That's fine. We should have the devices by then. We will go ahead with the Hugh Hamlin installation as soon as we get the request."

"I appreciate that, Jamie."

Philip arrived at Dorothy's office that afternoon. They had to come up with a plan to extract a confession from Hugh and Bonnie while the MCM monitor was enabled. Dorothy was concerned about the timing.

"I still don't understand why you think the technician will have the IVT feature on when they blab."

"Well, profound stress is likely to provoke a fast heart rhythm, and Hugh is extremely excitable."

"OK, but just because he gets stressed and the monitor gets activated doesn't mean that Bonnie will be there and that they will tell us what we need to know."

Philip had such a smug look on his face that Dorothy knew he had something up his sleeve. "The plan will work," he said, "if we come up with just the right stimulus. As to timing, you and I are going to have to be, let us say, proactive."

At that precise moment, Hugh and Bonnie were taking their two poodles for a late afternoon stroll through their neighborhood. Since their marriage, life had been good. They had more money than they could ever spend. The older kids' difficult adjustment was confined to brief isolated outbursts, while the younger children had only vague memories of Moira. Bonnie liked to remind Hugh that the trial psychologist had indeed exaggerated the effects of Moira's messy death on their development.

To ensure their collective amnesia, Bonnie emptied the house of anything that might remind the children of Moira, then instructed the staff to make no mention of her. She and Hugh resumed their careers, but in reality, only Bonnie was pushing hard. Hugh explained that he didn't want to take on any difficult projects, and never traveled for business because he "needed to be available for the kids." Hugh's father concurred and continued to pay him a fat salary. Hugh went to the office late, came home early, traveled with the kids, played golf, and had drinks ready when Bonnie came home in the evening. They never talked about John or Moira.

Their neighborhood walks gave them the chance to catch up on the day's events. This particular evening, Hugh had gotten a call from Henry Wong's office to move Hugh's appointment up a few weeks. "Sounds like Henry is going to be away for a few weeks, so they are accommodating people before he leaves."

Bonnie was idly curious. "Gee, I thought docs push their patients' appointments later when they are going away."

"You know Henry. He is probably anticipating some kind of scheduling problem. I hate going to the doctor's office."

"This visit should be pretty routine. You have been feeling well lately, haven't you?" Bonnie asked.

"I still get those palpitations when I have to rush or I don't get enough sleep. Otherwise, I have been OK, I think."

"I am sure everything will be fine—just try not to get yourself all worked up. That will just get you in a twitter."

During Hugh's appointment the following week he tried to heed Bonnie's advice. He told the nurse about his palpitations but tried to make them sound innocent. She recorded the information along with his vital signs and hooked him up to the electrocardiogram machine. "Dr. Wong will be here in a minute for your EKG and exam."

Hugh was petrified of having his EKG recorded. He lay on the examination table fearing the worst. By the time Henry came in, he had worked himself into a state of high anxiety. Wong could see how uncomfortable he was but instead of saying anything to soothe Hugh, he went directly to the machine and activated it. As he expected, Hugh was having multiple premature beats from his ventricle or bottom chamber. Henry had seen them before and had chosen to ignore them. This time, he wasn't going to do that.

"Hugh, have you been having palpitations frequently lately?" he asked with a feigned look of concern.

"I have, especially when I am under stress, like right now."

"There seem to be a whole lot of them today."

"Yeah, feels like two guys are having a fistfight in my chest. But I thought you said that I didn't have to worry about them."

"You are having an awful lot of them. I think it would be a good idea for you to see Milan Kuco again."

"Wait a minute. Last time he said you were right, and I didn't have anything to worry about. What changed your mind?"

"Nothing. It is just that all kind of important information has come out lately about this problem and I think we should take advantage of new approaches if we can."

Suddenly, Hugh was beside himself. "Damn it. I don't like this, Henry, not one bit."

Although Henry was the consummate professional, he didn't like patients addressing him by his first name. Quickly, the atmosphere in the exam room went from bad to worse. He completed his examination silently, and did some office lab testing. Hugh barely noticed. All he could think about was his heart rhythm.

As he left the examination room, Hugh had a request of Dr. Wong. "If you are going to send me to that guy, at least do me the service of getting me an appointment before the end of the decade. The last time I had to wait forever."

Henry wasn't interested in doing Hugh any favors. But getting him in to see Milan quickly was exactly what Philip wanted. Henry forced a smile. "I'll call Milan's office to see what I can do."

Two days later, Hugh and Bonnie were in Milan's office. Hugh stewed in the examination room before the EKG and, as with the Wong visit, he provided plenty of extra beats for the tracing. Milan looked over the recordings and then addressed Hugh and Bonnie. "I have to agree with Henry. I am concerned about all these extra beats. At some point, they could all come in a row and cause your heart to stop pumping."

"You mean I could die from these things?" Hugh was practically jumping off the exam table. Bonnie could do little to calm him.

"We have to take this matter seriously." The big man struggled to deliver the message gravely. To ensure that he did, he reminded himself that the person sitting in front of him destroyed the career of a preeminent physician, and had succeeded in stripping Milan's friend of his job, his family, and his reputation.

"I think our first step is to determine how much of this arrhythmia you are experiencing during normal activity."

"You mean you want me to wear a monitor? I have had plenty of them and nothing bad has ever shown up."

Milan maintained his serious look. "The monitor I have in mind is different, and more sophisticated than any you have had before." Milan went on to describe the MCM device and how it would allow for continuous monitoring of Hugh's heart rhythm for several days. Milan said nothing about IVT. Bonnie listened carefully and asked only a few questions of clarification, but it was obvious she didn't see any problem with him using the device. Hugh on the other hand had been shocked into silence.

"An MCM person will bring the device to your home, have you sign an agreement, and show you how to use it. It's easy so I am sure you won't have any trouble."

For Philip's sake, Milan maintained a concerned look on his face during the consultation. The frowning bear wasn't too worried about Hugh catching on—he was beside himself with worry and was convinced that he was going to expire at any minute.

"What happens if there is a problem with the monitor?" Bonnie asked.

"You will be contacted immediately by the company and they will notify us as well so we can intervene if necessary."

"What does 'intervene' mean?"

"Well, there are several alternatives including medicine, a special kind of pacemaker, or maybe even open heart surgery." Milan deliberately explained the invasive procedures in great detail. By the time they left the office, Hugh was in a state of high anxiety.

When Jamie Ascot arrived at the Hamlin's mansion three days later, Hugh was frantic to find out how bad his heart rhythm was, and whether he'd actually need the procedures Milan had described. Jamie wanted to slip away with as few questions as possible and was pleased to learn there would be no interference from Bonnie who was away on a business trip. It didn't take Jamie long to set up the device and show Hugh how to use it. As Philip had directed, she didn't mention the IVT capability. She applied the chest leads and showed Hugh how to replace them after a shower. At Hugh's request, she immediately activated the monitor. Then she took the agreement out of her briefcase.

"Mr. Hamlin, this agreement authorizes the use of the device in your home. It states that you understand how it works and that you consent to having it. It also confirms that MCM will be billing your insurance company."

Hugh snatched the agreement out of her hands. "Show me where to sign."

Jamie pointed to the last page. He signed, laughing nervously "Someday I am going to sign my life away," he joked.

Jamie took the papers back without comment, leaving a copy for Hugh. As she did with all of her patients, Jamie tried to be upbeat. "I am sure it will be fine. I think you will find our system to be user-friendly so there is a very good chance that we will be able to record a rhythm when you are actually having your symptoms."

"God, I hope so. This thing really has me rattled, especially since my doctors are so obviously worried. The first time I saw them, they were pretty laid back about the whole thing. Now they are talking about a serious operation or giving me some kind of device."

Jamie smiled as she packed up her things. "Remember to call

us if you have any trouble and we will take care of it."

On her way back to the office, Jamie called Philip to let him know that the device was in place. "He has it on and I think he will be cooperative. He is anxious to get an answer."

"What about the IVT feature? Is it activated?"

"Yes, and the technicians are familiar with it. Mr. Hamlin is the sixth patient we have placed on this service, and we have been able to record the patient's voice when they have had an arrhythmia. I am sure we will be able to do the same for him."

"Remind the technicians that they shouldn't try to talk to him. He is very excitable and I don't want to upset him any more than he is."

"They've been told. I am sure they will do as you have asked."

Philip rung off and immediately called Dorothy. "The trap is set. Now it is up to us to spring it."

Dorothy had some experience with stakeouts, and was worried. "This isn't going to be easy, Philip. When do you want to start?"

"Let's give Hugh a day to get used to the device. They both need to be at home and in the same room. I think it would be easier to shake him up late at night. So, how about if we make the first call tomorrow evening?"

Dorothy agreed. "We aren't going to be able to actually see them in their bedroom, so we need to wait until the light goes out, and then make the call."

"How do we know where their bedroom is in that huge place?"

"I was able to get the floor plan on line. Bonnie was the first owner, and it is a cookie cutter design. The builder still has two more on the market. According to the plans, the master bedroom suite is in the front on the right-hand side of the house on the second floor."

"How do we know that Hugh or Bonnie will answer the phone?"

"According to the agency, their staff doesn't stay overnight anymore. They leave about 10, after the children are put down. Are you in good voice? I want you to sound as mysterious as possible."

"Don't worry. I just need to rehearse a little and think about what I want to say," Dorothy replied.

"We need to make it good, because we will probably have only two or three cracks at it. After that, chances are pretty high they will go to the police or hire somebody to go after the phone intruder."

Dorothy remained skeptical. "I can't believe they are really going to fall for this, but it's your show, Philip. And remember it is the last gasp."

The next evening, Dorothy picked Philip up at his home in her dark green Jaguar S-type—less suspicious in that neighborhood than Philip's Japanese bomb. They watched the house for a couple of hours. They saw Bonnie go through the automatic gates at about nine o'clock and figured that Hugh was already at home with the kids. They sat nervously listening to the radio until about midnight. Eventually, the bedroom lights went off, and Dorothy pulled out one of three untraceable cell phones that she had gotten from her father. She dialed the number. After four rings, a drowsy Hugh picked up.

"Hello."

"Is this Mr. Hugh Hamlin?"

"Yes. Who is this?"

"Mr. Hamlin, we know that you and Bonnie Romano conspired to murder your wife Moira and we know how you did it."

Hugh's voice went up about 20 octaves and several decibels. "Who in the hell is this? I have no idea what you are talking about!"

"Mr. Hamlin, I think you know exactly what I am talking about. You and your wife have a lot to answer for." With that, Dorothy hung up.

When Hugh heard the line go dead, his heart went into a severe arrhythmia. Dutifully, the technician at MCM made a note of the arrhythmia, and according to protocol activated the IVT feature. Bonnie was startled when Hugh started yelling into the phone. When he tried to explain what had happened, Hugh couldn't even croak out a sentence. The only sounds were his groaning and Bonnie questioning him about what had happened. Because the IVT feature had a 90-second timer, by the time Hugh recovered his voice and answered Bonnie, the device had turned off. Philip learned all this the next day when he called Jamie and asked if there had been any developments with the IVT experiment.

"Well, we activated it several times but the most dramatic was last night with Mr. Hamlin."

"What happened?" Philip tried to sound calm but his own heart was pounding with anticipation.

"Well, he has been having a lot of arrhythmias all along but then he had a doozy with a run of ventricular tachycardia, about 20 abnormal beats in a row and it was very fast. That is the first time we have ever seen that. Happened about midnight."

"Did you get a good recording?"

"We sure did but we didn't pick up a voice transmission from him. We heard a lot of groaning and a woman in the background asking him what was wrong. The technician got very worried when she heard this and placed a call to Mr. Hamlin. His wife picked up and said he was OK. The technician alerted Dr. Kuco. I don't think that anything else happened. Do you have specific questions about the IVT?"

"No, I just wanted to make sure it is working and it sounds like it is. I'll give you a call in another day or two to see how it's going."

Philip was disconsolate when he told Dorothy what had happened. "I don't understand. The damn thing was on because they could hear him moaning and Bonnie screeching in the background. But he didn't say anything. What do you think happened?"

Dorothy tried to reassure Philip. "I have no clue. But remember I predicted it would take more than one attempt. I guess we go back to work tomorrow night."

The next evening, they repeated their routine, driving around the block every few minutes in case Hugh alerted the police or arranged for personal protection. Philip and Dorothy didn't notice any extra security, so about an hour after the bedroom lights went out, Dorothy called again. This time, she didn't give Hugh a chance to think. She immediately blurted out her accusation. Hugh hung up without a word.

Dorothy thought about calling back immediately but suppressed the impulse. She turned to Philip and shook her head. "He hung up immediately. I wonder if he is on to us."

Crestfallen, Dorothy drove Philip home. He slumped into a chair and sat in the dark, depressed that his plan was not working. Several minutes later, he went to the kitchen for a glass of milk and noticed the light on his answering machine was blinking. Except for Dorothy, he didn't get many messages. This one was from Jamie. The message was brief but said everything. "Hi, Philip. I wanted you to know that Mr. Hamlin had a major arrhythmia again tonight. We recorded a strange conversation. I really don't know what it means, but I wonder if you could come to the center early in the morning to listen to it before the staff arrives?"

Philip stared at the machine. What was on that tape? He would have to wait several sleepless hours to find out.

CHAPTER 27

That night, Philip didn't even try to sleep. Hugh Hamlin had said something, but what was it? He replayed the message again and again but couldn't decide why Jamie had called him. He considered calling her but didn't want to alert her or anyone at the center. Besides, Jamie deserved her sleep.

He paced the floor, went to an all-night pharmacy and bought shaving cream and a new razor, then went home and watched old movies. By daybreak, he was in the shower and at six o'clock, he was sitting in his car with a cup of steaming coffee in front of the MCM facility. Jamie pulled up a half hour later, waved him into the building, and together they went up to the executive offices. Jamie parked Philip in her office. "Let me get the tape and bring it back here, and we can play it on my machine. I'll also bring the EKG recordings."

Philip could not have cared less about Hugh's arrhythmia, but he played along. "Yeah, it will be good to correlate his symptoms with whatever arrhythmia he had at the time. That's what the IVT is all about." Philip wondered if he was persuasive. Jamie seemed satisfied and left to fetch the material.

Philip fidgeted in his chair until Jamie returned to her office. She put the tape on her machine and handed Philip the EKGs. "At first I really thought that the two of them were talking about some kind of crime, but they must have been discussing a movie or a book. Or maybe the sound is from a TV show they were watching. Anyhow, that certainly is an interesting set of tracings, don't you think?"

Philip hadn't even looked at them, but quickly glanced down and feigned concern. "You can say that again. Absolutely amazing!"

"OK, so here it is. Listen carefully because there's a lot of static on the line." Philip leaned forward. A few seconds of static were followed by a shrill voice, undoubtedly Hugh. "What the fuck is going on? Who is calling us with this horseshit?"

A woman's voice, trying to sound controlled said, "Calm down, Hugh, you're going to give yourself a heart attack. Getting excited isn't going to help!"

"I am having a fucking heart attack. My heart is beating about a million times a minute, and I can't count how many skipped beats I'm having. How in the hell do you think that bitch found out about Moira?"

"I think this is a crank call, and nothing more."

"A crank call? Are you nuts? She came right out and told me we did it. How could a crank know that?"

"Maybe it's one of those damn maids who used to work here and loved your ex-wife. Maybe she's just taking her best shot at getting some extortion money. If this were serious, we would have heard from her a long time ago. And besides, how can they possibly prove it? There is no body, no weapon, and no witnesses. And I don't know about you, but I'm not about to confess."

"Damn, I hope you're right, but this thing scares the living shit out of me. Just to think that somebody out there actually knows what we did. It doesn't make me feel better just because you think they can't do anything about it."

"Like I said, relax. We..." The voices stopped and static resumed.

"That's the end of the recording," said Jamie. You can see where I got the idea that they were talking about some bad thing they did. But there has to be another explanation? Do you think they were playing a game or something?"

Philip sat speechless staring straight ahead. For a split second, Jaime thought he had had a stroke. After another moment, she heard him whisper a polite request to replay the tape. This time, he listened carefully to every word, trying to decide if they had actually incriminated themselves. By the third run through, he was convinced they had confessed to the murder of Moira Hamlin. It took a few seconds for Philip to finally realize this was the most valuable recording of his life. He needed to compose himself quickly to deflect Jamie's suspicions.

"I'm sure they were talking about some show they went to or something like that, but I'll check it out with Milan." Philip wasn't sure she was buying his explanation, but he didn't have time to worry about Jamie. He had to get moving.

"By the way, is this a copy or the original?" Philip asked as nonchalantly as he could.

"It's a copy. The original is on our hard drive."

"Can you make one more copy for me?"

"Sure. Do you want copies of the EKGs, too?"

"Of course. That's the whole point, right?" Philip managed a smile. "Jamie, you've done a wonderful job with this project so far, and I promise when these results are published, your name is definitely going on the paper."

Jamie was thrilled. She seldom got that kind of recognition. Philip was hoping that treating her as a colleague would help deflect what she heard on the recording. "Philip, that's nice of you. I really appreciate it."

Philip underscored the need to remind the technicians about confidentially, and then left MCM with two copies of the tape. Jamie would keep another locked in her desk.

By the time he reached his car, Philip's hands were trembling. He tried to unlock the door but instead pressed the lock button repeatedly. After he finally managed to throw himself into the front seat, he realized he was sweating profusely and yet chilled to the bone. He looked around furtively before finding and fumbling with his cell phone. He finally reached Dorothy who was on her way to her office. Philip's panicked, shaky voice connoted a real emergency. He directed her to detour to Judy's office.

Judy was hanging up her coat when the phone on her desk rang. "Judy, can Dorothy and I come right over? I have something I want you to listen to."

"If you make it snappy. I have a meeting with the DA in about an hour."

"The timing might be perfect," Philip told her. "You may want to add something to the agenda for your meeting."

Judy had no trouble guessing what Philip had for her. The question was how compelling the evidence would be

Dorothy arrived just before Philip burst into the receptionist's office. Neither woman had ever seen him so manic. Without shedding his jacket, he pulled one of the copies of the tape out of his pocket, jammed it into the machine on her desk, and turned it on. The whirring of the tape was the only sound in the room.

Philip studied their expressions as the drama unfolded. Then Dorothy grinned expansively, and Judy cinched her lips together. When it was done, he rewound it several times and instructed them to listen again. "Does that sound like a confession?" he whispered.

Judy spoke first. "They used Moira's name, and they talk about all the elements, and then state that they don't understand how anybody would know about it unless they confessed. I would have to say you nailed them."

Philip sat silently with his head down. Large beads of sweat plunked on the floor. Dorothy's voice punctuated the tense silence as the devil's advocate. "Would either of you say we misconstrued?"

"I considered that," Judy said. "But they were pretty explicit."

After a poignant moment, Philip looked up and wiped his forehead impatiently. "OK, now what?" he croaked.

"Well, my meeting with the DA this morning is going to be a whole lot more interesting. I talked to him about this several days ago, so he knows what's going on. He was pretty convinced that nothing would come of your idea. I think this will change his mind."

"Will he go for an indictment?"

"Hard to say. This will be tough to put aside, but Hugh Hamlin's family is politically powerful. Jacob is tough, though, and he doesn't like to back off."

Judy's read of Jacob Springer was accurate. Jake had never wanted to be anything but a prosecutor. As a small boy, he was mesmerized by lawyer shows he watched on an old black-and-white TV. His parents, newly arrived Jewish immigrants, dreamed of the day their only son would go to law school and become a powerful advocate for folks like those in the TV stories.

Jacob was bright and tenacious. At Penn law, he concentrated on criminal law, then took a clerkship with the DA. Once he decided that his cause was righteous, his resolve was unshakable. He hated politics but worked hard and eventually became DA.

He was not wildly popular but was roundly respected. He also had the highest conviction percentage of any DA in county history.

Jake's management style was no-nonsense; he hired good people whom he trusted like Judy, then let them do their jobs. At regular meetings with his ADAs, he caught up on their cases and gave valuable guidance. When Judy arrived, he was sipping coffee from a beat-up mug he loved. His sleeves were rolled up, and he was staring at his computer screen with reading glasses perched on the end of his hooked nose.

"What's new, Judy?" Jake asked offhandedly.

"Remember I told you about the Hamlin case last week?"

"Is that about the woman who supposedly died of natural causes with some circumstantial evidence that she may have been murdered? And there was a doc playing sleuth as I recall."

"I think that you had better listen to this." Judy explained the genesis of the tape and then handed him the cassette.

Nonchalantly, Jake inserted the tape. By the time it it whirred to completion, his mouth was agape. "Holy shit, Judy, this is a great big story."

Judy nodded. "It sounds to me like True Confessions. The burning question now is if it's enough to bring an indictment and have them arrested for first-degree murder."

Jake spun around in his chair. "That depends on whether this tape will be allowed in as evidence."

"Judge Silverburg was pretty confident that it would be admissible, since Hamlin signed the agreement when he was given the cardiac monitoring device."

Jake was wary but agreed. "Well then, I guess we go ahead and put things in motion. How are you going to handle the arrest?"

"I plan to call Hamlin and tell him we will be seeking a warrant for his arrest based on new evidence. I'll give them the chance to surrender voluntarily for processing. They'll make bail, and then the fun will start."

"See what you can do to limit the media exposure. It could get dicey."

Back at her desk, Judy dialed Hugh's office. She hung up, paused a few minutes, and then dialed again. She did this several times, having a hard time getting over her ambivalence. No one should get away with murder, but on the other hand, several lives were about to be ruined. Having lost their mother, the Hamlin children could conceivably see their father and their stepmother go to jail. Judy knew she was about to deliver a huge blow. On the fourth cycle, she finally let the phone ring.

Hugh's secretary asked what the call was about. When Judy told her she was from the DA's office and that it was personal, her call was put through immediately. Hugh took the call but his voice was audibly strained. "Why are you calling me?"

"Mr. Hamlin, my name is Judy Thomas, and I am an assistant district attorney in Montgomery County. I suggest that you remain silent and listen carefully. We have reason to believe that you committed a capital crime. We are about to ask a judge to issue a warrant for your arrest and the arrest of Bonnie Romano, who we believe was your accomplice. I suggest you call your attorney immediately. Since I'll will be calling Ms. Romano as well, you will have to decide whether you want joint representation."

There was no response—just heavy breathing on the other end.

"I will call you at your home this evening at seven o'clock with instructions for surrendering to the Montgomery County police tomorrow morning for arraignment. Bail will be decided at that time, and if you are able to post bail, you will probably be home in a few hours. I would caution against fleeing. As of this moment, your place of business and your home are under surveillance, and if you try to leave the area in the next 24 hours, you will be detained. I suggest you talk to no one about this except your family and attorney. Above all, avoid the media. Is this clear?"

More silence. Judy needed to know that Hugh was still on the phone and conscious. "Mr. Hamlin, did you hear all of that?"

"I did. Goodbye."

Judy put the phone down perplexed. Hugh had not protested or pretended there was a mistake. Had he anticipated this or was he just shocked beyond words? When Judy called Bonnie Romano, the response was much different.

"Ms. Romano, I am Judy Thomas. My office will be obtaining a warrant for your arrest for the murder of Moira Hamlin and…"

Bonnie interrupted, "This has to be some kind of mistake. I don't know what you're talking about!"

"I am afraid this is not a mistake…"

"I have no idea what you are talking about. Moira Hamlin was not murdered. She died of an arrhythmia."

Judy raised her voice in frustration. "I assure you, Ms. Romano, there is no misunderstanding. You and Hugh Hamlin are going to be indicted for conspiring to murder Moira Hamlin."

Bonnie abruptly ended the conversation. "You will be hearing from my lawyer, and you can be certain that there will be legal action for harassment and for making a false allegation."

Judy wasn't surprised by Bonnie's response. Few criminals admitted guilt, especially this early in the process.

As soon as Bonnie smashed the receiver down, the phone rang. Hugh barked, "Did you just get call from the DA?"

Bonnie took over. She cautioned Hugh not to say anything on the open phone line. "Leave your office now and meet me at home immediately."

Ironically, Judy's call had thrown Hugh's heart rhythm out of whack, so at that moment, the technician activated the IVT feature, and his brief conversation with Bonnie was captured on a tape that no one would ever know or care about.

Bonnie knew she would have to calm Hugh before they called a lawyer. They needed to get their stories straight. Behind the paneled den's closed doors, they spent an hour strategizing and dissecting the puzzling turn of events.

"They can't have any physical evidence. This has to be connected to that damn phone call last night," Bonnie posited.

"But how? Did I say anything that would incriminate us? I hung up right away."

"It's too coincidental. Whoever made that call has to be involved. I just don't know how."

They called Len Barkley, their malpractice attorney, to get his recommendations for a criminal lawyer. After Bonnie explained their situation, Barkley's answer was decisive.

"You need Bobby Barrone. He has handled a lot of high-profile criminal cases, he knows Montgomery County, and he's tough. Mention my name and tell him to get right on it. You have to find out what they have on you so you can get the case kicked out as quickly as possible."

Bonnie had heard of Robert Barrone. He represented underworld figures, celebrity murderers, terrorist assassins, and date rapists, anybody who could pay his huge fees. He was famous for "creative" strategies that tiptoed on the edge of reality and legality, but played well to naïve jurists. Most of all, he was pugnacious, and intimidated both his adversaries and judges.

Barrone was on his way to the airport to take a deposition in a Florida case when Bonnie reached him on her cell phone. Barrone had already gotten an email from Len Barkley and was aware of Hugh and Bonnie's situation. He listened carefully to the whole story and concluded that the DA's office had a rabbit to pull out of the hat.

"Ms. Romano, has there been any hint that someone has evidence against you?"

Bonnie was cautious. "Can I assume you are my lawyer and what I tell you remains confidential?"

"Of course. I wouldn't let you tell me anything without that privilege in place."

"The last two nights, Hugh and I have gotten phone calls after midnight from a woman who said she knew we killed Hugh's first wife. The first time she called, we were in a state of shock. The second time, Hugh tried to talk to her, but she just hung up."

"Did Hugh say anything to incriminate himself?" Barone asked.

"No, of course not."

"Did you report the calls to the police or tell anyone else about them?"

"No. We thought that the woman was deranged and would just go away."

"Bonnie, I'm concerned about the integrity of your phone."

"I know. That's why I am calling on my cell."

"Not much better, I am afraid. We are going to end this conversation. I'll take your case but listen carefully. I don't want you or your husband to talk to anyone about this case, and I especially don't want you using your phones for anything except household issues. Is that clear?"

"Yes, I understand. What should we do next?"

"Nothing. Just stay calm. The next few days are going to be difficult. I was on my way to a deposition out of state, but I think I can reschedule. I'll be at your house this evening to talk to the ADA."

"Good. Good. I'm so relieved you are on board, Mr. Barrone. My husband Hugh is very excitable. You will need to make him feel like the case is under control. If he senses any uncertainty, his behavior will make him look guilty, which I assure you he is not."

"I understand, Ms. Romano, and I'll be careful with that. What time did Judy Thomas say she'd call?"

"She said seven o'clock."

"Good, I will come over about 6:00 so we can talk beforehand."

Bonnie gave Barrone her address and hung up. She decided to take a sedative and gave one to Hugh. She napped fitfully while Hugh sat in front of the TV.

In a morose way, Hugh glanced at Bonnie, who was sprawled unattractively on the sofa. A momentary wave of guilt and self-pity washed over him. What had he given up for this woman? Had it all been worth it? And for those few seconds he hated Bonnie for what she had done to him, and for what he had become.

CHAPTER 28

At the dot of 6:00, Bobby Barrone swept into their great room escorted by one of the maids looking very much the downtown attorney complete with pin-striped suit, slicked back hair, manicured nails, carrying a small leather attaché case over his shoulder. Bonnie greeted him, but a subdued Hugh stared at the TV and barely said hello.

Barrone immediately got down to business, asking for complete details about the case. Bonnie went through the entire story including her friendship with Moira, the "incident" that eventually killed her, and the ensuing malpractice verdict.

"So, the guy who took the biggest hit when Moira Hamlin died was Philip Sarkis. Could he have had anything to do with last night's phone call?"

"I have no idea. Hugh said the caller was a woman. I heard that Sarkis wasn't doing well. He was out of practice and scraping up money to pay damages. I can't imagine that he would have the resources to come after us."

"Is it possible that someone did murder Moira Hamlin?"

Bonnie paused and wondered if this was Barrone's way of asking if she and Hugh actually were the killers. She composed herself and answered as calmly as she could. "I can't think of who or why. It appeared she died because of the long QT syndrome and the doctor who took care of her didn't treat her properly. That's why we sued him and won."

"Has anyone tried to implicate your husband?"

"Hugh was incredibly concerned about her when she was in

the hospital after her cardiac arrest and did all he could to make her well. He loved her dearly, and she was the mother of his children. How could he be accused of such a terrible thing?"

"I don't know, Ms. Romano. But what I do know is that the DA's office has to have something definitive to get an arrest warrant. I guess we are just going to have to play this one out."

"What will happen tomorrow?"

"You'll give yourself up. They will read you your rights, and then you will be fingerprinted and photographed. I'll find out as much as I can before the probable cause hearing. That will determine if they can hold you over for trial. Hopefully, we can quash the case right there. Anything can happen in a jury trial."

Barrone told them he would take Judy's phone call himself. They could listen in, but he didn't want them to say anything.

When the phone rang a few minutes later, Judy laid out her directives. "Hugh and Bonnie should present themselves to the homicide detective bureau tomorrow morning. They will be processed and should be before a judge by mid-afternoon."

Barrone grunted his agreement and told Judy he would bring his clients in himself. "And by the way, I am going to represent both of them, at least for the time being, just so you know there won't be any other lawyers along tomorrow."

"That's fine. As long as the Hamlins know the pitfalls of that approach, I am sure that the judge will not object, and I won't either."

"I appreciate that, Ms. Thomas. And thanks for making this easy on my clients. I am sure this will get cleared up quickly, and it would be great if we can spare them the media circus."

Judy recognized manipulation and knew that Barrone's conciliatory behavior would end soon.

The next day, Judy and Chief Detective Mark Scotty met the threesome at the police station. Scotty placed Hugh and Bonnie under arrest, read them their rights, and ushered them into the police sergeant for processing.

A savvy police reporter happened to see the Hamlins on the way to fingerprinting and recognized them from the society pages. She confirmed Hugh's identity with friends at the front desk, and started asking questions. Before long, she had pieced the story together and called her editor. Within minutes, a brief account of Hugh and Bonnie's arrest was posted on the paper's web site.

Word spread to the TV and radio news bureaus, and reporters were dispatched to the police station.

By the time of the arraignment hearing, the courtroom was packed with reporters, eager for sound bites and film clips for the evening news. Barrone stood between his steel-faced clients. Bonnie had had a hairdresser come to the house early that morning, so she looked well put together in a charcoal grey suit. She had kept jewelry to a minimum. Hugh's somber suit and burgundy silk tie completed the serious tone, but Bonnie was afraid that his inflamed cheeks and nervously darting eyes would make him look guilty. While she tried to appear aloof and maybe even resentful, the photographers had a field day.

The hearing took only minutes. The judge in charge of processing cases for the day was Harry Mendelson, a mellow guy who was not the sharpest jurist. Following the clerk's recitation of charges, Mendelson asked for a plea from the defendants. Both croaked, "Not guilty."

Barrone followed with a request. "Judge Mendelson, my clients should have immediate access to the evidence that is being used to justify their arrest."

"I agree with you, counselor. I will schedule a probable cause hearing as soon as possible to determine if the defendants should be bound over for trial."

"Thank you, Your Honor."

"Ms. Thomas, do you have a recommendation regarding bail?"

"No, Your Honor. We will defer to you."

"Mr. Barrone, anything to say on this issue?"

"These are two prominent and upstanding people with no criminal record. They have children here and are not a flight risk. We ask that they be released on their own recognizance."

Mendelson paused, looked at Judy, and then continued. "Barring an objection from the prosecutor, I will grant your request, Mr. Barrone. But they must remain in the vicinity, and they must surrender their passports."

Judge Mendelson banged his gavel and left the bench. Hugh and Bonnie would indeed be home for dinner.

As Mendelson promised, the hearing was scheduled for a week later. After several suggestive stories appeared in the media, the public was mesmerized by the possibility of a murder on the Main

Line. Judy was mobbed by reporters every time she left her office, but she never elaborated on the "incriminating evidence" they assumed her office had.

Judy instructed her staff to divulge nothing until the probable cause hearing. She hoped that the shock of hearing the taped conversation in the courtroom would prompt Hugh and Bonnie to change their plea. At the very least, she didn't want Barrone's team to discover Philip's role in the taping until the trial. It was vitally important that the evidence against Hugh and Bonnie not be dismissed as Philip's contrived payback for their malpractice action.

The case was assigned to Judge Ann Marie Cartright, a conservative with a reputation of being hard on criminals. Judge Cartright hoped that the probable cause hearing might result in a plea bargain, in her mind a much better solution to a case with this much notoriety. Judge Annie, as she was known, made her opinion clear in her preliminary meetings with the attorneys. Neither side believed that the case would be resolved so easily.

But in a stunning turn of events, two days before the probable cause hearing, Judge Cartright's clerk informed the attorneys that Judge Annie had been replaced by President Judge Silverburg. Judy was incredulous. Why had he changed his mind and taken the case himself?

Silverburg refused to answer her phone calls, and his secretary couldn't find time for her to speak to him. Besides, his clerk pointed out, it would be improper for the judge to speak with the prosecuting attorney without the defense attorney present. Yes, there would be a pre-hearing meeting a few hours before court, but Judy wouldn't have a chance to find out what Judge Silverburg was up to.

Judy suggested to Dorothy that Dick Deaver put a tail on the judge. "I'd like to know if Silverburg goes anywhere or sees anyone that would indicate why he changed his mind and took the case. I can't do this through regular channels. Tailing a judge is not in the usual job description of police officers."

As soon as the courthouse opened on the day of the hearing, the halls outside Judge Silverburg's courtroom were filled with reporters. When the judge abruptly closed the hearing his excuse was that divulging cardinal pieces of evidence to the public might jeopardize jury selection, if the case got that far. The pre-hearing meeting of the attorneys in chambers was perfunctory. Judge Silverburg merely laid out the procedures.

"The prosecution will be permitted to present evidence that can then be challenged at cross-examination by the defense. There will follow summary arguments by both sides, and I will then take the matter under advisement."

Judy watched the judge closely during the meeting. Silverburg gave no hint he had prior information about the case. He looked like he was starting from scratch, never even glancing at Judy.

The attorneys left chambers and headed for their respective tables in court. The judge gaveled the proceedings to order and Judy began her case. She had decided to start her presentation with some of the evidence from Dorothy's interviews, and the material Philip had unearthed in his conversations with the Flanagans. As she expected, Barrone argued that the evidence was not of sufficient weight to support the plaintiff's case. "This information Your Honor, is hearsay and does not support an indictment for murder."

But Judy was just setting up the tape evidence. When she finally turned on the tape player, Hugh and Bonnie's voices could be heard clearly in the quiet courtroom. The reaction was as dramatic as Judy had hoped. Hugh and Bonnie looked horrified and could not answer Barrone's urgent whispered questions. "Is that you talking? What were you saying?" Even the courtroom staff, hardened by years at the bench, gawked in amazement.

When it was over, Judy asked the Judge if he wanted it played again. Before Silverburg could reply, Barrone was on his feet. "We request a recess Your Honor. We need to learn more about this tape, and I need to confer with my clients so we can formulate a response."

Judge Silverburg granted his request. "Very well. We will reconvene tomorrow at 10 am."

A flustered Barrone told Hugh and Bonnie to go home, stay indoors, and answer no calls except his.

Barrone spent the rest of the day with his staff trying to figure out what he had just heard and where it had come from. In her introduction, Judy had said it came from a medical monitor that Hugh had been given a few days before.

The recording, they eventually learned, had come from a monitor Hugh had been given by his cardiologist. The company was MCM, and Philip Sarkis was listed as a member of their advisory board. The agreement Hugh had signed when the monitor was placed clearly permitted his voice to be recorded in the event of a major cardiac arrhythmia.

Bonnie and Hugh were able to confirm that the arrhythmias had occurred and the voice transmission had been made immediately after the mystery phone calls. Hugh had been tricked into agreeing to a voice transmission. He and Bonnie had been "stimulated" to confess by a crank call.

Barrone immediately concluded that Sarkis was the culprit. Why not? He obviously had the cooperation of Hugh's physicians, but he had must have had other help. If Barrone was going to get the case kicked, he needed to discover the entirety of this complicated attempt to outsmart the Hamlins.

As soon as court convened the next morning, Barrone asked to approach the bench. "Your Honor, we have reason to believe that my clients were deceived by someone who wanted to invade their privacy. The conversation we heard here yesterday was obtained illegally, and must be excluded."

Barrone went on to explain his theory of how the tape had come into existence. Judy countered by pointing out that Hugh had agreed to the taping by signing the agreement, and the recording was made legitimately when he had his arrhythmia. Barrone argued that Hugh and Bonnie had no way of knowing that someone in a remote location had turned on a recording device.

The two attorneys went back and forth in their summary statements, each scoring points. Judy thought Silverburg avoided eye contact with her and seemed to be hurrying through the proceedings. Did he look guilty, or was he a little too quick to react to a complicated set of circumstances. In any case, Silverburg put an abrupt end to the debate.

"Counselors, I think I understand the issues. Ms. Thomas, if you have no further evidence to present, I will take this matter under advisement and render an opinion tomorrow morning at ten."

Bang went the gavel, and Silverburg almost ran out of the courtroom. Judy called Dorothy and Philip that afternoon. They had all agreed that the two of them should stay far away from the proceedings unless the case came to trial. Judy clearly wanted to avoid anything that looked like an organized plan to entrap Hugh and Bonnie.

Judy couldn't stop thinking about Judge Silverburg. She wondered if she had damaged the case by contacting him previously. It had seemed like a good idea at the time, and he had promised to stay out of it. Now he was very much in, and everything was riding on his judgment. No matter what he decided, Judy was in deep ethical jeopardy. She tried to explain her predicament to Dorothy and Philip on the phone.

"I was really shocked when Judge Silverburg took the case. I discussed this with Jake and he agreed that I should just go ahead with the hearing. I had no basis to get Silverburg to recuse himself and if I insisted, it would have been my word against his anyway. Besides, he may be doing this to make sure that Hugh and Bonnie are held over, in which case he can opt out before the trial starts."

Dorothy agreed. "That makes the most sense. When you last spoke with him, it sounded like he was in our corner."

"But he's hard to read. He must be a great poker player."

Philip was quiet, so much different from the frenetic person who had played the tape for them. He listened to the interchange between Dorothy and Judy on the speaker phone.

"At least we'll get an answer," he said without obvious emotion. "I want those two to get what they deserve, but I also want the world to know that I was not responsible for Moira's death. If this case doesn't make it to trial, the public won't hear that tape, and everyone will assume the DA's office was just looking for a little publicity."

Judy sympathized with Philip but pointed out there was even more at stake. "Philip, Jake and I think they murdered Moira, and we want to see justice done too. But if this case is thrown out because of the way the confession was obtained, we are going to have a political mess on our hands, not to mention the legal action the Hamlins will take. So, nobody is going to sleep well tonight."

Philip and Dorothy segued to her apartment. They needed to be together. After dinner, they just held each other in bed, talking about the case and how far they had come. Once again, Philip was more composed than Dorothy expected. They agreed Hugh and

Bonnie's arrest was an accomplishment, but they needed to get their story public. After that, Philip could rebuild his life.

"Once my FDA suspension is lifted, I might think seriously about going into the drug industry," he said. "There is so much to learn about patient safety and how to market safe drugs."

Philip pulled Dorothy closer, and they drifted off into a deep and much needed sleep.

The scene at the courthouse was as chaotic as the day before. The unruly media was jostling for space, desperate for information. The air was rife with rumors about a taped confession, but details were sparse.

Cameras whirred and flashed as the accused couple arrived. Philip watched the TV in Dorothy's office as Bonnie stepped out of the chauffeured black Range Rover. A few seconds later, Hugh solemnly followed in her footsteps. She turned back and took his hand, more like a mother guiding a bewildered child. Barrone's assistants joined the Hamlins in what was courtroom drama at its very best.

After all parties literally fought their way to the courtroom, the proceedings convened. Hugh had taken a sedative before he left home, so he sat staring at the floor, while Bonnie tried her best to look calm. Judy and Barrone leafed though their files. When the judge entered the courtroom, he had a ring binder under his arm and immediately gaveled the proceedings to order.

"This is a most difficult issue, and I have wrestled with it mightily," he began in sonorous tomes. "On one hand, the taped conversation, provided that the prosecutors can authenticate it, contains what sounds like a confession to a murder. Without the tape, the supportive evidence is weak. On the other hand, there is a serious question as to whether the defendants' rights were violated during the taping of their private conversation. The defendant, Mr. Hamlin, did sign an agreement in which he gave permission for his voice to be recorded. Even if he had read it thoroughly, he would not have known when the recordings were going to be made and for what purpose. In addition, Ms. Romano signed no such waiver but because of the recording, she is a defendant in the case.

"So, while in my heart I have serious doubts as to the innocence of the defendants, I have no choice but to exclude the tape as evidence. Since there is no other compelling evidence in this

297

case, I have no reason to hold the defendants over for trial in this matter. If the prosecutors can come forward with new information, the court would be happy to reconsider. For now, Mr. Hamlin and Ms. Romano, you are free to go."

Hugh and Bonnie sat quietly as the judge finished his pronouncement, but Judy was on her feet almost before his last words were out of his mouth. "Your Honor, may I approach the bench?"

"Ms. Thomas, this hearing is over, and nothing you can say will change my decision."

The judge gaveled the proceedings to a close and left the bench for his chambers. Judy looked as if she were going to have a seizure. She was visibly trembling and red in the face. Without a word, she darted for the judge's chambers, pushingright past the elderly tipstaff. She barged into the room just as the judge had taken off his robe. Two security officers came in behind Judy and grabbed her by the arms.

"You can't come into the judge's chambers without permission," one of the officers said. They turned to take her out the door.

The judge raised his hand. "Let her stay. I will speak with her. Ms. Thomas, since this case is officially dismissed, we can have this conversation off the record, but I want you to know that it will have no bearing on my decision. For that reason, defense counsel need not be here."

Judy had enough composure to wait until the security people had left the room. "You bastard! What the hell did you just do in there? You had prior knowledge of the case and should never have taken it. I should have screamed bloody murder when you did, but I was afraid of pissing you off. I even deluded myself into thinking that you took the case to do the right thing. What a joke! I can't believe that you let them off after you told me the evidence was OK."

"Ms. Thomas, first of all, I will remind you that you are talking to a senior judge, and you will keep a civil tongue in your mouth. Furthermore, I have no idea what you're talking about. I had no prior knowledge of this case. I took it on because of the public's scrutiny, and I rendered an opinion based on the facts."

"Really? Well, that is not my interpretation. We spoke weeks ago about this case off the record; you assured me you would never sit in judgment, and you did just that."

"Ms. Thomas, I will again warn you about your demeanor. Tone it down unless you want to sit in a jail cell tonight. I did take this case, and I think you and Mr. Springer decided to indict the Hamlins on shaky evidence at best. That is why we had to have an evidentiary hearing. You were given sufficient opportunity to present your case, and you lost.

"But you have now opened your office to criticism and maybe even some legal action by the defendants. If you want to be angry, Ms. Thomas, be angry with yourself for doing a crappy job. And if you want to do anything about my verdict, file an appeal. I doubt that it will get you far, but it will give you something to do instead of running your mouth."

Judy fought to control herself. Arguing with Silverburg was like screaming at an umpire after a bad call—it might make you feel better, but he wasn't going to change his mind. She also knew that he was right about the appeal. A senior judge had ruled that the defendants' rights had been trampled, and it would be hard for an appeals court to justify revisiting the taped confession. But Judy had one last shot to take.

"I can see I am not going to change your mind or get you to admit that what you did was wrong. But before I leave, let me just give you a little bit of advice. When you decide to meet with the father of a defendant about a case you plan to hijack, don't do it at a public place like the Union League. People might jump to the right conclusion."

Dick Deaver had placed the judge on low-level surveillance. One of Dick's investigators saw Judge Silverburg having a chatty lunch with the elder Hamlin at the Union League, a Center City institution where many of the rich and powerful spent time. Dick's detective didn't know what to make of it and had simply put it in his notes. When Silverburg took over the case, he told Dick, who in turn informed Judy.

Although Judy couldn't prove anything, she decided to see if she could get a reaction. As soon as the words were out of her mouth, Judy knew she had hit home. Judge Silverburg's face turned crimson, and he exploded from his desk chair.

"How dare you intrude on my private life, you little shit! My personal life is none of your damn business, and I won't be intimidated by your ridiculous accusations. I've known Gene Hamlin for years, and we see each other on occasion. It means nothing."

"Oh, I am sure, Judge. But you have to admit that you two had something interesting to talk about."

"Look, you little piss ant. If you think that you are going to intimidate me with this garbage, you are seriously deranged. I think you know your career at the DA's office is over as of right now. If you want to keep your license to practice law, I suggest you get your sorry ass out of here right now and keep your mouth shut. If you so much as hint that I was involved in any impropriety, I will destroy your career. This conversation is over."

"There was one thing, Judge, I couldn't understand. If Gene is such a good friend, how come you didn't warn him that his kid was going to be spied on before it happened?"

"What the hell are you talking about?"

"But now I know why. You figured that if his son got indicted, you could offer to step in and get him off the hook for big bucks. You aren't Gene Hamlin's buddy—you're just another slimy judge on the take. You are a disgrace!"

As Silverburg came around his desk, Judy decided to take a parting shot as she opened the door to leave. "So how much was it Your Honor?"

Silverburg stopped short. "How much was what?"

"How much did Hugh Hamlin's daddy have to pay you? Are you an expensive whore or do you work cheap?"

Judy didn't wait for the answer, but she heard something crash against the door just as she closed it behind her.

CHAPTER 29

The spacious hall outside the courtroom was jammed with reporters bent on getting the Hamlins' reaction to their victory. But they also wanted to know about the mysterious evidence that had nearly led to a murder trial. Barrone had instructed Hugh and Bonnie not to answer any questions. When the case ended, he intended to escort the couple out of the courthouse but stayed behind to hear what Judy Thomas was saying to the judge.

Hugh and Bonnie pushed their way out the courtroom door. Before Hugh could stop her, Bonnie made a beeline for the nearest set of microphones.

"I would like to make a statement. First of all, I want you to know how happy we are to be exonerated. The DA's office came after us with some tape-recorded conversations in which we supposedly admitted to murdering Hugh's wife, Moira. That is a lie. I don't know who masterminded the plan to illegally tape our private conversations, but my husband and I will make it our business to find out. I also want to make it clear that our words were taken out of context and had nothing to do with the death of Moira Hamlin. The evil people who tried to destroy our happy home will pay the price."

"Who do you think framed you, Ms. Romano," asked a plucky reporter standing next to her.

"The people who were really responsible for Moira Hamlin's death, the people at Gladwyne Memorial. They were found negligent, and appropriately punished, but they conspired to get back at the Hamlin family and to cover up the sloppy care that was the real cause of Moira Hamlin's death. They will face the consequences of making these outrageously false accusations. That much I promise you."

As Barrone left the courtroom, he was horrified to see Bonnie at the microphones. He managed to pull her away and to make a brief statement. "Bonnie and Hugh Hamlin are emotionally distraught, as you can well imagine. They will not be answering any more questions today."

Barrone pulled Hugh and Bonnie down the steps of the courthouse into their limo. As the three settled in, Barrone closed the glass barrier to the driver's cockpit. Bonnie let out a yell that caused Bobby and Hugh to jump several inches out of their seats. "I've been dying to do that for the last weeks. Can you believe what we just went through? Those bastards almost put us away, but we kicked the crap out of them!"

Barrone was fuming. "I have never seen anything so stupid in all of my life." Bonnie thought he was angry with the DA, but then realized he was furious with her.

"What the hell were you doing back there? Can't you listen to anybody? Threatening to go after people at GMH was more than stupid."

"But we have to go after them for what they did to us. They just about killed Hugh."

"Maybe you will get revenge and maybe you won't, but that was the wrong place to vent your spleen. What you said is going to be blasted all over the papers and TV, and you are going to look like a vindictive bitch. Not only that, you also announced to the world that there are tapes with some interesting shit on them. Now the media will try to get them. God help us all if that happens. "

"But, Bobby, I was just trying to set the record straight. My career and reputation are on the line here. I want people to know that I am blameless."

"You should have said nothing. There is no point in getting everybody steamed up. That is not going to make you look innocent."

Hugh had been thinking the same thing, but would never have had the nerve to criticize Bonnie. He sat in awe of Barrone as he dressed Bonnie down, and then made the mistake of jumping in. "Yeah, I told you to keep quiet and just leave it alone."

Bonnie might take it from Barrone, but not from Hugh. "Look, all I have done through this whole thing is to keep things together and all you have done is fuck things up. You had to go to the doctor because you were afraid of some ridiculous heart problem. How many times do they have to tell you not to worry about it? You gave them the opportunity to frame us. And now you have the nerve to complain about my behavior?"

"How the hell was I supposed to know that Wong and Kuco were out to get me? I thought that they took some kind of oath to take care of patients, not to help put them in jail!"

"Doctors do take an oath — to stick together. We are going to nail those assholes to the wall. I am sure the state medical society will not look favorably on doctors ordering unnecessary tests to help their buddies."

"I wish to hell you two would just shut up and listen," Barrone interjected. "It isn't Henry and Milan that you should care about. They can defend what they did because they ordered a test that was indicated clinically. Hugh asked them to find out what his arrhythmia was all about, and they did just that. The real culprit here is Sarkis. He is the one who set you up. If there is somebody that you should want to pay back, it's him, for Christ's sake."

Barrone had captured Bonnie's attention. "I don't doubt that Sarkis would have loved to get us back, but how do you think he pulled it off?"

"We spent most of yesterday piecing things together. One of the people in my office knows a technician who works at MCM, and got us information about the recording device Hugh was given. She heard that Sarkis was doing some off the record consulting for MCM on a new feature that is being incorporated into their monitoring device, called IVT, instant voice transmission. It was listed on the agreement Hugh signed."

Bonnie shot a dagger at Hugh. "I didn't see that in the agreement," he said.

"It was there all right—and in bold print," Barrone confirmed. "They may not have pointed it out to Hugh, but it was definitely written down. Philip worked with the GM over there, a woman named Jamie Ascot. According to our source, they were 'collecting data' on the new IVT design. Hugh happened to be one of the patients who had the IVT feature activated."

"But it wasn't just the IVT. It was those damn phone calls. We never would have said anything to incriminate ourselves except for that. Who called us?"

"I'm pretty sure the woman was Dorothy Deaver."

"Never heard of her."

"Her father owns a private detective agency, so it wouldn't be hard to believe they were gathering information about you."

"So they tricked us into saying something incriminating while the tape was on. Why do you suspect this Deaver woman?"

"My investigators told me that Deaver and Sarkis have been real chummy, hanging out lately at her office. He spent at least a few nights at her place."

Bonnie hated the idea that somebody had gotten the better of her and that Hugh's father had to bail them out. It was a good thing they had gotten that prick Silverburg to roll over, she thought. A half-million sent to some off shore account was a bargain. Otherwise, they would have been looking at some serious jail time. Barrone knew nothing about the critical bribe, and she saw no reason to tell him now.

"There are still some things I haven't been able to sort out," Barrone mused. "Like Judy Thomas, for example. I wonder if she knew about the case before the taping, or was she approached after they had it?"

Bonnie knew the answer to that question too, but she wasn't going to share it with Barrone. Silverburg had told Hugh's father about Judy's initial conversations with the Judge. Silverburg said he had underestimated Sarkis. He never thought he would be able to get a taped conversation of Hugh and Bonnie using that ridiculous MCM device. If he had, Silverburg told Gene Hamlin, he would have discouraged Judy and that would have been the end of it. Once the tape was made and the Hamlins had been arrested, Silverburg figured that Hamlin senior would want to protect his son. It was a service the Judge was happy to provide, for a price. He also thought it would be fun to put that bitch Thomas in her place.

Barrone went on. "Once Judy Thomas and Jake Springer were presented with the information, they had every right to issue a warrant and have you arrested. If you want to contest this in retrospect, you will have to contend that their legal argument was flawed."

"Should we actually do that?"

"It will be tough. Remember, the arraignment judge, that idiot Mendelson, didn't have a problem with the evidence, and he issued warrants for your arrests. Besides, Thomas got reamed out by Silverburg. I overheard Silverburg giving it to her in chambers right after the hearing was over. Jake Springer will take at least a minor hit in the media. Hopefully, he will save his own ass and fire her. That may be the best we can do."

Bonnie didn't like what she was hearing, but Barrone was right about where to fight her battles. Barrone continued his musings as he looked out the limo's window. "In fact, their case had a lot of momentum when Judge Annie picked it up. She's a strong advocate for the prosecution, so if the case had stayed with her, we could have had a very different outcome. It was a good thing that Silverburg stepped in when he did. I just wonder why in the world he did that?"

Barrone gave Bonnie and Hugh a smile and a wink. Bonnie noted Barrone's gesture, but it was lost completely on Hugh, who finally piped up. "So it sounds like we should let things blow over and decide later about going after Sarkis."

Barrone nodded. "That's the best approach. I know you're angry, but you should put it aside for now and enjoy your victory a little. Maybe get out of town for a couple of days and soak up some sun."

Hugh liked the idea. "Sounds good. Bonnie, shall I see about getting a flight for this weekend?"

Bonnie managed a small smile. It was going to take more than a weekend get-away to salvage her bruised psyche.

While Hugh and Bonnie were making plans, Philip and Dorothy were reeling from the devastating verdict. They sat in silence, watching the live broadcast of the mayhem outside the courthouse.

A phone call from Judy startled them. "I can't talk long—I have to get back to the office to do some damage control. Let's just say that it was a travesty. Judge Silverburg blew us out of the water. I had a little confrontation with the bastard after the verdict that I will tell you about later. But I think that the case is effectively over."

As he listened on the speakerphone, Philip chanted, "I can't believe it" so many times that Dorothy finally implored him to stop. "That isn't helping, Philip. We have to stay focused and make good decisions."

Judy advised them to say nothing. If they were lucky, the Hamlins would just let the matter drop. "If they decide to come after you, the tape will probably be made public, and I don't think they want that to happen. But we shouldn't provoke them."

Judy promised to call them again that evening and rang off. They continued to watch the scene on the courthouse steps. Every news station had reporters conducting interviews and commenting on the case. There was a frantic rush to discover the content of the tape. Dorothy suddenly sat forward in her chair. "Oh my God, I think I just saw Vincente and Giancarlo Romano standing off to the side of the crowd. Did you see them?"

"I wouldn't know them if I fell over them."

"I am going over there. I need to know if they were at the hearing."

"Dorothy, Judy told us to keep a low profile. She doesn't want us to be seen."

"She doesn't want you to be seen. I am a lawyer, remember? What's the big deal about my going to the courthouse?"

"Well, be careful."

"I know, Philip, I am afraid of those people, too. But if they were there tracking this case, I need to know."

Dorothy put on her coat, took her briefcase, and walked briskly the few blocks to the courthouse. Some of the crowd had dispersed, but many reporters remained on the steps hoping to interview someone from the DA's office. At first, Dorothy was relieved not to see the Romano brothers. But as she glanced over her shoulder, she walked headlong into Vincente.

"Ms. Deaver, how are you today?" he asked. He had a long black woolen coat buttoned to the top with a charcoal scarf knotted under his chin. The dark colors highlighted his silver gray hair.

Dorothy regained her balance and stuck out her hand. "Mr. Romano, how are you? It is good to see you."

"It is entirely my pleasure, Ms. Deaver. I apologize; I was not looking where I was going. I'm having a hard time extricating myself from all of this madness." An uncomfortable silence fell

306

between them as Dorothy tried to decide if she should talk to the old man or walk away.

Finally, Dorothy summoned her courage to speak. "Are you by yourself?"

"No, Giancarlo is with me, but we got separated in the crowd. In fact, my clumsiness was because I was looking for him."

"And what brings you gentlemen to the courthouse today?"

Vincente was his usual soft-spoken self. "Oh, we had some unfinished family business to take care of. We are still trying to collect on an old debt. We had a little bit of a setback today, but I am sure things will straighten out. They usually do."

Dorothy looked warily at Vincente, trying to read his thoughts.

"How about all of this excitement over the Hamlins?" Vincente continued. " In your legal opinion, what will happen next?"

"Hard to say," Dorothy replied, trying to keep a blank expression. "Judge Silverburg appears to have ruled that important evidence was not admissible, but I don't know what it was or why he ruled as he did."

Dorothy knew immediately that Vincente was not buying her story. He was unhappy that Dorothy had not kept him up to speed on the case. "It must be frustrating for you and Dr. Sarkis to see them released. A pity. Well, I hope that you are able to resolve the issues and get the justice you seek. Be patient, and things are likely to go your way."

"I hope so, Mr. Romano."

"And now I must find my brother. We have to get back to work. There is much to do. I wish you all of the best. Cent' Anni, Ms. Deaver."

"Cent'Anni, Mr. Romano." Dorothy watched Vincente locate his brother and walk to the black sedan at the curb.

Dorothy decided to go back to her office. Philip had already left to spend the afternoon with his kids. That evening, Dorothy told Philip her courthouse story over dinner at her apartment.

"That is quite a duo," Philip remarked. Dorothy nodded. She was concerned by the sudden appearance of the Romano brothers. It was no coincidence that they were at the Montgomery County Courthouse. They lived in Philadelphia, so what kind of business would bring them to suburbia? "Do you think they wanted to see what happened to Hugh and Bonnie firsthand?" she asked.

"That wouldn't surprise me. And that stuff they gave you about an "old debt" could be his way of saying Bonnie needs to get her just desserts."

"They didn't look too disappointed," Dorothy pointed out.

"I bet you they will take their own advice and wait patiently, but eventually they will get the justice they think they deserve."

"I suspect you're right. They seem like nice old guys on the surface. I can't really explain why my knees were knocking while Vincente was talking to me."

After dinner, they switched on the local news. The Hamlin acquittal was the top story including Bonnie's courthouse interview. She sounded like a martyr rather than a murderer. Philip was especially upset to hear that Bonnie was planning retribution. "Do you think they will go after Henry and Milan?"

"I wouldn't be surprised," Dorothy said. On the other hand, if they find out you had something to do with this, they might even zero in on us. Bonnie is truly evil and just might decide to torture you for a while."

Judy called as they were watching the news to give them the details of her final conversation with Judge Silverburg. Dorothy took the call while Philip snoozed on the sofa.

"After I accused him of taking a bribe, he let it be known that he was going to get me fired," Judy recounted. "I told Jake this afternoon that he could let me go to limit the office's exposure. Jake said he would think about it over the weekend, but he was inclined to tell the judge to go screw himself. I don't think we can prove he took money from Gene Hamlin, but Silverburg would have to explain why he was having lunch with the plaintiff's father just before he took over the case."

"What did Jake think about the verdict?" Dorothy asked.

"He wasn't surprised. He feared that the tape was questionable even though Philip had done nothing illegal. We'll just have to see if they come after us. How are you guys holding up?"

"Honestly, Philip has been pretty quiet. I know he is worried about what will happen to Henry and Milan."

"I think their exposure is limited but that won't necessarily stop Hugh and Bonnie. They might try to get the medical societies to censor the doctors. Who knows? My concern is legal action against you and Philip. It won't be hard for them to figure out you were the instigators. Why don't you and Philip go away for a few days? Let things decompress a little."

When Dorothy later made the suggestion to Philip, he snapped. "I am not in the mood to go anywhere. I can barely think straight."

"Well, I'm not staying in this apartment all night. I am going to take a walk and do a little evening shopping." She left Philip sitting in front of the TV set watching a basketball game.

When Dorothy returned two hours later, Philip was bouncing around the apartment. "Let's go to Cape May," he suggested.

Cape May was a quaint little town at the tip of the New Jersey peninsula brimming with Victorian architecture, cozy restaurants, and a non-commercial boardwalk. "I booked a room at a bed and breakfast for two nights. We can leave in the morning, drive down to get there by noon, and come back on Monday so you can work most of the day. What do you say? It's a great time to go. The season hasn't started yet. We'll have the place to ourselves."

Dorothy was incredulous. "Why the sudden change of heart?"

"Judy was right. We should get away."

"Philip, when I left here, you were catatonic, and now you are manic. What's going on?"

"Well, I was just thinking that things will eventually work out. So we just have to be patient and upbeat. I am officially turning my morose button off forever."

"Philip, I don't know what to say."

"Dorothy, the most important thing has come out of all of this is that I know I really care for you. We took our best shot at the Hamlin thing and struck out. That doesn't mean we can't go on and be happy together. Cape May will be the first event of our new life. I think that we should crack a bottle of champagne and celebrate. What do you say?"

"When I was walking back here, this was just about the last thing that I thought would happen. Champagne will put me in a better mood for a trip to the shore. But first I need a shower to wash this miserable day out of my head."

They sipped champagne and fell asleep in each other's arms. They overslept and arrived in Cape May in the late afternoon. The weather was spectacular, clear and brisk, without a cloud in a vivid blue sky. After stowing their bags at the B&B, they took a long walk on the beach.

"Philip, this was a great idea," Dorothy said as they walked arm in arm on the firm gray sand. "All I want to do is read, have a great dinner, and relax."

"The world is a million miles away," Philip answered. "I hope it stays there for a while."

In the world Philip was referring to, Hugh and Bonnie were packing for a trip to Bermuda for a few days. Hugh had a friend who owned a gated estate house on a pink sand beach complete with servants. They would take the first flight on Sunday morning, and be in Bermuda in time for an early afternoon golf game at the venerable Mid-Ocean club, a stone's throw from where they were staying.

"I have a limo picking us up at six," Hugh told Bonnie as they prepared for bed.

"Why don't we just drive ourselves?"

"I didn't want to leave my car at the airport for four days. Bobby Barrone hooked us up with the limousine company he uses."

"Bobby to the rescue." Bonnie was still seething about his tongue-lashing after the hearing.

After a quiet evening of eating pizza and watching videos with the kids, Hugh and Bonnie went to bed early and slept as soundly as they had for months. Gone was the angst over late night phone calls or a high-stakes criminal case. All they had to do was get in the limo, board the plane, settle into their first-class seats, sip a couple of Bloody Marys, and concentrate on relaxing.

It had been months since they had been intimate. Stress had robbed both of their libidos. Hugh hoped that having Bonnie a little pissed off at Sarkis might add a little spice to the soup. In the old days, she seemed more energetic in the sack when she was really pissed at somebody. Seeing that bitch Thomas humiliated by the judge could add a couple of extra inches to his hard-on, too.

Even if this trip was pure spur-of-the-moment, Hugh hoped it would be something they would both remember for a long time.

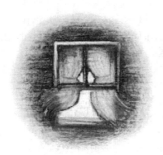

CHAPTER 30

The following Sunday morning dawned in spectacular fashion. The sun quickly warmed the air from its perch in a cloudless rose-colored sky, while beads of dew glistened on the new green grass.

Almost as if a clarion call had directed them, the city's inhabitants, accustomed to sleeping in on Sunday mornings in the cold, awakened that day to take advantage of the glorious weather. Hundreds of people headed to the banks of the Schuylkill River to bike, hike, and roller skate. To facilitate them, the curving drives that flank the river are closed to cars to make room for "weekend warriors" pursuing their favorite forms of recreation.

Among these was the sport of rowing. Crew has always been important in Philadelphia. In fact, some of its most famous citizens rowed in and won international games, including the Olympics. The drive on the east bank of the river was named for Jack Kelly, a legendary Philadelphia oarsman, who was the brother of actress Grace Kelly, later Princess Grace of Monaco. His achievements are memorialized with a statue depicting him rowing a single-man shell as a young man.

Springtime regattas along the Schuylkill River attract rowing teams from around the world. Nearly every academic institution in Philadelphia supports a crew team that uses the river for practice and competition. To accommodate this activity, the eastern bank showcases an array of historic boathouses, used not only to garage the shells, but also to serve as gathering places and headquarters for the rowing clubs. When little white lights illuminated "Boathouse Row" in the 1970s, the dramatic view the vignette created on the far side of the river instantly became an iconic symbol of the city. Since then, it has graced countless posters, book covers, and postcards.

On that morning, members of the St. Joseph University crew were on their way to the river for Sunday practice. The students slept as their bus made its way to Kelly Drive. After an intense afternoon practice the day before, and a raucous beer party at the boathouse Saturday night, they were understandably tired. Mandatory practice meant being rousted out of bed at eight, fed a warm breakfast, and loaded on the shuttle for the nine o'clock drill. The Hawks had performed well in the preliminary events that year, but the major regattas, including the NCAA championship, were coming up.

The bus passed through the traffic barricades and threaded its way through throngs of bikers and joggers claiming the road. It pulled into the driveway and disgorged its groggy passengers who slowly trudged up the stairs and into the bays to collect their shells. The coach was already at the water's edge, standing next to the motorboat from which he directed the practice. "Is it too much to ask to get your ass in gear so we can start practice?" he shouted.

A coxswain and a few members of the eight-man heavyweight boat collected the first of the shells and brought it down to the water. They set the boat into a launcher with tracks and small wheels, and allowed the boat to slide gently into the river. They pushed from behind and as they put their weight into it, the boat lurched and unexpectedly refused to move. Thinking the launch mechanism was jammed, they pulled back and tried again. This time the boat went a little further but there was a loud clang. Irritated and puzzled, the coach hurried over and told them to pull the boat back —there was obviously something in the water.

As the coach stepped over the launcher and peered into the river, he spotted what may have been a shiny rear bumper. "Holy crap, I think somebody dumped a car off our dock!"

He quickly called out to one of his students. "Jimmy, can you see the number on that license plate?"

Jim Price got on his belly and strained to see the plate beneath the murky water. "Can't see real well, coach, but it definitely is a Pennsylvania plate that starts with LM."

"That should help the cops."

"What does it mean, coach?"

"It means that somebody ditched a limo here, and judging from the size of this monster, I bet you that the son of a bitch is a stretch. Let's call 911 and tell the police to get over here pronto."

Philip and Dorothy also awakened early. Once again, Philip's behavior was proving too bizarre for Dorothy. Although they had originally planned a long, lazy morning in bed, last night Philip had turned into a frenzied, almost demonic activity planner.

At the end of their Saturday evening walk on the beach, they struck up a conversation with another couple, and quickly discovered they had a lot in common. Joan Skinner was a New Jersey cardiologist who practiced at a small hospital about 30 miles inland. Her husband Duane practiced family law. They owned a small weekend house in Cape May and came here frequently. After talking for a few minutes, Philip invited them to dinner without consulting Dorothy. She didn't complain, but Philip went on to propose at dinner that they meet for an early bicycle ride on the boardwalk followed by breakfast at the famous Cape May Pancake House. He suggested they get an early start to enjoy the great weather. Dorothy had no idea that he meant six o'clock, but here they were, the first in line to rent bikes, waiting for their new friends to arrive.

"Philip, what the heck is going on? Why are you dragging me out here in the middle of the night?"

"Well, I wanted to get in a good ride before bikers have to get off of the boardwalk."

"There is no curfew for biking on the boardwalk in the off-season. We could have slept another couple of hours."

"I forgot. We will definitely take a nap before dinner."

"I also don't understand why you glommed onto these people. They are nice, but wasn't dinner enough?"

"I just thought you might enjoy a little company, that's all."

"All I wanted was to enjoy time with you, dopey. So let's see if we can disengage ourselves after breakfast and keep the afternoon to ourselves."

So after the long bike ride followed by guiltless stacks of pancakes, the couples said goodbye, and pledged to keep in touch.

The rest of the trip was as Dorothy had anticipated. They sat on the beach, read junk novels and dozed, taking occasional walks

313

in the surf. That evening, they dined alone in a bistro four doors away from their hotel. After dinner they finished their novels on the front porch, then sipped sparkling water, and chewed contentedly on saltwater taffy.

They slept late the next morning, and after another fortifying breakfast, packed their car and drove back to Philadelphia. There wasn't much conversation, each enjoying the CDs Philip had chosen.

As they pulled into Dorothy's parking lot, they were alarmed to see two police cruisers in front of her building.

"Uh-oh. I hope that everything is all right," Dorothy said. "I wonder if we had a break-in."

Philip was dismissive. "Lots of reasons for them to be here."

But when they got out of the elevator, two uniformed Lower Merion cops were stationed outside of Dorothy's apartment door.

"What is the problem?" Dorothy asked.

The younger of the two asked, "Are you Dorothy Deaver?"

"Yes, and this is my place. Why you are here?"

The officer continued as if there had been no reply. "And you sir, are you Dr. Philip Sarkis?"

"Yes"

"Sir, ma'am, you can enter, but be advised our chief detective is in there. He'll fill you in."

Dorothy entered her apartment warily. Although there were no signs of forced entry and everything seemed intact, she knew instantly that things had been moved around. Chief Detective Scotty was sitting on her sofa with a newspaper.

Scotty rose to greet them. He was short with dark features that included black eyebrows that looked like furry caterpillars. His suit and tie were nondescript He shook Dorothy's hand first. "Hi, Ms. Deaver, Dr. Sarkis. My name is Detective Scotty. I'm sorry to have surprised you. We have been trying to reach you, but nobody, including your father, knew where you were. A judge issued a warrant to search your place."

"We decided to go to Cape May after my office closed on Friday. I never thought to tell anybody where I could be reached."

"It created the impression you had run away."

"That was an oversight on my part, detective. But why on earth did you assume we ran off?"

Scotty ignored her question. "Do you generally do things like that on the spur of the moment?" he asked.

"No, not usually, but we both felt like we needed to get away for a couple of days."

"We tried to get you on your cell phone. I guess you turned that off too."

"There wouldn't be much point in letting people pester me on my phone, so yes, it was not on."

"Just so you know, we obtained a search warrant for Dr. Sarkis' residence as well. As you can see, we made an attempt to put things back where we found them."

Philip had been listening passively and finally chimed in. "Detective, perhaps before we continue this conversation, you could explain what this is about?"

"Certainly doctor, but first, can you tell me your exact whereabouts the last two days?"

"As Ms. Deaver said, we were in Cape May staying at a bed and breakfast. We drove down late Saturday morning and just returned."

Detective Scotty took out his notebook and started to take notes. "Gosh, I love the Jersey shore this time of year. It is so peaceful. So were you down there alone?"

"We were by ourselves. We did have dinner on Saturday evening and breakfast on Sunday morning with another couple."

"I'm sorry, but could you tell me who they were and when you were with them?"

Philip was calm but Dorothy was unraveling. "Really detective, this is getting a little tedious. Why do you need to know these things?"

"All in good time counselor. It would be really helpful if you could answer my questions first."

"Fine. Their names were Duane and Joan Skinner and they live in Vineland, New Jersey. We have their numbers if you want them."

Philip cut in. "After we had dinner with them we decided to hook up on Sunday too. We met them at about 6:00 in the morning and were with them until about 10:00 on Sunday."

"Please write their numbers down for me and we will check them out. Were both of you with them the entire time?"

Dorothy's dam broke. "Except when we were sleeping. Now see here detective, are we being accused of a crime?"

"Well, Ms. Deaver, not officially. And if this alibi holds up, you won't be charged with anything."

"Detective, I think you are toying with us. You are using terms like 'alibi' so obviously a crime has been committed. Are you going to tell us what happened or are you going to make us guess?"

The detective closed his notebook, crossed his legs, and removed the smudged half glasses from the end of his long nose. He addressed the question with calm indignation.

"Quite the contrary, Ms. Deaver. I strongly suspect you are the one playing a game with me. The last time I checked, Cape May had TVs and radios. I am having a hard time believing that you aren't blowing air up my skirt. You must know what happened up here yesterday morning. It has been all over the news."

"You are dead wrong, detective. Dr. Sarkis and I didn't watch TV in Cape May and we didn't listen to the radio on our drive home today. So maybe you can make like Walter Cronkite and give us the news bulletin?"

"Sure. It seems that Bonnie Romano and Hugh Hamlin were found dead in the trunk of a submerged limousine near Boathouse Row."

Dorothy's face drained of color as she fell backward into an armchair. "Oh my God, that is unbelievable! Are you sure it was them?" Scotty noticed that Philip had not changed expression.

"It was them all right," he answered. "They were tied up neatly, gagged, and stuffed into the trunk together. They must have been alive when the car was submerged because they died by fresh water inhalation. You know, drowning. Pretty miserable way to go, don't you think? Somebody must have been really pissed off at them."

"Oh my God!" Dorothy exclaimed. "Who could have done such a terrible thing?"

"Well, Ms. Deaver, it was professional. Hugh and Bonnie were picked up at about 6:15 am by a limo service recommended by their attorney, Bobby Barrone. They were headed to the airport for a flight to Bermuda. The last time they were seen alive was when they got into the car. Sounds like you were pedaling bicy-

Lethal Rhythm

cles in Cape May with your new friends when this all went down."
"Cut the sarcasm, detective."
"Sorry about that, Ms. Deaver. The coroner is pretty certain that death occurred between 6 and 7 am. The car was found by a rowing team at about 9 on Sunday."
"We told you the truth, detective." Dorothy asserted. "Is there a particular reason why you don't believe us?"
"We'll check your story," Scotty said matter-of-factly. "We also got permission to examine your phone records as part of our search warrant. We are running the numbers now."
The detective took out his notebook and leafed to the relevant page. "Oh yeah, I did mean to ask you about one other thing, Ms. Deaver. There was a call to your apartment on Friday at about 8 pm from a phone booth in South Philly. Do you recall what that was about?"
"Dr. Sarkis and I were here on Friday evening. I don't remember a call," Dorothy answered.
"How about you, doctor? Do you remember a call?"
"Yeah, Ms. Deaver went shopping. It was a wrong number."
"That's funny," Scotty observed. "The call lasted four minutes."
"The bastard wouldn't take no for an answer. He kept on insisting that his sister lived at this number and he wanted to talk to her. I think he was loaded."
Dorothy was not happy with the way the conversation was going. She exploded. "What the hell is going on, detective? Are you insinuating that Philip or I had something to do with this crime?"
"Well, Dr. Sarkis certainly had a motive."
"Don't be ridiculous. That malpractice case was years ago."
"Well, the way I figure it, the malpractice thing had to be a blow. Ruined his career, didn't it? And now after the criminal case against them collapses, Ms. Romano makes a public announcement that she is coming after him, and maybe his new girlfriend too. Do you think that could have motivated him?"
"What makes you think I had anything to lose, detective?" Philip countered. "They had already taken away my career, my family, my house, my friends. What did I have left? As for the 'fair damsel' idea, Dorothy Deaver can take care of herself."

317

Scotty listened impassively, taking notes.

"Look, detective," Philip continued. "Dorothy and I had nothing to do with this. Sure, I thought Hamlin was getting away with murder, but it is a big stretch to conclude I killed him. I was nowhere near here when it happened."

"Yes, I admit that if your alibi holds up, their blood isn't directly on your hands, so to speak. But this was a contract hit—you know, murder for hire—so I couldn't clear you completely based on your alibi alone."

"Detective, this is really nuts! I wouldn't know how to find a hit man let alone hire one. Check my financial records. You'll see I am tapped out and have been for some time. So unless there is a pro bono assassin you know about, I think you are going to roll snake eyes on that theory."

"That may be, doctor. I am merely telling you what we have been considering over the last 24 hours. You have a motive and we couldn't locate you. For all we knew, you used Ms. Deaver's assets to pay for the hit and for transportation out of the country. If we got a little carried away, I apologize."

Philip wondered if Detective Scotty was sorry or if he was pulling a "Columbo" to get his guard down. But he also figured this would be a good place to end the interview.

He stood up. "Detective, I thank you for the information and for listening to our side of the story. Ms. Deaver is upset and we have to recoup. If you need to talk to us further, we will make ourselves available, I promise."

"I appreciate that doctor, and again I apologize if I upset you. I don't have anything else now but I would encourage you to stay in the area for the next few weeks. Wandering off without notifying us first will make my colleagues suspicious, if you know what I mean."

After Detective Scotty departed, Dorothy slid down in her armchair, and draped her arm over her eyes. Philip walked over to the large picture window and looked out at the budding, sun-drenched gardens.

When Dorothy spoke, it was softly, almost like she was thinking out loud. "Philip, what did you make of all of that?"

"How the hell should I know? I can't believe they think we hired somebody to kill Hugh and Bonnie. That is the kind of stuff that happens on TV, not in real life!"

"Don't be naïve, Philip. You heard him. They were killed two days after they threatened to ruin the people who came after them—that would be us. Springer knows we had a motive. We have to be suspects. Who else would want Hugh and Bonnie dead as much as we do?"

"I never wished they were dead."

"I know, but they were executed, so you have to think that whoever did it wanted revenge."

"They were evil. Somebody else might have had it out for them."

"As far as the public was concerned, they were exemplary people," Dorothy explained. "When we did their background checks, we didn't come across any other major scrapes. So who else would have wanted to harm them so badly?"

Dorothy sat up suddenly. "Oh my God, the Romanos!"

Philip paused for a moment and answered without expression. "Well I guess you can say they had a motive to kill Bonnie, but not Hugh. What else points to them?"

"Are you serious? Didn't you hear Scotty say how professional the killings were? And do you think that the Romanos would give a rat's ass about killing Hugh? They probably figured they were doing the world a favor."

Philip sat on the ottoman and took Dorothy's hand. "I think you are getting carried away with yourself."

"Should I call Detective Scotty and tell him about the Romanos?"

"Dorothy, listen to me. You will under no circumstances bring this to the police. I am not going to let you put us both in jeopardy."

"Philip, I am an officer of the court. I have an ethical obligation to present this to Scotty."

Philip's calm veneer crumbled. He became agitated and shrill. He leaned over Dorothy, red faced and angry. "You will do no such thing. Have you no idea how dangerous talking to the police is?"

"Philip, you are scaring me."

"Look, telling Detective Scotty about the Romanos is pointless. We don't have any evidence. So how will that help the police?"

Dorothy wanted to be persuaded. It was not a good idea to get the Romanos stirred up. "Maybe we should think about it for a few days?"

"That's more like it," Philip said soothingly. "Let things cool down and we can decide what to do later."

Dorothy nodded but was not totally appeased. "Philip, over the last few days, your mood has been all over the place. You have gone from depressed to manic to happy and now to frantic. And it seemed to start after my shopping trip on Friday night."

"I have no idea what you are talking about. My mood has been fine."

"Was that really a wrong number on Friday night?"

"Yes, it was."

Dorothy wasn't mollified. She was quiet for a few moments, then turned to face Philip directly. "I'm sorry, Philip, but I'm not sure I believe you. I gave you the Romanos' number. I think you either hatched a plan with them on Friday night, or you found out that they were going to take care of the Hamlins themselves. Is that what made you so happy when I got back?"

"That's ridiculous."

"And I am afraid that the sudden decision to go to Cape May, and insisting on hanging out with another couple we hardly knew was all about setting up an alibi for us."

"Dorothy, I don't have to sit here and listen to this nonsense."

"For all I know, that Italian stud Bobby Barrone helped by supplying the limo driver who drowned them. I am deathly afraid that the Romanos are at the bottom of this, and somehow they pulled you into it."

Philip sat forward on the sofa, barely able to control himself. "Dorothy, you are hallucinating — how in the fuck did you dream up all of this crap? Bobby Barrone was their lawyer, for crying out loud. Why would he want to have them killed?"

"Wake up, Philip. People like the Romanos have all kinds of people in their debt. I am not the only one who suspects you. Detective Scotty thinks you were involved."

Philip shook his head.

"Philip, look at me. Can you swear to me that the Romanos didn't warn you about Hugh's and Bonnie's murders and that you didn't sit still and let it happen?"

Philip's demeanor changed abruptly yet again. Dorothy was beginning to think that he was a chameleon. His scowl disappeared and his expression and voice were calm.

"Dorothy, I will only say this one time. I swear on the heads of my children that I knew nothing about those murders. I was just as surprised as you. I feel bad for those kids—first they lost their mom and now their dad and stepmother. I wouldn't do something like that. I must say that I am disappointed you suspect I could. I am a doctor, for Christ's sake. I don't kill people, I save them."

Dorothy wanted to believe that Philip had answered honestly. "I am sorry, Philip. I am upset, and you have been acting strange. I know you have been through a lot. Maybe I let my imagination run away with me. I accept your explanation."

But dismissing it from her mind would be difficult. As she lay in bed that night, listening to Philip's breathing, she wondered if the ugly suspicions she had about him would eventually destroy their relationship. How could she be with somebody she didn't trust? Or would she finally be able to convince herself that Philip hadn't known about the plan to get even for John Romano's murder, and hadn't manipulated an alibi?

And even more importantly, was Philip really trying to avenge Moira Hamlin's death? Or with his last legal recourse taken away, had Philip decided that the only fair retribution for the ruination of his precious career was the cold-blooded murders of Bonnie Romano and Hugh Hamlin?

PETER R. KOWEY MD

Dr. Kowey is an internationally respected expert in heart rhythm disorders. He attended medical school at the University of Pennsylvania and trained in cardiology at Harvard. For the last 30 years, he has developed a large referral practice in Philadelphia. He research has led to the development of dozens of new drugs and devices for the treatment of a wide range of cardiac diseases. He has authored hundreds of scientific articles and textbook chapters. LETHAL RHYTHM is his first work of fiction. He and his wife Dorothy have three daughters, and live in Bryn Mawr, Pennsylvania with their three Portuguese water dogs.

MARION L. FOX

Journalist and nurse, Marion Laffey Fox is a graduate of the University of Pennsylvania, Co-author with Dr. Truman G. Schnabel, Jr. of *Its's Your Body, Know What the Doctor Ordered* and author of *Philadelphia World Class!*, she has contributed to *USA Today, The Christian Science Monitor, Town & Country, Architectural Digest, Travel & Leisure, Forbes*, and *Vogue*. She is a contributing editor of *Coastal Living* magazine and *Entree* magazine. Ms. Fox is a trustee of the Lankenau Hospital Foundation and the Franklin Institute Bower Awards Committee.